Advance Praise for *State of Lies*

"In *State of Lies*, Siri Mitchell has penned a page turner that I literally couldn't put down. I confess I kept reading when I should've been writing my own novel. My heart breaks with Georgia Brennan as she suffers blow after blow when a past she didn't even know she had catches up with her. Readers will applaud her resilience and determination to solve the mystery and save the lives of the people she loves—even when the face of the boogeyman turns out to be someone she never expected. Don't miss this thrilling ride!"

—KELLY IRVIN, BESTSELLING AUTHOR OF
TELL HER NO LIES AND *OVER THE LINE*

"In *State of Lies*, Siri Mitchell has created a story that will suck you in and not let go. With twists and turns, international intrigue, and danger galore, this book reads like a psychological thriller mixed with healthy doses of suspense. It's also wonderfully written with an attention to detail that had me seeing my former haunts in Arlington, Virginia."

—CARA PUTMAN, AUTHOR OF
THE HIDDEN JUSTICE SERIES

Praise for Siri Mitchell

"Stunning . . . this story is sure to impress."
—*PUBLISHERS WEEKLY* ON *RUINS OF LACE*

"A fascinating story not only about lace, but about obsession, corruption, and self-worth. The ending is tantalizingly ambiguous."
—HISTORICAL NOVEL SOCIETY ON *RUINS OF LACE*

"A well-paced and interwoven story . . . Anthony [Siri Mitchell] creates a narrative that subtly educates, poses stimulating questions and entertains."

—*KIRKUS* ON *THE MIRACLE THIEF*

"Fast-paced and engrossing . . . The book's wealth of historic detail will transport you back in time, and Anthony's plucky heroines will have you alternately biting your nails over their plights and cheering over their triumphs. Hope, faith, courage, inspiration, love—this book has it all. Highly recommended!"

—SHERRY JONES, AUTHOR OF *THE SHARP HOOK OF LOVE*, ON *THE MIRACLE THIEF*

"Christy-nominated Mitchell's latest flawlessly crafted novel is a quietly powerful tale of love, faith, and hope set in Puritan New England. With its brilliantly formed characters and vividly detailed setting, this tale combines the best elements of inspirational and historical fiction into a richly emotional, unforgettable story."

—*BOOKLIST* ON *LOVE'S PURSUIT*

"Christy Award winner Mitchell makes a successful historical debut, immersing readers in the rich historical detail of Queen Elizabeth's court."

—*RT BOOK REVIEWS* ON *A CONSTANT HEART*

"A skillful mix of tense family drama, historical romance, and memorable characters that will stay with readers."

—*LIBRARY JOURNAL* ON *A HEART MOST WORTHY*

"A well-written, enthralling historical novel, *The Messenger* will not disappoint."

—*PORTLAND BOOK REVIEW*

STATE
OF
LIES

OTHER BOOKS BY SIRI MITCHELL

Kissing Adrien

Chateau of Echoes

Something Beyond the Sky

The Cubicle Next Door

Moon over Tokyo

A Constant Heart

Love's Pursuit

She Walks in Beauty

A Heart Most Worthy

The Messenger

The Ruins of Lace

Unrivaled

Love Comes Calling

The Miracle Thief

Like a Flower in Bloom

Flirtation Walk

STATE OF LIES

SIRI MITCHELL

THOMAS NELSON
Since 1798

State of Lies

© 2019 by Siri Mitchell

Published in Nashville, Tennessee, by Thomas Nelson. Thomas Nelson is a registered trademark of HarperCollins Christian Publishing, Inc.

Interior design by Lori Lynch

Thomas Nelson titles may be purchased in bulk for educational, business, fund-raising, or sales promotional use. For information, please email SpecialMarkets@ThomasNelson.com.

Library of Congress Cataloging-in-Publication Data

Names: Mitchell, Siri L., 1969- author.
Title: State of lies / Siri Mitchell.
Description: Nashville, Tennessee : Thomas Nelson, [2019]
Identifiers: LCCN 2019007287 | ISBN 9780785228615 (paperback)
Subjects: LCSH: Murder--Investigation--Fiction. | Man-woman relationships--Fiction. | GSAFD: Mystery fiction. | Suspense fiction.
Classification: LCC PS3613.I866 S73 2019 | DDC 813/.6--dc23 LC record available at https://lccn.loc.gov/2019007287

Printed in the United States of America

19 20 21 22 23 LSC 5 4 3 2 1

*For Milt and Joyce
and for Tony, always.*

Since quantum physics allows for multiple possibilities simultaneously, these possibilities should then keep existing, even after a measurement is made. But they don't. Every possibility but one vanishes. We do not see any of the others around us.

—Christophe Galfard, *The Universe in Your Hand: A Journey Through Space, Time, and Beyond*

FEBRUARY

Sean was already pulling his shirt off over his head as he came into the bedroom.

I held up a corner of the comforter as an invitation. But not too far. The damp of a drizzly week had seeped into the house.

He stepped out of his jeans and then slid in beside me.

I nestled against him. Felt him cringe as my cold feet brushed up against him.

"Sorry."

He pulled me into his embrace. "One of these days they're going to fall off." He nuzzled my neck.

I wrapped my arms around him. "They already did. These are the replacements."

I felt his lips curl into a smile as he kissed me again.

Sean was doing that thing he does—the one that made my toes curl—when my phone twanged out the beginning notes of "Sweet Home Alabama."

My mother.

I gripped his shoulder and tried my best to ignore the phone because married sex was my personal holy grail. Always elusively tantalizing, just out of reach. I'd even put it on Sean's weekend to-do list, just after "sharpen the knives" and right before "fix the sink." It was okay because our son, Sam, was still in preschool; he didn't know how to read. That afternoon, however, our window of opportunity was about to come sliding down right on top of our fingers. Sam was down for the count due to a cold, though I expected him to wake up soon.

But the phone kept ringing.

The drums started thumping and the cymbals clashed.

I must have wavered because Sean folded me within his arms. "Georgie. Don't." He nibbled at my neck. "If you want me to, I'll throw the phone across the room for you."

"No! Shh. You'll wake up Sam—"

He rolled, switching our positions, leaving me on top.

"—and he needs the sleep to get over that cold he's been fighting."

When I put a hand to his chest and stretched for the phone, he captured my reaching arm and planted a kiss on the inside of my wrist. "She doesn't know we hear her. We could be at the mall. We could be having drinks with friends. We could be at the movies." He kissed me on the lips. "We could be doing this."

His hypnotic brown eyes began to sway me, and then mercifully, the phone stopped twanging.

He relaxed; I relaxed. Things were just getting interesting again when the phone erupted with a drum cadence that quickly segued into a marching version of "You're a Grand Old Flag."

My father.

Both of them were calling me? That wasn't a good sign. I shifted beneath Sean. "Just give me a minute, then—"

"We're in the middle of something here."

"I know." I sat up, trying to pull the sheet with me. "I know. I'm sorry." I stretched for the phone.

Sean gave up and rolled toward his side of the bed.

I swept my hair from my face with one hand as I answered. "Dad. Hi."

"Peach? Your mother wants to talk to you."

"I know. I heard. But I couldn't—"

"Do me a favor. You know how she is. Call her." He hung up before I could say anything else.

Couldn't he have just passed her his phone? Or told me what she wanted?

Sean was right. I shouldn't have answered.

But in the interest of forestalling another interruption, I returned my mother's call.

"Georgia Ann?" Her Southern accent hadn't mellowed with age. Come to think of it, nothing about her had mellowed with age.

"Hi. Sorry, I just—"

"Did you get that picture I texted you from the magazine? The one of that hairstyle? That model has the same long nose you do, and I've been telling you for practically forever that . . ."

I sent a glance over my shoulder in Sean's direction as she continued to speak.

He lifted one of his black brows and then settled on his back, folding his arms behind his head.

"Well? Did you?"

"Sorry. What?"

"The hairstyle. The one I sent you."

"It kind of looked more like a wig."

Sean sighed and closed his eyes.

"Extensions, I think. But that wouldn't be so bad, would it? You're so busy with Sam. A few extensions would give it some body. And you wouldn't have to mess with it. Besides, if you find someone who can match colors, how could anyone ever guess?"

I cupped my hand around my mouth when I answered, trying to keep Sean from hearing what I'd given up sex for. "I am not getting extensions." And my nose wasn't *that* big. "And I'm kind of in a hurry. Can I call you back later?"

"I just wanted you to be the first to hear the good news. Your father heard it straight from Scott Edwards."

"Scott Edwards?"

"From *Scottie*. The secretary of defense?"

"Right." *That* Scottie Edwards.

"He's resigning. Might not even hold out to the end of the year and . . ." She chattered on.

I'd given up sex for military gossip? I hated myself. I really did. And I wouldn't have blamed Sean for hating me too.

"And guess what?"

"Mom, I really don't have time right now."

"I'll just tell you: the president has taken Scottie's suggestion of nominating your father as his replacement—"

"Great! That's great. Dad must be really—"

"—so we'll be moving to DC."

"DC? Wow!" DC? No! I was a big girl, all grown up with a family of my own until my parents appeared. And then? I might as well be ten years old again. At least in my mother's view.

Sean's brows had collapsed.

I answered his unasked question with a look of horror as I replied to my mother. "I don't know what to say."

"I know! It's all so exciting. I knew you'd be happy for your father. Speaking of, he'd like to talk to Sean sometime."

"I'll let Sean know, okay? But really, I need to go."

"Say no more." Punctuality was one of the virtues my mother held sacred. Right up there with Respect for Your Elders, Patriotism, and Really Good Hair Dye. "We can talk tomorrow."

I was just about to sign off when her words registered. "Tomorrow?"

"When we get there."

"There *where*?"

"To DC. We fly in around three."

"You're coming *here*? *Tomorrow*?"

"We'll let you know when we land. Can't wait to see you!"

I switched my phone to silent, then burrowed back under the covers and scooted over to Sean's side of the bed. I told myself not to worry about their visit. I would deal with them when they showed up.

"They're not going to call again, are they?" Sean shifted to face me and ran his hands up my arms.

"They . . . uh . . . they might."

"Hmm?" He was nuzzling my ear again.

"They might call back. Mom said Dad wanted to talk to you." I nipped at his neck. Pressed closer.

"Me? Why?"

"I don't know." I pulled his face toward mine and kissed him. "They'll be here tomorrow, though; he'll probably tell you then. Sounds like he's going to be the next secretary of defense."

Sean kissed me back. "Sorry. What?"

I traced the tattoo that ran around his bicep. "Secretary of defense. Scott Edwards is going to resign. The president's going to nominate my father to take his place."

"Mommy?" Sam's plaintive cry filtered through the door.

We froze and then sprang apart as if we were teenagers about to be caught by our parents.

∞

By the time Sam emerged from the cozy burrow of his bed, Sean was already at the front door, sliding his feet into his old hiking boots.

Sam ran over to him. Somewhere between his room and the front hall, one of his socks had come off. His honey-colored hair stuck up in back where it had been pressed against the pillow. "Where are you going? Can I go?"

Sean held something up, then shoved it into his pocket. "Have to fix the sink." He glanced up as I approached. "Isn't that what comes next?"

I'd put it on the list to jog his memory. He'd told me back when we first moved in that he would fix it. I was trying my best not to nag.

"If I'm going to do it, I need to find the right parts."

Sam was hopping up and down. "Can I go?"

"Not today. Too cold out. Stay with Mom and keep warm."

Sam gave me the side-eye. The look said, in no uncertain terms, that staying home with Mom was not a very good consolation prize.

I cleared my throat. "Um . . ."

Sean turned toward me as he zipped up his coat.

"Can we circle back to the things on the list that we didn't quite get to finish?" I felt so sneaky, talking in code.

The corner of his mouth quirked. "We could just push them back to next weekend. Make a new list."

"No. We can't."

He wanted to laugh. I could tell. But he laid a hand on Sam's head. "Let's play Legos when I get back, Super Sam." He sent me a glance. "And maybe we can check a few more things off your mom's list too."

He leaned over Sam to kiss me and then walked out the door.

Two hours later, Sean still hadn't returned.

I tried his phone.

It went to voice mail.

Again.

Hey. It's Sean. Let me know where to reach you so I can give you a call back.

<beep>

2

I wandered into the kitchen and eyed the faucet, wonder-ing if whatever Sean had taken with him would keep it from running. A careful turn of the handles showed it hadn't made any difference.

Rain was pummeling the window above the sink. At least I wasn't out in it the way Sean was. But even so, our old 1920s bungalow came with a built-in draft that circulated about two inches above the floor. It also came with twelve-foot ceilings. Draft; high ceilings. Life was a trade-off.

Sam was hungry and I couldn't delay dinner forever, so I dished us up our servings and we ate together in front of the TV exactly the way I swore to my mother that I never did.

When I tried to steer him toward bed later, he balked. "Dad said we'd play Legos."

"And you will. But it's your bedtime soon and you can't play if you're asleep."

"Daddy said!"

I put a hand on his head to calm him. "I know he did. He'll kiss you when he comes back. And I'm sure he'd love to play with you tomorrow."

As Sam finished up the episode of his TV show, I called Sean's phone again. He didn't pick up.

Eventually I shooed Sam down the hall to his room. Once prayers were said and one . . . two . . . *three* stories read, I kissed him good night and then curled up on the couch in the living room, pulling a blanket over me. Our dog lifted her head, eyeing me as if wondering whether it would be worth the effort to join me.

Apparently not.

Shifting, I parted the curtains and stared out past the front porch into the night. Raindrops glittered like tracer bullets as they fell through the streetlight's diameter, but the light's glow didn't illuminate the ground. It just left silvery smudges on the asphalt.

I let the curtains settle back into place. Tried to talk myself out of the uneasiness that was starting to flutter around in my gut.

Finding a part for an old faucet at one of those home warehouse stores couldn't be easy. But calling me wouldn't have been hard.

I wished it would stop raining.

Drivers in the DC area were notorious. "Powdered Idiots," Sean called them. "Just add water."

Our dog, Alice, huffed a sigh.

"Amen."

She flicked an ear. I wouldn't have called a 150-pound mastiff Alice, but she'd already had the name when we got her.

I'd just started reading a well-thumbed copy of my favorite Asimov novel when I heard footsteps on the stairs outside.

My apprehension lifted away like a helium-filled balloon. Throwing off the blanket, I vaulted toward the door, ready to shush Sean. Sam didn't usually wake up after he'd fallen asleep, but wouldn't it have been just our luck for him to do it that night?

I yanked the door open. "Shh! You're going to—"

It wasn't Sean.

Two men dressed in identical blue uniforms, each holding a rain-flecked hat, stood in front of me. Their faces were sallow in the porch light. "Mrs. Brennan?"

Alice had gotten up and ambled over to see what was happening. As she nudged me aside with a push of her head to my hip, the men took a step back.

"There's been an accident."

I leaned out over Alice and glanced up and down the rain-slicked street. An accident? "Where?" I hadn't heard any sirens. Didn't see any flashing lights.

They exchanged a glance. "Not here. In Falls Church."

"Then why are you—" Realization hit me with the impact of a sledgehammer. "Sean?" With his name came the last bit of air I had in my lungs. Clearing my throat, I tried to swallow an enormous lump of fear. "Is he all right? Where is he?"

"His car was hit. He didn't survive." They exchanged a glance. "We're sorry."

"What are you saying?" I looked from one to the other, trying to decode their words because I couldn't understand them. "Sean's not dead. That can't be what you're saying because he's not— No. *No*, it's just— He just went to get a part." I was so cold all of a sudden.

Alice stepped forward onto the porch, moving the men farther away from the door.

I had to try several times before I could force more words out. "It was a part for the faucet. It's not working. He took the part off so he could match it, to get a replacement. Only sometimes it's not easy because everything in the house is so old. Sometimes there aren't any replacements. Or they have to be special-ordered. It can take a while. So he's not dead. It's just taking a while. He said he'd be back."

"I'm sorry, Mrs. Brennan. Can we come in?"

I felt like I should offer them something. You didn't invite someone into your home and not offer them something. Not if you were raised properly; not if you were raised by my mother. "Can I . . ." Having made it into the living room, I thought for a moment before remembering what it was I wanted to ask them. "Tea? Coffee? Would you like something?"

"No, ma'am."

My teeth were starting to chatter. I clenched my jaw to try to stop them. But then my mother's training kicked in and I opened my mouth again. "Could you, would you like to . . ." I disguised a full-body shudder by gesturing toward the Alice-distressed brown leather couch that sat in front of the window. "Please."

"We just need to ask you a few questions."

I heard what they said. I must have. I remember answering

questions. And I must have asked them some in return because they told me what they knew.

The accident was a hit-and-run.

Sean's car was totaled.

He was dead.

They handed me a card with the phone number of the medical examiner's office. Asked me to go the next day to identify the body. As they were leaving, one of them paused in the doorway. "Will you be okay, ma'am?"

Sean was dead.

"What?" What was he saying? His mouth was moving, but I couldn't hear any words.

He put a hand on my arm.

I looked down at it.

"Is there someone we can call for you?"

I looked back up at him. "No. Yes." What was the question again? "No. No, I'll be fine. I just have to . . ." My hand was groping for something to hold on to. It found something. A leash. I seized it. Held it up. "If you'll excuse me, it's getting late. I have to walk the dog now. Before I go to bed."

I didn't normally walk Alice at night. Sean did. But if he wasn't . . . if he didn't . . . Alice needed someone to take her out. Sam was sleeping; there was no need to wake him. I only went down to the end of the block. I'd forgotten to take my umbrella, but I had remembered my phone. I called Sean again, willing him to answer, willing for it all to be a mistake.

It kept going to voice mail.

Hey. It's Sean. Let me know where to reach you so I can give you a call back.

<beep>

I didn't know what else to do, so I just kept calling, waiting for him to pick up.

When I got back to the house, I decided to try a different number. I called my mother instead.

"Mom? They told me Sean died."

"Georgia Ann?"

"Sean died. Sean's dead, Mom. He died."

She gasped. "What?" It was a guttural, Southern *whut*.

"He went to the store to get a part for the faucet and his car was hit and he died. Mom?" I'd made a list in my head while I was walking Alice. There were things I needed to do. Lots of them. I just couldn't remember what they were right then. "Mom? What do I do? I'm not sure. I don't know what to do now."

"You just hold yourself together."

"Yes, ma'am."

"We were flying in tomorrow anyway. I'll call and make them put us on an earlier flight."

"I just keep thinking I should have fixed the faucet. I could have fixed it when we first moved in and none of this would have happened. I've always been better at fixing things than he is."

"Georgia Ann, you listen to me, do you hear?"

"Yes, ma'am."

"This is not your fault."

Not my fault. She sounded so sure of it that I wanted to believe her.

"Mommy?" The call came from the hall. "Mommy?" It was Sam.

I closed my eyes. I hadn't even thought of Sam. What was I going to tell him? What was I supposed to tell our son?

"Georgia Ann? Are you still there? Georgia Ann! What's happening?"

"Mommy?" Sam appeared at the entrance to the living room, bleary-eyed and pale, sniffling from his cold. "Mommy? Where's Daddy? He was supposed to kiss me when he came home."

3

I was sitting in the conference room at work surrepti-tiously trying to write my grocery list while my boss, Ted, was talking about our upcoming two-day red-team exercise. We were supposed to be playing devil's advocate on a group of proposals to make sure we weren't so in love with them that we'd overlooked the obvious or failed to anticipate our customers' criticisms. But Sam and I had just gotten back from a weekend trip we'd taken with my parents to the Eastern Shore and the refrigerator was bare.

I'd been doing better handling my parents in small doses since Sean had died. My father passed through DC regularly to visit companies on whose boards he sat or for whom he served as a consultant on classified projects. The trip to the shore, however, had been about a day too long. They just would not let up on trying to get Sam and me to move in with them once my father got confirmed as secretary of defense. They had bombarded me with a barrage of reasons throughout the weekend.

I forced myself to loosen my grip on my pen. Tried to relax my jaw.

Every few moments I sent a glance up at the whiteboard, which was illuminated with PowerPoint slides.

And then I wrote down the next item on my list.

Bananas.

"Georgie, you're going to be red-teaming with Mark, Bill, and Carl on the inertial navigation proposal."

"Right." *Applesauce.*

When I refocused on Ted, he was talking about my quantum encryption project.

"How's the test prep coming?" He was looking at me.

Our company was one of several contractors working on a quantum encryption project for the Department of Defense. The Chinese had taken the lead in quantum communication technology and there was an all-hands-on-deck effort to leapfrog them. If our product worked as we'd been promising, then it would put us one step closer to that objective. The goal was to use entanglement to make transmitted information self-report hacking attempts. If everything went as planned, if it passed its upcoming tests, it would be the ultimate in proactive cybersecurity.

"There's the test scheduled at White Sands in January. We had to cancel the last one because of a subcontractor issue. Everything looks set this time, though." He asked me about the details of the delay, then he changed the slide. He moved on to something else.

Cereal.

Multitasking was bad. I knew it was bad. My mother always said doing two things at once was like trying to catch a greased pig; it wasn't going to end well. When I was little I'd wondered why anyone would want to grease a pig and why anyone would want to catch one. But in my house, you didn't ask questions. You just fell in line and marched along.

I glanced up at the board.

And suddenly I couldn't breathe.

It felt like the bottom was dropping out of my soul. I locked my gaze on the whiteboard, trying to concentrate. If I could just concentrate, if I could just keep myself in the moment, then maybe everything would stabilize.

I tried. I heard Ted talking, but I couldn't decipher what he was saying.

I was used to grief creeping up on me unawares, but it hadn't yet done so at work during a meeting. As I stared at the slide, at the jumble of words, I could feel the tingling of rising tears. I blinked at them.

When that didn't work, I crooked a finger and pressed it beneath my eye, pretending to scratch an itch I didn't feel.

"Georgie?" Ted said my name as if he were repeating it.

"Yes! What?"

"Did you have an opinion?"

Opinion on what? I tried to focus again on the slide. Tried to discern what the topic was, but the words were meaningless. I couldn't even make them relate to each other. "Um . . . there are some things I would need to look into before I can offer an opinion. Can I get back to you on that?"

"On our next meeting? Just taking a vote. Next week or the week after?"

"Oh. Um . . ." My vision started to tunnel. My ears started to buzz. I wasn't going to be able to do it. I pushed away from the conference table, shoved my phone into my pocket, gathered my notebook to my chest. "Sorry." I forced a cough. "Water." I dashed down the hall to the bathroom, where I took refuge.

Any woman working in a male-dominated workplace learns to appreciate the women's bathroom. It's the only place where she can be herself. It was the only place where I could afford to show my grief.

Most of the time I couldn't do it at home. Not the way I wanted to. I couldn't yell and scream and rail against the accident that had taken Sean from me. When I left in the mornings, it was to take Sam to school on my way to work. When I returned in the evenings, it was always with Sam in hand. He stayed at school after classes ended, in an extended-day program, until I could pick him up after work.

I dropped my things on the counter by the sink and sought the privacy of a stall. I shoved the metal door closed. Before I could engage the lock, it bounced back toward me.

I shoved it again. Harder.

It swung back, clipping me in the chest.

I gasped, curling into the pain. Then I reached out and grabbed the door, slamming it shut again. The whole frame shook.

I did it again.

And again.

And then once more for good measure.

But it flew past the stop and bashed into the door of the neighboring stall.

I stood there panting for a few moments. Then, swiping at my tears, I took hold of the door and forced it back into position. I went and pulled my pen from the spiral on my notebook and used the cap to tighten all the screws.

Then I rinsed my face in the sink and patted it dry with paper towels. An advantage of never wearing makeup? I never had to worry about my mascara smudging. It was the one thing my mother had finally given up on. I gave myself a long, hard stare in the mirror, probing for any sign of weakness. Tried a smile.

Wobbly.

Tried again.

It would have to do.

At least I worked with a bunch of men. They would never notice.

∞

The get-down-and-get-dirty process that was grief, the two-steps-forward-three-steps-back, had become the rhythm of my life. Most of the time weekends were better. At least during the day. There was so much to do at home that I rarely had time to think.

That Saturday Sam was with my friend Jenn, so I decided to finally tackle the kitchen sink. It was a day that felt slightly more like summer than fall. I'd opened the windows to let the breeze freshen the air. Then I got out my pliers and applied them to the faucet I had finally found the nerve to fix.

Didn't budge.

I went back down into the basement and dug around for my strap wrench.

I'd found out that work—physical work—was good therapy. I hadn't found the time to see an actual therapist, but I'd read all the books I could find. They offered the same advice. I was supposed to be patient with myself, validate all my emotions, and remain connected to the people around me. And I was.

My neighbors Jim and June had become surrogate parents to me and grandparents to Sam since my own lived so far away. My best friend, Jenn, and I saw each other a couple of times a week.

I couldn't be anything but grateful for the friends we had.

But as I fastened the strap around the pipe, I heard footsteps scuffing up the stairs to the front porch. Since Sean's death, it had been a sound that left me with a sense of profound dread.

When I heard the sound of footsteps, my neck began to prickle and my hearing began to fade. In a strange sort of way I was entangled with the memory of the night Sean had died. Though time and space separated me from his death, my body kept reacting as if it had just happened.

I'd learned that it was best to breathe deeply and try to carry on.

The doorbell rang.

Leaving the wrench dangling, I walked through the dining room and living room to the front door. Opened it to find Mr. Hoffman.

"I thought to come by today. I hope you will forgive me. I know today is difficult."

Difficult. That was the perfect word. It had been eight months exactly since Sean had died.

"There's nothing to forgive." I shook the hand he'd gravely offered.

Alice tried to push her way between us. I pushed her back with my knee. Then I opened the door wider to let him enter.

Out in the street, a gray car drove by, leaving the rustle of scattering dogwood leaves in its wake. As I shut the door, a smile lifted the corners of Mr. Hoffman's mouth and animated a face otherwise void of expression. He was wearing his usual dark suit, hat, and solid-colored tie. He was splendidly old-fashioned and quaintly European. He'd escaped from East Germany back in the sixties and found his way to America, where he'd opened a toy shop down in Crystal City.

Next to him, my frayed jeans and my Think Like a Proton and Stay Positive T-shirt looked even scruffier. "I'm trying to fix my faucet."

He shifted the bag he was carrying to his other hand and removed his hat, revealing the bald spot that had been slowly consuming an otherwise enviable mane of hair. He tucked the hat under his arm. "We have a saying in Germany on faucet."

I raised a brow.

"When faucet drips one must call the plumber."

I laughed. "We have that saying here too." I gestured toward the back of the house with a sweep of my chin. He followed me. "Coffee?"

He demurred with a frown and a shake of his head. "Please." He nodded toward the sink. "Continue. I must not stop you."

The aerator finally came loose with a couple of forceful pulls. I unscrewed it and held it up to the light. "A lot of buildup in there." It hadn't been cleaned in a long time. Maybe never. The good thing about mineral buildup was that it acted like cement. It kept everything together. Bad thing: it messed up the seal.

"Little Bear is not here?"

"He's at a friend's. Due back anytime." I was using Sam's playdates to tackle the enormous to-do list that had accumulated since Sean had died. I kept telling myself I just had to do one thing at a time. But it seemed like every time I crossed one thing off, I added two things to the list in its place.

"Then this, I give you. To give to him." He gestured to the bag he'd placed on the floor at his feet.

I didn't have to look inside to know what it was. "Mr. Hoffman—you really have to stop!"

He shrugged. "He is a boy who misses his father."

"And another toy is going to help?" Actually, another wooden train to add to his collection of playsets probably *would* help. For a while.

Like many things in life, those too were my father's fault.

Dad had presented Sam with his first wooden train set just a few months after he was born. And over the years it had been joined by many others.

When he worked from DC, he'd come to dinner on Saturdays, new toy in hand, and play trains with Sam. Then, after Sam went to sleep, he'd stay and talk with Sean.

I was just the conduit for bourbon.

There was a period of time when Sean's reserve unit deployed and my father was so otherwise occupied that the additions to the playset had ground to a halt. Sam had begged me for something new, but I hadn't been able to find anything of similar quality online. I finally asked my dad where he'd found them. To my relief, his source was a toy shop—Mr. Hoffman's shop—just down the road, in the mall in Crystal City.

That's when I found out he'd escaped from East Germany with only the clothes on his back. His wife hadn't been so lucky. Before he'd been able to get her out, she'd died of pneumonia behind the Iron Curtain. Once he told me that, we'd had him join us for Easter. And Thanksgiving too.

He was a kind, dear man.

I took a mug from the cabinet, dropped the aerator in, and poured vinegar over it. I was hoping it would dissolve enough of the mineral deposits that I could clean it up and put it back on.

The doorbell rang again.

"That's probably Sam. You can give it to him yourself. Be right back."

My friend Jenn and her son, Preston, had returned Sam to me.

I stepped out onto the porch and leaned out over the boys to give her a hug.

When I wore a button-down shirt and jeans it always looked like I was planning on digging around in the yard. When she wore a button-down and jeans, like she was that day, it always gave me the impression of yachts, horses, and expensive estates on the Eastern Shore. She had that thing going on. But that afternoon she looked rumpled. And unhappy.

She kept me close. "Is there any way you could watch Preston for just an hour? I have some things I need to talk about with Mark. So we can come to an agreement on the divorce."

The crimp in her mouth and the line between her eyes let me know she wasn't looking forward to this talk.

"Sure. Yes. Of course."

I stepped aside so the boys could go in. Before they could tear through the house, I caught Sam at the elbow. "Mr. Hoffman's here. Why don't you go back to Sam's room, Preston, and let Sam come say hi first."

As Sam and I walked into the kitchen, Mr. Hoffman held the bag out to him. "Something for Little Bear."

"Cool!" Sam ran over and took the bag from him.

The delight on Mr. Hoffman's face as he watched Sam unwrap the gift? It transformed him. Sam didn't have a very good grasp of the calendar; there was no way he would have known how many months Sean had been gone. But it had been sweet of Mr. Hoffman to bring him a distraction.

Sam pulled a train and an add-on playset from the wrapping. "Wow! Thanks!"

Mr. Hoffman leaned forward. "And tell me: How is hockey lessons?"

"I'm really good!"

When Preston came wandering in, Mr. Hoffman stood. "I must go." He kissed me on the cheek. Nodded at Sam. The two boys ran off down the hall while I walked Mr. Hoffman to the door.

After he left, I went back to work on the faucet. I took the aerator from the vinegar and scrubbed it free of the accumulation of decades' worth of hard-water deposits. Then I applied a toothbrush to the threads of the faucet, trying to do the same thing. But as I screwed the newly cleaned aerator back on, I realized something.

Sean had lied to me.

5

The thought landed in my stomach like a deadweight.

He'd lied to me.

Whatever it was that he'd put in his pocket the night he'd gone to the store and never returned, it didn't have anything to do with the faucet, because those parts hadn't been touched in years. And whatever he'd put in his pocket hadn't come back to me with the effects from the coroner's. At least I didn't think it had.

I stood there at the sink staring out the window into the sun-drenched autumn afternoon wondering what Sean had actually been doing when he died.

As I tried to understand the implications, I started to tune in to Sam and Preston's conversation. They were in the living room.

"Dad says my hockey bag would be a good place to hide."

Sean had told Sam that? When? I put a hand on the counter and turned toward the dining room.

"Like for hide-and-seek?" I didn't blame Preston for sounding confused.

"Just if I ever had to hide."

Preston seemed to accept the explanation. "Want to play hide-and-seek?"

"Okay. Maybe my mom would look for us."

Not a chance. And I went into the living room to tell him so. "Hey, Sam? You said Dad told you your hockey bag would be a good place to hide?"

"Yeah."

"When did he say that?" I tried to sound nonchalant.

"When we played the game."

"The game? What game? Hide-and-seek?"

"The Bad Guys."

"The Bad Guys?" I was starting to sound like a demented parrot. "I don't think I've ever played that game." I looked at Preston, hoping to enlist an ally. "Have you?"

He shook his head.

I knelt beside Sam. "How does it go?"

"So you're in the—you have to pick the room." Sam looked at me, prompting.

"The room? Of the house?"

"Mom." He should have said, *Duh*.

"Okay. Um . . . here. The living room."

"Okay. So you're in the living room and the bad guys come. What are you going to do?"

"What kind of bad guys are these?" And why had I never heard of this game?

"The *bad guys*."

"Uh . . . well . . ."

"You're dead."

"What?"

"You're dead. You took too long. Now it's my turn."

Preston protested. "It's *my* turn!" He raised his hands and jumped. "It hasn't been my turn yet." He jumped again.

"Preston's right, Sam. It's his turn. But just— I need a second here to get used to being dead. That happened kind of quick, don't you think?"

"That's how it happens, Mom. And you don't get second chances. It's Preston's turn now." He turned to his friend. "So where do you want to be?"

I interrupted. "I still don't understand how this works. Could *you* do the living room? So I know how it goes? What do you think, Preston?" I wasn't beyond using peer pressure to plead my case.

Sam sighed the heartfelt, world-weary sigh of a six-year-old. "Okay. I'm in the living room and the bad guys come so I hide in the couch."

"The couch?" Preston and I looked at each other. It didn't seem like that great a hiding place.

"Like this." Sam dove into the couch, shimmying down into the crack between the seat cushions and the loose pillows. He burrowed in and pulled the pillows over himself. By the time he was finished, he'd completely disappeared. "Can you see me?"

"See you? I can hardly hear you."

He tossed the pillows off and pried himself out of the cushions.

"Let me try!" Preston repeated the disappearing act.

I put a hand to Sam's head. "Just out of curiosity, what did Dad say about the couch?"

"He said it was pretty good. Not as good as some of the others, but if you're in the living room when the bad guys come, it's good."

"So you're just supposed to, what? What are the rules? You stay there in the couch until the bad guys leave?"

Preston was crouched on the hearth, trying to pull a big pot over his head. I walked over and took it from him.

"Only if you have to. Because maybe the bad guys will go into another room and then you can run away." It was such a reasonable explanation that I had no doubt Sean had spent some time explaining to Sam how those things worked.

The hairs at the back of my neck stood on end.

"If they leave the living room, I run out the front door to Mr. Jim's house and I ring the doorbell until he or Miss June lets me in."

"Do *they* know about this game? About the bad guys?"

"Then I tell them to call the police."

"Do they know about this?" My voice had taken on a shrill edge that I couldn't quite control.

He shrugged. "You told me Mr. Jim sees everything."

He did. Most things. That's partly why he and Miss June had a spare key to our house; I could trust him. But I didn't think bad guys were on Jim's radar. Not the really bad ones.

"My turn! My turn!" Preston was jumping up and down.

Sam turned to him. "What room do you want?"

"Your room!"

"My room's great! There's lots of places to hide in there."

They raced into the dining room and then swerved down the hall while I stood there trying to count just how many kinds of wrong that game of Sean's was.

6

Sean had been dark and handsome in a mysterious sort of way. He had a five o'clock shadow at noon. And bedroom eyes just about any time of day. He was the sort of man you might overlook until he looked right back at you. That's when you discovered he had a gaze that could see inside your soul. And the sort of slow, sensuous smile that was a serious turn-on.

But when we first met, I hadn't been able to figure him out.

He wasn't constantly eyeing his cell phone the way most people in DC did. And he didn't seem to be looking for better options when he was with me or thinking of what he was going to say next. He didn't monopolize the conversation or play more-in-the-know-than-thou the way people in the area often did. In fact, after several weeks of dating, I realized I really didn't know anything about him. And wasn't a girl supposed to be suspicious of a man who never mentioned his family? Or his job? Or his hobbies? Or anything about himself at all?

With his dark eyes, dark hair, and swarthy skin, he might have been from anywhere.

So one night, as we were walking back from a restaurant to the apartment I shared with Jenn, I went for it. "I have to ask. Are you— I mean, your family. Where are they from?"

His lips lifted in a half smile. "I'm black Irish."

I blinked. "What?"

"Black Irish. Not Italian. Not Hispanic. Not Arabic."

Apparently, though, he spoke Italian. And Spanish.

He took my hand and fit our fingers together as we walked along.

"It's just— I feel like I don't know very much about you."

He sent me a sidelong glance. "What do you want to know?"

Everything.

So he told me. He'd been in the military, special forces; he'd gotten out. He had family—of course he had family, everyone had family—it was just that he'd grown up on the other coast.

Sean had a PhD in history. He worked for the army as a historian. He did have hobbies. *A* hobby. He liked to read: history, any kind.

Friends? He'd never mentioned friends. But that was normal, wasn't it? For someone who had grown up on the other side of the country and never had time to do anything with anyone but me?

"But what do you really know about him?" Jenn asked me the question one Saturday morning about six months after I'd met Sean. She was doing yoga in the living room. Her eyes were filled with concern as she regarded me, upside down, from a pose.

"*Pfft.* Everything."

"I mean, really. How much?"

"Enough."

"Because he's the silent, mysterious type, and sometimes mysteries aren't like, 'Oh, who keeps sending me flowers anonymously?' Sometimes they're more, 'Oh, who keeps torturing all these cute little kittens?'"

"Jenn, he's fine. Trust me."

To my great relief, Jenn shut up about Sean. But eventually I felt like I had to tell my parents about him. My father was still in the military and they were living in the area at the time, so of course my mother insisted that we come for dinner. And that I stay afterward.

Within five minutes of meeting Sean, my mother had managed to convey all the important information: she was from Mobile, born a Sinclair. Some people thought the Sinclairs were French, but they really weren't. Although she'd been brought up country club, she'd somehow ended up officers' club. No one in her family had thought my father would ever amount to anything, but she'd known better. Just look at him now; he was everyone's hero. Regardless, family was important, wasn't it? And a person would do anything for family, wouldn't they? She flashed her beauty-queen smile.

As always, her blonde hair was flawless. Her lightly tanned skin glowed against the red of her jumpsuit and the gold of her bangles and earrings that night.

As she started to ask Sean about his family, my father sent me a wink and diverted her attention. Mentally, I breathed a sigh of relief.

"Look here, Mary Grace! The poor man doesn't care about all that. Here's what you need to know, son: we're having brisket for dinner."

My mother smiled. "And slaw and coconut cake. Which I made."

My father raised his beer glass in her direction. "Which you made. To perfection."

She beamed. "What would you ever do without me?"

"Eat pork rinds and peanuts?"

"Be nice." She sent a glance to Sean. "People have always said we're like sweet and tea."

"Or bats and hell." My father mumbled the words under his breath as he brought the glass to his lips.

My father was gung-ho about life in general. The moment he sat down, he'd invariably get right back up. His favorite exercise, aside from running marathons, was pacing. My mother's job was to manage. She managed everything. If he was guns blazing, full speed ahead, she was the coolheaded analyst who always proceeded carefully, checklist in hand. He was big picture. She was details. All in all, they made the perfect team.

A very attractive, very perfect, quite formidable team.

At least they waited to talk about Sean until after he left. My father looked at the door that had just swung shut, lips pursed, eyes narrowed. "At least his discharge was honorable."

How would he know that Sean's discharge was . . . I felt my mouth drop open. "You checked? Mom!"

She kissed me on the cheek. "Your father loves you, sugar pie. Let him do what he has to do."

My father left the front hall and went into the living room. "He was awarded a silver star. Did you know that?"

I couldn't stop an eye roll. "No. I didn't ask for his evaluations." Not the way my father had apparently done. The stars he wore on his uniform guaranteed him just about anything he asked for.

Dad took up a post in front of the window. "He did the serious sh—"

"JB!" My mother tsked.

"What? It's true."

I joined him.

Sean glanced up before getting into his car. He pulled himself straight and threw a salute. Dad nodded.

For heaven's sake! I left my father standing there and followed my mother into the kitchen.

∞

If I had still harbored the slightest, tiniest, slimmest reservations about Sean, our wedding wouldn't have soothed them. On the Slater side of the aisle: a veritable Who's Who of the Washington and military establishments. On the Brennan side? His sister. A handful of co-workers and the overflow from my side.

My mother approached me just before she was walked down the aisle. She fluffed my veil. Straightened my gown. "I only have one piece of advice."

I'd been hoping that, considering the occasion, I might get by with no pieces of advice that day.

But she grabbed my hand, leaned toward my ear. "In any marriage, there are some things you might not want to know. Understand me? So don't you go asking questions that you don't want to know the answers to."

Before I could think of any reply, she'd pasted her beauty-pageant smile back on and was adjusting the groomsmen's boutonnieres.

I didn't know what to think of my mother's advice, so I decided not to think about it at all. Jenn, my maid of honor, had been flirting with a senator's aide as she waited for her own cue to walk down the aisle. Somehow she'd turned her scoop-neck bridesmaid gown into a shoulder-baring one.

I poked her in the ribs with my elbow. Gestured with my bouquet toward Sean, who was waiting at the front of the church. "See? He's not some sort of ax-wielding serial killer."

"I never said he was ax-wielding."

"You thought it."

"He always struck me as more of a knife-wielding kind of guy."

"Seriously, Jenn."

"Seriously? It's your wedding day. Why are you worried about knives and axes?"

It wasn't until later in the evening, at the country club where my mother had planned the reception, that I had a chance to talk to Sean's sister. She was too reserved to be described as friendly, but she and Sean shared the same brown eyes and the same Brennan smile.

I lifted the massive skirts of my dress and sat down next to her for a moment. I thought I'd been in the market for a simple and plain wedding dress. Somehow my mother had talked me into an extravaganza of ruffles and lace and even more ruffles and lace, and when I looked in the mirror just before I walked down the aisle, I thought it might have been a mistake.

Sean's lifted brow as he offered me his arm at the front of the church during the ceremony just proved the theory.

I'd leaned close. "Pretend this isn't me."

His mouth had quirked. "Really hoping it *is* you under all of that. Kind of why I'm here today."

I stuffed the extra froth of petticoats underneath the table as I leaned close to his sister and thanked her for coming. Kelly was her name.

"I didn't want to miss it. He never said much, but Sean always wanted a family."

It wasn't an odd thought to share. Most people grew up imagining themselves married, having children one day. But she said it in such a strange way. "Didn't you have one?"

"Not really. Not after Mom and Dad died. We got farmed out to relatives. You know how it is. I went to stay with Aunt Colleen and Uncle Bill. Sean got sent to Uncle Mac and Aunt Sue. Then we were together for a while, but Sean was kind of a handful. When we got put into foster care, he sort of fell in with the wrong crowd. Then he enlisted." She shook her head to dismiss the conversation. "But you don't want to talk about all that today."

"I knew your parents had died." Sean told me when we'd been planning the wedding. "But I don't think I've ever heard how."

"He wouldn't have told you. He still feels guilty about it."

7

Guilty about it? Visions of axes and knives floated through my head. "Why? Um, *why* would he feel guilty?"

"It's just that he was so small."

The backs of my ears began to tingle. From across the room, Sean caught my eye and raised his champagne glass in my direction.

"Small? How small?"

"He was six." She said it as if that explained everything.

"I see."

She plucked at her sleeve. "We've all told him there's nothing he could have done. And he saved me, so . . ." Her smile flickered. Died.

Her demeanor didn't exactly shout Crazy Person, but she kept saying the strangest things. "I have to be honest. I've never heard any of this. Do you mind telling me what happened?" So I could have the marriage annulled right away if I needed to?

"Oh." She sent me a searching gaze. "Sure. It was a robbery. I guess they thought no one was home. But we were. The lights were off because my parents had promised Sean a camping trip. But it was raining that weekend, so they'd decided to do their camping in the living room instead. They'd already set up the tent. Sean was coming downstairs when the thieves came in the front door. Sean watched them shoot Mom and Dad, then he went upstairs and took me from my crib and hid me underneath the bathroom sink."

"He saw them do it?"

She nodded. "He went over to the neighbors after, crying, saying the bad guys came."

The only real argument Sean and I ever had happened that first night of our marriage. I brought up the death of his parents.

"I just wish you would have told me yourself."

He was sitting on the bed in the hotel room, pulling off his bow tie. "It wouldn't have changed anything." Those were the words he said, but his eyes were asking me a question. *Would it have?*

"Why should it have?"

He glanced away, but I saw his shoulders relax.

"But it seems like—" I huffed a sigh in exasperation. "That was a big deal. And it changed everything for you. Both you and Kelly. I just feel like if I didn't know that about you, then . . ." I let my voice trail off.

He said nothing.

"Parents, family. They're really important."

"I can see that." He sent a sardonic look toward my wedding dress, which seemed to be expanding like Gorilla Glue, trying to take over the hotel room.

I ignored the barb. "And if you're that closed off about them, then maybe it's something you still have to work through. Maybe you haven't gotten over them."

"Maybe I've never gotten over my parents, but you've never gotten out from under yours."

The sting of his words stole my breath. I blinked back tears as I replied, "My strategy has been to keep my distance." I didn't like what happened, how easily my resolve wavered, when I was drawn into their orbit.

"How's that working for you?" He shrugged out of his jacket and stalked over toward the closet.

But he had to pass me on the way, so I reached out. "It's difficult! They're just so . . . so . . ." They were just so everything that they defied description. "And anyway, how would you know what it's like?" I clapped my other hand over my mouth as soon as I'd said it.

He stepped away from me and held his own hands up as if in surrender. "I wouldn't." He slipped by and hung up his jacket.

The first, some might say foundational, law of physics is that objects in motion tend to stay in motion unless acted upon by an external force. It was vitally important to me that we not start our lives together moving away from each other.

"I'm sorry." I went to him. Put my arms around his waist. Pressed my cheek against his back. "I didn't mean to hurt you. But I don't want you to keep hurting yourself with your memories either." He'd thrown me a zinger, but what he'd said was true. I released him. Stepped back. "So let's try to help each other. Over." I pointed at him. "Out from under." I pointed at me. "Deal?"

We might have shaken on it, but it was our honeymoon. We came up with a different way of sealing our bargain.

Considering his past, it was perfectly logical that Sean would teach Sam to play the Bad Guys. But in another sense? It was completely and horribly wrong.

We weren't living in an industrial, crime-ridden city of the 1980s like he had been when his parents were killed. Our house was smack-dab in the middle of one of the wealthiest counties in the nation. Kids walked to elementary school in our neighborhood. And middle school and high school too. They rode their Big Wheels down the sidewalks and tossed footballs in the streets. There were community movie nights and food truck festivals and bonfires in the park. If Sean had been looking for a safe place to raise Sam, he couldn't have settled in a better area. But clearly, none of that had been enough. Sean had still been worried about something in the months before he died.

I was still trying to figure everything out when Jenn came to pick up Preston.

She looked beyond me into the house. "So where are the kiddos?"

"Playing Bad Guys."

She sent me a quizzical look. "Bad Guys?" She raised her brow. "Do tell."

How to put into words the unease that I felt? It wasn't normal to teach your child the Bad Guys game. But Jenn had enough problems of her own. She didn't need to add mine to them. "It was a Sean thing. He used to play it with Sam." I shook my head. "But never mind. How did it go?"

"It's not. Going." She bit her lip. "I don't know if I'll be able to get residential custody."

That was news to me. "What do you mean?"

"I'll share custody, but you know my schedule. It's crazy. Senator Rydel's a great guy, but working for him will never be nine-to-five. And you know Mark. He's all about being a dad. Since he's got the more flexible schedule, what's the judge going to say?"

As Jenn stood there recounting her meeting, I tried to sympathize in the right places. But my mind kept crunching the new pieces of data I'd discovered, trying to reconcile those glimpses of Sean with the man I'd once known.

Why hadn't he told me about his fears? What other kinds of secrets might he have been keeping?

By evening, my unease had morphed into something bigger and darker. I may have banged my pots around as I washed them, and I might have slammed the doors to the cabinets as I put the dishes away. After the kitchen was clean and every spare crumb obliterated by antibacterial kitchen spray, I stood there wanting to *do* something. Solve something. Fix the disequilibrium that had been created.

Using my wrist, I pushed at the hair that had escaped both my ponytail and the confines of my headband.

I went into the dining room and ripped the placemats off the table. And then, as I stalked to the back door to go shake them outside, I nearly tripped over Alice. "Sorry."

All the warmth of the afternoon had been lost to the autumn night. After I shook the mats clean, I took a deep breath of frost-laced air before going back inside. After throwing them back on the table, I returned to the kitchen. Squeezed out my sponge, put it back in its holder. Then I slapped my palm down on the countertop.

Alice was watching me, ears cocked.

"I'd been doing so well, don't you think? Fixing the faucet. Cleaning out Sean's desk." I still hadn't dropped his phone line from my account, but I would. Eventually. I'd called his voice mail almost every night that first month after he'd died. I'd just needed to hear his voice.

My mind had been so fuzzy back then. Without Sean, I'd just been going through the motions.

Then, a few months later, my synapses had begun to fire in fits and starts as I began to take notice of the world around me. As of that afternoon? I was fully engaged, my thoughts razor sharp and singed around the edges with frustration over all the unknowns that were cropping up in my world. "What am I supposed to do, Alice?"

She sighed and settled her chin on her paws.

"I wish I could talk to him about everything. Maybe there was some perfectly reasonable explanation."

People always say you never forget your first. Well, that was Sean: my first, my only.

I hadn't even been thinking about love the night we met at the Clarendon Ballroom.

I'd been thinking about black holes. Because, why not?

The concept of the black hole is a mystery made more enigmatic by a misnomer and more complex by competing theories.

Black hole is an oxymoron. They're created by dying stars. And it's not that black holes signify a giant nothingness, but rather a giant everything-ness. A black hole is the densest mass in the universe. They aren't called black holes because they're unfathomably deep, but because they're unfathomably dense. And they just keep adding to their density.

There's everything *and* the kitchen sink in there. There's so much matter crammed into a black hole that nothing can get out. Not even light. That's what makes them invisible.

That means black holes can only be studied by observing their effect on the matter around them. Millions of black holes exist undiscovered—in our galaxy alone—simply because nothing has passed by close enough for us to detect them.

The funny thing is, people talk about black holes all the time. Even when they don't know they're doing it. Everyone who wishes they could stop time? The only point at which time ever stands still is at the edge of a black hole. Just before mass tips over the "edge" and is drawn into one, time freezes. If people knew that's what their time-stopping moment would be, they wouldn't make that wish.

How many black holes are there?

One hundred *million*. A new one forms every second. There's one at the center of our galaxy.

You'd think scientists would be able to figure out what happens to the things that get pulled inside black holes, but no one actually knows. Energy can't be created or destroyed; we know that for certain. But inside a black hole, it can be honed and compacted down to a single, solitary point. Dump in the entire United States. Throw in Africa and Europe and Asia too. And in the end? They all get compressed down to a single point.

The paradox is mind-blowing.

And yet whatever is taking place inside of them must have some sort of process. Even if it defies description, it can't defy explanation. If someone could just turn their brain inside out long enough to comprehend all the complexities, then physicists might be able to better explain the phenomenon.

Why couldn't that person be me?

Jenn had long ago attached herself to a lawyer type wearing the newest pastel incarnation of preppy chinos. And I had long ago given up on meeting anyone other than a junior Capitol Hill staffer or congressional lobbyist.

So, black holes.

I brought out the topic the way other people pulled out a Sudoku or a crossword puzzle, hoping that time and experience might reveal a different way of looking at things. There was always the chance that a series of unrelated events or mindless daily tasks would provide the trail of crumbs that would lead to comprehension of the scientific mysteries of dark matter, dark energy, or the reversal of time.

And, possibly, a Nobel Prize.

I sighed and glanced out over the wall. The rooftop bar overlooked a bloated median in Clarendon that was meant to be a tree-lined oasis. It was home to an Orange Line metro stop, a fountain that burbled when it happened to feel like it, and an overlooked monument to those who had died in the last century's wars. I was probably the only one who wished I were down there instead of up on the roof.

Everyone else was laughing and drinking. They were making a surprisingly persistent attempt at pretending the song the DJ was playing was danceable.

Poking my straw at the fruit that had settled to the bottom of my ruby-colored sangria, I wondered how long I should wait before I dragged Jenn away. She'd made me promise not to let her go home with anyone but me.

Thirty minutes? An hour?

I gave a piece of pineapple a good poke. As I eyed the steadily growing crowd and all the gyrating bodies, my gaze swept past a man at the bar. Came back to focus on him.

Dark-haired. Dark-eyed.

Hel-lo!

9

I caught a glimpse of his face and he shifted, attention caught by something to the left of me. I still had a few high school tricks up my sleeve, though; I moved left, threading my way around dancing couples, hoping it would place me in his view. And it did.

He saw me.

We saw each other and everything changed.

It was one of those movie moments. He pushed away from the bar and started toward me and suddenly time became elastic. The music faded and people moved in slow motion as I swallowed, wishing I'd actually worn the cute dress Jenn had convinced me to buy.

Then time slammed back into place—the music overloud, people overclose, my cheeks overheated. As he came toward me, I wished he'd stop looking at me. But then, just as quickly, I hoped he wouldn't.

He nodded.

My mouth opened, but I don't think I said anything.

What was it about his eyes? They were dark. Probing. But it was more than that. It was as if I was the one he'd been looking for.

The lock of gel-tipped hair that lifted from his widow's peak? It only emphasized those gorgeous eyes. The tattoo on his bicep that played hide-and-seek with the sleeve of his polo? Intriguing. The fact that his jaw was outlined by a not-too-close shave? Magic. And yes, Robert De Niro, he was talking to *me*.

And he *kept* talking to me! (Honestly, that normally didn't happen. I wasn't very good at flirting.)

When he asked if I wanted to leave, I happily threw all my mother's advice right out the window, as if I didn't have a world-class brain.

Don't ever let a stranger buy you a drink.

He wasn't a stranger; his name was Sean.

Don't ever leave a bar with someone you don't know.

I did know him. His name was Sean.

Always go home with the friends you came with.

I would have, but Jenn had just given me a thumbs-up and disappeared with the guy in pastel chinos. And that left me with Sean.

When all else fails, take a taxi home with the spare twenty you keep in your wallet.

If I hadn't spent that spare twenty, I might have. But again, there was Sean, who seemed more than happy to walk me home. It was odd, really. There'd been no one at all and then, all of a sudden, there was Sean.

I wasn't drunk. I never got drunk. But I was buzzed and I was happy and when he offered to take me home, I accepted. Why? Because somewhere, deep down, I understood that I wouldn't be able to keep feeling like the only girl in the world if he stopped looking at me.

Now I couldn't even think of our first meeting without wondering if there was something I should have seen from that very first night. Was he a liar when I first met him? Was there something he'd been hiding even then?

You never know enough about a person when you first start dating to understand what they're made of. They're a black hole of sorts. You know they're composed of a density of associations and people and experiences, but you can't actually see any of that. You know everything about them reinforces a certain theme of their character. But you can't see that either. Not at first. Not until you get closer. And by that time they have pulled you in past the point of no return and you've lost your objectivity. You've become part of their density, and when that happens you can no longer escape.

So I had questions without any good answers and no foreseeable way of finding any either. But it was clear that there was something, some *things*, about Sean that I hadn't been able to see.

If it had just been the lie about the faucet, I might have gone into our room and rifled through his clothes—which, yes, were still there—looking for signs of lipstick or sniffing for the scent of an alien perfume. Or any perfume, really, because I didn't wear any. Much to my mother's chagrin.

But it wasn't just the lie.

It was the idea that Sean thought Sam might be in danger.

Sean had worn a green beret. It's not like he didn't know what danger was. It might seem strange that I'd never asked him much about his time in service. Probably made me seem impossibly naïve, because that's what pillow talk was for, wasn't it? But I was raised in a military family by a four-star general. Any information I was given had been strictly on a need-to-know basis. And one of my family's cardinal rules was Don't Question What You've Been Told.

Over a million Americans hold top secret security clearances. Among them were probably many of my friends and neighbors. So in the DC area? You didn't pry. People told you what they could. They might say what three-letter agency—Department of Defense, Department of Homeland Security, Department of Agriculture—they worked for, but that's usually where the information stopped.

When Sean had told me that he'd "done stuff," I'd left it at that because people with top secret security clearances honestly don't even tell their wives what they do for a living. Not everything.

So, knowing Sean's background and that he was worried about Sam's safety? That was big news. That meant I should be worried too.

It led me to question my understanding of reality as I folded laundry that night.

In order to make sense of our unanswerable questions in physics, we scientists have begun to think we might have to jettison all of our assumptions and leave behind everything we know. The answers are staring at us—they are right in front of our eyes. Everyone knows they are; we just can't see them because they've camouflaged themselves in our reality. The key to unlocking the mysteries has to be things we've seen a million times and always managed to overlook.

So that was the challenge. How could I unknow the Sean I'd married? How could I re-see the man I'd once known? I needed to look, not for clues, but for something obvious. Something, perhaps, that had been there the whole time.

10

It took longer than normal to get Sam to bed that night.
His counselor told me it might take a while for Sam to let himself fall asleep again without a fight.

Subconsciously he was afraid I might die while he was sleeping too.

I called my parents and put them on speakerphone. Sometimes that worked. My father asked Sam about school. Asked me about work. I mentioned Mr. Hoffman had brought Sam another train. Sam sang a song he'd learned at school that included the names of all fifty states, in alphabetical order. Then he sang it again. They reminded him that they'd be coming into town again on Friday and would play with him. But when we said good night, Sam was still wide-awake.

We cuddled for a while on the couch as we stared up at the constellations of glow-in-the-dark stars I'd stuck to the living room ceiling. When he started nodding off, I carried him to bed.

But then *I* couldn't sleep. I kept thinking about Sean.

I'd been looking back at the beginning of our relationship to try to figure out what I'd been missing. It hadn't gotten me very far. I decided, as I lay in bed, that maybe I should start at the end, with the night Sean died. Maybe from there I'd be able to pick up something, some thread, that would unravel everything back to the beginning. It was the same way scientists observed explosions in the universe and then followed them back through billions of light-years to determine where they'd come from.

So I threw on a bathrobe and went into the office and pulled out the documents from the accident. The police report. The medical examiner's report. The death certificate.

As I sat there on the cold wood floor in my pajamas, I read through the medical examiner's report. The descriptions of the actual autopsy meant nothing to me. And I wasn't quite sure what I was looking for.

Sean had died. End of story. But I skimmed the pages anyway. They stated his sex, height, weight. Eyes: brown. Hair color: black. Noted his tattoo, scars, moles. There were descriptions of the evidence of injuries. Next were pathological findings.

He'd been found in the driver's seat. He had blunt-force injuries. One of his lungs had been punctured. I went on to the next page. There had been no video surveillance. No witnesses that they could find. The verdict? He'd died of blunt-force injuries to the head due to a motor vehicle accident.

It was signed and stamped by the medical examiner, Dr. Kyle Correy.

Attached to the report was an inventory of personal effects. The items he'd been wearing or carrying were listed on the left-hand side of the page. The right side noted that they'd been "given to father-in-law." I'd asked my father to identify Sean on my behalf.

The inventory had been taken by the medical examiner as well. I read through the list:

Black coat
Blue plaid shirt
Jeans
Brown leather wallet
Keys
Phone
White socks
Brown boots
Briefs
Watch
Gold wedding ring
Pocketknife

They were all still in the cardboard box my father had signed for. But what would it hurt to go through them again? I pulled the box from the corner of the closet where I'd let it gather dust and went down the list, pulling the items out as I came to them.

With every item came a whiff of that indefinable combination of soap, shampoo, and laundry detergent that had, when combined with the heat of his skin, resulted in a scent that was uniquely Sean.

I had to pause a couple of times, take a few deep breaths, but I got through it.

Everything was there but the pocketknife.

I turned the box upside down.

No knife.

I unfolded all the clothes, averting my eyes from the rust-colored bloodstains. Then I felt in the pockets of the jeans and coat to make sure it hadn't been concealed inside.

Nothing.

I paged back through the report and made a note of the medical examiner's name and phone number.

Had anything else failed to come back to me from the autopsy?

I grabbed his wallet and went through it.

Driver's license. Library card. Visa. ATM card. Medical insurance card.

Nothing else.

No receipts. No money.

I picked up the key chain: the car key, house keys for both the front and back doors, key for his bike lock. And one more. A key for what? I fingered it for a moment. Key to his office? It was small and thin. More like a key to a padlock? A filing cabinet?

Probably something at work. And if that were the case, then I needed to return it.

I worked it from the ring and set it aside.

What else was missing?

Struck by inspiration, I went to get my purse from the bedroom, then came back and dumped it on the floor beside the box. I took my wallet and pulled everything out of it.

I had most of the same things in my wallet that he did and some cash in addition to several receipts.

I took my money and the receipts and set them aside. I put my sunglasses on the pile too, along with my mini notebook, pen, assorted hair ties, lip balm, and the coins that lived at the bottom of my purse.

It was an exercise in uselessness.

Nothing was missing from Sean's effects but his Leatherman pocketknife. I sent a quick glance over in the direction of my piles. What about his sunglasses?

He hadn't been wearing them. It had been raining that day.

But then where *were* his sunglasses? I would have noticed them if he'd left them in the house.

I tore a page from my notebook and wrote it down: *sunglasses.* Then I wrote *Leatherman* underneath it.

Oh! Where had I put his attaché? I found it on the floor in the pile of things I'd removed from the closet when I'd brought out the box. I took everything out of it and stacked the contents next to the things I'd found in his wallet.

A couple of pens. A few binder clips. A ruled notepad. It wasn't nearly as packed as it could have been. Or maybe he'd just never carried much in it. I couldn't remember.

Once again, I grabbed hold of my own attaché and compared my contents with his.

Mine had power cords, my security badge from the office, some folders with notes from the office, my work laptop.

Laptop! His was missing.

I added it to my list.

But it was a government-issued computer. Maybe he'd left it at work that weekend. A definite possibility.

Anything else?

My attaché had a security badge. He'd had one too. He'd worn it on a lanyard, putting it on every morning before he left. It usually spent weekends in his attaché. But it wasn't there. And he hadn't left it on the dresser either, the way he sometimes had. I would have noticed long before. I added it to the list.

Mystery item: *key.*

Missing items: *sunglasses, Leatherman, laptop, security badge.* What had happened to them?

11

The next morning I called the medical examiner's office.
It was a Sunday, but I was guessing they were open for business 24/7.
I asked for Dr. Correy.

There was a long pause.

"I don't want to interrupt him. If he's in the middle of . . . of . . ."
An autopsy? A body? I shuddered at the thought. There was a reason
I'd gone into a *theoretical* science. "If he's in the middle of something
I could leave my number and ask him to return the call."

"No. That's not— I mean, you can't."

"I'm happy to call back."

"He's not here."

"Can you tell me when he'll be in?"

"No. It's not that." The voice on the other end dropped. "He was
fired."

"Fired?"

"After he was arrested."

"He was arrested?"

"I mean, yeah. He was taking people's things."

The conversation was making no sense.

"It's not as if they needed them anymore. Not that it was—"

"Dr. Correy was taking things? Whose things?"

"The dead people's. Not like, I mean, you never know what you're
going to find when you do an autopsy."

I had no idea what to say to that.

"Sometimes people hide things. In their . . . you know."

"In their wallets?"

"No! In their cavities."

"Oh." Oh!

"Drugs. People hide drugs. Sometimes Dr. Correy found them. Instead of reporting them, he'd sell them."

Just the thought made me feel icky. "Did the doctor ever use any of those drugs he stole?"

"Don't think so."

"There isn't any chance— It's just, he's the one who performed the autopsy on my husband, and it makes me wonder if—"

"Doc was really good. At autopsies. You should have seen him with that saw. *Zizzz-zizzz*. If it wasn't a 'specially difficult case, he'd be in and out like no one you'd ever seen. Don't worry. If Doc Correy autopsied your husband, he was good to go."

∞

While Sam played with his trains that afternoon, I did an internet search on Dr. Correy, medical examiner. He'd been indicted and pled guilty to charges of racketeering and conspiracy to distribute. He was serving a three-year sentence in a federal prison. That seemed quite generous for a convicted drug dealer. If he'd gotten time off for good behavior, they'd awarded it before he'd even been assigned to a cell.

Strange.

The federal prison was at the extreme southwestern edge of Virginia. It was not reassuring that Sean's medical examiner had been a drug dealer. But I didn't have time to drive down there and ask him about it. And beyond that, what would I say?

My husband didn't happen to tell you what he'd been doing right before he got hit by that car, did he? He was, in fact, dead when you autopsied him, right?

It didn't seem like he'd actually been taking drugs himself. He'd only been selling them.

But strange was strange.

Twenty-four hours earlier, there had been no strange people in my life. Now there were two: the bad guy or *guys*, which Sean had been afraid of, and the medical examiner.

I googled the number for the prison, called, and asked if I could speak to him. Or at least leave a message.

"You want to leave a message? For who, now?"

"For one of the prisoners. His name is—"

"Oh, we don't do that. Nope, nope, nope."

"But I *really* need to talk to him."

"Then you *really* need to get *him* to call *you*." *Click*.

So maybe that hadn't been my best idea ever.

How could I get Dr. Correy to call me if he didn't even know me?

I could write him a letter and ask him to call me, which might entail a several-week turnaround. Or I could contact his attorney. I found the phone number of the attorney's office and added it to the contacts on my phone. Then I added it to my to-do list for Monday.

∞

Reading the medical examiner's report hadn't helped me understand what Sean had been doing when he died. But that didn't mean I had to stop looking for information. As Sam did some coloring, I read through the police report on Sean's accident. When I'd received it, I'd only given it a cursory glance before shoving it into a drawer of his desk. At that point, it was redundant. It had only told me what I'd already known: Sean was dead.

That night I actually read it.

He'd been killed at Seven Corners, which had taken no one who heard about it by surprise. Five major roads converged at that point into one of the worst traffic snarls in northern Virginia. It was a concrete and asphalt nightmare framed by potholed access roads and parking lots that fronted superstores and other blights on modern existence.

The accident had occurred at the intersection of Leesburg Pike and Broad Street. Sean's car had been traveling southeast on Broad Street. He'd been hit on the driver's side by a car traveling up Leesburg Pike and—

Something didn't seem right.

Pulling my phone from my pocket, I googled Seven Corners and zoomed in, trying to make sense of a truly funky intersection. One road split, two went up and over, and a fourth entered from a side, while the fifth just barreled through underneath them all. Okay. So if Sean had been on Broad Street and . . . Why had Sean been on Broad Street?

Broad Street was *past* Home Depot.

I zoomed in even closer. There was no way a car traveling on Leesburg Pike could have hit him. Because at the point where Leesburg Pike intersected Broad Street, it wasn't called Leesburg Pike anymore. It had a different name.

Wasn't that something a police officer would have known?

But a bigger question remained. Where had Sean been coming from?

12

Monday came in the way only Mondays do: with protests, regret, and a vow to do the next weekend better. Clothes, breakfast, vitamin gummy; brush teeth; coat, backpack, shoes. That was the morning routine. But Sam waved off the backpack and sat down on the floor to tug at the Velcro fastenings on his sneakers.

The order didn't matter, as long as he walked out the door with both. That's what I told myself. But I drew the line at superhero capes.

I didn't think his teacher, Ms. Hernandez, would appreciate it. But mostly I was worried that some of the kids might make fun of him. Or try to take it and wear it themselves.

Considering that he was still working at making sense of Sean's death, and that Sean had called him Super Sam, I would have done almost anything, offered any bribe, in order to keep that cape at home.

I pulled it out from the collar of his coat and then turned him around so I could undo the tie beneath his chin.

He batted my hands away.

"Why don't we leave this at home today?"

"Because I can't be Super Sam if I don't wear it. And I have to practice for Halloween!"

"You know what? Superman didn't always wear his cape. But even though no one else knew he was Superman, he knew it. And that was the important thing." The other important thing was that I'd gotten the knot undone and the cape lay in a puddle on the floor behind him.

I leashed Alice, then she and I walked Sam to school past 1920s farmhouses and bungalows with wide front porches; storybook brick Tudors from the 1930s with their arched front doors and steeply pitched roofs; and brick colonials from the 1940s and '50s in sizes small, medium, and center-hall large.

Here and there, raised ranches from the 1960s and a rare split-level from the 1970s made an appearance. And—often whispered about, but largely ignored, like a sprawling seatmate on a regional plane—a few mini mansions bumped up against county height restrictions and strained against the outside edges of their too-small lots.

Alice and I walked back home along her preferred route of boxwood- and liriope-lined walkways. Chris Gregory and his Maltipoo joined us.

Chris walked his dog around the same time I walked Alice, along the same route. There were dozens of Chrises in our neighborhood. People you talked to because you were walking in the same direction. People you shared your life with for ten or fifteen minutes every day.

My out-the-door-at-the-very-last-possible-minute schedule assured that I was usually heading into the school with Sam while Chris had already dropped off his son. Although, once or twice, I'd managed to see his son ignore him as he'd waved good-bye.

I'd found out Chris was a professor at one of the local universities and a fountain of knowledge about all things Boy. He wore a leather-billed baseball cap over his sandy hair and had a penchant for pairing Northwestern T-shirts with his cargo shorts.

He slid a look toward me. "How are things?"

I shrugged. "You?"

"Same. I wanted to offer, with Sean not there, if there's anything you need help with. Kristy was always asking me to do things around the house. You know—change a lightbulb, kill a fly."

His wife, Kristy, had died several years before.

Chris and Kristy. What could be cuter?

But she must not have been handy like I was. Sean and I had an unspoken agreement. The person most bothered by something became the person responsible for the fixing of it. So when the towel rack in the bathroom started tilting toward the floor or the front door started to stick, Sean got out a hammer or a wood file and went to work. But when the fridge started gurgling or the air conditioner stopped working, I got out my multimeter, my power drill, and my set of screwdrivers and unfastened the panels labeled *Do Not Open— Danger of Electrocution* so I could take a look inside and figure out what was going on.

Sean had been the first one to comment on the dripping faucet. It wouldn't have taken me long to fix it, but that faucet had been his.

Chris's hazel eyes crinkled at the corners as he slanted a smile at me. "It would make me feel useful again. And I've got this great set of screwdrivers."

That made me smile.

He glanced at his watch, then inclined his head. "Anyway. Just let me know. Sorry to ditch you, but I've got to go."

As his stride lengthened and his pace quickened, I wondered what it would be like to establish a life with someone so normal. So solid. Someone who was exactly what he seemed.

Alice and I looped toward home. Along the way, a garbage truck stalked us, halting with a grinding shudder and starting up again with a hydraulic hiss. When it drew even with us, we stepped from the sidewalk into a yard, waiting for it to pass.

Alice tensed.

I tightened my hold on the leash and ordered her to sit.

That's when I remembered.

Trash!

I hadn't put out the trash.

I'd meant to. But the previous night I'd been focused on the police report. And that morning there'd been the issue of Sam trying to leave the house with his cape around his neck.

Alice's muscles bunched and then, before I could take any deterrent measures, she'd whipped the leash from my hand and was off down the road, scampering after the truck, legs a-blur.

"Alice!"

She didn't used to run after garbage trucks. She only started after

Sean died. We all had our ways of dealing with grief. Without Sean as her alpha, her preferred method was to pretend that she'd forgotten all of her obedience training.

"Alice, stop!"

Skidding to a halt just before our house, she sat down—with an odd, sharp bark—in the middle of the street, just the way Sean had taught her to do on command.

A pleasant surprise.

As I recovered the leash, she stretched her neck up and let out another short bark. The garbage truck disappeared around the corner, two garbage men hanging on to the back.

I trudged up to the house, scowling at the yellow fall crocuses that had magically appeared the previous week in the front yard along the fence. They were supposed to have been spider lilies. I knew that because Sean and I had planted them with Sam.

I hated fall crocuses. When crocuses pushed up out of the earth in the spring, it was cause for celebration. When fall crocuses did the same, they seemed like latecomers, irritatingly out of season. The party? It's over. Ended months ago. Everyone's gone home!

I was so focused on despising them that I almost ran into my trash cans.

But I hadn't wheeled them out. I was certain I hadn't. I flipped the lids shut and hauled them back up the driveway anyway. God bless Jim. He must have rescued me. Again.

I'd thank him later.

As I came back around the house toward the front yard, a gas company van drove up. Slowed. Parked on the street in front of the house.

Men in white coveralls popped out of the back as if it were a clown car. One of them waved me over.

"Can I help you?"

"Is emergency."

13

"With my *gas*?" I peered past him out to the street. Orange cones had already been placed along the perimeter of my property. "What emergency?"

"System say need repair."

The neighborhood was nearly a hundred years old. Something was always breaking down. One week the fire hydrants would be flushed out. The next week the power company would shut down the lines for a few hours to put in a new transformer. Just as soon as the county repaved a street and filled its potholes, the water company would come along and dig a trench right down the middle to pull up an old pipe or replace the main. If you thought too long or hard about the aging infrastructure, you'd never be able to sleep at night.

I led him through the house to the kitchen. Alice wanted to come too, but I ordered her to stay.

Surprisingly, once more, she obeyed.

We walked down the bare, scarred wooden stairs to the partial, cinder-block basement. Pulling the string for the light, I pointed past Sam's train table to the gas pipes, which snaked along the wall.

He gestured toward the meter. "Is old."

It most certainly was. I'd asked the gas company about the regulator before we'd moved in. They said they'd be happy to replace it. On our dime. Unfortunately, by then we'd already spent all our dimes buying the house, so I'd made myself feel better by reading up on the decades-old, mercury-regulated device. It had the effect of making me feel worse. I finally made my peace with it by inspecting it every week and building a cage of sorts to keep Sam and his friends away from it. Mercury didn't have a discernible smell, but it did leave traces and would give off toxic fumes if it spilled.

I removed the cage and gave it a once-over, then glanced at the floor beneath it. "I don't see any spills or leaks."

"Is, uh . . ." He waved a hand toward the regulator.

I raised a brow.

"Inside."

"The leak? That's impossible." When the units fail, they fail because they've been improperly moved. The spills are *external*. I'd read all about the incidents near Chicago back in the early aughts.

The man shrugged and nodded at his clipboard. "Is on list."

"For what?"

"For fix."

"How?"

"We fix."

"With a new one?"

He nodded.

Uh-oh. The problems in Illinois had been made worse when poorly trained contractors removed the old mercury regulators. "So you're going to use a vacuum cleaner, right?"

"Yes."

Good grief! "Okay. Know what? I don't see any signs that this is leaking and I need to get to work. Leave me the number of your supervisor and I can call to get this sorted out."

Upstairs, Alice was barking like a fiend. Over across the basement near our bedroom, where an outdoor crawl space abutted the cinder blocks, floorboards squeaked. What was she doing over there?

14

Twenty minutes later, I was showered, changed, and ready
for work. But I was also thirty minutes late. As I locked the front
door, Jim hailed me from across the street. Sunlight glinted off his
glasses. His old, paint-splattered barn jacket was buttoned up against
the morning's chill.

I waved back. "Hey—thanks for putting out my trash this morning!"

"What?" He put a hand to his ear.

"The trash. Thanks for putting it out."

He shrugged. "Didn't do it. Not this week."

If he hadn't done it and I hadn't done it, then who had?

I puzzled over it on the drive to work. None of my other near
neighbors would have even noticed my trash wasn't out. I finally
decided I must have pulled them out without remembering, crediting
the lapse to the interminable twists and turns of the grieving process.

Setting my uneasiness aside, I told my phone to call the gas company's customer service line. Five minutes later, as I was turning into
the parking garage at work, I was connected to an actual person.

I hit my blinkers and pulled to the side so I wouldn't lose my
connection.

Of course, every car behind me felt the need to honk on their way
down into the garage.

I pressed a finger to my free ear as I explained about the repairman.

"We don't replace old meters, although we can recommend a
contractor."

"I know you don't. He wasn't there to replace it; he said it needed
to be repaired."

"We don't repair old meters."

"He said my meter was on his list."

"His list of what?"

"Repairs."

"We don't repair old meters."

Being trapped in an endless loop of conversation with a person was worse than being trapped in an endless loop with an automated answering system. "Can you check to see if my house was scheduled for work today?"

"Can I have the work order number?"

"I don't have a—" I took a deep breath so I wouldn't yell at him. "There is no work order number. Could I give you my address?"

"How about the account number?"

"I don't have my account number at the moment."

"Can you give me the address?"

I gave him the address. And after five minutes of incredibly frustrating conversation, it only took him about five seconds to confirm that my house had been issued no work order and that it was not on anyone's list of anything to be concerned about.

"So you're saying you didn't send them."

"No, ma'am."

∞

Once I got to work, I shut the door to my office and placed a call to the medical examiner's attorney.

"And you need to talk with Dr. Correy why?"

"My husband was one of his . . . um . . ." Patients? Clients? "He performed my husband's autopsy."

"And you want to what? Thank him?"

"No. There was something missing in my husband's inventory, and I wanted to—"

"Let me guess. Your husband had drugs on him? In that case—"

"What? No!"

"—the feds might be very interested in talking to you about your husband's drug—"

There was a knock on the door. Ted poked his head in.

I held up a finger.

He gave me an okay sign and closed it.

"No, he wasn't— That's not what I called about. Dr. Correy's inventory listed a Leatherman pocketknife. My father signed for it when he picked up my husband's effects."

"And?"

"And it wasn't there when I got the box."

"Listen, I can't help you."

"Is there no way you could contact him and ask him to—"

"I did my job when we made the deal with the feds. I'm not his office assistant, okay?"

"Wait. He had a deal with the—"

"Can't you people just leave the guy alone?"

You people? "I was just wondering what might have happened to the Leatherman, that's all."

"Who did you say signed for it again?"

"My father."

"Then why don't you ask him?"

15

My boss, Ted, leaned into my office as I hung up. "We missed you this morning, for the beginning of the meeting. The customer was here."

"I'm sorry. I just—"

He came into my office and plopped into the chair in front of my desk. "Thing is, we were counting on you. Classic entanglement theory as it relates to cybersecurity. Remember?" He shifted, placing his elbow on an armrest, propping his chin up with a loosely held fist. "You're the only one who can answer all those questions in detail."

"I know. I'm so sorry."

"Can't tell the customer"—he cleared his throat—"*prospective* customer, that we could do the job better when you're not doing the talking."

"I know. I—" What was there to say? I'd screwed up. "I'll follow up with them and see if they need anything else. I've been working the clearances for the test in January. Everything's submitted. Admin says we're good to go. I've been told the chairman of the House Intel Committee wants to come." That's how big a deal it was. And it added a whole other layer of anxiety. "Our subcontractor says there shouldn't be any problems. They've checked and rechecked." Ad nauseum. A lot was riding on the test. If everything worked the way it should, then the system would go into production almost immediately. Which meant lots of money, lots of jobs, lots of growth for the company. It would put us in a prime position, riding the leading edge of the technology.

He eased himself from the chair. "Listen, I know it's hard with Sean gone." He sent me a keen-eyed glance. "Do you need to cut back on hours?"

"No! No. I can manage."

"I understand. I really do. They say it takes time." He gave a half shrug and headed toward the door. "You could go to part-time. We'd find a way to make it work. Think about it."

Part-time did sound nice. And I did think about it. For two seconds. That's all it took to remind myself that somebody had to pay our bills. There had been insurance money when Sean died, but I'd used most of it to pay off the car and refinance our mortgage so I could afford the payments on my salary. With the little bit that was left, I'd done some things like fencing in the backyard for Alice and replacing several of our ancient windows. The rest I'd dumped into my 401(k) and a college savings plan for Sam.

My boss disappeared out the door only to reappear a second later. "Before I forget, where do we stand on your contract for next year?"

From long experience, by *we*, I knew he meant *you*. Whether the test was successful or not, the funding for my part in the current phase had almost been used up. I'd had to find a new contract to work on in the coming year, so I submitted a proposal for a quantum encryption project and I won it. But winning a government contract was a double-edged sword. "It's been awarded, but since Congress hasn't approved the budget, they're operating on a continuing resolution." Like they *ever* approved a budget. "The money hasn't been released. Word is, they're going to pass the appropriations bill next week. Then it's a go."

"So we're good?"

I gave him a thumbs-up. Then I called my contract officer and asked if he'd heard anything new about the vote on the appropriations bill.

He scoffed. "It's been twenty years since they've passed an appropriations bill on time, the way they're supposed to. I'd like to see *them* operate on 75 percent of *their* last year's budget."

"How long do you think it's going to be?"

"Till we get the real budget? Who knows."

"Because I can't charge against my new contract until the funding comes through."

"Believe me, you aren't the only one."

I hung up feeling much less hopeful than I had been. I might be forced to take vacation until I was funded. Which normally would be fine, only I didn't have any left. I'd used it up during those first few weeks after Sean's death, and I'd been working through lunch ever since to accumulate extra hours for when Sam got sick or an appliance broke or any myriad other things happened that weren't big enough to qualify as an emergency or a rainy day but seemed to crop up every week since he'd died.

Without the funding, I'd be out of a job, and not many employers were looking for quantum physicists. People tended to look at you strangely when you spoke of things like time travel, parallel dimensions, and wormholes as matters of fact. As my father said, with a wink, when I announced my college major, "Why? Are there too many people out there with useful skills? You have to major in unuseful ones instead?"

Why?

Because I wanted to get to the bottom of things. I wanted to know the reasons.

Most people would conclude that my research didn't really matter. Regardless of what I discovered, the world would keep turning the same way it always had. But those of us who were traditional quantum physicists poked at the foundations of our science for the sake of principle, invalidating assumptions one by one just to see what would happen.

When we removed one assumption too many, when our theories suddenly started to fall apart, then we'd know where we stood. We'd know what was foundational and what wasn't.

❦

Before I left work, I wrote Dr. Correy a letter, printed it, and put it in outgoing mail.

As I drove home, I thought to send out an email to the neighborhood loop and ask if anyone else had run into the gas people. I didn't have any other way of figuring out who they were.

Next problem? My meeting with Sam's teacher that evening.

Despite Sam not wanting to fall asleep, his occasional lapse into present tense when he spoke about Sean, and his reversion to wetting the bed, I'd thought he was doing a pretty good job processing his father's death. That's what his counselor had told me.

And that's what I'd told Ms. Hernandez when she asked for the meeting.

But she asked me to come in anyway.

She was working at her desk when I walked into the classroom. Standing, she teased a folder from a pile in front of her, then gestured toward one of the miniature round tables that dotted the classroom.

She was a vivacious woman with vivid features and an ever-present smile. The children took to her like sunflowers to the sun. The fact that she wasn't smiling as she took a seat next to me was not a good sign.

"I just wanted to talk to you about Sam." Her dangly earrings trembled as she tilted her head toward me. She pressed her hands to the folder. "In the afternoons I call the children aside one by one and ask them for their happy thoughts." She opened the folder. "I write them down and have them color a picture about them." She passed me some papers. "What I'm trying to do is help them order their thoughts and strengthen their motor skills in advance of writing."

I began to read.

Daddy says I'm Super Sam. I have a red cape.

I picked another.

When Daddy plays trains with me.

She gave me a few moments before she spoke again. "I would have kept these until the next parent conference, but I thought it might be better to show them to you now."

The happy thoughts were each different, though they all had to do with Sean, but the picture was always the same. Sam had drawn the same thing over and over again.

"It's been six months since his father died?"

"Eight."

"That a child would speak of a dead parent in the present tense sometimes is normal. Especially for a child so young. But combined with his illustrations, I'm a little bit concerned."

I was too.

"Usually children at this age draw pictures of their families or pets. Their house or apartment building."

Sam's pictures had none of those things.

"I was hoping you might be able to help me figure out what he's drawing. He keeps telling me it's 'the firm.'" She frowned. "It might look like he's scribbling, but I've watched him. He's clearly not. It's, uh . . . it could be slightly alarming, the color he keeps choosing."

Black. He drew them all with a black crayon.

"Not necessarily, of course, but considering that his father recently died—" She looked at me, brows drawn together. "It's concerning."

My heart ached for my son.

"I've watched him do these. He's not angry. He's not clenching the crayon." She ran a finger over one of the images. "You can see that he's not pressing down very hard. I just would like to understand. And to help if I can. Do you know what he's trying to draw? Do you know what he means by 'the firm'? Which firm he might be talking about?"

He'd drawn a long black spiral, or series of circles, that stretched from one end of the page to the opposite corner.

"I've just never seen a student draw something like this before. On purpose. Then associate it with a happy thought."

I could only shake my head. "I don't know what it is. I wish I did, but I don't." I told her I'd ask Sam's counselor to talk to him about it. Then I left.

I made it down the hall to the bathroom before I started to cry.

After grabbing a hunk of paper hand towels, I locked myself into a stall and tried hard not to make any noise. I couldn't quite keep from sniffling, but I did manage to squelch most of the sobs as I dabbed at my tears with the towels.

One thing I knew. We were going to get through it.

We had to.

16

By the time I put Sam to bed that night, I was ready to kick
something. I'd found all sorts of odd things associated with Sean's
death, but none of them seemed to be connected to the questions
I was trying to answer. I had to talk it through with someone, but
there wasn't anyone I could trust.

I didn't want to give my parents one more reason to worry about
me. They had enough to do with my father's upcoming confirmation
hearing in November. It was only three weeks away. My neighbors,
Jim and June, had been lifesavers, but they already did too much for
us. I didn't want them to think I was having a breakdown. Jenn? She
had too much going on with her job as chief of staff to a senator, let
alone her divorce. And at that moment she was completely anti-male.

One thing, one *more* thing, still bothered me.

You people.

The medical examiner's lawyer had lumped me in with *you people.*
People who, for whatever reason, were calling the lawyer about his
client. And either there were so many of them or whoever *they* were
had called the lawyer so many times that he was beginning to feel
harassed.

Why?

There were too many *whys* and not enough *becauses.*

I had the feeling that the *whys* might matter, but I didn't know—
wait for it—why. The ratio of things I knew about Sean to the things
I didn't seemed to be rapidly decreasing. It was unnerving. I'd had
the same feeling when I started to study dark matter.

That's when I'd found out that physics can account for only
4 percent of the universe. Nobody knows what makes up the other
96 percent. Ordinary matter, the kind we can define and measure

and experiment with, actually *isn't* the most common kind. Of course there are theories—physicists have lots of theories—but that mysterious, undecipherable, unexplainable 96 percent, that dark energy and dark matter, is something upon which we're entirely dependent.

I didn't like knowing that I hadn't even known what I didn't know about Sean. I'd depended, to an extraordinary extent, on someone who was becoming increasingly opaque.

∞

I needed more information. I called Sean's old office at Ft. McNair and left a voice mail message for Brad asking for a callback. He was the person Sean had worked with most closely at the army's Center of Military History. Then I called my father.

"Peach. Hey. We're looking forward to coming out your way in a few days. Just have to finalize some appointments up on the Hill before we get there."

"Sam can't wait to show you his new train." We talked for a few minutes about his confirmation hearings, then I got down to business. "I have a question about when you went to the morgue. Do you remember there being a Leatherman in the box of things you brought back?"

"Don't think so. Don't know that I'd really have noticed, though. But hey, Clyde and Harry and the others are having some Halloween thing for their grandkids on post at Fort Myer. Do you think Sam might like to go?"

"Clyde and Harry?"

"Westerman and Ladowski. You know. The joint chiefs."

Right. Yes. The joint chiefs of staff. That collective governing body formed by the heads of the branches of the military, otherwise known as Clyde and Harry and the Others. "I don't think so, Dad. But thanks for asking."

"Sure. No problem. Gotta go. I'm live on cable in five."

Before I could say anything else, he was gone. At least he hadn't put my mother on the phone. I wasn't up to hearing about all the things I could be doing better.

It's not like I had expected Sean's autopsy to be the key to some secret code. But still, I'd been hoping for something more. For some hint as to what Sean had been doing.

∞

Alice woke me up in the middle of the night, barking her short, sharp bark. It was the one that told me she knew she'd get in trouble for it, but for whatever reason, she'd decided it was worth it.

"Alice!" I hissed her name.

She lumbered to her feet, left her cushion-bed, and scratched at the hardwood floor.

"Stop!"

I'd been hoping she'd turned a corner on the obedience thing, but she just looked at me, whined a bark, and scratched again.

Sighing, I got up and went to the bedroom door. "You need to go out? Is that what this is?" I was halfway down the hall before I realized she wasn't following me. Turning back, I found her right where I'd left her.

I flicked on the light.

She was staring at the floor, head cocked, ears at attention.

"Alice!"

She flinched as if I'd startled her, gave me a long look, and gave off another sharp bark.

"Shh!"

Still staring at me, she lowered the front of her body toward the floor and dug into it with both paws. Her long, quavery whine ended with a yip.

I took her by the collar and tried to lead her back to her bed.

She wouldn't budge.

So I walked around her, bent toward her behind, and gave it a mighty push.

She scrambled away from me, came back in a U-turn, and curled up right on top of the place she'd been scratching. After a few more whines and barks, she settled into sleep.

She was acting the way I felt. Out of sorts. Disoriented.

Our world had seemed so safe and ordered. But like a dying star, going through the motions, sending out its last rays of light, I felt like my reality was collapsing. I was being drawn into the darkness of something I couldn't fathom.

17

The only way I knew to solve a problem was by asking questions. Sean had been afraid of something. Someone. Bad guys. In my search for the truth, I didn't want to ask the wrong people my questions. I did, however, need some answers.

So the next day, during lunch, I called someone I knew was safe. I went outside and walked across the street to the Crystal City Water Park, where I sat down in a chair by one of the fountains and called Sean's sister, Kelly.

"Georgie! I've been thinking so much about you lately. How is Sam?"

I gave her the executive summary version.

"And how are you?"

That was where things were getting tricky. "I was wondering, do you have a minute?"

"I have about twenty minutes. That's how much longer the baby's going to sleep." Sean had missed the birth of his nephew by three months.

"Could you tell me a little more about Sean? About your childhood?"

She went back over the part I knew—about their parents' deaths, about being passed around to relatives.

"But what happened after that? You told me once that he fell in with the wrong crowd." Were those the people Sean was afraid of?

"Well . . . the wrong crowd. Yes. I'd say so."

I waited for her to expand on that idea, but she didn't. "Could you tell me a little more?"

"I don't think it's anything he'd want Sam to know. It would be a shame to remember him that way."

"I won't tell Sam. I promise."

"It was something he really tried to put behind him. It seemed like he was trying to close that door when he joined the army. I don't think he'd like me talking about it."

Which was probably why *he'd* never talked to me about it. "It's just— I was hoping maybe understanding Sean better would help me process everything." A cool wind stirred the trees and tugged some of my hair from my ponytail. I pulled the zip on my jacket all the way up to the top of the collar.

"What can I say?" There was a long pause while I hoped she'd say *something*. "He was in a gang, Georgie."

"A gang? You mean a *gang* gang?"

"It's not like he wanted to be. He tried not to be. He really did. But where we grew up wasn't very nice."

"But he didn't do things, did he?" Surely he hadn't done things. Gang things. Girls, guns, drugs. Not my Sean.

"Honestly, I don't know what he did. He never told me and I never asked."

My mother's words came back to me. *In any marriage, there are some things you might not want to know.* "But he got out."

"Yes. By that time I knew what gangs were. And I was really scared for him. I kept begging him to get out, but you couldn't leave the gang. And if he'd tried, I don't know what they would have done to him. I was only in sixth grade. And I was with a foster family; I was stuck there. Looking back on it, I think he was worried that if he tried to go, they'd come after me. They probably would have. And there was this one boy. He was not a good person. He was in Sean's gang . . ." Her words tapered off, and I was worried that might be all she was going to say. "He wanted me to be his girlfriend. But Sean found out about it. He told me he was going to take care of it. That I wasn't going to have to worry about that guy, about any of it, anymore. I was so excited. I assumed Sean was going to take me away somewhere with him."

The regional train must have pulled into the station behind the park because a horde of people suddenly appeared. They walked en masse to the sidewalk and dispersed in all directions.

If Kelly had been in sixth grade, then Sean would have been a senior. "That was just before he enlisted, right?"

"Yeah. But I didn't understand that at the time. To me, it felt like he'd just disappeared."

"So he did leave the gang." He'd found a way to do it. "But what about that boy? He didn't bother you after Sean had gone?"

"No. He never bothered me again."

"That must have been a relief."

"Well, yeah. Sure. I mean, they died, so . . ."

"What do you mean *they* died? Who died?"

"That boy. And his best friend."

"When did they die?"

"It was just before . . . just after?" A pause hung in the air. "I think it was just before. I don't know. So much happened right then. Like I said, Sean enlisted. I didn't see him again for years. But one of my aunts took me in right after, so I ended up moving. But I think, at least I'm pretty sure, it happened just before he left."

"*Both* of them died?"

"Yeah."

"How?"

"They were shot. It was some sort of gang thing."

My heart stopped beating for one long moment as the implication of that statement made impact. Then it started again in double time.

In the background, a baby cried.

"They never sleep as long as they're supposed to, do they? Don't tell me. I don't want to know."

She made me promise to call again soon and hung up.

What were the chances that Sean had absolutely nothing to do with those gang members' deaths? The ones who'd been interested in his sister?

I considered what I knew about Sean. The medal he'd received during his service had been awarded for gallantry in action. The vehicle he'd been traveling in had been hit in an ambush. It overturned. He'd dragged his fellow soldiers to safety, killed the dozen enemy combatants who'd ambushed them, and used their own vehicle to transport him and the wounded soldiers out of danger.

All by himself.

That was heroic.

And I would know. I'd grown up around heroic people, people who risked their lives for the safety and liberties of others. Could I really say, if Sean had been responsible for those long-ago gang deaths, that it was any less heroic? If he'd done it, he'd done it to save his sister; he'd done it to get out of a gang. And after having been in foster care for so long, to have an aunt suddenly agree to take Kelly? I didn't think it was too generous to attribute that to Sean as well.

I was not going to think less of him for doing what he'd done back in high school, nor think more of those two gang members who'd been trying to coerce a *sixth grader* into a relationship.

When his sister had been in danger, he'd done what he had to do.

The resourcefulness and determination that had led to Sean's medal had also led to a bachelor's and a master's and a PhD. But back there, in that gang? That's where his resourcefulness and determination had developed.

I had to work with the facts I could find. Those facts told me Sean had been afraid of someone. Those facts told me he'd lied to me. But they also told me something about his character. In conjunction with Kelly's story, they told me he would do literally anything to protect someone he loved. I was beginning to see the outlines of a pattern.

18

Later that afternoon Brad returned my call.

"Georgie. Hey. How you doing?"

I appreciated it when people asked, but by that point, I figured they didn't really want to know. "We're doing all right. But hey—I was sorting through some things the other day and I found a key I think might belong to the office. And I realized I never returned Sean's badge." Not that I could have, had I wanted to, because I didn't have it. But how would Brad know that? "Do you want me to bring them in?"

"I'm pretty sure he would have turned those in when he left."

"When he left? You mean at the end of the day?"

"At the end of his job."

End of his job? "Because I know he brought his badge home every night."

"He probably had one from his other job too. But I'm sure we're fine."

"What other job is that?" There was a long enough pause that I wondered if we'd been disconnected. "Brad?"

"Yeah. I'm here. It's just— How do I say this? I thought you knew. Sean stopped working here last year. About six months before he died."

"When you say he stopped working there, I don't understand."

"He left."

"But he was still working. He was working somewhere. He went to work every day."

"He did say he had something else lined up."

I hated to put him on the spot, but it was the first I'd heard of it. "Do you remember when that would have been? Exactly?"

"Sure. Yeah. It was toward the end of August. I remember taking him out for lunch during Restaurant Week. You know, in DC? Cut-price menus at all the fancy restaurants?"

"He wasn't *fired*, was he?"

"Fired? No. Don't think so. It didn't seem like it. He was just moving on. Sort of vague about the job he was going to, but that's not unusual around here. Whatever it was, I got the impression that he was just switching agencies."

After the call I sat there behind my desk, holding on to my head with both hands. It seemed best. I was trying to grab hold of my thoughts. Maybe I was wrong. Maybe the core of Sean's character *wasn't* the desire to protect. Maybe it was a pathological drive to obfuscate. To lie.

I'd always kind of seen myself as A Seeker of Ultimate Truth. I'd taken pride in it. But the new information about Sean? I almost wished I'd never uncovered it. Any of it. I sat there trying to look at everything objectively, and the problem was, I couldn't figure out one way for it all to make sense.

Someone knocked on my door. Opened it. "Georgie?"

"Ted. Hi!" I took my hands from my head. Tried to make it look like I'd been smoothing back my hair.

"Meeting at eleven? You coming?"

"Yes. Sure. Yeah. Just give me a minute."

The door shut and I heaved a sigh, closing my eyes and rolling my chair way back so I could rest my head on my desk.

What was I supposed to tell Sam about his father?

I could hardly play the role of adoring, trusting wife when my perfect life had been blown to pieces.

Actually, probably I could.

Most definitely.

I sat up, opened a drawer, and rummaged around for a pen.

Pretending would be easier than telling him the truth. Because what truth would I tell him? "Hey, Sam, turns out your father was a big liar"?

Saying that could be problematic. Because it might create a ticking bomb of self-loathing that would explode upon impact in adolescence. So maybe not.

I sent a file to the printer.

But what if I didn't tell him the truth? What if someday way, *way* down the road I met an actual nice guy, someone like Chris, and fell in love again? Maybe not *again* again, because obviously I hadn't really fallen in love with Sean if the Sean I knew wasn't a true representation of the real Sean. I'd fallen in love with an illusion. So if I happened to fall in love with a real, honest, truthful person? What would Sam think?

That I'd thrown over the memory of his sainted father.

What defense would I have? Other than that I was a fickle woman, faithless to the memory of her beloved first husband?

I closed my eyes once more and forced myself to breathe. I didn't know the truth. Yet. I opened my eyes as I thought about the implications. So the best thing to do was nothing.

Nothing. I wasn't going to do anything. "There's nothing to do."

I'd said it out loud. My head didn't burst. The world didn't explode. For the moment, everything was all right.

I grabbed a notebook and my water bottle and headed out down the hall. As I walked, I tried to ignore the voice in my head, but I couldn't quite silence it.

Who were you really, Sean Brennan?

19

Jenn came over that night with my half of our farm share.
Her au pair picked up the box on Wednesdays.

I hustled us all inside, out of the cold. "Tell me there's some
Halloween candy in there. I could have sworn I bought some last
time I went to the store. And the time before that too. But I can't
figure out where I put it."

"No candy. But there's broccoli and carrots and turnips." She
dropped the large, waxed cardboard box onto my kitchen countertop.

I peered inside. "Turnips? Great." I wasn't a fan.

"Hey—I'm taking Preston down to that toy store in Crystal City
on Saturday for story time. Want to come?"

"To Mr. Hoffman's? Maybe."

"Margarita?" Jenn opened my fridge, not bothering to wait for
my reply. She brought out the mix, poured it into a pair of glasses,
then mixed it with a generous pour of tequila. Jenn and margaritas
and I went way back. "So spill it." She pointed at herself. "Best friend.
Maid of honor. Person you can tell anything to, otherwise known as
me. That would be *moi* in French. Come on. What's going on?"

I should have known I couldn't hide anything from her. It had
always been that way. We'd met in high school and had been part
of a group that included the daughter of the Pakistani deputy chief
of mission at the Pakistani embassy; the daughter of the president of
the American subsidiary of a big multinational conglomerate; the
daughter of . . . I'd forgotten what her mom had done, but she'd been
mentioned in the *Post* a lot; and me. Typically Arlington. I'd lost
contact with the others soon after high school, but Jenn and I kept
rotating in the same orbit. "Bad day. Bad week. That's all."

"Seriously, G. What's the deal?"

Did I really want to tell her? If I told Jenn, then it would all seem real. It would be like opening a door to a haunted house. I didn't know what might come out. Besides, she had enough to deal with on the Hill. She had a hand in everything Senator Rydel did and was trying constantly, as any chief of staff would, to weight the scales of political power in his favor. She was a master in the Byzantine art of keeping track of who owed favors to whom. And my father's upcoming confirmation hearing was probably making everything worse. Since Rydel was the head of the Armed Forces Committee and would be chairing the hearing, that was now on her plate too. She didn't have time to deal with my extracurricular stress.

I shook my head.

"We're still good, right?"

"It's just that I've been wondering . . ."

She straightened as if bracing for something. "Spill it. Just say it and get it over with. It's more efficient." She rolled her eyes. "That's what my father says, anyway."

Jenn had issues with her father. He was a big, serious, intimidating Supreme Court justice who'd only gotten more serious and more intimidating after her mother had died during our sophomore year. It wasn't easy pleasing someone who demanded perfection. It was even harder to find ways to get his attention. Back in high school Jenn had seesawed between trying hard to coax him into her life and shutting him out because she didn't think she deserved his time or attention. Since she'd left home after college they'd reached a sort of truce, although sniping had a tendency to break out now and then.

But if I couldn't talk to Jenn, then I couldn't talk to anyone. And I had to talk to someone. I decided to take a chance. "Do you think Sean ever cheated on me?" The thought had been lurking in the back of my mind.

Her brow furrowed and it took a moment before she responded. "Why would you ask that? You and Sean, you were like, I don't know, all those perfect 1950s TV couples. You weren't just Georgie. And. Sean. You were GeorgieandSean."

"I don't know. Just some things I've discovered lately."

"About *Saint Sean*? I can say this as the honest truth: I don't think he ever looked at anyone but you."

"But he was hiding something from me, Jenn."

"How do you know?"

I shook my head.

"Did he say something? Before the accident? Is that what this is about?"

"No." I shook my head. Tried to shrug it off. "It's probably just me being paranoid."

"Did somebody else say something? You want me to beat them up for you?"

I laughed and determined to put the topic away.

Jenn and I finished our margaritas, then she rounded up Preston.

As I walked with them out the door and onto the porch, Sam lured Preston down onto the lawn where they ran around like loons. As we were standing there, I caught sight of all those fall crocuses waving their spring-colored petals at me, showing me a detail I hadn't noticed before.

I must have pulled a face because Jenn raised a brow. "Something wrong?"

"I just—" I sighed. *"Those flowers."* I gestured out toward the fence. "I hate fall crocuses. I thought they were going to be spider lilies."

"So dig them up."

"We naturalized them. They were supposed to be naturalized." But they weren't. They mocked me from their ruler-straight rows.

She gave me quizzical look. "Yeah, flowers are natural."

"Naturalized. Planted as if they'd grown naturally."

"Which kind of contradicts the idea that they were planted at all. What do they call that? Oxymoron, right? Compassionate conservatives. Practical progressives. Principled politicians."

"The point is, we gave Sam the bulbs and had him throw them up in the air. Wherever they landed, Sean planted them."

"And?"

"And those are planted in rows. And they aren't lilies."

"So maybe he bought the wrong kind. Mark was famous for doing stuff like that. Send him to the store for toilet paper and he'd come back with a bag of potato chips."

"No. I saw them. Have you ever seen a spider lily bulb? They aren't the same. You can tell the difference. And it looks like he dug them up and replanted them."

"You know how Sean was. Always anal about— No, wait. That's *you*."

"Ha-ha. But that's what I mean."

"Okay. So he dug them up and replanted them. But why does that have to *mean* something?"

"Jennifer—we planted all those bulbs! Dozens of them. Why would he replant them? And when? And he knew I hated that kind of crocus. Why would he do that?"

Jenn's look of concern was being overshadowed by confusion. "He was probably joking. It's no big deal."

I might have believed her if Sam hadn't been there. But he'd had so much fun helping that day. And the Sean I knew never would have tried to erase that memory.

20

There was about an hour of daylight left. I texted June and asked if they would mind watching Sam for a while. She met us at the door, wearing a pair of Halloween-decorated sneakers. She enfolded him with a hug. "It's my favorite Sam!" As I left they were discussing whether to make cookies or brownies.

I found the shovel in the shed. It was hidden behind the rake and the plastic sled. I tugged on some garden gloves and went to work. "Jerk!" I muttered the word as I forced a shovel into the ground and jumped on it to drive it down farther. Blinking back tears, I overturned the dirt onto the grass. Sean had called me from the store to verify what kind of bulbs I wanted. I'd told him spider lilies; the red ones, not the pink ones.

And still he'd somehow managed to end up with yellow crocuses. So that meant he'd bought both? Because I knew we'd planted spider lilies.

Good grief, how many had he planted? If it had been just a dozen, I might have left them. As it was, the whole artificial-looking display insulted both my sense of aesthetics and my sense of fair play. I peeled my quarter-zip fleece off and draped it over the fence. My Don't Trust Atoms, They Make Up Everything T-shirt had seen better days, but then, so had the crocuses.

I jumped on the shovel again, but the ground wouldn't yield. Moving it a bit to the right, I tried again. That time it worked. Levering the soil out, I turned it over on top of the pile I'd created.

When I dug back into the ground, though, I hit that same hard patch of earth. Was it a stone? A brick? It wouldn't have been surprising. Whoever had built the house ninety years before had used the front yard as a trash heap for construction debris. Whenever we did yard work we couldn't dig anywhere without finding bricks and boards and nails.

Using the shovel more like a trowel, I excavated around the spot and was finally able to lift off the layer of earth from its top. It wasn't a stone or a brick. It was a box. A metal box.

Kneeling, I brushed the dirt off and exposed a corner.

"Hey!"

Jumping at the greeting, I turned to find Chris and his Maltipoo on the other side of the fence.

I stood. "Chris. Hi."

"Need some help?" He'd already released the latch on the gate.

"No." I tried to push the mound of dirt back into the hole with my foot. "All done."

He eyed the crocuses that I'd thrown into a heap. "I'm not really a flower guy, but aren't you supposed to let them, I don't know, stay in the ground while they bloom?"

"I meant to dig them up earlier in the season, but I never got around to it. They're the one flower I just can't stand."

"So you're ripping them out midseason."

I shrugged, then dumped a shovelful of dirt back into the hole on top of the box. "My yard, my rules."

"Remind me never to cross you."

I picked my way out of the bed—away from the box—toward the driveway and the shed behind the house, hoping he'd follow.

He did. "Where's Alice? She okay?"

"She's inside. She's fine." Mostly. When she wasn't trying to dig a hole through the house. Which reminded me. "Have you ever had mice?"

"As in pets?"

"As in pests. Something's driving Alice crazy in our crawl space."

"My neighbor had raccoons last winter. It's amazing, the tiny holes they can fit through. Rats too."

If I ever found a rat in my house, I would move out. Immediately.

"I could take a quick peek. See if there's anything down there."

"You know, I might just take you up on that." If anyone had to confront a creature, better him than me. "But I've got to get Sam to the rink tonight for a lesson."

"Sure. No problem. I'll see you tomorrow." He gestured with his thumb toward the end of the block. "Gotta get going too. Soccer practice."

As soon as he had turned the corner, I went back to the flower bed and dug the box free.

Kneeling, I brushed the dirt from it. It looked like a metal cashier's box. The finish was still shiny, untouched by corrosion. I might have convinced myself that it had been left there by kids playing buried treasure if it hadn't been placed right beneath all those replanted fall crocuses.

I nearly opened it right there but thought better of it. After glancing up and down the street, I shook the rest of the dirt from it and took it with me into the house.

In the kitchen I set it in the sink and put on my cleaning gloves. I didn't want to be at the mercy of any bugs that might come crawling out. But there was no need to worry. It was locked. If only I had a key.

But I did.

I had a key. I had the mystery key from Sean's key chain.

I peeled off the gloves, ran to the office, and dug the key out of the cardboard box. Then I slipped it into the lock with a trembling hand. The top swung open easily, silently. The inside was pristine. It contained just a single book enclosed in a gallon-size Ziploc. I undid the fastener and slipped it out.

It was some sort of diary or journal.

I opened it.

Sean's handwriting.

21

I set it on the counter. Ran my hand across the pages as if touching them would somehow put me in direct communication with him. I flipped through it. Only a quarter of the pages had been used.

The alarm on my phone beeped.

Time to get Sam ready for his hockey lesson.

I put the phone into my giant catchall of a purse and went across the street to get Sam. June gave him back to me along with a dozen still-warm brownies. I sent him to his room to get dressed for skating. Sooner than I expected, he bumped back down the hall, dragging his bag behind him.

"Are you sure you need all of that? It's going to take you half an hour just to take everything out and put it on."

"It's only my helmet. And my stick. And my pads and—"

I took the bag from him. "It's fine." He was small for his age, but even so, it seemed like the bag shouldn't be taller than the kid who owned it. I would have swung it forward to tap him on the butt, but I was afraid I might give myself a hernia.

Once we got to the rink, we stood in line to get skates. I wrestled them onto his feet and must have tied and retied them ten times to cries of "But they're too loose" and "Now they're too tight."

"Is your name Goldilocks?"

He giggled.

"You ready?"

He nodded. At least I thought he did underneath that massive helmet.

I held his hand as he tottered on his skates through the glass double doors to the rink. There, he joined the crowd of wobbly-legged kids waiting for the session to start.

"Want me to stay until they let you on?"

He nodded.

I held Sam's hand as he shuffled along toward the door. Then I watched, holding my breath, as he put a tentative foot to the ice. He grabbed the rail and wouldn't let go, but as he inched away from the door, he glanced back and sent me a triumphant wave, which very nearly caused him to lose his balance. I stayed to make sure he made it to his lesson in one piece.

Once he did, I went up to the glass-fronted mezzanine and found a seat overlooking the rink. And there, I pulled the book out of my purse and opened it.

The book I was holding wasn't a journal. In fact, I wouldn't have said Sean had even made entries. The pages were filled with numbers and names.

Some had been crossed out.

Others had a question mark drawn beside them.

They were all written in the same format.

E/Abbott/David/DS
E/Ornofo/Lee/DS
E/Beckman/Beck/DS
E/Wallace/Reginald/DS
E/Conway/Paul/DS
2/Denunzio/Bobby/BW
2/Jenkins/Peter/BW

It was like a logbook. A roster.

Or a record of some sort of investigation?

I felt my eyes widen. I shut the book and buried it at the bottom of my purse. Glancing around, I looked to see if anyone had been watching. A woman's glance intersected with mine. She smiled and then her gaze shifted to the rink.

I picked up my purse and transferred it to my lap, threading my arms through the strap.

But as I sat there watching Sam pick his way back and forth across the rink, something niggled at me.

I brought the book back out and flipped through the pages again until I found it.

E/Conway/Paul/DS

Conway.

It seemed to me I'd heard that name before.

⚮

After I put Sam to bed, I picked up the book again. I took a picture of all the entries with my phone so I could look at them without having to access the actual pages. Sean had gone to a lot of trouble to hide it, so I figured I should do the same. I'd find a safe place to put it.

I turned back to the Conway page.

Abbott
Ornofo
Beckman
Wallace
Conway

On a whim, I turned on my computer and typed in the names as I flipped through the pages.

A search returned nothing but the random hits a person would expect with common names like Abbott and Conway.

Costello. Twitty.

I searched several of the combinations of names and numbers from Sean's notes.

Nothing there either.

I woke myself that evening with a snore. After going through Sean's book, I'd been too wound up to go to sleep. I'd turned on the TV instead and fallen asleep watching cable news. I woke to the sound of my father's voice. It took me a moment to realize it was coming from the TV.

"Listen—we've tried being enemies with Russia. We tried it during the Cold War. Was the world any safer? Why don't you ask the children of the eighties, who grew up having nightmares about nuclear wars."

The news anchor was frowning. "So you're saying we should *trust* Russia? Because that's what I'm hearing."

"Trust them?" My father held up his hands as if that was going a bit too far. "I think trust has to be earned. What I'm saying is, why can't there at least be a dialogue? Talking never hurt anyone. And talking about small things can sometimes lead to bigger things. That's all I'm saying." He leaned forward, tone earnest. "I'm not talking about making promises. Not talking about signing treaties or defense agreements. I'm just talking about . . ." He stopped and chuckled. "I'm just talking about talking."

I turned off the TV and went to get myself a glass of water from my perfectly working faucet. Out in the night, past my backyard, a light went on in the house behind mine. A man appeared in the window.

He lifted a hand.

I nodded and clicked off the light.

It was strangely comforting to know that there was someone else besides me awake so late. Especially since I'd found out that Sean had done something. Some *things*. Things that were undecipherable.

And definitely not like him.

Or maybe they were completely in character. Things that I had been so certain of the previous week were now open to question.

As I climbed into bed, I tried to corral my thoughts, but they were restless. I hadn't yet fallen fully into sleep when I heard something. Some noise that reverberated through my head loudly enough to wake me.

I lay there listening, trying to turn the sound into something familiar.

But it hadn't been the refrigerator or the radiator or any other thing that I was used to hearing. I knew that because it had come from beneath me.

From the crawl space below my room.

I sat up and turned on the light, hoping, I suppose, that illumination would help with clarification. I drew my knees up to my chest. The sheet up to my chin. It was an ages-old reaction to the fear of monsters underneath the bed.

Alice had heard it too. She listened along with me, head lifted, ears cocked.

What was it?

I was listening so hard that I could almost hear myself listen.

It hadn't been a creak, a squeak, or a rustle.

Alice whined.

Wanting to listen, hoping to hear it again, I hissed at her to stop.

She pushed herself to her feet, left her bed, and started pawing at the floor just like she'd done two nights before.

"Alice!" I whispered her name. When that didn't make her stop, I snapped my fingers at her. "Alice." She turned around and lumbered back to her bed.

I'd heard *something*. An animal, maybe? A mouse running between the floorboards?

There it was again!

Some sort of shifting. Not a shifting *of* the floorboards. A shifting *beneath* them.

Alice froze as I swept my blanket aside and eased toward the side of my bed, closer to where the sound had been.

It wasn't a mouse. I'd heard mice before. They scratched and scurried. This thing, whatever it was, hadn't been that. It was a heavier sound, with more force behind it. It had been something bigger.

Alice let out one of her quavery barks.

I heard a metallic *clink*.

I picked up my phone from the bedside table and dialed 911. Then I pulled Alice away from her post and took her into the living room with me. Whoever was out there would have to make it past Alice and me before he could even think about going down the hall for Sam.

While Alice sprawled on the couch and went to sleep, I pulled back an edge of the curtain and stood there, heart pounding as I stared into the darkness, waiting for the police to arrive.

22

"But you had to have heard them, Jenn. You're only three blocks away." I switched my cell phone from speaker as I heard Sam flush the toilet. He'd be coming down the hall for breakfast; no need for him to hear about what had happened the night before. I lowered my voice. "They sent two squad cars."

"I didn't hear a thing."

In the background I heard the sound of . . .

"What are you doing?"

"Teeth."

"Sorry. Didn't mean to catch you in the bathroom."

"'S okay."

"There were lights and sirens. Thank goodness Sam didn't wake up."

"Did they catch whoever it was?"

"No." I'd been afraid they wouldn't. Because who would hang around when he could hear the cops coming?

Jenn murmured something I couldn't hear.

"What?"

"Sorry." Her voice was more distinct. "So what'd they say?"

"They said there may have been someone, but they couldn't find any signs." Which was probably cop code for "just another crazy lady."

"None?"

"No footprints. No signs of forced entry into the crawl space. But then, it wasn't locked. There was no lock." Stupid, stupid. Putting a lock on it had become priority number one. "And that side of the yard is mulched."

"You want to spend a few days at my place, G?" Her voice seemed to echo. I heard heels clicking across a floor. "I could put you two up on the couch."

"We're fine. There's nothing to be afraid of." Funny just how little reassurance those words provided.

"I'd be afraid. Just saying."

"I'll put a lock on the crawl space. Should have done it before. It was probably just a drifter looking for someplace to spend the night." The more rational I sounded, the more afraid I felt. But I was thirty-six years old. I wasn't supposed to be afraid of the dark anymore.

"It wouldn't be a problem. It really wouldn't."

And I really wanted to say yes. But I knew I shouldn't. "We'll be fine."

"Just so we're clear, when the police find you and Sam murdered and they come to question your best friend, I'll tell them I offered, but you declined."

Chris asked how our night had been as I was walking home from school that morning. I just smiled. "Fine." I didn't want to think about it any more than I already was. But when I got home, Jim was waiting for me at the front gate.

"You okay?" He peered at me from behind his glasses, worry sketching lines between his eyes. "Heard the sirens last night."

"I'm fine. I had a prowler."

His brows peaked. "You should have called. I would have sent June right over with her rolling pin."

I laughed.

"Seriously. You should have."

"We pay enough in taxes, I figured I should make the police handle it."

"Did they catch him?"

"No."

"He get inside?"

"In the crawl space. That's where I heard him."

"Want me to take a look?"

"I don't have time right now. I've got a meeting at work. Can't be late." Not to another one.

"Doesn't take two people. I'll check it out for you while you get your things."

"You wouldn't mind?"

"'Course not!"

"You don't have to."

"Hey, kid, I want to, okay?"

By the time I'd made a lunch for myself, exchanged my yoga pants for a pair of jeans, and grabbed my attaché, Jim was nailing the door shut. "I'll swing by Cherrydale Hardware and pick up a lock later in the morning. But this should do the trick for now. Once I get that lock on, I'll leave the key on your dining room table, okay? I'll let myself in with your spare."

"You don't have to do all this, Jim."

"Maybe not, but I want to."

"Thank you. I can't even tell you—" I couldn't finish my sentence. I felt too much like crying.

He patted me on the shoulder. "Hang in there, kid. It'll be okay."

❧

It didn't feel okay. It didn't feel okay all day long. And it still didn't feel okay when I picked up Sam from school. But I tried not to let it show.

"Mom!" He ran over, backpack bouncing, when he saw me. "Mom! Ms. Hernandez wants to know what you do. She's looking for parents to talk about their jobs. I told her you were a fizziest. She didn't know what that was, so I told her you're a scientist. And now she needs to know what kind."

"A physicist."

"That's what I *told* her. I told her you work with holes. She said she needs to talk to you."

"It's *worm*holes. Although they're not really what I work on."

"But that's what I told her."

Because that's what I'd told him. What kid wants to know that their parent just sits around all day and thinks really hard? So I'd told him about parallel universes and wormholes and black holes. "I'm a special kind of scientist. I try to explain things that are hard to understand. Kind of like magic."

"So maybe I can tell Ms. Hernandez that you do magic tricks!"

"It's not really magic tricks."

"You could say it was. And I'd let you wear my cape."

I stopped walking, pulled my son close, and kissed him on top of the head. Hard. It was easier to keep from crying that way. "Thanks."

❧

Jim came over that evening to make sure I'd found the key on the table. After he'd gone, I left Sam playing in his room with Legos, grabbed a flashlight, and went to see what Jim had installed for the crawl space.

A large Keep Out sign was nailed to the door, and it had been secured with a very big, very formidable-looking padlock.

I unlocked it and opened the door. Then I clicked on the flashlight and squatted, peering inside, just to make sure everything looked okay.

Nothing to note except a glint. Back in the corner.

Were they eyes?

I beat the flashlight against the wall, hoping whatever it was would scurry away, but it didn't move. I shifted the flashlight up and down, back and forth.

Still glinted. Still didn't move.

I so didn't want to crawl around down there. I was fine with electricity and motors and machines and lasers, but I was not fine with spiders. Or mice or rats or other things.

"I'm coming in!" I said it with a confidence I didn't feel.

23

"I'm coming in there right this second." I paused, listening for any noise that would require an actual, certified pest removal expert.

Nothing.

Crouching, I stepped over the threshold and swept the space with the flashlight. I hadn't been down there in a long time. Outside had been Sean's domain.

At least it wasn't musty. It smelled of damp earth and old wood.

Duckwalking, I headed toward the corner where I'd seen the glint. My light bounced around as I tried not to let any part of my body or clothing touch the ceiling or the dirt floor.

Huh.

There weren't any cobwebs.

And it wasn't all dirt at my feet. Here and there, bits of sawdust powdered the ground.

Termites?

I hoped not. Not on top of everything else.

I swept the arc of light up to the ceiling. Was that . . . ? I took one duck-step closer and put a hand to the ground to get a better look at a shadowed area between two long wooden support beams.

I didn't see any evidence of termites, but there was a cable running along the length of the crawl space, right up against one of those beams. Following it with my light, I traced it back to where it took a right-angled turn and headed down the outer wall toward the door.

Taking a look outside, I saw where it went up the side of the house and then joined a set of other cables that ran from the house to the electricity and telephone poles along the street.

Back in the crawl space, I traced it in the other direction toward the other side of the house. Exploring further, I could see where that long central cable was joined by another that came from the basement.

A circuit?

But we'd had the house rewired after we'd bought it. And there was no reason why any of those new wires would have been routed through the crawl space.

I shined the light up toward that cable again.

Definitely a puzzle.

My flashlight hand sagged and something caught the light, reflecting it.

The glint.

Setting the flashlight on the ground, I rolled forward from my feet onto my knees. One hand on the ground, I reached out toward the object with the other, fingers closing on it. I brought my prize into the flashlight's beam.

Then I brought a trembling hand to my mouth.

Sean's Leatherman.

I closed my eyes as I remembered.

∞

"Ow." I shifted positions on the couch, placing space between my hip and whatever it was that had gouged me. "What *is* that?"

Sean was already reaching for me, pulling me back into his embrace. After a month of dating, it had become my favorite place to be. "What is what?"

I slid a hand up under his shirt and around his waist.

He cringed. "Cold hand!"

"Warm heart." I smiled, pulling my hair away from my face as I pushed away from him. "What is this thing that keeps poking me?"

I edged up his shirt and grabbed at whatever it was near his belt.

He glanced down. "My Leatherman." He sat halfway up, wrapped an arm around my waist, and pulled me back beside him, nuzzling my neck.

"Your Leatherman?"

He sat up, adjusted himself, then pulled it off his belt, offering it to me.

"It's a pocketknife."

He scoffed. "Does it look like a pocketknife?"

It was shaped like a pocketknife, albeit quite a bit larger. And it had all those metal pull-outs on both sides, with slits in them like a pocketknife. I started pulling them out. A saw. A knife. A wire cutter. Pliers. Some sort of little brush. All the kinds of things that would come in handy in a research lab. I'd figured out what to ask for at Christmas!

"Why do you wear this?" He didn't work in a lab. He was a historian. He worked in an office. And spent a lot of time going through files in archives.

"Why do I—" He snatched it from me as if worried I might break it. "It's an old habit. From my army days. Any soldier worth his rank wears one of these. I mean—" He broke off as if he couldn't find the words. "Okay. Before we go any further, we don't *wear* them. We *carry* them."

I tried my best not to laugh.

He turned to face me. "They do a hundred things." Now he was sounding like a used-car salesman. "Your father must have one of these."

It was my turn to scoff. "My father has people to carry one of those for him."

He smiled. "Fair enough."

I kept on pulling out tools. A wire stripper. An awl. A screwdriver. Several of them. "A wire crimper?"

"For crimping wire." He took it from me, folding everything back up.

I learned something new about myself. Men with pocketknives. It was kind of dorky. And adorable.

Sean had never gone anywhere without his Leatherman.

Ever.

It could be considered a weapon, granted. So he couldn't take it anywhere there was a metal detector or a security checkpoint. But anyplace he *could* take it, he did.

On the weekends it was one of the first things he put on in the morning and one of the last things he took off at night.

He'd shoved it into his pocket as he left the house the night he was killed, hadn't he? I was sure he had, but maybe I was wrong.

I had to be wrong because I was holding it in my hand.

But then, the Leatherman had been listed on the inventory from the morgue, even though it hadn't made it back to me in the box of Sean's effects.

How did any of that make sense?

I put a fingernail to one of the slits and pulled out a tool.

Screwdriver.

Maybe the medical examiner had been mistaken. Maybe the Leatherman had never been among Sean's effects.

I discounted that theory almost before I'd finished thinking it. That didn't make any sense either. Some things, almost anybody brought into the morgue might have: keys, a wallet, shoes. But a Leatherman?

You wouldn't make a mistake about something like that.

So somehow the Leatherman had disappeared between the medical examiner's office and the cardboard box. Then reappeared.

In my crawl space?

Like I'd told Sam, my job was trying to explain things that are hard to understand.

But the disappearance and reappearance of the Leatherman just wasn't possible. Not in our universe. Not without the presence of something like a wormhole.

24

I tucked the Leatherman into my pocket, took one last look around, and backed out of the space. I pushed the door shut with a scrape and closed the padlock.

Then I went inside and performed an inspection of my basement.

I'd found a cable of unknown origin. That much was clear. Its function, however, was a complete mystery. As was the date of installation. It looked new . . . ish. But how new was new? Had Sean had something put in that I hadn't been aware of?

I called both the phone company and our cable TV/internet provider. Nothing had been recently installed.

In frustration, I grabbed a pair of wire cutters and stood staring at it with indecision.

There was no reason for the cable company to install a wire that ran from the basement into the crawl space. The only point in that would be to provide either service or access. I discounted service. Obviously there were no computers or TVs in the crawl space and there never had been.

Access? Possible. But why go all the way out there and then to the street, when the cable box was easily accessible on the outside of the house?

I heard the thump of small feet across the floor above my head. "Mom?" The call floated down the stairs.

"Down here."

"Mommy?"

"I'm down—" I raised my voice. "I'm in the basement!" I reached up and snipped the piece of the cable that ran through the wall and into the crawl space. No green lights flickered on the router. No red lights appeared. It hadn't made any difference. "Coming!"

∞

Later that night, after sleep had finally claimed Sam, I tested all my cable connections. In spite of my having cut that cable, my internet, TV, and Wi-Fi were all up and running.

Someone who was not the gas company, the telephone company, or the cable company had a very odd interest in my basement. A very marked interest in keeping tabs on what?

On information being accessed by my computer?

Was that why the not-gas-company people had wanted access to the basement?

A cold sweat of fear broke out on my forehead.

Who were they? Why would anyone be interested in me? And why now? Whatever Sean had been involved in, whomever he'd been involved with, they had to know he was dead.

My computer, and quite possibly my Wi-Fi, had been compromised. I'd severed the connection, but that didn't mean whoever *they* were wouldn't try again. If I assumed they would, then I would keep myself from doing anything stupid.

I rebooted my router, then reset my password and renamed the network. I adjusted the Wi-Fi settings on my phone.

Phone!

My phone was even more susceptible. Every time it was turned on it could function as a tracking device. And every time I made a phone call, it pinged a cell tower. Of course, monitoring my cell phone required a court order. Or a personal decision on my part to download an app that would share my phone's location with family and friends or help me find my phone if I lost it. I went to my phone settings and app manager and made sure I hadn't granted those permissions.

I could power off my phone when I didn't absolutely need it, but that would risk me missing emergency texts from the school or a call about Sam or even a phone call *from* Sam. My phone number was the only one he'd memorized. Considering how often he mixed up his words, I didn't trust that he could memorize a new phone number without mixing it up with the old one. I needed to know he could reach me in an emergency situation.

One thing was certain: I also needed to figure out what Sean had been involved in. Because, apparently, it now involved me. And soon, whoever *they* were would figure out I'd blocked their access.

I took advantage of the window of opportunity to do one more search on Paul Conway. I was hoping it would jog my memory. There were hundreds of Paul Conways, but I got a hit on a local internet news site. The link led to an article on a hit-and-run fatality that had happened the previous night.

Paul Conway was the victim.

25

I had a lunch meeting the next day in Ballston and decided to swing by home on the way back to work. I could hear Alice whimpering even before I opened the door. Once I stepped inside, it took me a minute to understand what I was seeing.

And another minute to take it all in.

Alice had been muzzled with a Velcro tie around her snout; her legs had been zip-tied together. And the living room?

There was no place left for Sam to hide from the bad guys.

The sofa cushions had been sliced, the pillows punctured. The curtains had been torn from their rod.

Sean's campaign desk had been overturned. My hovering Bluetooth speaker had been grounded; a dent marred its smooth surface. And my replica da Vinci clock was shattered.

A hole had been punched through the plaster wall by the fireplace. The TV had been knocked over.

Nothing, absolutely *nothing* was as I had left it that morning.

A white-hot rage swept over me.

Alice was eyeing me with a look of profound shame. I knelt beside her and freed her from the muzzle. For her legs I needed scissors. Or a knife. But as I moved toward the dining room, intent on finding one, she barked and let out a long, rolling growl.

I froze.

So intent had I been on freeing her that I hadn't stopped to consider that whoever had ransacked the house might still be there. I retreated to the door and then, leaving Alice, I fled to Jim and June's.

"What?" Jim put a hand to my forearm. "Just slow down. One thing at a time."

"I need a knife." I also needed to find some way to keep my teeth from chattering.

June had come from the kitchen to join us. "What kind do you need? Paring knife? Bread knife? I've got this great—"

"They tied up Alice and I have to get her free."

Jim and June exchanged a glance. "Tied up Alice?" Jim peered down at me, concern etched between his eyes. "Back up and start again from the beginning."

By the time I'd finished, June was calling the police. Jim had retrieved a gun from somewhere and was shoving it into his waistband. He saw me watching him. "Don't worry. I know how to use it."

Over June's protests, I went back to the house with Jim. While I freed Alice, he inspected the rooms. We were standing together on the front porch when the police pulled up.

Though the living room had been vandalized and Sean's study was a complete wreck, I couldn't say for certain that anything had been taken.

"Did you check your jewelry, ma'am?" The officer paused in her writing while she waited for my answer.

"I don't have any." Aside from my wedding ring. My mother had given me lots of jewelry over the years. Necklaces. Bracelets. Earrings. As soon as she sent them, I'd donated them to local charity silent auctions.

"Any cash in the house? Credit cards?"

"No."

"Electronics? Any of those missing?"

"Missing? No. Broken? Yes."

"Anything else of value?"

Memories? Souvenirs of my life with Sean? A sense of security that would take a long time to restore? "No."

She told me she would file a report. After she left, I got in touch with my insurance company. Then I called a locksmith to come change out all my locks and add deadbolts, agreeing to pay extra for immediate service.

June and Jim helped me clean up the mess. I didn't want Sam to see anything out of place when he got home. I found an old college poster down in the basement to tack over the hole in the wall. While June ran the vacuum cleaner up and down the hall, Jim duct-taped the sofa cushions back together. When he was done, I fit them back into the couch, wrong sides up. I crossed my fingers that Sam wouldn't notice.

I sent June and Jim home with a promise that I would call them if I noticed anything suspicious.

I knew I should call my parents. I knew I should tell them what had happened to the house. They would have wanted to know. But if I did, they'd swoop in and make us stay with them. All my reasons for not moving in with them would be moot.

But would that really have been such a bad thing? Why couldn't we stay with them a few days? Why shouldn't I let them help us?

Because after a few days we'd still have to come back home.

I'd still have to get used to living in a house that had been broken into and pondering questions that didn't have any answers. I'd still have to be brave and strong. I'd still have to figure out how to keep on keeping on.

It was something my parents couldn't do for me.

∞

The chill, crystalline morning yielded to a blustery evening. The wind pushed at my car as I drove from work to school that evening to pick up Sam. Ms. Hernandez was waiting with him. She pulled me aside to fill me in on something that had happened earlier in the day.

I waited until after dinner to address it with Sam.

"Is there dessert?" He was looking up at me with hopeful eyes.

"I need to talk to you for a minute."

"Then can we have dessert?"

"Yes. Then we can have dessert."

He sat there in his booster seat, cape tied around his neck, waiting for me to continue.

"Ms. Hernandez told me about something that happened in class today. Sam, did you push someone at school?"

He sucked at his bottom lip. "Guess so."

"Why?"

He shrugged.

"Can you tell me what happened?"

"She was mean."

That shouldn't have made it any worse, but it did. "What happened?"

"She said mean things to me."

"What things?"

He shrugged again. "Things."

"Sam!"

He looked up at me, startled.

"I need you to tell me the truth."

"She said Daddy was dead."

"The thing is, Daddy *is* dead." It was one of the hardest things I'd ever had to say. "You went to Daddy's funeral. Don't you remember?" He'd sat right beside me. We'd held hands the entire time.

He said nothing.

Maybe he didn't remember. Maybe he'd been more emotionally impacted by his father's death than I'd thought.

"He's in a hole now."

Relief washed over me. Of course he remembered. "That's right."

"He went into the firm hole."

"*Firm* hole?" Sean had been cremated and I'd explained they were going to put him in a little hole in a big wall and put a plaque on top of it. The wall was made of stone. I supposed it *was* an unusually firm sort of hole.

"You know." He looked at me as if he was waiting for me to say something. "You go in one side and come out the other. Like a tunnel."

"A *worm*hole?" *Dear God.* "You think he went into a wormhole?"

He was playing with the strings of his cape. "Yeah."

"The thing is, Sam . . . The thing is . . ." I couldn't tell him wormholes weren't real, could I? I'd always tried hard to tell him the truth. No one had ever found one, but theoretically, they could exist. There was a possibility.

His eyes sought mine. "Welp, what if . . . what if when Daddy went into the firm hole—"

"Wormhole."

"What if, when he went in, he was still alive?"

How to tread carefully? "If he was still alive when he went in, then it would be possible that he could come back out."

His face brightened. "That's what I told her. He just went into the hole, that's all. That's what I said. But she wouldn't believe me. She said her grandpa went into a hole and he was still there and he wasn't ever coming out and—"

"Sam, Daddy would have had to have been alive if we expect him to come back out. And we know that he wasn't."

His gaze sank toward the table.

"You know that he wasn't. Remember?"

He nodded.

"So your father *didn't go into a wormhole.* Do you understand?"

"But if he went in there before he died and he was still alive, then—"

"Sam, your father didn't."

"But how do you know?"

"Because he died, sweetie."

"But how do you *know*?"

"Because his car was hit and he died. Remember?"

"But if—"

"So if Dad was dead, then he couldn't be anywhere else. He couldn't be in a wormhole. Do you understand?"

"But—"

"He's not coming back. He can't."

"But if he went into the hole—"

"Sam!"

He looked up, eyes wide in that small, dear face. "But—"

"He didn't go into a wormhole. He's dead! Your father is dead. He's dead and he's *not coming back*!"

He slid from his booster seat and tore off down the hall, cape flapping behind him.

"Sam!"

26

I would have given Sam anything. I would have moved heaven and earth if I thought I could. I would have lied, cheated, or stolen if I had to. I wanted Sean back just as much as he did. Mostly so I could yell at him for what he'd done to his son.

And to me.

Bedtime was a subdued affair that evening. As Sam brushed his teeth in the bathroom, I did a quick check of his closet. Knelt and looked underneath his bed. I don't know what I would have done if I'd found anything odd there, but it made me feel better.

Sam came into the room and pulled his pajamas out of his drawer. When I tried to help, he gathered them up and turned away. When he got in bed, he turned away from me and refused to say his prayers. I said them for him.

"Sam, I'm sorry I yelled at you. I shouldn't have done that."

There was no response.

"Sometimes adults don't know the right thing to say. Sometimes they get scared. And sometimes when you're scared, it's easier to yell than it is to say something the nice way."

He turned to look at me over his shoulder. "You get scared?"

Yes! I'd spent the rest of the previous night awake, listening for noises. I was sleeping with Sean's Leatherman under my pillow. And someone had just ransacked our house. But still, maybe I shouldn't have admitted to it. Maybe my being scared would make Sam more scared. No matter, it was done. I'd said it. Best thing to do was to own it. "I do get scared. Everyone gets scared sometimes."

He rolled toward me and put an arm out to hug me around the waist. "It's okay, Mommy. That's why we have Alice."

I kissed him. "You're right. That's why we have Alice."

"And if you get scared in the middle of the night, you can always come and sleep in my bed with me."

Tears slid from my eyes at the words of my kind, brave boy. "And what would you tell me if I did?"

He let go and settled onto his back. The hall light shone in his eyes as he looked at me. "I'd say, 'Mommy, it's okay. Don't worry. Everything's going to be all right.'"

The wind whipped into a temper that evening as it sometimes did. I heard it the way I heard planes going into and out of Reagan National Airport: from a great distance, as a hum in the background. Then, quite suddenly, it was beating against the house.

I jumped.

My heart had just dropped back into its normal pace when the floorboards creaked somewhere in the front of the house, in the living room.

Alice didn't even flick an ear.

I reminded myself that we lived in an old house. It was just settling.

But the wind stirred up a great restlessness inside of me. Suddenly I felt much too isolated. I wanted to talk to someone besides myself.

I wanted to talk to Sean.

I wanted to tell him about the break-in. I wanted to tell him what I'd said to Sam. I wanted to tell him off. To demand he tell me what the heck he'd been doing the night he died.

But I couldn't. He was dead.

That's what I'd told Sam, wasn't it?

I vowed that in the morning I would finally take his number off our phone plan. It was time. But that night, listening to the wind howl through the trees and beat against the windows, I just needed to not be alone. I needed to hear his voice one last time. I picked up

my phone to dial his old number and realized I had a voice message
of my own. I thumbed over to my voice mail log to see who it was.

Sean Brennan.

At 6:43 p.m.

How was that even possible?

I brought up the call information; it listed his old number. I went
back to the voice mail log and pressed on his name. Held the phone
to my ear.

Hey. Georgie. There was a long pause. *Do you still trust me? I need
you to know that*— His words became garbled, as if he'd turned away
from the phone, and then the message ended.

27

Sean?

Had I just heard . . . Was that *Sean*?

How could it be?

Sean was dead.

As I was trying to figure out what had just happened, the voice mail ended with a beep.

I stared at the phone in my hand, trying to think of a reasonable explanation for what I'd just heard. But the more I stared, the more my hand shook.

I set the phone down on my bedside table and pushed it away.

Swiped at the sweat that had formed above my lip.

My ears felt thick. They were buzzing.

Maybe my doubts about Sean's trustworthiness were manifesting themselves in audible voices. Maybe I'd been wanting to speak with him so badly that I'd brought him back to life.

I tried to pick up the phone but dropped it.

With a shaking hand, I retrieved if from the floor and brought up the message again.

Hey. Georgie. Do you still trust me? I need you to know that—
<beep>

Sean.

It truly sounded like Sean. And the call had been made from his phone number.

It was as if something in my brain had crossed circuits and I was receiving messages from the twilight zone.

But that wasn't possible. I tried to refocus myself on what *was* possible.

Maybe Sean's phone had been stolen during the break-in. I hadn't even checked to see if everything was still in the box. I went to the office and pulled it out of the closet to check.

It was still there.

But maybe someone had traded out his chip for theirs.

I took the phone into the bedroom and used one of the tools on Sean's Leatherman to take it out. I used my phone to verify that it was his.

That meant the call had to have come from Sean's phone.

Where had I been at 6:43? Eating dinner with Sam.

Fear knotted my stomach.

Had someone been in the house, in the office, while we'd been in the dining room?

I tried to power up the phone, but the battery was dead.

There was no way the call could have come from Sean's phone. It wasn't possible.

And there was no way Sean could have made that call. He was dead.

I sat on the bed, phone cradled in my hands.

What should I do?

First thing I couldn't do: tell my parents. They were coming into town to get ready for the confirmation hearing, and I'd invited them for dinner. But crazy was not something the Slater family did. Period. End of story.

I couldn't tell Jim and June. They worried about me enough as it was.

I could tell Jenn, but she'd looked at me so strangely when I asked her if she thought Sean had ever cheated on me. I didn't want to have to explain all the other odd things that had been going on. So that left no one.

No one but me.

I couldn't sleep that night. I have to admit I didn't try very hard. I was afraid to. I was worried I would wake up certifiably insane. But I had more than enough distractions to keep me from those thoughts. The next day, Friday, was Bring a Parent to School Day. And after that, my parents were coming to dinner. I called in sick to work so I could have the day off. They assumed I had a physical ailment. I didn't tell them I was afraid it might be mental.

Ms. Hernandez beamed her thousand-kilowatt smile in my direction when she saw me. "I've put you right after Dr. Thomas."

I wished she had put me before Dr. Thomas. Dr. Thomas was a veterinarian and she brought real live animals. After she put the guinea pig and the baby chick back in their cages, Ms. Hernandez asked Sam to introduce me.

He took my hand and pulled me up from my place on the carpet beside him. "Welp, this is my mom. She's a doctor too, but she can't help anyone."

That was me. Academically brilliant but practically useless. It didn't, however, keep me from performing the magic tricks Sam had requested. I made a glass fill itself with water, I turned liquid into gas using a bicycle pump, and I made a boiled egg slide through the narrow mouth of a glass jar. I wished I could figure out the magic that had created Sean's message as easily. The only thing I could figure: someone was playing a cruel trick.

After me came Mr. Carter. He was a journalist with the *Post* and he came armed with handouts: bookmarks, colorful cartoon books, and puzzle pages that explained the importance of the First Amendment.

Later, as I was standing in the lunch line with Sam in the cafeteria, Ms. Hernandez motioned me over. "When the students go outside to play, would you mind coming by the classroom?"

I ate my lunch in record time and waved at Sam as he ran from the cafeteria out onto the playground. In the classroom Ms. Hernandez was sitting at one of those tiny tables, waiting for me. She pushed a folder across the table. "He's still drawing these."

I opened the folder.

It was another long black spiral that stretched from one end of the page to the opposite corner. But this time there was a difference. This time I knew what it was.

Realization sank into my stomach. I couldn't keep the tears from coming. I dabbed at them with the cuff of my sweater. "They're worm-holes. He's been drawing wormholes."

28

I waited until Sam came back from recess before I left. I didn't want him to freak out if I wasn't there. As I walked home—coat collar turned up, hands shoved deep into my pockets—my cell phone rang.

I turned into the wind as I answered so my hair would stop blowing into my face. "Hello?"

"Mrs. Brennan? This is Kyle Correy."

Kyle Correy? Kyle *Correy*! The medical examiner from Sean's autopsy. I'd written him a letter. "Yes. Dr. Correy. Hi."

"You asked me to call you? About your husband?"

"Hi. Yes. My husband. You did his autopsy. And you also took his inventory. I had thought there was something missing, but I found it." Or maybe *it* had found *me*. "I'm sorry. Sorry to have bothered you."

"No. I remember." He paused. "Could you do me a favor? I'm sure you've got it all figured out by now . . ." His voice trailed off. When he resumed talking, it was in a whisper. "But the feds didn't want that to get around. It was different from the others."

I stopped walking. "Sorry?"

"Everyone knows I swung a deal. But not many people, not even my attorney, know about *that*. So please, let's keep it that way."

"Dr. Correy, I don't understand what you—"

"I have to go. Sorry."

"Wait! Dr. Correy?"

Silence.

I stood there on the sidewalk trying to figure out what had just happened.

I'd been operating under the assumption that Sean's death was a hit-and-run.

Had I been wrong?

Dr. Correy had seemed to suggest that there was some sort of relationship between the feds and Sean. Some sort of relationship they didn't want anyone to know about.

Maybe Sean's death hadn't been an accident.

As I sat there, it felt as if the world was collapsing in on me.

I tried to push it back. In order to think, I had to focus.

What else had Dr. Correy said? *The feds didn't want that to get around. It was different from the others.* What did that mean? That Sean's death didn't have to do with drugs? Or that whatever deal Correy had made, when it came to Sean, it had been done in a different kind of way?

And why didn't the feds want it to get around? What were they trying to hide? Who were they trying to hide it from?

I didn't have enough information to determine what Dr. Correy had meant when he said that.

And what about the other part? *I'm sure you've got it all figured out by now.*

What was there to figure out? And why was he so sure I would have been able to do so?

∞

I spent the afternoon tidying the house for my parents' visit. As I cleaned, I worked on solving the mysteries of Dr. Correy's words and the notes in Sean's book as well as trying to make sense of the mysterious voice message.

I needed a theory that would explain everything.

The voice mail message almost made me want to change my mind about the existence of parallel universes.

Had someone somehow recorded him speaking before he died? And then used it to create a message? But then, how had they been able to use his phone number? I was still paying for that phone line. The number was still assigned to my account.

I shook my head in an effort to focus on the problem at hand.

Dr. Correy.

Sean's notes.

And the prospect of something disturbing, something nefarious, that Sean had gotten mixed up in. Maybe whoever was trying to wire my computer and ransack my house was looking for something, some information, that Sean had left behind.

Information like the notations in the book.

I took Alice for a long walk as I tried to sort it all out.

Midafternoon I was interrupted by a call from my mother. She was calling from their layover in Atlanta to make sure I had something "smart" to wear for my father's confirmation hearing. I assumed she wasn't talking about my Resistance Is Not Futile—It's Voltage Divided by Current T-shirt.

I kept going back to the names and numbers from Sean's book. If I knew what the two-letter designations after each name were, it might have helped. It would have given me some hints as to what Sean had been doing. As it was, I felt like I was trying to define dark energy.

Physicists knew dark energy existed—for numerous reasons, it had to—but beyond that? We knew nothing about it at all. In the same way, Sean's notations had to mean something, but it was easier at that point to say what they weren't—a grocery list, a car, a ball—than what they were. I didn't know how to start thinking about them; there was nothing to put my hands around.

29

I let Sam stay at school until the end of extended day. I'd already paid for it and, considering the things that had been happening, he was safer at school than he was at home.

My parents arrived soon after I picked up Sam. I saw them pull into the driveway and alerted Sam. He already had his new train ready and waiting to show my father.

My mother came bearing gifts. "Just a little something." She dipped toward me so I could look inside the leather tote she was carrying. The little something turned out to be some cheese straws, a gallon of sweet tea, and container of pimiento cheese.

She winked. "I know you never have any."

I didn't. Hadn't. Not for a number of years. I kissed the cheek she offered as I took them from her.

"So I thought I might as well bring my own." She smoothed her hair as she glanced around the room, raising a brow when she noticed the galaxy of stars on the ceiling.

I didn't want to hear her thoughts on those. "I'll run these into the kitchen."

Sam was already well into telling his grandfather about his new train.

Out in the kitchen, I set the tote on the floor and put the cheese and sweet tea in the fridge. When I lifted out the package of cheese straws, I saw— "Mom? Mom!"

"Georgia Ann?" Her reply came floating from the living room.

"Mom? Come here!" Right now!

She appeared a moment later. "Sugar pie?"

I gestured toward the tote at my feet.

She came over to peer down inside it.

"Did you know that was in there?"

"The gun? Well . . . you can take the soldier out of the army, but you can't take the army out of the soldier."

"Mom!"

"Your father has a permit to carry."

"And I have Sam. What were you planning to do with it?"

She lifted a slender shoulder. "Take it with us when we leave."

"But why did you bring it here?"

"With the world the way it is? You just never know."

"Do you always take—" Parents! "You know what? I'm going to put it here." I stretched up toward the refrigerator and placed her bag on top of it. "And when you go, you'll take it, and you won't bring it back."

She smiled. "All right."

"I mean it."

She went back to Sam while I took a few moments to get myself together. Deep breaths; some ice cold water patted on my face. Once I had myself under control, I rejoined them. My father had already shed his sports coat and was playing with Sam's new train.

But my mother wasn't having it. She'd taken out her phone. "Come on, everyone. I need a picture for Instagram. And the blog. And Facebook."

She gathered us together. Then she stood back from us, hand on hip. "Tsk. Georgia Ann, does your child not have any socks to wear? Samuel, go find something to put on your feet!" She shooed him off to his room. "And comb your hair while you're there!"

Once Sam came back, dressed to her standards, she took a selfie. And then another. And then—

"Mom! Seriously." She was annoyingly techie. But she ran a military-spouse support website and spent a good part of every morning clicking through the apps on her phone, visiting the sites and pages of all her acolytes in the military community and leaving comments.

My father was fiddling with the wheels of Sam's new train. "When did Sam get this?"

"Saturday. Mr. Hoffman brought it for him."

My father's brow rose. "To the house? Because it seems like the wheels are already a little loose." My dad cupped a hand to Sam's shoulder. "But it's no problem, buddy. Nothing a screwdriver can't fix." He glanced over Sam's head at me.

"Downstairs. In the toolbox beneath the workbench. But—" I stepped toward them, offering to take it.

My father pushed to his feet with a groan. "Don't worry about it. We can do it, can't we, Sam?"

Sam had taken the train from my father and was clutching it to his chest.

My mother intervened. "Georgia Ann, you never answered my question from before."

I dutifully turned toward her as my father and Sam went to fix the train. "Which question was that?" There were lots of questions she'd asked that I'd never answered.

"The confirmation hearing. What are you planning to wear?"

That question. I caught myself mid–eye roll.

"Because you just know, sitting right behind him, that we'll be on television the whole time. I've already made an appointment for us at a spa downtown. I'm going to have them give you just a little trim. I was thinking a couple inches off the bottom and some more layers. With hair like yours, layers are the only thing that help. And I really need you not to frown while we're sitting there." She pointed at me. "Like that. It makes you look like you're scowling. And everyone will see you and they'll wonder why. Just—" She paused, remolded her features into a look I could only label angelic. "You can do that, can't you? I know you can."

"I, um . . . Alice! She needs to go for a walk."

At the sound of her name, Alice lifted her head from her paws.

I nodded toward the door. "Let's go for a walk."

Her ears flicked forward. She stared at me as if questioning my sanity. She'd already been for a walk earlier. A really long one.

I had to grab the leash and walk over to her in order to clip it to her collar. And then I had to plead with her to get up.

"You sure she wants to go?" My mother asked the question with a frown as she stared at me over the top of her reading glasses.

"She's going. I'll be back in fifteen minutes. Maybe twenty. Then we can all go out to dinner. My treat. How's that sound?"

Before she could say anything else, I slipped out the door.

The wind had picked up. And with the sun's decline, it had turned frosty. In my haste to get away, I hadn't thought to grab a hat or gloves. In retrospect, it might have been better to stay and deal with my mother. We turned left, away from the school, at the end of the block. It took us past Mrs. T's house.

I hadn't thought about Mrs. T in forever. She'd lived in a bungalow that was the same era as ours. She was big on walking, and her route took her past our house in both the morning and the evening. Soon after we first moved in, she'd decided that Sean was her personal project. She baked him cakes and knitted him sweaters and recorded television shows for him about the Dalai Lama on her VCR. She flirted with him outrageously. It wasn't difficult to understand why. When Sean smiled, it was like Christmas and the Fourth of July combined.

After she let it slip that her ninetieth birthday was fast approaching, Sean had started checking in on her in person every Friday, to see how she was doing, to make sure she was okay. We discovered she made a mean martini. *And* played a competitive game of Nertz. And just like that, Friday-evening cocktail hour at Mrs. T's had begun.

She'd passed away several years before Sean died. Her son had rented the house out for a while, then decided he could make more money by selling it. Her old house with its tattered garlands of Tibetan prayer flags and its collection of stone Japanese lanterns had been torn down during the summer and a new mini mansion was being built in its place.

As we reached her lot, the last of the contractors' mud-splattered pickups was pulling away.

Mrs. T wouldn't have liked the McMansion. I stood there for a moment, trying to take it all in. It was too big. It was too much. Alice must have sensed my inattention, because she bolted toward the front yard, pulling her leash from my grasp.

"Alice!"

She ran up the front steps and disappeared into the house.

"Alice!" I picked my way through the debris that was strewn around the front and climbed up onto the porch.

I pushed the door open wider and put a foot to the threshold. Took a listen.

Heard nothing.

Slipping inside, I closed the door behind me, then stood in what would eventually be the front hall. "Alice!"

A whimper came from a room off to my right.

"Alice?" I walked into it.

A yelp came from the room beyond.

"Alice, what have you—"

At the back of the house was a great room with soaring ceilings and a full wall of windows that provided a view into the backyard.

Alice was there, lunging at a construction worker who was trying to calm her.

I jogged toward him, trying to explain myself. "Alice! I just— Sorry. Alice—stop! I know we're not supposed to be here, but my dog got away and— Alice, sit!"

Alice sat, but her tail kept thumping.

The construction worker took off his hat and tucked it under an arm.

I reached for the handle of the leash. "I'm sorry she jumped—"

He put a hand to his sunglasses and pulled them off.

"—all over—" All the air left my lungs. I gasped. Felt my knees buckle. "Oh my—"

30

He was beside me in a minute, grasping my arm, keeping me upright.

"Sean?"

"Georgie, I—"

It was *him*. It *was* him. Underneath the beard and the too-long hair, it was truly and unmistakably him. But still, as he put a hand on my forearm, I moved away. "Don't touch me! Don't!" I recoiled, retreating in the direction of the wall. "Don't touch me! I can't—" I turned away from him, folded my arms around my waist, and closed my eyes. I wasn't okay. I wasn't going to be all right. I leaned my forehead against the wall for a moment. It was solid. Cool. I turned to face him and slid down the wall, sobbing.

He reached out.

I held up a forearm to fend him off. "Don't!" My chin began to tremble. "You're not alive." I whispered the words.

"I am alive."

My mouth was drawn down like a bow, my voice dissolving into hysteria. My whole body was trembling. I was deathly cold. "Don't you—" I could hardly speak. Sobs, deep and guttural, were pulsing upward from deep down inside. "Don't you just come here—" I grimaced as I wrapped my arms around myself, trying to hold everything together. "Don't just come here and—" A sob broke through. "And tell me that you're alive and show up as if—as if—I should be *glad*? Glad that I had to bury you? Glad that I had to listen to my son try to explain to me why he thinks you're alive when you're dead?"

"I'm not—"

"But you're not! You're *not dead*."

He squatted and tried to put his arm around me.

"Don't try to apologize. Don't—" My resolve crumbled. "You were dead."

"Georgie?"

"Don't."

"Georgie." His voice was closer.

"Just—"

His arm came around my shoulders.

"You can't—"

He went to one knee and pulled me to his chest.

I clung to him, weeping. I wept for him and for me. I wept for our son.

When he tried to pull away, I clutched at him. "Don't go!"

"You listened to my message."

"It was you. I tried everything I could to make it not you, but it was you."

"I've been trailing you for two weeks, but there's always been someone around. We need to talk."

I sat up, putting distance between us, and swiped at my tears with my forearm. Then, drawing a shuddering breath, I nodded.

He sat down next to me, back against the wall.

Alice came over and curled up beside him, placing her head on his thigh with a sigh.

He gave her one of those rubs behind her ears that she loved so much. "Remember that Gulf War project?"

I nodded.

"I was helping write the army's history of Desert Sabre. Pulling together documents. Collecting oral histories."

Where had Sean been all this time? What had he been doing?

"Georgie?"

I blinked. Nodded. "Desert Sabre. My father was there."

"And I was writing about his battalion, down to the company level, looking back through everything I could get ahold of—oral histories, field reports, orders of the day."

If I hadn't interred Sean, who had I interred? Who had I— I heard myself gasp. I'd had someone else cremated!

"Georgie, are you okay?" Brow furrowed, he touched my arm. "Are you—"

"Fine. I'm fine. Haven't been sleeping. There was someone in the crawl space on—"

"That was me."

"That was—that was *you*?"

"I was trying to—"

"Wait. Stop." Everything was starting to make sense now. It was as if I'd been looking at everything backward and upside down. "Alice chases the garbage truck. She started doing that after you died."

"Because it's me."

"*You're* the one who hauled out the garbage cans this week."

He nodded.

That was *him*? "Those were all *you*? All those times she chased the truck? You'd been there? *Right there?* The *whole time?*"

"I needed to make sure you were okay. So I pay one of the guys off every Monday morning so I can make sure that no one is—"

"So you've been, what? Working construction here? In my own backyard, all this—"

"No, I've just been wearing this the past few days so I could blend in. Lots of construction in the neighborhood."

"—time and moonlighting as a garbage man once a week? Did you never stop to think, *Gee, Georgie looks a little sad. I know! Maybe I should let her know I'm alive!*"

"I couldn't because—"

Maybe that's what Dr. Correy had meant. Maybe he assumed that I already knew Sean hadn't died. Why would he have assumed that? Because I was *Sean's wife*. "I cremated someone and put your name on him. I don't even know who he is."

"Just— I need you to listen." He shifted to face me and gripped my hand. "I can't keep you here much longer. I noticed there were—"

"The Leatherman. It was on the inventory from the medical examiner's office, but it never made it to the house. At least, I didn't think it had, but then I found it under the house. It's because you—"

"—because I took it with me when I left the medical examiner's office. When I didn't die."

"Then how did— The autopsy?"

"I only have a few minutes and I need to explain." He squeezed my hand. "Are you with me?"

The questions could wait until later. "Yes. Okay. Yes. I heard you: Desert Sabre."

"Right. I was working on your father's part in the war. It seemed like a no-brainer, assigning that to me. I had an inside connection."

I nodded.

"So I started contacting soldiers in his old unit, scheduling oral interviews, asking questions about the night they made that breach in the Iraqi lines."

My father's company had stumbled on the Iraqi Republican Guard during a scouting mission the first night of that war. The Iraqis outnumbered them, but the company fought them off and blew up their base, destroying their weapons. That's how he breached their lines and that's what put him on the road to the four stars he eventually earned. It was the one story from that war almost everyone knew. "Okay." It all sounded like standard historian work to me.

"That's when things started getting weird."

"Things? What things?"

"Just . . . little things. All of a sudden I had to turn in a daily report on who I'd talked to, what questions I'd asked. My files were being accessed without my knowledge. Some of my source material disappeared."

"Did you tick someone off? Was someone jealous of your assignment?" That seemed remarkably petty. Even for the army. "Maybe someone just wanted to keep tabs on how the project was going."

"Maybe. But no one else's materials vanished. And no one else had to file a daily report."

"What kind of questions were you asking?"

"Nothing unusual. State your name. What was your rank and duty? What are your memories of that first night of the war?"

"You were *given* this assignment, though, right? Someone asked you to do it. It's not like you were freelancing."

"I was given the assignment."

"I don't understand."

"I don't either. I don't understand any of it. But when things start disappearing and people start following you—"

"People *followed* you? You were just doing what everyone else was doing."

Sean nodded. "But the company I was researching was your father's. And I think something happened out there in the desert. Something that shouldn't have."

31

Outside, footsteps scuffed up the front stairs to the porch. Paused. A voice called out, "Georgie?"

Alice pushed to her feet. Barked.

Was that . . .

Sean rose to a squat and lunged toward the shadow along the far wall.

From my location I caught a glimpse of Chris's face through the front door.

Sean sprang toward me, grabbed my hand, and pulled me to a sliding glass door at the back of the house that should have led to a porch but at that moment led to—nothing but empty space. The ground was a half-story down. Inside my shoes my toes tried to grab on to the door's track. My free hand clawed at the cutout, trying to leverage me back from the hole.

But Sean's hand clamped around mine. "Jump!" The word was low but vehement, and his momentum was already carrying me with him over the threshold. As he hit the ground, he let go of my hand and reached upward. Pulling me to his chest, he broke my fall and then rolled us away from the house. And even then, he kept moving, heading toward a pile of discarded lumber and scraps of trim that had been stacked at the back of the lot.

Alice galloped along at our heels.

Once we ducked behind it we were out of view of the house.

"It was only Chris."

"Who?"

"Chris."

"Who's Chris? I don't know any Chrises."

"Chris. The dog-walk guy."

Sean's brow folded.

"We walk our dogs together."

"Georgie?" Chris's voice came from the direction of the house. "You okay?"

"He must have seen me chase Alice up the stairs."

Sean grabbed my hand for just a moment. "Go home. Be careful. Meet me tomorrow; walk at dusk. Wear dark clothes. I'll find you."

Hidden from the house, he disappeared around the far side of the pile before I could say anything. I scrambled after him, but by the time I could take a peek, he'd gone.

As I rounded the pile, I saw Chris standing in the opening for the sliding glass door, staring down at the ground.

"Hey!" I waved an arm.

He looked up. Saw me. "You okay? I saw you come in here. Didn't see you come out."

"Alice chased a squirrel into the house. They really should lock these things up when they're working on them."

He made the jump to the ground. Then he walked through the side yard and down the street with me, back home.

⚮

"Georgia Ann? Is that you?" My mother's words were accompanied by the click of her heels, and she soon appeared from the dining room. "I was just doing a little tidying up and I went into Sam's room. Did you know he didn't make his bed?"

"He doesn't know how, Mom."

"You were three when I taught you that!" She blinked at me, put a hand to her hip, and gave me a once-over. "What happened? You're a hot mess!"

Coming over, she put a hand to my chin and turned my head to pick something out of my hair. Tsking, she held out a tuft of dried grass.

"I, uh—" I put a hand to my head, feeling for more. "I fell."

She licked her thumb and used it to smudge at something on my face. "You all right?"

No. "Yes. Yes. Yeah. I'm fine." I shied away from her touch, trying for a smile. I'm not sure it worked. "I'm fine." Doubting I could pull off nonchalance, I tried a different tactic. "So! Where are we going for dinner?"

She stood there looking at me, eyes narrowed. "I don't like your color. And your eyes are puffy. You look like you've seen a ghost." She flapped a hand toward the couch behind me. "Go on and sit down. I'll bring you some tea."

"So I said to him, I said, 'Sergeant, I don't care what you *can't* do, I'm only interested in what you can.'" My father was regaling Sam with stories from his past. I was pretty sure a military career wasn't going to be in Sam's future, but Sam never passed up a chance to hear a story. Not even those he'd heard before. My father chuckled as he shook his head. He glanced around the table to make sure we were listening.

My mother and I had heard it a million times, and I was mulling over what Sean had told me, but Sam was rapt with attention. He picked up a piece of Korean-style fried chicken and started pulling meaty strands of it from the bone. That's what we'd decided on for dinner: takeout.

"And do you know what Sergeant Conway said? He said, 'Then I don't think I'm going to be of much interest to you, sir. Because I can't get the phone to work.' Can you believe it? There we were, trying to fight a war, and I couldn't have gotten an order if I'd wanted one because the phone wouldn't work!" My father wiggled his eyebrows at Sam.

Sam obliged by giggling.

"Wait. Dad?"

"Hmm?"

"Sergeant Conway. Do you remember what his first name was?"

"Started with . . . an *M*? No. Started with a *P*. Pete? Pat?"

My mother surprised us by answering, "Paul."

He blinked. "How do you remember things like that?"

"Because the first hundred times you told the story, you used his first name too."

"Huh." He gave Sam a wink. "So there we were, sitting in the middle of the desert, stuck tighter than a hair in a biscuit . . ."

My father continued, but I didn't hear him. The only thing I could think about was Paul Conway. That's why the name had sounded familiar. I'd been hearing about him for years.

"Peach?" My father had fastened his eyes on me.

"Hmm?" I'd been trying my best not to talk. I was afraid that if I opened my mouth the words *SEAN IS ALIVE* would leap out before I could stop them. Right then I was afraid I'd babble something about Paul Conway too.

I forced my lips into a smile instead.

"Got any intel on dessert?"

"Dessert. Right." I collected the plates and took them with me into the kitchen where I put them in the sink. I retrieved the carton of ice cream from the freezer and took it out to them.

My mother frowned. "Bowls?"

I blinked. "Yes. Sure." I went back into the kitchen, but by the time I got there I'd forgotten what I needed. Sean's revelation kept running through my head in a loop. *I think something happened out there in the desert. Something that shouldn't have.*

The thing was, the actions of my father's company were widely known. My father talked about that night all the time, just like he had with Sam. He wouldn't do that if something odd had happened.

Unless he didn't know about it.

Bowls.

And spoons. *That's* why I was there.

I got them and returned to the dining room. Then I scooped the ice cream and handed out the bowls.

"Do you keep up with anyone from your company, Dad?"

"Which one?"

"The one from the desert. The one you were telling Sam about. Anyone like Paul Conway?"

"From E Company?" He thought for a moment. "Can't even remember the last time I talked to anyone from there. Probably that History Channel retrospective. The twenty-five-year anniversary show, maybe? But that was mostly people from the headquarters level; it wasn't any of my troops."

"Would you ever want to see any of them again?"

"What? People like Conway? Sure." He winked at me. "I'd even buy him a beer. Ask him how life's been treating him."

I tried to ignore the chill that crept up my spine. "They were good guys, then?"

"The best. Never served with any better."

32

Being the sole recipient of his grandparents' attention
that evening tired Sam out. He went to bed without any problems.

As I came back into the living room, my father stood and unfolded a blue T-shirt with a flourish and held it up across his chest. "I brought you another one, Peach."

"She doesn't want another T-shirt, JB." My mother was shaking her head.

I read the words. "Quantum Entanglement Is Neither Here Nor There." I smiled. "Good one."

He balled it up and tossed it to me. "You can never have too many T-shirts."

"I kind of think I might. But thanks." My wardrobe of pithy physics-themed shirts was entirely due to him.

He was the first to admit that he knew nothing about physics, but whenever someone asked about me, he'd say, "Georgie? She's a genius. Don't know where she got it from, but it's true."

He sat back down in Sean's old chair.

My mother got up. "I'm just going to powder my nose before we leave for the hotel." She passed by my father on her way.

He reached out for her. "Best thing I ever did was marry you."

She bent down, took him by the chin, and kissed him. "Don't you ever forget it."

"Like I could." He kissed her back and then sent me a wink. "You're always reminding me."

She straightened. Laid a hand on his shoulder and sent me a glance. "Can you believe this man didn't know a butterfly from a boutonniere when I first met him?"

He took her hand. "It was in first grade."

"Well. It's been my life's work, but I think all those rough edges are just about buffed off." She ruffled his hair and turned to walk away.

He pinched her on the butt. "All but the ones you like."

It used to be that I was both profoundly embarrassed by and incredibly proud of my parents. Who else had a mom and dad who looked like Ken and Barbie? And who else could say their father was a general and their mother was a no-kidding beauty queen? However, it had been embarrassing in the extreme when they kissed in front of my friends, or when my mother wore her fur coat to shop for groceries.

In college, *incredibly proud* had evaporated, leaving only *profoundly embarrassed*. It wasn't cool at the time to cheer America's swagger on the international stage. And when your professors were grappling with new theories of light and matter, beauty pageants just seemed so trivial.

By the time I met Sean, I was swinging away from embarrassment and back toward proud. To have two parents who took care of themselves just as carefully as they took care of those around them? Who were still deeply in love with each other? The more I'd seen of the world, the more I'd realized just how rare they were.

But I was a grown-up with a son of my own. And I knew that people weren't good or bad. People were people. They were good *and* bad. All of us had weaknesses and strengths.

My parents' strengths were many.

Ever since I was old enough to notice, my parents had been tirelessly, *relentlessly* patriotic. Military-themed symposia, panels, seminars? My father had been part of them. Visiting professor, cultural ambassador, talking head? He'd done all that too.

And my mother had been at his side the whole time—comforting military spouses, cajoling Congress for more support for veterans, and fundraising for myriad nonprofits.

If there was good to do in the military community, they had done it.

Their weaknesses?

Appearances seemed so important to them. But considering who they were, wouldn't appearances have to be important? In order to advocate for others, to present yourself as an expert in something, you had to be a person who could be trusted, didn't you?

Even *I* didn't wear yoga pants and my Physics—I Can Explain It to You but I Can't Understand It for You T-shirt to customer meetings.

Sometimes their squabbles became heated. And my father could be a little controlling.

But all couples experienced friction, didn't they?

Even Sean and I had had our moments.

Moment.

And part of the job description of a general was to control.

Knowing Sean, there had to be something behind his suspicions. If he said something happened in my father's company, then something probably had. The question was, why didn't my father know about it?

Sean was alive!

The moment my parents pulled out of the driveway, I said the words aloud. I whispered them to myself. "Sean is alive!" Okay, I might have more than whispered them. Alice's ears pricked as her head swiveled toward the door.

I was every emoji on my phone, all at the same time.

Ecstatic that he was alive; mad that he had let me believe he was dead for so long. I still didn't understand why he'd done that. But as soon as he could clear up what had happened during the Desert Sabre project, we could get on with our lives.

I heard a whisper in the back of my mind, but I was too busy exulting over Sean's appearance—planning how we would let Sam know and figuring out what to say to people like Jim and June—to listen.

Sean was alive!

It wasn't until I had slipped into bed and turned off the light that the volume on my exultation was turned down enough that I could finally hear.

Sean was no choirboy. Trouble followed him for most of his youth. If he thought something had been going on, then experience said he was probably right. And what had his instinct always been? What was at the core of his character? The desire to protect the ones he loved. Sean would have left us only if he thought he had to.

33

The next night Sean found me walking past an ivy-covered wasteland in a dip along the road that no streetlight could reach and no window seemed to overlook. I'd invited Jenn and Preston for dinner earlier in the week. Considering that Jenn was going through a tough time with her divorce, I hadn't wanted to cancel. But when they arrived, I asked her if she could keep an eye on the boys while I took Alice for a walk.

Finger to his lips, Sean led me through the vines to the far side of a decrepit old shed that was falling apart at the back of the property. Alice yipped and did a joyful two-legged dance as Sean tried to quiet her.

I put a hand on his arm. It was solid. Real. He was real. And I didn't want to be hiding in the shadows. I wanted to walk down the street with him and take him home to Sam. It made me angry that I couldn't.

"I still don't understand any of this, Sean. We had a funeral. You were cremated." *Someone* was cremated. "After you left that voice mail message, I thought I might be making you up, that I was having a breakdown."

"No, Georgie."

"How did you leave that message?"

"It was a caller ID spoof. I didn't want to do it that way, but I needed to talk to you. I was going to ask you to meet me, but then I got interrupted."

"What is this? What's going on?"

"I don't know. I didn't have time to find out."

"Then what *do* you know? You're saying someone was worried about you finding something out. You're also saying you *didn't* find anything out. You've got to give me something. Something to think there was a reason you've been dead for eight months. I cried real tears for you. My heart broke for you. Sam can't sleep because of you. I want to know there's a reason why." My tone was sharp. My fists were balled. I took a step back, consciously uncurled my fingers as I waited for him to reply.

He turned away from me, ran a hand through his hair again. Turned back. "Here's one thing I can tell you: the Iraqi Republican Guard didn't have any defenses in the area where your father was."

"But they had to have been there. He made a breach through their lines."

"I know. And he destroyed an arsenal of top-of-the-line weapons. It's all documented."

"Maybe those Iraqis were originally somewhere else. Maybe their new location just hadn't been logged."

"That's what I thought too. I might still be thinking that, sitting at the table in our house drinking coffee every morning and walking my son to school, if someone hadn't intervened."

"Do you know Sam thinks you're still alive? He thinks you're in a wormhole somewhere and that at some point you're going to—" My emotions had overcome my capacity for words. My throat closed. I took a deep breath. "Have you seen Sam since you died? Have you talked to him?"

"No. Why would I—"

"Why didn't you talk to me? Why haven't we done this before now?"

"Shh."

I lowered my voice. "Why didn't I know any of this? I'm your wife! I thought we were in this marriage together."

"We are. I just couldn't—"

"You do not get to walk out the door and leave. Not without telling me."

"Why would I have left you if I could have stayed?"

"I don't know. But you destroyed our family, Sean. Whatever this is, you let it in and then you left."

"I'm sorry, I just—"

"No. I'm sorry. I'm sorry I've wasted eight months trying to get over you, telling myself I should move on, trying to fix myself by reading— I've been reading *nonfiction!*"

"I know I should have—"

"I am beyond mad at you."

"Georgie."

"What have you been doing for the past eight months?"

"I've been disappearing. Covering my tracks. Trying to stay alive. And I've been trying to figure this all out. I have been reading every book about the war, watching every interview, tracking down every article I could find. And I've been trying to stay out of sight at the same time. And keep an eye on you. And make enough money for food and somewhere to stay. None of it's been easy."

He was telling the truth. I could read it in the slant of his shoulders and the haunted look in his eyes.

"Someone ransacked the house. Tore it all apart."

"Someone ransacked the—"

I held up a hand to preclude his questions, because I had questions of my own. "Do you have any idea what they might have been looking for?"

"They were probably looking for information. My notes?"

"What were you doing in the crawl space the other night?"

"You were gone the weekend before—"

"My parents took us to the beach."

"—and the first night you were gone I noticed activity. There was someone in the basement. Someone in the crawl space. I wanted to see what they'd been doing."

"They tried to wire your computer."

"I know. I know what they've been doing. What I still don't know is why."

34

Dark energy was at work again. Sean didn't know who he had provoked or why, but we knew he'd happened onto something that mattered because of the reaction that had occurred. Something invisible was at work and it was powerful.

"Tell me about work. Your files were accessed. Things disappeared from the archives. Someone was following you."

"They had me write up my research. And once they had all my materials, they transferred me to a different job. Out of the army. It was straight DoD. They sent me to the Pentagon."

The new job.

"That was last August? When they transferred you?"

He nodded.

So at least that cleared up one question. But it left so many more. "What did they want you to do in the new job?"

"Update the list of all the military-related museums in the country and put together a spreadsheet of their addresses, contact information, and boards of directors."

Busywork? Ouch. "And why didn't you tell me about it?"

He sent me a sardonic look. "Why do you think?"

"You worked it for half a year. That was important. I would have wanted to know. I embarrassed myself just last week calling Brad about something."

"About what?" His gaze sharpened.

"Keys. Your security badge."

"Why?"

"I realized you'd lied about the sink the day you died. You weren't trying to fix it that afternoon. That thing you took with you. It wasn't a part from the faucet. What was it?"

"It was a thumb drive."

"Well, it never came back from the medical examiner's. And that led me to wonder what else was missing, or not, from what you'd left behind. So I went through everything. I found a key I couldn't identify, but I didn't find a security badge. And I knew you'd had one."

"What did you say to him?"

"To Brad? I don't know." I searched back through my memories, sifting through the emotions I'd been experiencing. "I just told him I was sorting through some things and found a key I thought might belong to the office. And that I realized I'd never returned your badge."

"But you just said you *didn't* find my badge."

"I lied, okay? Crucify me."

"Just—" He stretched out a hand, tucked some hair behind my ear. "You asked if you should return it?"

I nodded.

"So he must think you have it."

"Right."

"Okay, I should be fine then."

A chill crept up my spine. "*What* is going on, Sean?"

"You found my notes, right? In the front yard. In the book?"

"Yes, and—"

"I knew someone was following me and it felt like I needed to hide it somewhere. I knew if crocuses came up in the fall, you'd want me to dig them up. I could access it then if I had to. And if anything happened to me before, I wanted you to know why."

"That's just it. I have no idea what any of it—"

"It's in a safe place? It needs to be in a safe place."

"It is. I put it—"

He gripped my hands. "Don't tell me!" He took a deep breath. "Sorry." He drew me close, enfolding me in his arms. He planted a kiss on my forehead. "Sorry. But as long as it's safe, it's better if I don't know where it is. It would be even better if *you* didn't know where it is. Safer. Maybe we should just burn it."

Suddenly not even his embrace felt safe.

He let me go.

I stood beside him, back against the shed, slipping my hands into my sleeves to keep them warm.

Alice sighed and sat down in front of us.

"So I changed jobs, but I couldn't let it go. That's when I started that list of names. I was looking for anyone connected with your father. Anyone who could help me figure it out. Back in October, I got in touch with the FBI."

"And?"

He lifted a shoulder. "And they wanted my help in passing them all the information I'd found."

"But you said the army took it all."

"They took my files, but I knew what I'd read. At first, the FBI wanted me to find out who was wanting me to cease and desist, at what level that decision had been made."

"So you were working the new job, and also working for the FBI?"

"*With.* I was working *with* the FBI."

With. Knowledge dawned with startling clarity. "You were an FBI source?"

He frowned.

"Sorry. *Asset.* You were an asset."

"They were *my* asset. *I* was trying to get *their* help. That's what I was doing that night."

That night. "The night you died."

"You'd just told me that afternoon that your father was going to be nominated as the new secretary of defense. I thought the FBI should know since whatever had happened out there had involved his company. So I went out and met my contact. The FBI took care of the car accident. They even swung a deal at the coroner's for a fake death certificate and autopsy report."

That's what Dr. Correy meant.

"They needed the DoD, the army, to think I was dead; someone over there was getting nervous."

"Wait, wait, wait. The Department of Defense tried to kill you?"

"No. The FBI just wanted to make it look as if I had been killed."

"They did a good job of it. My father identified your body."

"What?"

"He identified your body. I couldn't do it. I couldn't go. Sam wouldn't let me out of his sight. So I asked my father to do it for me."

Sean's eyes narrowed. "But there was no body. The agency told the medical examiner to write out a death certificate and fill out the transfer paperwork for the crematorium. It was supposed to seem like my body had already been sent. When you came to identify me, he was supposed to give you my effects and a phone number in case you wanted to lodge a complaint. It would have been a number at the FBI. But your father said he'd *identified* my body?"

We stared at each other for a long moment.

I was trying to sort it all out. "Maybe he just got caught in the plan. The FBI thought I'd show up, but he went in my place. Maybe he thought I'd be even more upset if I knew there'd been some mistake with your body."

"What did he tell you when he came back?"

"From the medical examiner's? He said they had to know what to do with you. That there was no point in having a viewing, considering the effects of the accident, so he asked them to cremate you." There was something distinctly odd about discussing someone's cremation when they were standing right in front of you.

He sighed and ran a hand up the back of his head. "Anyway, the plan was that I'd be able to move around more freely if I wasn't being watched. But—"

"By the Department of Defense? They were the ones watching you?"

"Yes."

What kind of world did we live in?

"But then something must have happened because the FBI reprioritized; things with me were put on a back burner. I wasn't interested in that, so I disappeared."

Disappeared? "What does that even mean?"

"It means that I made sure even the FBI didn't think I was alive anymore."

"Why? How?"

He sent me a sidelong glance. "I had ways."

Ways. The hairs at the back of my neck stood on end.

"But now they're looking for me again. Both the DoD and the FBI."

There was something about what he was saying that didn't make sense. "If the DoD didn't want to hear what you discovered and the FBI didn't care to follow through on what you found out . . ." I forced myself to think it through, one piece at a time. Realization came with an overwhelming sense of dread. I had to force out my words. "You *can't* be alive, can you? Because you think that someone thinks you know something. And whoever it is—maybe even the FBI—doesn't want that something known and would kill you for it all over again."

He didn't answer.

"Only, you don't know. You don't know what they think you do. But if they find out you're alive, then—"

"Then they could threaten *you*, you and Sam, in order to make me reveal myself. So I took you both out of the equation. I made sure there was no reason to threaten you."

I took you both out of the equation. He'd done the same with Kelly. He'd disappeared from her life when he thought his presence endangered her. Without hesitation, without warning. "That's why you had to die."

"A second time. And that time, I had to stay dead."

I had it. I understood it. All the pieces of the puzzle had fallen into place. But I still couldn't make any sense of the picture. "So then why are you back? Why now?"

"Because I think they suspect I'm alive. It's what I was afraid of. Maybe I should have stayed away—I tried to stay away—but I just can't stand by and watch anymore. And you needed to know what's going on. They're using you as leverage. This could escalate."

35

Standing there by the shed, we talked it through. "You've been at this for eight months. More than eight months. The only thing you know is the Republican Guard shouldn't have been where it was?"

"I also know somebody thinks I know more than I do. I can infer that person, those people, want the information—whatever it is—to stay hidden."

"Agreed."

"Beyond that? Whoever it is must be in a position of power. If they were able to demand reports on my progress and access my computer, take documents from the archives, they had to be doing it from a level above my pay grade."

"You're thinking officer or civilian?"

"I'm not sure."

"And it has to do with my father's old company?"

"It almost has to, doesn't it? That's what I was working on."

"I asked my father about Paul Conway last night. He was one of the names in your book."

"He was a sergeant."

"Right. But he died. Hit-and-run at the beginning of last week. My father didn't show any signs of knowing that, though."

"This might not have anything to do with your father. Not directly. I've been trying to find out more about the commanders further up the chain. Maybe someone had information about that Republican Guard position. Maybe your father should have been given that information. Maybe that's what this is all about."

"Does that make sense, though? Everything turned out all right in the end for everyone. Maybe we should just ask him. Maybe it would help us figure it out."

"By you asking him questions all of a sudden? If they tried to shut me up, what would they do to him? And what would you tell him when he asks why you think there's a problem? That your dead husband was just wondering? We need to keep me out of this and you as far away from it as possible."

He was right.

"With your father's nomination, people are probably poking around his career anyway, trying to see what they can find."

"Everybody likes my father."

"But not everyone likes the president. Think how many people would like to embarrass him."

"You think it's the *president* who had you reassigned?"

He shook his head. "There's no way to know."

"What could have gone hidden for this many years when a whole company of men was involved?"

"We don't know it was the whole company. It could have been just one man. And he could have been someone at the battalion or brigade level."

"We need to figure out what this is. And then we need to make it known."

"That's all I've ever wanted to do. But I've been working on this for months and I can tell you everything about the war but that."

"Let me help."

"I can't. I refuse to put you in more danger than you already are. I never should have left that message on your voice mail. I shouldn't be here now."

"But you did. And you are. And now I know. We're in this together. Tell me how to help. How did it all start? If we back up, then maybe—"

"It started with the project. But you don't have access to the archives."

He was right. "But you said you did interviews. Let me talk to the people you talked to."

"They weren't helpful. If they had been, then I would have figured it out long before now."

"It's worth a try. You never know. What if I ask a question you didn't? Or they think of something they forgot to tell you?"

He shoved his hands into his pockets. "I'll give you a name. It's the first person I interviewed. I don't have a phone number, but you can find it. Lee Ornofo. He lives near Philadelphia. Ask him about that first night of the Gulf War." He leveled a look at me. "Be careful. Whoever is behind this, we have to assume they're watching and listening."

Lee Ornofo.

It was one of the names in Sean's book.

Sundays were Samdays as far as Jim and June were concerned. After Sean died, they'd made a point to do something with Sam every Sunday. It let me have time to get things done.

That Sunday I went to Central Library, signed up for computer time, and started googling. Considering that extraneous cable I'd discovered, I didn't trust my home computer network.

I couldn't find an email for Lee Ornofo, but after tracing the name to a radiosport organization in Philadelphia, I was able to find contact information from their website. I went out to the car so I could have some privacy. People walked in and out of the library, stacks of books in hand. Two teenagers hit a ball around the tennis courts beside me. I phoned Mr. Ornofo, explaining that I was doing a report on Desert Sabre. "Are you the Mr. Ornofo who served in Captain Slater's company?"

"I am."

"May I ask you a few questions about your time in Iraq?"

"Sure. Yeah. I served. I did." He sighed. "That was back when they give you a parade when you came home from a war. Marching band. Convertibles. The whole shebang." He coughed. "Different times now."

"I'm just trying to understand the war better, how exactly it went. That sort of thing. Would you mind helping me?"

"You with that project? The one that other fellow was with?"

"I'm working with the military history office. Just following up. You spoke with someone last year?"

"That's right. Happy to help. What do you need to know?"

"Let's just start with the basics, Mr. Ornofo. Name, rank, position. All of that." I opened up the notebook I'd brought.

"You can call me Lee."

No, I couldn't. I hadn't been raised that way.

He gave me the information, then I asked him what particular job he'd done.

"I was the company RTO. The radio telephone operator."

"What did that mean, practically speaking?"

"Meant I was the captain's shadow." He cleared his throat. "Anywhere he went, I was there too. Stuck like glue."

I asked him to describe February 24, from the time he woke up until the time he went to bed that night.

He laughed. "Well, I didn't go to bed, that's the first thing. So I didn't wake up either. Desert Storm was a month and a half. Started in January. Desert Sabre was the actual ground campaign. The war itself. It was fought in five days. Probably didn't sleep five hours for the duration."

"As RTO, you were used to receiving communications from headquarters?"

"Sure. Message traffic. Orders. We communicated with the other companies too. And kept in contact with all our platoons. There were five of them in our company. And I kept in contact with the commo too." He replied to my unspoken question. "That's the communications sergeant. Wouldn't have wanted to be him."

"Why not?"

"Sand. And all that wind. Later on in the afternoon and evening—that's when everything started to go south."

"How so?"

"We didn't have our ground-to-ground comms. At least not dependably."

"What did that mean for you?"

"Didn't really matter what it meant for me. It's what it meant for the captain. We had a job to do, but we couldn't do it if we couldn't coordinate with our platoons. And the battalion couldn't do its job if they couldn't coordinate with us. See?"

"Makes sense."

"You tend to think the battalion commander gives an order and the companies like ours go out and get it done. But it's not like that. 'Specially not out there."

"So what happened?"

"The commo would know better than me. He got all the communications. Everything from the battalion on down. My job was just communicating for the captain. I sent out what he wanted to say, and when someone wanted to say something to him, I took the message or put the phone to his ear. The commo made sure all the message traffic, all the calls got through."

"And who was the commo?" I waited, pen poised above my tablet of paper.

"Conway. Paul Conway."

36

Paul Conway. **My knuckles turned white as I wrote his** name. "So the company stumbled onto a Republican Guard unit that night. How did that happen? Do you remember? You must have been there because you were with the captain the whole night, right?"

"Mostly I was with him the whole hundred hours. Yeah. So things started off as planned, everyone all lined up. Nice and straight. Tidy, you know? Then someone runs into an enemy position. Slows 'em down till they can wrap it up. Pretty soon, some units who don't encounter any resistance are out ahead; other units get hung up, they fall behind. Relatively speaking, you see?"

"Sure."

"Then the comms start going in and out. We weren't receiving messages. Or only receiving partial messages. Drove the commo crazy."

"What did you do?"

"You just press on, do what you're supposed to do until someone tells you otherwise because that's what everyone's expecting you to do."

"So you pressed on."

"Yeah. Captain was a little uneasy. Early on, the companies could see each other. Later on, you could see the dust-ups. Know what I'm saying? Explosions. Smoke, when there was contact with the enemy. After that, couldn't see anything at all. And it was dark that night. Sand in the air. Cloud cover. Radio was on the fritz. Seemed like an order came through telling everyone to pull back, but it cut out. We couldn't confirm receipt. Captain and I just looked at each other. Shrugged."

"Wait. You got an order but you didn't do anything about it? Why?"

"Because the general, he was all set before the whole thing started on how important it was to do the job. Just keep doing the job. He didn't want anyone getting all hung up. Had to keep up the pace, keep going, because of the strategy. There were multiple countries' forces involved. If we weren't all where we were supposed to be at the time we were supposed to be there, then the plan wouldn't work. So we hear half an order and it just doesn't make sense. Why would the general tell everyone to pull back when he'd been dead set on going ahead full throttle before it all started?"

"So what did you do?"

"We talked it over."

"You and the captain?"

"Yeah."

"He asked for your opinion?"

"Yeah."

"Did he do that a lot?" The father I'd grown up with had always had a plan. Had always known what to do. He never asked anyone's opinion, never asked anyone's permission. He just stepped out and expected that everyone else would follow along.

"Ask me what I thought? Sure. And sometimes he'd just talk, work his way around to a decision. That's part of the job. To be the guy the captain can talk to. The RTO is like a black hole. Lots of stuff goes in through the ears, but none of it's ever supposed to come out."

"So what did he decide?"

"He decided to just keep going. That's the only full order we'd received. And that's when we discovered that minefield and met up with the Iraqis."

Minefield? I made a note to ask Sean. "What happened then?"

"Well . . . turns out, they had us surrounded. But the captain, he went out to talk to them."

"And you went with him?"

"No. In that case I didn't. He left me behind."

"So you don't know what was said?"

"Not exactly. But I know the end result. The captain found us a breach. It's what the general had wanted. Once we got our breach, everyone else could go through."

Maybe that's all there was to this. Maybe my father was just embarrassed that they hadn't obeyed an order. My relief, however, was short-lived. That didn't seem like enough to need to kill someone like Sean over. "But it didn't cause anyone any heartburn that he hadn't obeyed the order to fall back?"

"Thing about the captain is, once he decided something, he was all in. I stayed with him for a while as RTO after. Through the desert. Into that mess in Bosnia. After that, they booted me out. Whatever it was I brought back from the desert, I wasn't any use to the army anymore."

I didn't get it. "What did you bring back?"

"Nobody knows. Felt like I was an old man at thirty years old. Gulf War Syndrome. That's what they called it. At least it wasn't just all in my head. Shame to leave the captain, though. Felt like I was letting him down. He was a major by then. Best officer I ever had the pleasure to serve under. He might not have known exactly where everyone else was out there in the desert, but I can tell you, no matter where we were after that, he always seemed to know where the enemy was. It's like he had some sixth sense or something." He coughed again. "Captain Slater? He was good people. That's about all I know."

∞

My father had gotten himself way out ahead of the line and then he'd chosen not to obey an order. He'd come across the enemy and gone to talk to them by himself. But what did that signify? I still hadn't heard anything that was worth killing Sean over.

But I had heard about Paul Conway, and that bothered me.

A lot.

Because Paul Conway was dead.

Paul Conway probably knew more about what had happened that night than Lee Ornofo did. And now he would never be able to tell anyone.

37

"Georgie!" The receptionist caught me as I was passing through the lobby on Monday morning. She waved a slip of paper at me.

I smiled my thanks and took it from her as I continued on down the hall. I'd only taken a few steps before I turned right around and went back to see her. I held it up. "I'm not quite sure what this says."

"That was your ten o'clock who called."

"My ten o'clock what?"

"Meeting. Your ten o'clock meeting. Said he didn't have time to come by the office, but he could meet you down at Starbucks."

"Starbucks?"

Her brow folded. "Isn't that what I put down?" The phone rang. She held up a finger as she answered.

I waited as she transferred the call through.

"Did he leave a name?"

She shrugged. "Just said he was your ten o'clock."

"Did he say *which* Starbucks?"

"I just assumed you'd know. I'm sorry. I should have asked."

"He didn't leave a number?"

"I just assumed . . ." By that point she was getting flustered.

"Don't worry. It's not important. Thanks for—" I held up the message.

Starbucks.

There were three in the general area.

I'd just have to assume that the Starbucks in question was the closest one. The one beneath my building, in the Crystal City Shops. It was the same mall that housed Mr. Hoffman's store.

The identity of my ten o'clock appointment?

It was a male; that's what she'd said. I wanted to think it was Sean. But what if it wasn't? Who else might it be? It could be those nameless, faceless DoD or FBI people Sean thought were after him.

If I didn't go, then I wouldn't be putting myself in any danger.

But I might miss an opportunity to talk to Sean.

I went early. That way, I was there first.

I got a venti brew. If anyone tried anything funny, a huge cup of hot, scalding coffee in the face could be my first line of defense.

Second line of defense? I took a seat along the mall-facing counter back in the corner where it met the interior wall of the store. That way I could see everyone who came in, and if anyone tried to drag me out of the store, I'd have a chance to make a scene.

I watched from my perch for half an hour. Ten o'clock appeared to be break time, so there were lots of professionals, company lanyards looped around their necks. There were military people. Artsy types. There was a guy draped in an oversize hoodie and a woman with really long red fingernails. Retail associates from other stores in the mall stopped in, name tags pinned to their shirts and sweaters.

The guy in the hoodie leaned against the stool next to mine while he waited for the barista to make his drink.

I shifted away from him.

He was talking to someone over a Bluetooth headset that was stuck in his ear. "So what did you think of my guy?"

I kept my eyes on the entrance to the store as I waited for Sean. "You had the chance to talk to him?"

I shifted once more, securing my purse between my elbow and the wall.

The man shifted too, adjusting his Bluetooth, putting his heel to the rung of the stool. "I don't have much time, Georgie. Did you get to talk to him or not?"

At the sound of my name, I jerked. Tightened my hold on my coffee. Then I looked past the baggy jeans, past the hoodie and the beard, and . . . "Sean?"

38

He put a finger to his Bluetooth and glanced over toward the counter. "Don't look at me."

Uh. Okay. "Yes." I opened my purse and pulled out my phone. Pretended to pull up a number and dial. Then I put it to my ear. "Hi. Yes. I talked to him."

This was not the Sean I'd known. The Sean I'd known was articulate. And rational. And most definitely not paranoid. "Yeah. It was very interesting. Did you know there was a minefield that night?"

"Not one of the things that everyone talks about, but yeah."

"And my father didn't draw back when he was supposed to."

"Comms went out. I know."

"Apparently my father talked through a lot of his decisions with his RTO. That's something I can loop back to if we need it."

"Anything else?"

"He stayed with my father. Went with him to Bosnia. Did you know that?"

"No."

I asked him a question I should have asked long before. One that was vital to our collective safety. "How did they figure out you're still alive?"

"I don't know."

"Was it my phone calls? I called you every night that first month."

The barista called out someone's name. Sean slipped from the stool and sauntered over, hand in a pocket, to get his drink. When he came back, he sat fully on the stool, positioned to see out the window. "No. It couldn't be. When I call in to access the voice messages, it's from a different number every time. That voice mail box is like a dead drop now." He put a finger to the Bluetooth again as he held his cup in one hand.

I pulled out a pad of Post-its and a pen as I spoke. "But they think you'll show up at the house." I wrote on the top Post-it. Slid it out in front of me so he'd be able to read it.

I'm scared.

I was scared about what it all meant for Sam and me, but I was also scared in a broader sense. I was scared of what was out there lurking.

"Yeah. I get it. I really do. You've just got to trust that I'm doing what I can."

"I don't know what to do."

"I need you to be careful."

Right. I turned my back to him while a tear slipped down my cheek.

"I'll figure out what to do, but in the meantime, just be careful . . ."

"They're not trying to kill us?"

He didn't answer for a long moment.

My knuckles grew white as my fingers clenched around the phone. "Are they?"

Something brushed against my arm.

I glanced over and saw that he'd stood.

He hitched up his jeans and put his finger to his Bluetooth again as he grabbed his coffee. "I think they're using you to bait me." His eyes scanned the passersby who strolled the mall.

"It seems to be working."

There had to be a solution. A way that Sean could come back to life again. The FBI might suspect that he lived, but they couldn't truly know for certain. And if the DoD figured it out? My son had already lost his dad once. I didn't know if I could handle him dying again. For real. I had to know he understood that. "I'm in."

He squinted. "What?"

I pulled the pad of Post-its back. "I'm in. Whatever it takes." I put them back in my purse as I spoke. "I'll do whatever it takes, but you have to promise not to die again."

He fiddled with the cardboard sleeve around his cup. "I can't—"

"I can't go through that again. I won't."

"Can't promise you anything."

I held the phone out in front of me and pretended I was making another call. Put it to my ear. "I don't care if you can't promise. I need you to do it. Just say it."

"Georgie—" He flipped the lid off his coffee. Put it back on.

"Say it."

"I promise."

"Good. Okay. Now we just need to figure out what it is that everyone thinks you discovered."

He grimaced. "Get a phone. A throwaway. Leave the number on my old voice mail."

39

I needed to figure out what Sean had discovered and why people were so intent on keeping it hidden. And if I wanted Sean to be able to come back from the dead, if I wanted Sam to live in safety, then I would have to figure out how to make all of it known. No one kills to protect information that's freely available.

First things first. Back at the office, I muted a conference call in which I was peripherally involved so I could contact a security company. A supervisor with an eye toward customer service, plus the guarantee of a much higher-quality system than I could afford, made the impossible possible. Waving a credit card was like waving a magic wand. They scheduled the consultation *and* installation for the next day. I crossed my fingers that Jim would be able to supervise.

I would feel safer if I knew who was watching me. Not in a global sense but in a particular one. I wanted a name I could recognize, a face I could identify. That way I would know who to look for.

In the absence of definite knowledge about the bad guys, I needed to play defense. Anyone could create a hypothesis. That's where conspiracy theories usually started. And ended. In order to turn Sean's suspicions into a plausible theory, I needed facts.

At lunch I went out and bought two prepaid phones. I called Sean's old number and left contact information for one of them on his voice mail. The other I decided to use for talking to people like Lee Ornofo.

I stopped by Mr. Hoffman's on the way back to the office. He greeted me, asking about Sam.

"My father was playing with him the other night and he mentioned there's some sort of train that has things you can take on and off?"

He frowned. "I don't know this one."

"Things like boxes? Crates?"

"Ah!" He walked behind the counter and pulled out a well-thumbed catalog. I probably could have found it faster online, but I loved that in his shop at least, things were done the traditional way. He flipped through it and turned it around toward me, pointing. "This one."

It looked pretty cool. It was a cargo set with an engine and a couple of cars. "Do you have it? I want to give it to Sam for Christmas." Mr. Hoffman's store wasn't large; his stock was limited. If he didn't have it, if he had to make a special order, sometimes it took a while to arrive.

He went to the shelves to take a look. Then he went into the back. He came out empty-handed. "I can order it." He made a phone call as I browsed and arranged to have it delivered to the shop later in the week.

My burner phone vibrated as I was walking back to work. I pulled it out. A text from Sean. It was blank, but at least I had his phone number.

∞

When I came out of the school from dropping off Sam the next morning, Chris was petting Alice. She nudged his hand aside when she saw me. He turned and then straightened. "Hey."

"Hey." I freed the leash from the holder.

We fell into step with each other as we headed out toward the street.

He glanced over at me from beneath the leather brim of his hat. "How's Sam doing with everything? Keith wasn't much older when Kristy died."

"His teacher's keeping an eye on him. And he's been working with a counselor."

I asked him about what kind of help he'd gotten for Keith. By the time we made it back to the house, the security van was waiting on the street.

Chris nodded toward it. "You have a system?"

"I'm going to. Just as soon as I can have one installed."

"Been getting quotes?"

"I'm just going to do it. Consult and installation on the same day."

"Don't sign up for anything yet. Let me give you the name of the company who did mine."

"I already basically gave them my credit card and told them to charge whatever they wanted."

"Tell me you didn't."

"With Sean gone, I just want to feel safe."

"You could feel safe for cheaper. I can guarantee it. Want me to see if I can haggle for you? Work the price down?"

"You're sweet, but in this case, the cost of being able to sleep at night? It's priceless."

He shrugged, waved good-bye, and continued toward home.

I watched him walk away. He'd seemed concerned about my not being taken advantage of. Which was nice. And kind. And maybe it spoke more to my state of paranoia than anything else that I couldn't just accept his interest at face value.

He'd shown up at Mrs. T's. He'd been interested in my new security system. In terms of how much it was going to cost me. I caught myself frowning. Sean had ruined me for nice people who just wanted to look out for their friends.

❧

The installation began. Jim had agreed to come over and stay at the house so I could get to work.

I took my lunch break in my office, closing the door. That's when I pulled Sean's book out of its hiding place behind my bookshelf. It was easier to read the actual pages than to zoom in on my phone to see the entries.

The letters and numbers finally made sense. E was E Company. 2 was 2nd Battalion. DS was Desert Sabre. BW. I assumed that was the Bosnian War. The names, I guessed, were all people my father had commanded.

There was nothing to indicate that Paul Conway's death had anything to do with Sean's inquiry into Desert Sabre, but why not take precautions as I made contact with the people on the list? If there was a truth to be revealed, those people could tell me what it was. I googled the names, filling in ranks and positions when they were available. Noting phone numbers when I could.

∽

Before I picked up Sam, I stopped by home and met Jim. He came equipped with operating manuals and instructions about programming the system, setting a security code, and contacting the monitoring center.

"So if you're home, you turn the system off. That way you won't activate it. And when you head to bed or when you go out, you turn it on."

Mostly I was worried about when I was at work. That seemed to be when strange things happened.

"If one of the sensors gets tripped, then they'll call you from this number." He pointed to it in the manual.

I entered it into my phone's contact list.

"Remember: you had them set the alarm to silent."

I had. I'd debated whether I should. But because the security company called the police when the sensors were tripped, I figured they'd have a better chance of catching an intruder if the alarm wasn't clanging a warning.

"So all you have to do to disable the alarm is punch in the code." He showed me the four-digit number. "The year I was born."

His security code lasted the length of time it took me to change it later that evening. I knew I'd never remember his birth year. I changed it to the year Sam was born instead.

I had new locks and deadbolts on my doors and sensors for every room, window, and door of the house. By the time I brought Sam home from school, I felt like I might actually be able to sleep.

∞

My new phone buzzed as I was getting ready for bed.

There should be a better way to earn money than panhandling

40

What?

It was from Sean. It had to be. Same number as before. But I had no idea what he was trying to say.

A better way to earn money than panhandling?

I tried free association. Panhandling. Money. No money. Poor. Homeless. Street. Corner.

Street corner!

I thought—I *hoped*—I knew what Sean wanted me to do. There was an intersection about five minutes away, in Pentagon City, just after the exit ramp from the interstate. A man stood there every morning panhandling. Cars would back up in the left-turn lane, giving him the perfect opportunity to walk up and down the median and ask for money.

I'd made the comment more than once that some company could have a captive advertising audience if they'd just pay the man to hold up their sign instead of his. And that way maybe he'd be able to earn some decent money. *A better way to earn money than panhandling.* I'd just have to cross my fingers that I'd guessed right.

A storm blew in during the night. I'd expected to run into Chris at the school the next morning, the way I usually did, but I didn't see him. Not surprising considering that the entire fifth-grade class was bunched together on the curb huddling under umbrellas, duffels and pillows in hand, as they waited to be whisked off to the county's Outdoor Lab for an overnight. He was probably still inside, filling out last-minute forms or hauling luggage.

I walked home by myself and got ready for work.

Sure enough, as I waited in the left-turn lane at Pentagon City, I saw the man at the edge of the intersection. He was wearing the usual battered camouflage jacket and Nationals baseball cap. Rain dripped from the brim. As he stood there holding a handwritten sign, he hunched his shoulders against the wind. Today, however, the man looked a lot like Sean. I tried to time it just right so that I'd have the full rotation of lights to speak to him. But still, I had to stall for a couple of seconds before the light went red.

Several horns blasted in protest behind me.

Sean walked over, holding his sign.

I rolled down my window.

He leaned toward me.

My phone rang.

I ignored it.

"Can you maybe just leave a voice mail for me? Instead of sending crazy texts?"

"Burner phones aren't hack-proof. They can be traced."

True. I eyed the traffic light. Still red. "I had a security system put in. I need to identify who it is that's doing all these things. Then we can figure out whether it's the FBI or the DoD. We can be working on this from both sides."

The phone stopped ringing.

"I just want you and Sam to be safe."

The intersection cleared. My light would be turning green soon.

My phone pinged. Text message.

"You should talk to Abbott next. I couldn't figure out what to think about what he told me."

I glanced at my phone. Home Security. Intruder Alert. "I have to go."

"What's wrong?"

"Someone just broke into the house."

He gripped the door. "Let me come."

"You can't. You're dead."

As the light turned green, I whipped around the median, making a U-turn, and barreled back onto the interstate.

41

I could have left it up to the police, but I was so close to home. I wanted to see who it was. If I saw him—them, whomever—before the police scared them off, then I would know who I was up against.

After parking the car several houses down, I jogged up the driveway and around the house to the back door. I opened it as quietly as I could and then stepped inside and listened.

Alice wasn't barking like she would have if a stranger had forced their way in. She wasn't even whining the way she had when she'd been muzzled.

Maybe the system had glitched?

I tiptoed into the dining room.

That's when I heard a voice. It was out in the living room.

My phone rang. I grabbed at it, turned the ringer off, and sent it to voice mail.

The voice stopped talking for a long minute. Then it started again. This time I could hear it clearly.

"Georgie?" Is was a she, not a he. "Hi. This is June. Jim and I are over at your place and—"

I walked into the living room to see June and Jim standing by the front door.

The look on June's face as she noticed me was one of utter confusion. "I was just—" She took the phone from her ear. Looked at it. Looked at me. Held it up. "I was just calling you."

Turned out they'd gotten a big Halloween yard inflatable for Sam. They'd decided to leave it inside so it wouldn't get wet. They'd used the house key but plugged in the old security code. I gave them the new one. We got it all sorted out.

But not before the police got there.

It was getting to be a regular thing with me.

That afternoon I got word that everyone was cleared for the big test in January. I put in a request with the travel office for plane tickets and hotels. Congress was still moving forward on passing a funding bill, so I was good there. But I had phone calls to make and emails to send and a list of new government requests for proposals to scan. Several to start working on. And I had a presentation for one of the American Physical Society's conferences to outline.

When I came home with Sam that night, Jenn and Preston were sitting on the porch swing, shivering as they waited for us. A box filled with my half of our farm share sat in front of the door. At least I wouldn't have to go into the house by myself. I'd expected that installing the security system would make me feel more secure, but it hadn't.

Jenn hefted the box to her hip as I opened the door. After punching in the security code, I let everyone in.

Sam discovered the Halloween inflatable right away. He and Preston wanted to take it outside. I persuaded them we couldn't blow it up in the rain and herded them toward the kitchen instead.

"Sorry about the delay." Jenn followed me. "Got home too late last night to bring it over. But guess what's in our box this week— You'll never guess."

"Kale, broccoli, turnips, onions, and cauliflower?"

"O-kay, so maybe you will guess. But there is *one* surprise."

"No idea."

"Apples!"

"Really?" I took it from her and carried it into the kitchen. Apples were a gift from heaven. I didn't have to think about how to disguise them or make them yummy. They already were.

"I know, right? I'm thinking we should drink to them."

Rain splattered against the window over the sink. Where would Sean go on a night like this? Where would he sleep? What would he eat? Was he safe? "You'd drink to anything." I pulled a bag of veggie chips from the cabinet and shook them into a bowl for the boys.

Jenn raised a brow. "Let's just say I'm not picky. Usually people think that's a virtue, G."

I shot her a look over my shoulder. She'd been drinking far too much lately, in my opinion. "They say women are drinking just as much as men now, but because we have a higher fat-to-water ratio than—"

"Please, don't mention fat." She put up a hand. "Let's think positive thoughts: agave. There is agave in tequila. Agave is green. Greens are green, ergo, when I drink a margarita it's basically like eating spinach."

Divorce was tough. I got it. But she seemed manic. Borderline destructive. "I count at least three fallacies in your argument."

"That's just because you're a scientist. Normal people would agree with me. I say we deserve doubles."

"You can deserve a double. Make me a single." I pulled the tequila from the cabinet and set it on the counter next to her.

"Only if you promise to drink it twice as slow."

I held up three fingers in a Scout's promise.

She poured herself what looked like a triple shot to me.

We sipped the drinks while Sam and Preston chattered about the Halloween party that would take place the following Friday. Sipped some more as they told us the latest rounds of their hilariously unfunny knock-knock jokes.

Sean used to knock-knock Sam right back with even crazier, screwier jokes. Whatever wavelength Sam lived on, Sean had been a frequent visitor.

Jenn leaned toward me. "Do you mind?"

"Huh?"

Jenn snaked the bottle of tequila from the cabinet and poured herself another shot while the boys acted out a scene from some super-hero movie. When they ran out of the kitchen, Jenn trailed them, taking a seat at the table in the dining room.

Pushing thoughts of Sean away, I pulled out a chair across from her and sat down. "What's going on?"

She blinked in apparent innocence. "With what?"

"The divorce."

She made a face.

"I just worry about you."

She downed about half the tequila in one long swallow.

"Seriously worry."

She shook her head. "Don't." Jenn worked hard and partied hard. She always had.

"Have you talked to your dad lately?"

She took another drink. "Chief Justice Andrew Cunningham Baxter IV?"

I raised my brow.

Her gaze dropped toward the table. "No." It came out in a whisper.

When Jenn's mother died, her father had conquered his grief by pouring his heart into his career and his religion. Which left Jenn no one to help her through her own grief. No wonder she was messed up. In high school, we'd had parent envy. I gladly would have given her my type A parents for the bliss of benign neglect. She'd tried everything she shouldn't have at least once by then. But she'd finally figured out that being the best was a better way to get her father's attention. Therefore, Harvard. Therefore, Georgetown Law. Therefore, her position on the Hill in the office of the most powerful politician in Washington. Senator Rydel chaired the Armed Services Committee that would be conducting my father's hearing. He was rumored to be exploring a run for president. If that happened, if he got elected, Jenn would be able to ask for any position in his admin-istration she wanted.

"I really do worry." About her. About Sam. And about Sean.

"It's not worth it. I mean, think of how many times you've already worried about me. And here I am." She saluted me. "I'll be fine."

"You'll be drunk."

"Too late." She snickered.

At least I didn't have to worry about her driving. She and Preston only lived a couple blocks away. I leaned across the table and reached for her drink, but she held it out of reach.

"I just want you to be happy."

"I *am* happy. In my odd, perverse, screwed-up sort of way."

"Is it Mark? Has he changed his mind? Is he asking for full custody?"

"No. He's just about perfect. Except he married me. We still have to hold that against him." She took another drink.

Jenn wasn't the sentimental type. Especially not about her exes. "You realize you just said something nice about him."

She nodded glumly.

"Sean always thought he was a good guy."

"Sean." She sighed, closed her eyes, and leaned against the back of the chair. "Here's to Sean." She raised her glass. "The perfect gentleman who, even when presented with the possibility of a sure thing, chose fidelity." She tossed back the rest of her tequila.

42

"*What* did you just say?"

"What did I what?" She sat up, wiped her mouth with the back of her hand, and set the glass down, hard, on the table.

"That thing you said. About Sean."

Something flashed across her face as her gaze shot away from me. "What did I say?"

"Something about when he was presented with 'a sure thing'?"

"I said that out loud?"

I nodded.

"Funny story . . ."

"I don't think I want to hear it."

"No. Wait." She didn't seem drunk anymore. "I think you should hear it. I think you should hear how one day last January I came over when you were gone and asked Sean if he wanted to—"

I stood up. "You should leave. Now."

She put a hand to her eyes. "I'm such a mess. I can't even tell you—"

"No, really. You should leave." I stepped into the hall. "Sam?"

He answered a moment later, yelling, "What?"

"Preston has to leave." My call sounded more like a screech.

"Can we have five more minutes?"

"He has to leave *now*."

"But, Mo-om!"

I went down the hall to Sam's room and started scooping up Legos and tossing them into bins.

Jenn had followed. "If I could just—"

Glancing up, I saw her lean into the room. Alice nudged her aside and came in and stood beside me.

"You have to understand. Please, Georgie."

Understand? What could there possibly be to understand? Once she'd blown up her own marriage, she'd decided to blow up mine? I ignored her, focusing instead on Sam. "Don't worry about picking up. I'll do it."

"'Kay."

I looked over at Preston. "Your mom has to go."

His bottom lip edged out into a pout. "But we weren't done playing."

Jenn stepped forward to grab Preston's hand, pulling him toward the door. "Sorry."

I wasn't sure who she was saying it to, but I hoped it was Preston. Because sorry wasn't going to be enough for me.

∞

After we'd finished dinner—after *Sam* had finished his dinner—I took him to the public skate session so he could practice what he'd learned in his lesson the night before. I laced up his skates and helped him over to the wall of the rink where he could wait with the rest of the kids.

"I'll meet you down here when it's over."

"What if I get tired before that?"

"Of skating? You love skating!" And I knew I'd need the whole hour to process Jenn's revelation.

"Can you skate with me?"

"Tonight?"

I could barely see his eyes through his helmet. But I probably wasn't imagining they looked hopeful.

"I can't, sweetie. I didn't bring any thick socks." And my heart was breaking.

His shoulders dropped.

"I'll skate with you sometime next week."

"You will?"

"I promise."

One of the skate guards unlocked the door and swung it open.

I stayed until Sam made it to the end of the rink. The chill in the rink reinforced the chill in my heart. After verifying that there were two fluorescent yellow–hoodied skate guards on duty, I went upstairs to the mezzanine, which overlooked the rink. It was warmer there than it was rinkside, and I could keep an eye on Sam. I could have watched him the whole time if I'd wanted to. And I did want to. But my gaze kept veering off into nothingness as I contemplated Jenn's betrayal.

Forty-five minutes into the public skate session, I'd done absolutely no work on hunting down Mr. Abbott, even though my purse, papers, and phone were strewn across the seat next to mine. On my other side, a woman had sat down, book in hand. She was a typical skater mom, dressed in one of those puffy down jackets and a pair of fuzzy boots. She spent more time watching one of the figure skaters who was using public ice to practice than she did reading.

When I looked down into the rink the next time, Sam was stumbling more than he was skating, but he was making a valiant effort of it.

Far away, on the other side of the ice, two other kids were skating around in hockey gear. They were much more solid on their skates, elbowing in and out of the crowds, crisscrossing back and forth. Maybe someday Sam would skate like they did.

I glanced at the clock on the scoreboard that hung suspended over the middle of the rink. Five minutes of public skate left.

Looking down at the rink, I found Sam at the far end. He was holding on to the rail with one hand. The two would-be hockey players were at the other end, racing along, zigzagging around the other skaters. As I sat there watching, the taller one looked up in my direction. Following his gaze, I noticed a man standing by the mezzanine window.

The man gave them a thumbs-up.

The kid nodded, pulling at the arm of the other. They continued on, careening down the long side of the rink.

I looked over at the man again.

He was nodding as he watched them.

Seriously? Shouldn't he be reining in his kids rather than encouraging them?

Sam shoved off the wall and moved toward the crowd that was circling the ice.

"Watch out!" I knew he couldn't hear me, but it was the only thing I could do to help him.

I breathed a sigh of relief as he narrowly avoided colliding with a girl who had just completed a jump.

He threw his arms out, trying to balance.

"Just—" I held my breath.

An adult who was skating past paused a moment to steady him.

I promised myself I'd skate with him at public skate for the rest of the year. It would be less exhausting to be out there with him than to watch him.

A blur of red streaked into my vision.

Those kids.

They were bent forward, skating fast, and seemed to be heading right toward— Did they not see Sam?

I sat up straighter. "Don't— Stop—" Dumping my computer on the seat next to me, I stood. I put a palm to the glass and pounded at the window.

It didn't help. They couldn't hear me.

It seemed like it happened in slow motion. One came at Sam from behind and pushed him. As Sam flailed, the other came at him from the front, slamming into him. Then my son crumpled into a heap on the ice.

43

I headed for the stairs at a run.

When I got to the ice, those two boys were at the end of the rink, opposite Sam, and my son was still sprawled face-first on the ice.

"Hey!" I tried to wave down a skating guard, but he didn't see me. Nobody saw me.

"Hey!" I tried again. Gave up. Stepping out onto the ice, I started off down the rink toward Sam.

The skate guard came flying at me and slid to a stop with a scrape of his blades and a shower of ice. "I'm sorry, ma'am, you can't—"

"My son!" I pointed out to the end of the rink where a crowd was now, *finally*, gathering.

He skated off and soon returned with Sam.

I took Sam from him and carried him to the nearest bench. Propping him up against the wall, I knelt in front of him and pried his helmet off. "Are you all right?" I felt his head for bumps. Pressed trembling fingers to his face to feel along his jaw. "Did you know those boys? Did they hurt you?"

The buzzer sounded the end of the session and skaters exited the rink. I leaned forward, an arm on either side of him, trying to create a buffer as the bench filled. "Does anything hurt?"

He shook his head and winced.

"Where does it hurt? Can you see okay?" I rolled forward on my knees to get a better look at him. There was no bruising. No blood. "How many fingers am I holding up?"

"Two."

"How old are you?"

"Six."

"What day is it?"

"Thursday?"

Wednesday. But that wasn't a fair question. He mixed up the days of the week on a regular basis just the same as he mixed up yesterday and tomorrow. "Can you move your arms?"

He lifted them up.

"Can you move your head? Slowly."

He moved it up and down and then from side to side.

"Can you—" I paused, distracted by a pair of red hockey jerseys. It was those two boys. "Hey!"

I stood. Keeping one hand clamped around Sam's forearm, I used the other to reach for them.

They glanced at me, glanced at each other, then made a break for those double glass doors.

Luckily, they ran right into that man who'd been watching them from the mezzanine.

"You! Sir!"

He glanced over at me, then quickly looked away.

"Sir! Yes, *you*!"

The other children on the bench were staring up at me, mouths agape. Parents, kneeling beside them, busied themselves with untying skates.

I couldn't leave Sam by himself, and the man was standing his ground. But I was in a mood, and I could do Crazy Lady better than just about anyone. I raised my voice. "You told those kids to attack my son!"

He held up his hands as if in defense.

"I *saw* you! My son could have been hurt!"

The skate guard lurched over and offered an ice pack to me.

I rounded on him. "And *you*!"

He quailed, dropping the pack.

"You're a *skate guard*! How could you not see those kids were being reckless? Did you not notice how many times they—"

He held up his hands. "I— They were practicing hockey moves— they were just deke-ing."

"By weaving around all over the place?"

"That's what—"

That man was steering the boys toward the doors.

"That's what deke-ing is." His teenage voice climbed the scale a full octave.

Bolting from Sam, I caught up with the man and grabbed him by the sleeve. "I want your name."

He stopped. "Boys will be boys. They were just practicing."

I tightened my grip on his sleeve. *"Your name."*

"Mommy?" Sam had left the bench to follow me. He was holding a finger up to his nose. Blood was dripping out beneath it. "I think my nose is bleeding."

Letting go of the man, I knelt beside my son, drawing him close within the circle of my arm. "Let me see."

I'd left my purse upstairs, so all the hand sanitizer and Band-Aids and Kleenex I carried in it were useless. I shepherded him to the bathroom and used up most of a roll of toilet paper trying to stop the bleeding. By the time it had tapered off, the benches that had been filled to capacity were empty. The ice that had hosted the public skate crowd was now occupied by figure skaters executing graceful spins and effortless jumps. The Top 40 music had been replaced by a symphonic rendition of the latest Disney movie theme song. I felt as if I had emerged from a wormhole into a parallel universe.

I held out a hand to Sam. He grabbed on. "My things. They're upstairs." At least I hoped they still were.

The skater mom who'd been sitting beside me looked over with concern. "I saw it all. I'm sorry. Is your son okay?"

"He's fine." I wasn't. My hands were shaking. My knees felt like they'd come undone. "Thanks for keeping an eye on my things."

She smiled, then turned her gaze back to the figure skaters who were gliding across the rink.

I got Sam checked out at the emergency room. No sign of a concussion, just a mild sprain to his wrist where he'd tried to break his fall on the ice. It was soon clear my phone, however, hadn't survived its time at the rink.

At random intervals, the alert light would blink when I had no incoming email, and the camera flash even went off once. I resigned myself to asking the tech group at work to take a look at it.

In all my time at the rink over the past year, I'd come to recognize most of the parents. But I'd never seen that lady before. She acted as if she'd watched my things, but who had watched her?

At home I texted Sean. What I really wanted to do was call him, but he was right. Even disposable phones could be identified and hacked. And people who attacked children were just the type to do it.

S got hit at rink. No accident. S fine.

I meant to get ready for bed after I tucked Sam in, but I couldn't. My hands were shaking too hard to brush my teeth.

The attack on Sam hadn't been random and it hadn't been a childish prank. It had been deliberate.

I went into the kitchen to get a glass of water. Alice followed me, pausing in the doorway as if unsure what to do.

"I don't—I don't—" I put down the glass and gripped the lip of the sink. I couldn't seem to take in a breath. So I stepped back, bending over to let my head fall between my arms. "I don't know, Alice." I took in a deep, gasping breath and then lifted my head. "What do I do?"

Ransacking my house was one thing. But attacking Sam?

I glanced out the window over the sink, into the dark, out into the night where people were watching. Sean, perhaps. And the FBI.

Or the Department of Defense. Or grown men who told their children to beat up little boys.

I grabbed my glass. Or tried to. It toppled over into the sink and shattered.

"Alice—" I couldn't keep the sobs from coming any longer. I slid to the floor and pulled my knees to my chest.

Alice shuffled over.

I grabbed hold of her neck and buried my face in her fur.

The tears didn't last long because I knew they wouldn't help. And I knew it didn't make any difference how afraid, how terrified I was. The only way out was through.

I was surprised to see Chris at school the next morning with his Maltipoo. Wasn't Keith supposed to be at the Outdoor Lab overnight trip? As I bent to pull Alice's leash from the holder, he joined me.

"Is Keith all right?"

"What? Sure. Yeah. He's fine. Had soccer practice last night."

We started walking. "He must be really dedicated. That's quite a drive, isn't it?" The lab was at least an hour west of Arlington.

He shrugged. "It's not that bad."

"He must have been disappointed to leave."

"Homework waits for no man. Or boy."

"I thought—" It seemed, somehow, that he was talking about something different. Keith was in fifth grade, wasn't he? Had I remembered wrong? That would be embarrassing. Only one way to find out: ask. "Is he worried about middle school next year?"

"Middle school!" He blew out a breath. "He's not worried. I am, though!"

So he was in fifth grade, just like I'd thought. And if so, he should have been on that trip. Even Sam had heard about it. "Sam's already looking forward to the Outdoor Lab."

"Outdoor Lab? Is that in sixth grade?"

My step faltered as my blood ran cold. "Pardon me?"

"The Outdoor Lab. Sounds fun."

He didn't know. Chris didn't know about the Outdoor Lab.

"I, uh—shoot! There's something I forgot to give Sam. I'd better—" I gestured back toward the school.

"Sure. Okay. See you." He nodded and walked off down the street.

I jogged with Alice back toward the school until he was out of sight and then I stopped. I stayed where I was until my legs stopped shaking and the fear that had broken out in a cold sweat behind my ears had evaporated. Until I could think clearly. And even then, one thought echoed in my mind.

Chris doesn't have a son.

∞

I forced myself through the motions of getting changed, making my lunch, getting into the car.

Two things I needed to know. Who was Chris? And who had ordered him to watch me? We'd been walking our dogs together since when? The week after Sean died? Fear stole my breath. He'd been watching me for that long and I'd never once suspected.

Halfway to work, one of those red dashboard warning lights came on. It was an exclamation point enclosed by a circle. And parentheses. At the next stoplight, I pulled the car's manual out of the glove box.

Immediate attention was required.

Of course immediate attention was required. And I'd have to pay for it with all the money I didn't have. I pulled off into the nearest parking lot and called my mechanic. He was happy to take my car but vague about when he'd be able to fit the work in or get it back to me.

The next call I made was to Jim. He drove out and followed me to the mechanic's shop in his car, then dropped me off at work. He lifted a hand as I got out. "When do I pick you up?"

"I can take a taxi home."

"Not when you've got me as a neighbor."

I smiled my thanks. He'd been so good to us. They both had. "Five?"

"I'll be here."

By the time I got to work, I was already in a deficit. I hadn't slept well. Again. I had to turn my cell phone over to the tech group so they could figure out what was wrong with it. And my thoughts kept jumping randomly to Jenn, to Chris, and to the problem of what had happened over in Iraq.

I pulled out Sean's book and surreptitiously worked at deciphering his notations. It quickly became apparent that the names he'd struck through had died. Those notated with a question mark? I had no idea. So I texted him.

Looking at records. Question about ?s

His answer came a few minutes later.

Couldn't find any info

During a conference call, I created a new email account and then sent emails to some of the people in Sean's book. Toggling back and forth between the call and the emails didn't do my concentration any favors.

I heard back from David Abbott. He gave me a phone number for the USO lounge at Dulles International Airport where he volunteered. I pulled out the notes I'd taken from Lee Ornofo, then I gave Mr. Abbott a call as I ate lunch at my desk.

"You want to know about Desert Sabre? What can I tell you?"

"I believe you spoke to my colleague about the war. He was working on a history of the conflict, but he died not long after you spoke to him."

"Sorry to hear that."

"I was just wondering, could you tell me what you talked about?"

"The war. Mostly."

"You were with Captain Slater's company? Can you tell me about the twenty-fourth of February?"

"Day one? You want to know what it was like? Not what you expect. You think desert, you think hot. Sun. All that. Well, it wasn't. It was rainy. Rained more there that month than it did back home.

Least we didn't get stuck like some of the other units. So, yeah. Rain, early in the day. Then the rain stops and the wind kicks up. We had us one of those desert sandstorms. Went from miserable conditions to just pure misery."

"And what was your position?"

"I was a platoon sergeant."

"And what were the orders for the day? Do you remember?"

"Sure wasn't to take a mud bath. That was extra."

"So you woke up at, when?"

"We were awake. We were all awake. Don't think none of us slept. We knew the war was starting."

"So what happened?"

"What happened? What didn't! Start of a war isn't like the start of a race. One-two-three-bang! And you're off and running. More like one of those big marathons. Someone must be right up against the starting line ready to go, but most everyone else is piled up behind them just waiting. Sometimes takes a good twenty, thirty minutes for the guy in the back to get to the start line where he can do some running. That's how it is. So the war starts when the general says it starts, but we didn't get to move out until the guys in front of us started moving out because the guys in front of them had started moving. See what I mean?"

"Sure. Makes sense."

"And even then, to start fighting, you got to get yourself to the war. We were all waiting in Saudi, right? But to fight the Iraqis and liberate Kuwait, we had to get ourselves to Kuwait. So we're cold. We're getting rained on. Antsy. Finally start moving. Got to get through their first defenses. Just trenches in the desert, through the sand, manned by those Iraqis. Good thing: we got lots of sand to work with. Bad thing: we just plowed them over."

"Sorry? What did you say?"

"Plowed 'em. They wouldn't surrender so we just went right along their trench lines and plowed all the sand they'd dug out right back on top of them. Their fault, I suppose. If they'd have thrown all that sand they dug out over on the other side of their trenches, then we couldn't have done it. Us grunts didn't want to say it, but it didn't sit right. See what I mean?"

They *plowed* them?

"You sign on to be a soldier, you expect you might get killed by a bullet, but you don't consider that you might be buried alive. In sand. That's one thing I wish I'd never seen."

I resisted the urge to shudder.

"But after that? Things opened up real nice. Guys in front of us took care of the minefields, laid lanes out over them, and we were set to go. Wasn't that hard. The Iraqis we ran into, they weren't the Republican Guard. Most all of them saw us coming, they surrendered. Just like that. So we were going pretty good. Rain stopped. But then the wind started. Came on something fierce toward evening. Messed with the communications. Our company commo, he was having fits, trying to keep us connected to headquarters. Terrain started changing too. More dips and valleys. Some rocks thrown in. The battalion got spread out. Wasn't long before we were out there on our own."

"And what happened then?"

"Well, we stopped. You have to understand that all those sand dunes look the same. Not like here: Potomac to the east. Blue Ridge Mountains to the west. You can always kind of figure out the lay of things. And if there's any doubt, just look for the Washington Monument, right? Well, out in that desert, there was only sand. Here, you see sand like that, you look for an ocean. There? Nothing. It's odd. It's disorienting."

"It must have been."

"If you didn't see the sun rise, you'd have no idea where east was. And if you didn't know where east was, you didn't know anything. Those Iraqis, though, they seemed to have a sixth sense. Had some prisoners by then. We were trying to pass them back but couldn't find anyone to pass them to. Anyway, I'd noticed when we were sitting back there in Saudi two, three weeks before, didn't matter what time of day it was, when prayer time came, those Muslims, they'd get on their knees and pray toward Mecca. Really something to see. So we're sitting there, who knows why, night coming and I guess it's time for prayers, 'cause all of a sudden, those guys, they're down there in the sand. They were praying. Toward Mecca."

"Right." That made sense. Because Mecca for Muslims is, well, it's Mecca.

"Mecca was south and west. It's always south and west if you're in Iraq."

"Sure." I was a little spotty on my Middle Eastern geography, but that sounded reasonable to me.

"So if they're praying toward Mecca, and orders were that we attack from the west, we're supposed to be heading east, right?"

I nodded.

"So they're praying toward southwest and the company's sitting there, middle of the desert, and we're kind of pointed at an angle from them, maybe hundred fifty degrees, hundred sixty degrees."

"So?"

"So Mecca is *west*. We were supposed to be going *east*. Should have been going opposite, right?"

"You're saying that the company was going the wrong direction?"

"That's what I'm saying. Not by much, maybe, but still."

"Did you do anything about it?"

"Not a lot *to* do. I was a sergeant. Company commander was a captain. He wins. Still didn't sit right, though. So I went up and had a word with top. That's the company first sergeant. He said the captain was dead set we were going the right way. Top said to just go along. If it came to it, he said the captain's the one who'd hang for it, not us."

"Who was top? Do you know how to get ahold of him?"

"Top? That was Sergeant Wallace. First name? Sarge." He laughed.

I wrote it down. "So it was known among the NCOs that the captain was off course?"

"Oh yeah. But Captain Slater, he was one of those—if he was heading to hell in a handbasket, most folks'd say, 'How do I hop on?' It was the desert, you know? We had people lining us up with a compass, standing out there in the sand, directing us with their arms. Little bit off course here, little bit off there, and then we got so far ahead of everyone."

"Can I ask, did you know someone named Paul Conway?"

"The commo? Sure. He was a good troop."

"Do you know what he might have been doing that night?"

"Conway? He was just trying to keep everything working. Sucked to be him that night." He laughed. "But you should talk to him. He's the one who'd know what messages managed to get in and out."

45

Mr. Abbott had corroborated Mr. Ornofo.

The company had lost contact with everyone else.

Even so, that wasn't a major crime or even a minor one. It was more than a little embarrassing, leading two hundred men out into the middle of the desert and not being in quite the right place, but it wasn't court-martial terrible, not kill-to-keep-it-quiet terrible. The only thing it established was that my father wasn't where he was supposed to be. That was the theme: no one was where they were supposed to be. I can see why Sean hadn't known what to think. It seemed like it ought to mean something, but what? There had to be more to the story.

One of the tech gurus brought my phone back midmorning. She handed it to me. "You had some nasty stuff on there. Didn't find any record of anything having been downloaded, though."

"But you got it all off?"

"Yeah. 'Cause I'm kind of awesome that way." She flashed me a smile as she left.

At least all my communications with Sean were through my new phone. But I deleted my personal email account from the mail program on my old phone just to be safe.

Who had planted the malware? The FBI? The Department of Defense?

"Georgie."

"Huh!" I was startled out of my reverie by Ted.

"There's a—" His words were drowned out by the sound of a vacuum cleaner down the hall. We worked so often with classified information that cleaning staff had to be escorted. It was easier to have them come during the workday and make everyone take escort responsibility for their own office.

"Sorry, Ted. What?"

He stepped inside my office. "There's a problem with your contract."

"The appropriations bill. I know."

"Besides that. Someone's challenged the award. They say you had inappropriate contact with the contract officer."

What? "I didn't talk to anyone in the government after the request for proposal came out. Not until after they published the award of the contract."

"I know. Of course you didn't. But you're going to have to sort it out. Make some phone calls." He dropped the folder on my desk. "Just answer the challenge, will you?"

"I resent having to charge billable hours to someone else's un-founded accusations when—"

"Then you're really going to resent having to get it done before noon tomorrow."

"Seriously?"

He didn't answer. He was already out the door.

I made a few calls trying to determine who had challenged the award. I narrowed the possibilities down to two.

By that time it was noon. I dug into my purse for my sandwich. Looked at my phone. The old one. Then the new—

I'd missed a text from Sean. He'd sent it several hours before. It must have been during all the vacuuming. I hadn't heard it buzz.

Meet me downstairs

I grabbed my purse and left my office at a run.

I was heading for the Starbucks, like before, when someone stepped out from a store right into me. His coffee spilled all over my sweater and down onto my purse.

He stepped back. "I'm so sorry. I didn't mean to—"

I glanced down at the stain. "It's fine. It's all right." I looked at him. It was Sean. "Sorry I'm late. I didn't see your—"

He grabbed my arm. "Let me wipe this up for you." He pulled me over to a bench. Handed me a napkin. Then he took one himself and dabbed at my purse. "You need to tell me what happened with Sam."

"There's not much to tell. Two of those little hockey punks sandwiched him. He fell."

"He's okay?"

"He's fine." I used a napkin to squeeze the coffee out of my sweater. "It took a while to stop his nosebleed. That night I realized my phone was acting strange. It was spyware."

"From the rink? How did they do it?"

"When I ran down to get Sam, I left everything upstairs. It couldn't have been for more than ten minutes. Or maybe fifteen."

His gaze had settled over my left shoulder as he'd listened to me speak. "So they knocked Sam down on purpose."

"Georgie!" The call came from behind me.

I stiffened.

Beside me, Sean did too.

46

"Georgie, hey—" It was one of my coworkers. One who'd actually met Sean. We'd all gone to a baseball game together back in the day. "How's that presentation for the conference coming? I was hoping we could talk about it this afternoon. I had some ideas." His gaze settled on Sean.

Sean smiled. "Hey."

I gestured to my sweater, trying to distract him. "I ran into him as I was heading for Starbucks. Wasn't quite the way I'd imagined getting coffee, but—" I dabbed at it again with the napkin. "Anyway, yes. I'll swing by your office later."

"Great. Okay. Later."

I breathed a sigh of relief as he walked away. "Do you think he recognized you?"

Sean shook his head. "People only see what they expect to." His eyes scanned the crowd. "Flirt with me." He turned the full force of his attention back to me and I remembered exactly what it had felt like when I'd first met him.

"What?"

"Flirt with me. We'll draw less attention as we talk if it looks like there's a reason we're doing it."

He didn't know what he was asking. Even back when I was single and flirting, I wasn't very good at it. And somehow, just then, I couldn't quite catch my breath. He didn't look like a panhandler anymore. He was wearing a tailored sports jacket, trim trousers, and an open-neck shirt. His hair was slicked back. Had he trimmed his beard? He looked European.

He put a hand on my arm. Looked down into my eyes. Then his

gaze dropped to my lips. Went back to my eyes. "I like being with you."

My cheeks bloomed. "Sean."

"I do. It's been way too long." He flashed a smile again. "Did you learn anything from Abbott?"

He didn't seem like Sean. He was so suave. It was as if he were playing a role. But he was so good at it. It was like he'd done it all before. A lot.

"Georgie?"

I blinked. "Yes. My father let the company get off course."

"Right. I know."

"Is that why they ran into the Iraqis?"

"Less frowning. More flirting."

I smiled.

He smiled.

"Maybe the company was in the wrong place; maybe the Republican Guard was right where they were supposed to be."

He winked. "I checked that out at the Pentagon. Neither group was supposed to be where they were."

"They buried people alive, Sean. In the sand. Is that what this is about?"

"Everyone knows that. Nobody talks about it."

For good reason.

He smiled once more and extended his hand.

As I put mine into it, I felt him press something into my palm.

He winked. "See you around maybe?"

"Yes. Sure. Yeah."

He turned around, threw his empty coffee cup into a trash can, and walked away.

I plunged my hand into my purse, letting go of whatever it was he'd given me. Then I brushed at the coffee stain one last time. It was useless. I tossed the napkin away and continued on to Starbucks. At least that would provide a reason for my trip.

If anyone was watching.

As I stood in line waiting to place my order, I fished Sean's gift out of my purse. It was a hotel key enclosed in a cardboard pouch.

I'd never spent much time thinking about Sean's past. Not as it related to his relationships with women. He'd seen so many terrible things. Done, perhaps, some terrible things. He'd been in a gang. And he was *really good* at flirting. Just how much experience with women did he have? Granted, he'd turned Jenn down, but how many others had thrown themselves at him?

If I could have beat myself over the head with something, I would have. I didn't have time for that kind of nonsense. And I wasn't fifteen years old. But after talking to Kelly, after hearing Jenn's betrayal, after seeing Sean's performance, I was starting to question what we'd had. How could I trust *us* again?

∞

The hotel was connected to both the mall and the office complex. It was a fancy hotel, the kind we put our consultants in when they came to meet with us. I strode through the lobby as if I did it every day of my life. As if I belonged there.

I lectured myself as I rode the elevator up to Sean's room. I told my stomach that it was *not* allowed to turn over. I told my knees that they were *not* allowed to melt. I practiced what I was going to say when I saw him because I needed to ask him about Jenn. I wanted to hear what he had to say. I used my key to unlock the door, pushed it open, and then all those good intentions fell right out of my head.

Sean was there.

And he wasn't wearing his shirt anymore. Or his jacket. Or his shoes.

I held up a hand. "Don't come any closer."

He ignored me.

I pressed my back against the door and closed my eyes so I wouldn't lose focus. I wanted to be able to say what I needed to. "There's something I really need to talk to you about. I need to talk to you about Jenn."

His hand cupped my elbow.

My eyes flew open.

His gaze held mine. "What about her?"

"Sean. Seriously. You know. January?"

He sighed. Ran his hand up the back of his head. "It was that Saturday when you were doing that Kids and Science day downtown. Jenn brought Preston over. She'd been flirty before, but I'd kind of written it off as her trying to get attention."

"Jenn's flirty with everyone."

"I know the difference between fun flirty and sexy flirty. I'd been brushing her off. You know, deliberately misunderstanding the cues. But that day there wasn't any way to misunderstand. So I told her I wasn't available. End of story."

"And you didn't tell me, why?"

He took hold of my hand. "Because I figured I could handle Jenn, and whatever it was that you got out of your friendship with her was something you needed on some level. I just made sure I was never alone with her again."

He was trying to meet my gaze, but I didn't let him. I needed to sort it out on my own. Either I trusted him or I didn't. But I wouldn't be persuaded into it. "I just . . ." I put a hand to his chest.

He covered it with his own.

"I want to trust you, Sean."

"You *can* trust me."

"I'm not—" A sob was trying to work itself out and I didn't want it to. I swallowed. "I'm not good at any of this."

He let go of my hand and cupped my face. "Any of what?"

I closed my eyes. "I never even thought—it just always felt like—" My voice had gone ragged. "*I* wanted to be the one."

His hand slid to my shoulder. "You are the one."

"I just— I think I would have wanted to know."

"Then I'm sorry I didn't tell you." He scooped me up and carried me to the bed.

47

After, as I lay there next to him, I would have sworn I was
floating if my head hadn't been cradled in the crook of his elbow.

Sean pressed a kiss to my forehead.

"I don't want to leave."

He pulled me closer. "I don't want you to."

I slid my arm across his chest. "Should I worry about how you
paid for this? You did pay for this, right?"

"The important thing is that there's no trail that will lead to me.
Or you. Right now the only thing I want is for you and Sam to be
safe."

"I wish we could talk to Paul Conway. I think he's the key; he
knew everything. He's the one who sent and received all the messages. I don't think it's an accident that he died."

He entwined his fingers with mine. "I don't think so either."

I curled into his torso. "They don't get to choose what happens
to us."

"I couldn't save my parents, but I'm doing everything I can to
save you."

He was doing what he'd done when he saved Kelly. He was
withdrawing in order to pull away the danger. I could feel it. "I want
you back."

"I need you to understand. I might not get to come back." He
said the words slowly. Distinctly.

The illusion of safety, of togetherness, vanished. I propped myself
up on an elbow. "Why not?"

He glanced up at me and then rolled onto his side to face me.
"How can I? I don't even have an identity anymore."

"We figure this out and we tell the truth." I reached out and traced one of his eyebrows. "We tell the truth and it's not worth it for them to try to kill you anymore."

He rolled onto his back. "Sometimes I wish I'd just kept my mouth shut. Decided that it was just an oversight—that someone forgot to mark that Iraqi position. I could have convinced myself it didn't matter the Iraqis weren't supposed to be there."

"Once we figure this out, maybe if we told someone *else*. Someone different. Someone not at the Pentagon or the FBI. Isn't this the kind of story someone would publish?"

"Maybe. Probably." He looked over at me. "Let's say they did. It'd be a twenty-four-hour sensation. Then what would happen? I'd get arrested and prosecuted for leaking classified information."

"They couldn't—"

"The only one who'd know all those things, who could have pulled it all together from all the different sources—the message traffic, the people, the maps—is me. And how would I know them? Because I had access to classified materials. And worse, the other historians would be brought in to testify against me. There's no way for me to publish my story without revealing classified information."

"But wouldn't it be a whistleblower suit? Intimidation by the government? Conspiracy?"

"Maybe. But what kind of money would I need to defend myself in a case like that? And how many years would it take? And even if I were exonerated, what kind of job could I hope to apply for? I'd never be eligible for a secret clearance again. No one in the federal government would want to touch me. Academia? I'd always be the crazy conspiracy guy. So why would I come back?"

"You have to."

"Most people, had they put two and two together the way I did, would have looked at the other side of the equation. They would have realized it wasn't worth it."

"The truth is always worth it."

"Is it? Always? Really?" He searched my eyes.

"It has to be. The confirmation hearing is less than two weeks away. We need to know what happened. There has to be a way."

"All roads still lead to me. And classified information."

"But what if they didn't?"

He raised a brow. "How could they not?"

"What if they lead to me instead? That way you wouldn't be implicated."

"It won't work." Sean didn't even pause for a moment to reflect before discarding my proposal. He threw back the sheets and got out of bed.

I followed him to the bathroom. "It *will* work."

"It won't. You'd have to have access to message traffic and the files and interviews in the archives." He turned on the shower.

"Not necessarily. You could tell me."

"But what I know is based on that information."

"*And* all the research you've been doing in the past eight months."

"You'd have to know what people to interview."

"I do. I have the names in your book."

"But you'd have to know what the orders for the day were—"

"I can get that information."

"How?"

"It's like a geometry proof. You got there one way. All I have to do is figure out an alternative method."

"In academia we call that researching with a bias."

"That's quaint. In geometry it's called proving a postulate."

He closed his eyes and leaned back into the water.

I raised my voice so he could hear me. "Do you want to come back from the dead or not?"

He straightened, opened his eyes, and looked at me. "This isn't safe." His eyes softened. "If they'll kill me for what I know, what do you think they'll do to you? This isn't academic, Georgie. This is good guys and bad guys."

"And that's absolutely what gives me hope."

"Hope?"

"That's right. Because you're not dead yet, are you?"

"I might as well be."

"You aren't. And after I'm done, you'll be even more alive." I stepped into the shower with him, reached up, and took his face between my hands, treasuring the opportunity, knowing from experience that I might not ever be able to do it again. "I love you. And I want Sam to have his father back. That's why I have to do this. Just trust me. Okay?"

Underneath the desolation in his eyes was something I hadn't seen in them since he'd turned up alive: hope.

48

By the time I finished washing and drying my hair, Sean was gone. But that was okay. My body was still warm, my heart still singing from his having been there. I walked out of the hotel and back down to the mall. As long as I was passing by, I decided I might as well pick up Sam's Christmas present.

Mr. Hoffman came out from his storeroom as I walked into his shop.

When he saw me, he stopped. Then he smiled. "You are happy."

If only he knew. I blushed. Then tried to cover it up. "How could I not be happy? Walking into your store is like walking into a fairy tale."

He returned to his storeroom to get Sam's train. It was already boxed, bagged, and ready to go. "Little Bear is well?"

"I think things are going to work out for him."

❧

I went by Ted's office on the way back to my own.

"Hey—Georgie. Thanks. I need to talk to you." He took in a hiss of air through his teeth. "I hate to do this to you, but I just heard Congress is going to pass another continuing resolution today."

A continuing resolution? "You mean an appropriations bill." A resolution meant nothing. It wouldn't release the funding for my contract. I couldn't do anything, I couldn't get paid unless they passed the actual bill.

"Nope. It's going to be a CR."

"Another one? For how long?"

"Four months."

"Four—"

"I know. Sucks, right?"

That meant I wouldn't be able to charge any money against the new contract until February. At the earliest. "Can you put me on someone else's contract until then?"

"That's the thing. We saw this coming and already did the old shell game, you know? Switching people to other contracts until they can get funded on their own."

"And?"

"And thing is, we don't have any moves left. Your contract was a sure thing and it seemed like they were going to pass the bill, so—"

"It *is* a sure thing. It's already been awarded."

"Point is, we didn't come up with a plan B for you. I need you to go on PTO—"

He needed me to go on vacation? For *four months*? "But I don't—"

"—and since you don't have any left, I need you to go."

"Go. Go where?"

"Go home."

"Go *home*?" What was he trying to say? "Are you *firing* me?"

"Well, I'm . . ." He opened his mouth to speak, but no words came out. He tried again. "We're letting you go. Because of the contract. Or lack thereof. If it comes through . . ." He shrugged.

"When. *When* it comes through. It's coming through." But not until the appropriations bill passed.

He shrugged. "When it comes through, we'll have a welcome-back party."

"So you're—" I really was quite sure I hadn't heard him correctly. "You're letting me go. I'm fired."

"Not for any *bad* reason. It's not personal." He sent me a thumbs-up. "I'll give you a great recommendation if you feel like you have to find something else."

"But the fiscal year just started. Can't we run into the red a little bit and make it up—"

"Wish we could, but we've been told to clamp down on that sort of thing."

One of the security guys stopped outside Ted's door.

Ted gestured toward him. "He'll escort you out. He can help you carry the heavy stuff." Ted winked. "Okay?"

I simply stared at him. Not okay. Not okay at all.

There wasn't much to pack. Just a few pictures. My framed diplomas. Some well-thumbed college books I used for reference. The pen I liked the most.

It all fit into two cardboard boxes.

After downloading my personal files and Outlook contacts, I tossed the thumb drive into one of them. "Guess that's it."

The security officer held out his hand. "Badge?"

Right. I slipped it off and gave it to him. We were halfway down the hall when I remembered Sean's book. "Just— I forgot something. Be right back!" I sprinted down the hall before I remembered I didn't have the badge to access my office anymore. I had to wait for the guard to catch up with me.

But my badge had already been deactivated and he had to get special permission to let me back in. Then he had to watch me.

Did I ever feel like an idiot on my hands and knees reaching back along the wall behind my filing cabinet.

Nothing.

I moved even closer, jamming my shoulder up against the metal. Still nothing.

"What you got behind there? Stack of *Playgirl* centerfolds?"

"Just, um, my son. He visited. His ball. It rolled back there."

He leaned against the cabinet and levered it away from the wall for me.

There it was!

"Huh. No ball, but at least I found this book I'd been missing." I pulled it out and slid it down the side of the box.

I called the car mechanic from the lobby of my building, asking when the car might be finished. He said the parts they needed were on back order and since they'd torn the engine apart, they couldn't guarantee when they'd have it all back together.

I asked if they'd found anything unusual.

"Like?"

"A bug."

"A bug? What? You mean on the windshield or something?"

"A bug. An electronic bug. You know. For tracking someone?"

"Oh. Oh! Like in James Bond? That kind of thing?"

"Right."

"Nope. I mean, I haven't looked. But aren't they supposed to have red blinking lights? I would have noticed something like that. Unless, wait. No. Red blinking lights are the car bombs, right? Not the trackers?"

I told him not to worry about it.

The security guard asked me to stand outside since I was no longer employed by the company and I wasn't a visitor. I shivered in the wind while I waited for a taxi.

It's not like Congress hadn't punted on the budget before. And it wasn't unusual to have contract funding delayed due to a continuing resolution, but for Ted not to even *try* to find interim funding for me? That was strange.

And wasn't the timing just a little suspicious? The DoD or FBI had already tried to bug my computer and my phone. They'd already broken into the house. They'd beat up Sam to distract me. Why wouldn't they take my job away too? Most of the company's business came from government-funded contracts. How would Ted be able to say no if they asked him to fire me?

I texted Jim that I wouldn't need a ride home.

Ms. Hernandez texted me, asking if I could meet with her again.

I texted her back, setting up a meeting. I hoped Sam wasn't still drawing wormholes. I'd meant to sit down with him and try to talk things through again—without raising my voice—but then the house had been ransacked and Sean had come back from the dead and Sam had gotten beaten up by hockey hooligans. Maybe I really was a bad mom.

My mother called on the way home, as I sat in the back seat of the taxi clutching what remained of my professional life. Being fired from a job was definitely not Slater-condoned. Maybe my mother had been right about everything. Maybe I should have been following her advice. Maybe I should have studied business like she'd told me to. I sent her call to voice mail because she had an uncanny way of ferreting out the truth.

I walked into the house, dropped the boxes on the floor, and barely remembered to punch in the security code in time. Then I pulled Sean's diary out and took it into the kitchen with me. Taking Sam's box of Fruity-O's from the cabinet, I removed the bag of cereal and dropped the diary inside the box and put it back in the cupboard.

After retracing my steps to the living room, I peeled off my coat and let myself sink into the couch. "I'm not that bad a mom, Alice, am I? I've never forgotten to feed you, have I?"

I hadn't. Ever. At least not that I remembered.

"And you always get at least two walks a day."

In fact, Alice got more planned, more regular exercise than I did.

"I don't add sugar. To anything. I only serve real juice. And I have a CSA subscription. I've tried."

Really. I had.

"Isn't the thought what really counts, Alice?"

Silence.

"Alice?" Normally Alice gave some sort of response when I came home. And when I talked to myself.

"Alice?" I pushed myself to sitting. Where was she? I'd assumed she was close because she usually shadowed me around the house.

But she wasn't on her dog bed in the living room.

She wasn't in the kitchen where she sometimes liked to cool her belly on the old linoleum floor.

"Alice?"

As I walked down the hall to my room, I heard panting. Then I saw the mess. "Oh, Alice!"

49

Jim drove us to the vet and helped me carry Alice into the exam room.

"Are you sure she hasn't had any chocolate?" The vet gave me a searching look as I tried to keep Alice from pacing the length of the clinic's exam room.

"I don't know where she would have gotten it." I kept all of ours in a cupboard.

"She's been vomiting? Had diarrhea?"

I nodded.

"Tell me about her daily care. Have you changed anything? Food? Shampoo? Medications?"

"Nothing." I was kneeling on the floor beside her, trying to stroke her head, but she kept shifting positions—sitting on her haunches, then pushing to her feet—as if she just couldn't get comfortable.

"Has she been anyplace new? A dog park? Someone else's house?"

"No. And we've been walking the same route for years." I tried to embrace her, tried to ease some of her discomfort, the way I did with Sam, but it didn't seem to help.

"She hasn't spent longer than usual in one place on her walks? She couldn't have discovered any old food containers on the street or anything?"

I had no answers.

"Something's poisoning her system."

Fear clutched me. Something or *someone*?

"Do you keep fertilizers or pesticides within reach?"

"No."

Alice whimpered again, shifting her weight from foot to foot.

I stroked her head. Her ears.

208

She lay down and then immediately got back up.

The vet lifted Alice's tail with one hand and wielded a thermometer with the other. But before she could insert it, Alice began to seize.

∞

It took a while for the doctor to stabilize her, and there were some harrowing moments, but by the time I left the veterinarian's office, I was told she would recover.

I got back in enough time that I was able to walk down to pick up Sam right when school ended that afternoon. There was no reason for him to stay for their extended day program since I was home. I had to figure out how to cancel him out of the program anyway. Even if I managed to bring Sean back to life soon, with security systems and car repairs and vet bills and the loss of my job, we were going to have to save every penny we could.

Sam and Alice had always had some sort of telepathic connection. First thing he asked when he got home after school? "Where's Alice?"

I'd meant to ease into telling him. Could nothing go right? I shoved my keys into my front pocket and took off my coat, trying to buy myself some time. "She has to stay at the doctor's overnight."

Sam looked at me, concern coloring his eyes. "Why?"

"The doctor thinks she found chocolate somewhere and ate it." No need to tell him of my own suspicions. "She can't eat chocolate; it's not good for dogs." It wouldn't hurt for Sam to know that. "If they have too much they can get super sick."

His mouth dropped open. His eyes went wide. "Is Alice going to die?"

"The doctor says she'll be fine. But she got really sick and she'll need to stay there a few days."

Tears were welling up in Sam's eyes. "I'm sorry."

I knelt and gave him a big hug. "I'm sorry too."

"It's my fault." He wrestled himself out of my hug and took me by the hand and led me to his room. I had discovered Alice in the hallway, so I hadn't seen Sam's room until just then. The mattress of his bed had been pushed askew and the floor was littered with candy wrappers. "Sam?"

He was sobbing. "It's all my fault. Alice is going to die and it's all my fault."

"Shh." I tried to hug him again, but he wasn't having it. He beat my arms back and sat on the floor, pulling at his hair.

"Sam. It's okay. Alice is going to be okay."

Gulping back his sobs, he looked at me. "Are you sure?"

"I'm sure." Pretty sure. I sat down next to him.

He scooted onto my lap.

I put my arms around him and rocked him back and forth.

He turned and snuggled into me.

"How come you had so much candy for Halloween in here? I thought I told you we were keeping it all in the kitchen."

"I took it for Daddy. In case he was hungry after the firm hole."

I cheered him up with his Super Sam cape, tying it under his chin. Then I made him half a peanut butter sandwich as a snack.

When tears threatened, I thought up another diversion. "Hey! Guess what—I have a surprise for you. Want to see it?" I slipped my old phone into my back pocket, in case the vet called, and the new one into my front pocket in case Sean texted. Then I grabbed the bag containing the new train from one of the boxes on the living room floor.

"What is it?"

"You'll see." I'd been meaning to keep it for Christmas, but he seemed to need it just then. And so did I.

We went downstairs into the basement where he could play with it.

The delight in his eyes when he pulled it out of the box was worth it. "Grandpa was telling me about these!" He offered the train and its crates to me. "You can use them with the crane."

I handed them back. "Show me."

Sam took them from me and pushed them along his intricate network of intersecting tracks. He made the crane take off the crates, ran it around again, and then made the crane put them all back on. Pretty soon he forgot about me, so I sat cross-legged on the floor and checked my email. Already word had gotten around that I'd been let go. I drafted an email to send to all of my business contacts.

Sunlight had retreated from the basement windows; it was getting dark. I got up and turned another light on.

Somewhere above us, a floorboard creaked.

"Can you do this for me, Mommy?" He held up two of the trains. He was trying to secure the connection between them.

I cocked an ear toward the ceiling. Old house. Just settling. "What?"

He dumped the trains into my lap. "Can you make them fit together?"

"Sure." I picked them up.

But there it was again.

I put a hand to his arm. "Just a second, buddy."

I held a finger to my lips as I glanced up at the exposed ceiling. He followed my gaze with his own.

Another creak.

I set the trains on the table. Put an arm to his shoulder and eased him away from it. I bent so I was looking directly at him and spoke quietly. "This is very important. When you and Dad played that game, the one about hiding?"

He nodded. "The Bad Guys."

"Did you ever play it down here?"

He nodded again.

"I think we ought to play it, you and I. Can you show me how?"

"Not really, I mean—"

"This is a real game, Sam. Do you understand?" There was another creak upstairs. That time it sounded like it was coming from the dining room. "There's someone up there. And Alice isn't here to protect us."

50

"But Daddy says—"

"Can you tell me some other time? Right now I need you to hide."

"Welp, there isn't any laundry piled up." He glanced around behind him. "And you moved Daddy's big backpack and his bike, so—"

"Sam!" I hissed his name. "What did Dad tell you to do?"

He took my hand and pulled me toward the back of the basement where the water heater and boiler sat. But Sean had always been compulsive about keeping the area around them clear. I yanked him back. "There's no place to hide over there."

"Mom!" He tugged back so hard that my shoulder felt it.

I put a finger to my lips. The creaks were moving toward the kitchen now. Whoever it was might soon notice the stairs.

He let my hand fall and ran over to the water heater. Then he pointed toward a metal flap set high in the cinder-block wall.

There was a ledge beneath it, but even if I hoisted Sam up there, he'd be in plain sight. "I don't think that ledge is big enough for—"

"You're supposed to open it."

"What?" I spoke the word a bit louder than I meant to, but he was jumping at it, trying to reach it with his hand.

"Open it, Mom. Just push it open."

"But even if it opens, I don't think—" I gave it a push and it swung straight up into the outside air.

"Dad says it's a coal chute."

The door to the basement creaked open and a footstep fell on the stair. I boosted Sam up and he scrambled through. Then he lifted the door from the outside. "Come on, Mom!"

"Listen to me. I want you to run over to Mr. Jim and have him call the police. Tell him there's someone in the house."

"Mom! Come on!"

Now the footsteps were coming down the stairs. In just a few moments I would be seen. "I can't make it. Just go!"

"Stand on the pipe. Climb up."

I put my foot to the pipe. Two steps more and I was holding on to Sam's hand. "I don't think I can fit through here." I might have, pre-Sam, but my hips were wider than they used to be.

"Dad fit. Just go like a snake."

I wriggled a bit, testing the sides of the chute and the sides of my thighs. The chute wasn't very forgiving. My thighs, on the other hand, compacted quite a bit.

The chute was masked by a tall, chubby euonymus bush that hid us from the driveway behind its green and yellow leaves. The deep shadows of dusk also helped.

I eased the flap closed behind me and crouched next to Sam. "I never noticed that before."

"Dad says nobody remembers them." He put his head to the ground and looked out between the branches of the bush. "I can't see anyone."

Neither could I.

Holding on to Sam's hand, I led the way around the bush. Then, keeping to the darker parts of the yard, we moved out toward the street. As I pulled him along, I sent a glance back to the house. And as I was doing it, I ran right into—

"Oof!"

Chris. It was Chris.

I put a hand to his arm to steady myself. "Sorry!"

He'd recovered his balance and now he smiled. "Georgie. Hey." He glanced toward the house.

Was he the intruder?

No. I discarded the thought. He wouldn't have had time to meet us out in front. But maybe he was an accomplice. I followed his gaze, trying to figure out the best way to get rid of him. "We were just leaving." I gestured toward Jim and June's. "We really need to—"

He released my arm. "I was just wondering if—"

A door slammed. Then a strange light illuminated the backyard for an instant as a shadow went racing away toward the house behind ours.

The sudden contrast with the darkness hurt my eyes. Squinting, I put my hand up to block it even as I backed away from Chris. It wasn't safe to be on the street. I had to get Sam out; had to get him away. "Sorry. Can we talk tomorrow? Sam and I were—"

There was a percussive boom.

Chris put up a hand to shield his face. "What the—"

I felt it in my chest, like the slap of a wave, before I heard it. The sound started low, then mushroomed. It swelled, threatening to obliterate my ears, and then it retreated, leaving me staggering.

Ears ringing, I reached out for Sam.

He'd been knocked to the ground, but he was pushing up from his knees. Arm extended, brow crumpled, he reached for me.

I pulled him up, turned us away from the house, and folded my body around his as I felt to make sure he was okay.

"Mommy?" I felt Sam's mouth move against my cheek. He clamped his arms around my neck.

"It's okay. It's going to be okay." I spoke the words into his ear as I scooped him up and started running.

But it wasn't.

Heat licked at my backside. The pavement, the houses next to ours, stood out in graphic relief. Windows had been blown out of the cars that were parked on the street.

It was not okay.

Our house had just exploded.

51

"Why didn't I call about it? About the intruder?" My voice had climbed an octave in disbelief.

The police officer sat across from me at June's table, pen poised above his notebook. "That's right."

"Because I didn't have time. Literally." I clutched at the blanket June had wrapped around my shoulders. "We escaped from the basement and then the house exploded."

"You didn't notice any fumes beforehand?"

"I noticed the sound of someone walking around in my house. That's what I noticed."

"Setting that aside for the moment—"

"Setting that *aside*? Setting aside the fact that someone was prowling around my house? While we were *in it*?"

June put a hand to my shoulder as she leaned in and put a mug of coffee on the table in front of me.

I cupped it, pulling it close.

"There's no one who might be able to corroborate—"

"Chris Gregory was there. Outside the house with us. He saw it explode."

"Chris?"

"He's the one who called 911."

"And he's . . ." The police officer glanced out into the living room where Jim and Sam were working a puzzle. "Is that him?" He gestured toward Jim.

"No. Chris is—" Where had Chris gone? He'd been there, at the explosion. He'd made a phone call. "I don't know where he is."

"Do you have contact information for him?"

"I— No. He's just a neighbor. We walk our dogs together."

"Address?"

"He lives . . ." Where *did* he live? He always dropped me off on the way home and then continued on. I didn't know anything about him really. Except that he didn't have a son in fifth grade. "Um, he lives farther down this street." Or maybe the next one up? Or maybe he didn't live in the neighborhood at all. Maybe Chris wasn't even his real name.

Jim had pulled the curtains in the living room shut so Sam and I didn't have to see the firefighters or watch flames devour our house, but against the darkness outside, the curtains still glowed. And they still pulsed red from the lights of the fire trucks.

The police officer flipped his notebook shut. "It will probably take a while for everything to stop burning."

Everything. Every single thing I owned.

"We'll be in touch."

∞

I knew why my house had exploded. I knew who had done it. The FBI or the DoD. Agencies that shouldn't have been trying to intimidate me in order to reach Sean.

By the time my parents drove up, I was crying big, ugly tears of rage.

My mother pulled me into her arms.

I let her.

My father stood outside in Jim's yard, watching the house burn, one hand clutching his side, the other pressed to his mouth.

We stepped out to join him.

My mother tightened her hold on me. "At least you weren't at home."

Pulling away, I very nearly yelled. "We *were* home. We were in the basement when I heard someone in the house. Had we been two minutes later in getting out"—of our own house!—"we wouldn't be standing here now."

She blinked. "Pardon me?"

"We were *there*. At home. In the basement."

Somewhere inside the inferno, something popped. Flames flared. A window exploded.

The orange and yellow of the fire reflected off my mother's face. She clutched at me, drawing me close, and whispered my father's name.

He eyed her. Dropped his hand from his mouth and extended it to her. But she didn't see it. She just stood there holding me, transfixed by the flames.

My father glanced beyond her to me. "I, uh, maybe . . ." His shoulders slumped as if all the air had suddenly left his lungs. "I don't know. Why don't we get your things? Sam shouldn't be seeing this."

He wasn't. He was still inside with Jim. "I don't have any things."

My father's brows collapsed in uncharacteristic confusion. "What things?"

"Any things. I don't have *any* things. I have nothing." Nothing but the clothes we were wearing and two cell phones. Everything else was gone.

"Nothing." The word hung in the space between us for a moment. "Well." He cleared his throat. "I just think that it would do you a world of good to get out of here. Leave all of this behind you. Your mother and I have found a house. A big one. There's room for you. There's no reason you couldn't move in with us."

"We can't." My tears had dried up as the weight of reality had settled onto my shoulders. For myriad reasons we weren't going to do that. I chose the easiest one for protest. "Sam's school is here."

"But the new house is in a good school district and—"

"His friends are here."

"He can make new—"

"I'll have to deal with the fire. The insurance company. There might be things that can be salvaged. If there are, I want to know about them."

"But your father's right. Maybe this is a good time to start over."
My mother had reengaged.

"Start over?"

"Completely. Leave the past behind."

I choked down a laugh. It left me feeling strangled. "Leave the past behind?" My own father, her husband, was the reason I couldn't. Because somewhere out in the desert in Iraq, something had happened. "Sean wouldn't want me to." But if I wasn't careful, if I didn't say just the right thing when I told him about the fire, he was liable to throw all caution to the wind, come back to life, and have to die all over again. For real. I gestured toward the fire. "That was my life. Everything we'd built together." I wanted it all back.

"It's been eight months, Georgia Ann. Let us help you. We'll be here now. Let us take care of you."

"But Sean was trying—" I'll never know what I might have told them, what I might have admitted to, if my father hadn't interrupted me.

"Sean doesn't matter!"

I blinked.

"JB." My mother's voice was low. She was sending him a warning.

"Do you really think it was fate that led Sean to you? *I* sent him to that bar to find you. So whatever loyalty you think you still owe him is misplaced."

"You—you what?" The bottom dropped out of my world. My memories, the very foundation of my life with Sean combusted, turned to cinders, and disappeared through the huge, gaping hole my father had just blown in my heart. "But he'd gotten out." Sean had gotten out of the service by then.

My father dismissed my words with a frown. "Strong character. I could tell that about him. I'd thought I could trust him. I was hoping I could count on him. And truth is, I knew you were floundering—"

"I wasn't floundering!"

"—so I asked him if he'd do me a favor."

Asked him? He'd *asked* Sean? Then it might as well have been an order. No one ever refused a general anything. I'd thought I was blossoming. That I'd finally become the butterfly bursting from her chrysalis. That I was pretty. Maybe I was, maybe I wasn't. But it didn't matter. None of it had mattered. Sean had been sent on a mission. Like any good soldier, he'd done what had been asked of him. I was the mission; he'd done his duty. Which made me wonder. Was he part of all of this too?

52

I left my mother and father standing there, walked up the steps into Jim and June's house, and locked the door behind me.

After plying us with multiple mugs of hot chocolate and a dozen freshly baked chocolate chip cookies, they settled us into their guest room. It would have been nice if Sam had been a cuddler. I would have liked something to hold on to. But he was a spinner, rolling in his sleep. At least he always spun in the same direction. I kept myself out of his way as I stared into the dark, trying to wrap my mind around all there was to do. At one point I almost got out of bed to make a list, but then I realized my attaché had burned along with everything else.

I'd have to ask June in the morning if I could borrow a piece of paper. And a pen.

And shampoo. And a hairbrush. And a towel.

And a cereal bowl. And a spoon.

And maybe a clean pair of socks.

And some dental floss.

I'd have to ask the DMV for a replacement driver's license. I'd have to contact my bank for a new credit card and ask the post office to forward my mail to a new address. And then . . . and then . . . I couldn't quite remember . . . and finally, I fell asleep.

∞

I didn't text Sean about the house until morning; I didn't know what to think about him anymore. I didn't figure there was any way for him to help, and I didn't want him to do anything rash. Which is probably what someone had been hoping for.

I put some effort into figuring out how to tell him, but I finally gave up.

House exploded last night.

S ok

At J Js

It was Friday and that was both good and bad. I could send Sam off to school and he wouldn't have to see the smoking ruins of our house, but all his fears about leaving me had come back. Jim and June tried to make him feel better about everything by telling him it could be Samday every day now, but he wasn't buying it. They offered to take him to a movie and out for lunch over in Ballston the next day. That cheered him up.

I borrowed June's car that morning, went to Kohl's, and picked up some basic essentials. Pajamas, a change of clothes for us both. A purse for me. A backpack for Sam. I used a phone app to pay.

When I got back, I wandered over to the house. It looked as if someone had doused our entire lot with a bucket of charcoal-colored paint. My nose wrinkled at the acrid scent of burnt wood and burnt wiring.

"Georgie!"

I turned around to find Chris walking down the sidewalk toward me. "Hey. How are you doing?"

I slipped my hand into my pocket and grabbed my phone. I didn't think he knew that I was on to him, but I was wary just the same.

"I keep wishing I'd been able to do more for you than just call 911." He shrugged. "I'm sorry."

"It wasn't your fault." I tried to sound convincing.

"You guys okay?"

"The police were asking about you."

Did his eyes sharpen beneath his baseball cap? "Me? Why?"

"I told them you were there with us. They wanted contact information, but I realized I don't have any."

He pulled at the brim of his cap. "Right."

I pulled my phone out of my pocket, pretended to open an app while I opened my camera instead. I held the phone up, gesturing with it, and took a picture of him. "If you give me your phone number, I can pass it on to them."

"Sure."

I opened up my contacts and thumbed it into my phone as he gave it to me. "Thanks. Well. I should go. Lots of things I have to do. About the fire."

"Sure. If I can do anything, let me know, okay?" He lifted a hand by way of good-bye and left.

I let out the breath I'd been holding.

A lawn maintenance crew had gone to work blowing leaves in the yard next door to mine. They came every Friday. As the leaves began to swirl, I stood there staring at the ruins of my house.

The picket fence dipped toward the street as if trying to escape the wreckage. The gate had been blown off its hinges.

There was just so little left.

And what the fire hadn't destroyed—the massive support beams, the fireplace and chimney, the concrete laundry basin in the basement—wasn't anything I would have wanted to save.

Ten years of life together and there was nothing. I didn't have the strength to stand anymore, so I squatted. As I swept a hand over a pile of ashes, something brown and lumpy caught my eye. I pulled it out of the debris. A melted Lego brick. Next to it was a picture frame. It was a photo of Sean and me on our wedding day. The frame was blackened. A corner of the photo was singed.

One of the lawn workers approached the edge of the property line. His leaf blower sent a stream of powdery, acrid ashes in my direction.

I stood, spitting ashes from my mouth. "Hey!"

He didn't appear to notice.

Clutching the picture to my chest, I stomped over, skirting a pile of still-smoldering embers. "Hey!"

He turned.

"Can't you see what you're doing?"

He idled the leaf blower.

I looked past the work boots. Past the company jacket. Past the sunglasses. It was Sean. Of course it was Sean.

He held the leaf blower away and leaned close. "Argue with me."

Argue with him? He wanted an argument? Well, I had one for him! I raised my voice. "I always really liked our story. The way we met at the Ballroom. The way we found each other." I tossed the picture behind me onto a still-smoldering pile of charred wood. "My father told me last night that he put you up to it!"

"What?" He powered the leaf blower up a notch and swung it back toward the house, sending up another stream of ashes.

I kept pressing him. "Did he? Did my father ask you to find me that night?"

"What night? What are you talking about?"

I grabbed hold of his coat. "Did my father set you up with me?"

He twisted away.

"How am I supposed to trust you? What am I supposed to believe?"

"Georgie—"

"Is my father telling the truth?"

He pointed the leaf blower out toward the street. "No! You have to believe me, Georgie."

"How?"

"I am not the bad guy here." He gestured to the ashes. "Our house blew up. My son got beat up. I got run out of my job. You're not asking the right question. You need to ask yourself why your father would lie to you about something like that."

"I want to believe you." I closed my eyes. "I want to. Just tell me how."

Everyone trusted someone until they realized they couldn't. Everyone thought they knew what love was until they discovered they didn't. Everyone thought they knew the truth until they found out it was a lie. But how do you let go of one to take hold of the other?

"I have always tried to act in your best interests, Georgie. I might not have always succeeded, but I have always tried. Because I love you. And that's what love does."

Love. Sean claimed that he loved me. He'd never stood me up beside him to portray the perfect American family. He'd never used me to bolster enthusiasm or display patriotism or recruit supporters. He'd never made me part of an argument that made him look better than he was. If Sean had used me at all, it was to make *me* better, not him. When it came down to it, the decision to believe him was simple. It didn't have anything to do with anything he said. It had everything to do with all the things he'd done, including lying to protect his family. "I believe you." Maybe he wasn't Saint Sean, but he was something better. He was my Sean. "This is where it stops."

"This is where it stops."

I pulled my phone from my pocket, showed him the picture of Chris.

"He's FBI," Sean said. "Be careful."

53

As I walked back across the street to Jim and June's, I called the number Chris gave me. Just to see what would happen.

No one answered.

No voice mail picked up.

My mother called while I was helping June clean up from a batch of Rice Krispies Treats she'd made for Sam. "Georgia Ann. Sugar pie."

June waved me toward the living room. I handed her the sponge with an apologetic smile and went to sit on the couch.

"I just wanted to tell you how bad your father feels about last night. I want you to know that I'm on your side."

My side.

Maybe she was.

"He wants you to know how sorry he is. He shouldn't have told you that."

"Is he there?"

"Your father?"

"If he's there, I want to talk to him."

There was silence for a moment and then my father came on the line. "Georgia Ann?"

It was a measure of just how much trouble he was in that he didn't call me Peach. "Why did you do it, Dad? Why did you set me up with Sean?"

"Why?"

"Why."

"Because he was a good man. I could tell. I can always tell a good troop. He was everything I'd always wanted for you. If we'd ever had a son, I would have wanted him to be someone like Sean. It was time for you to find someone." My father was warming to the topic. "I told myself, if I'm picking family, I might as well pick the best."

It was clear to me that he was making it up as he went along. I was trying to figure out why. Regardless, one thing he'd said was true. "He was. Sean was the best."

He sighed. It was the sound of relief. "Can I take you out for lunch maybe?"

"I don't think—"

"Here. I'll pass the phone back to your mother. She'll set it all up."

My mother came back on the line. "Georgia Ann?"

"Dad wanted to do lunch, but today is not a good day."

"Tomorrow then. We'll both come by. We can go to McLean and show you the new house. Even if you decide not to move in with us, we want Sam to know there'll be a room just for him. Whenever he wants to visit."

"Tomorrow we can't. Have you already bought it? You don't want to jinx anything."

"You know your father. Senator Rydel might be a bear, but everyone likes him. We're not expecting any trouble with the confirmation."

∽

I asked June if she would mind if I borrowed their computer for a while. She set me up at their dining room table. I got out my phone and brought up the pictures I'd taken of Sean's diary. Then I logged in to my new email account and checked some emails I'd sent to several of the names in Sean's book. I called a couple of them as well. After several hours of talking to people who'd fought in Desert Sabre, I felt like I was spinning my wheels. Every person I'd talked to who had served with my father had known that their unit had been far out ahead of everybody else. Some of them had even known about the order to draw back. None of it was breaking news.

There had to be more to the story.

Maybe I was looking in the wrong places.

I wished I could just look at everything from a different angle.

Or maybe figure out how not to do what I was doing. If I'd had my notepad, then I would have taken it out and made more notes. But I didn't have it. I had to borrow some paper from June.

I wrote down the names *Conway, Ornofo, Abbott.*

What did they have in common?

They were all there during the first Gulf War.

What else?

They were all part of my father's company. And those were, quite logically, the people who could tell me what had happened. If anything had happened at the company level at all.

Frustrated, I drew a circle around their names. I needed to think outside that circle. Although they'd been there, they didn't have the information I needed.

Who else had been there? My father. Obviously. Who else? Almost two hundred other men. Whom I didn't have time to interview individually.

I put my fingertips to my temple. Closed my eyes. Forced myself to focus. I needed to speak to people who were not those three men. I needed to speak to people who were not the communications sergeant, a platoon sergeant, or the radio telephone operator sergeant.

My eyes sprang open.

There it was. I needed to speak to people who were not sergeants, people who hadn't been noncommissioned officers. Maybe I needed to speak to someone who wasn't my father's subordinate. Outside the circle that I'd drawn, I wrote down *peer* and *commanding officer.*

If choices had been presented that night and decisions had been made, just like Mr. Abbott had said, it wasn't the NCOs who had made them. It was the officers.

What else did those names inside the circle have in common? At least two of the three had really liked my father. Whatever had happened out there, they were likely to have given him the benefit of the doubt.

So what if I came at it from a completely different angle? If I was going to find out the truth, then maybe I should talk to people who hadn't liked him. At least it would provide me with a different perspective.

I just had to find out who my father's enemies were.

54

I called my father's staunchest supporter.

"Mom. Hey."

"Georgia Ann! Did you change your mind about lunch tomorrow?"

"No. But I was out running errands and, funny thing, I thought I saw that guy. The one who never liked Dad." It was a complete shot in the dark. For all I knew there might have been no one on earth who disliked my father, or there might have been hundreds. But it was worth a try to see what my mother came up with. "What was his name again?"

"Steven Edgars? Lord have mercy! If that man——" The pause was full of vitriol and venom. "If that man'd had his way, your daddy would be in Leavenworth to the end of his days, turning big rocks into little rocks. I've never a seen a soldier more just plain mean than Steven Edgars."

"Right. That's the name. He served under Dad?"

Steven Edgars. I wrote it down.

"Nothing but trouble."

"Just out of curiosity, what was it with him and Dad?"

"Oh, just—things not worth repeating."

"None of it's true, is it?"

"Georgia Ann!"

"I mean, how could any of it be true?"

"That man was poison. Pure spiteful poison."

"Didn't mean to bring back bad memories. Do you know what happened to him? After he got out?"

"Edgars? Who knows? Although I heard he started one of those watchdog websites. Always going on about corruption in the military. Figures."

∞

A few internet searches and I found him: Steven Edgars, CEO, Integrity in Government. It was an Alexandria-based company. I pulled up their website and read some of their press releases. They were mostly fact-based accusations that tended to veer off into rambling tirades against the federal government and the powers that be.

I imagined there were people like Mr. Edgars in every field. People who seemed reasonable at first glance but on closer inspection turned out to be just a little bit odd. If the goons at the Department of Defense and the FBI had considered him credible, he might have met the same fate as Paul Conway. Or Sean.

I signed up for another free email account, using a fake name, and sent an email asking him if we could meet.

Dear Mr. Edgars,

I'm working on an account of Desert Sabre and am in search of new source materials beyond those that have already been so widely referenced. It's been pointed out to me that you served in Captain JB Slater's company. Is it possible that we could meet?

Regards,
Gina Porter

Jenn came over that night, after dinner. Jim invited her in. She enfolded me in a hug and sat down right next to me on the couch, taking my hands into hers.

"I'm really worried. Jim said there was someone in the house? Before it blew up?"

I nodded.

Her face was pale, her eyes wild. "First the guy in your crawl space. Then your house blows up. You have to come stay with us."

I freed myself from her. "Jenn, I can't—"

"Say whatever you want. I'm a terrible person. I know I am. But you need someplace to stay. Come home with me."

I stood. "Are you insane?"

She blinked. "No. Why? No. The boys would love it. I really think it would be safer."

"Jenn. You tried to sleep with my husband."

"I know I did. I just want to make it up to you." She was pleading. "Can't we get past it?"

Make it up to me? Get past it? I could only stare at her.

She held up her hands as if fending off an argument. "I mean, I know I could never make it up to you. But we've been friends—we *were* friends—for a very long time. Please. I have to find some way to make this good."

"There's nothing that would make this good. You'll never make this good. We're not good."

"But I really need to—"

"I don't know how many ways I can say this. I don't know why you're not understanding this. We will never be good."

"Don't say no yet. Okay? Please don't. Maybe once the insurance people have come out and everything is settled?"

I said nothing.

"I want to help."

In some weird way, she probably did.

"Just tell me you'll think about it. I'm hardly ever at home. It would be like I'm not even there."

That, at least, was probably true.

"So we're good?"

Good? No. Not even close.

After Jenn left I put Sam to bed. At least he didn't put up a fight; there weren't any stars on June's living room ceiling to look at. I tucked the blanket under his chin. "You okay, Sam? It must feel strange, sleeping here. You probably miss your things."

"Daddy told me things are just things."

I smiled. Sean had always said that when Sam had lost or broken one of his toys. I kissed him on the forehead. When I was sure he was asleep, I wandered back down the hall.

Jim waved me over. "Hey, sweetie! Your dad's on the news."

When wasn't he?

"Come watch with me."

I sat in an armchair next to his.

It was mid-interview and the host was beaming at my father. "I can't think of any reason anyone would contest your nomination."

"You just haven't talked to my wife yet. She'd give you at least ten."

They both laughed, though the commentator quickly followed up. "Seriously, though." She leaned closer, as if hoping for a confidential word. "You're one of the only retired generals I can think of who hasn't thrown in with any of the political parties."

My father sat back, raised a hand. "Not my place."

"You must have a preference. Some opinion? An allegiance?"

"Sure I do. To the American flag. Truth is, the American people don't care who I vote for. They just care that they can count on me. Give me a commanding officer, give me a marching order, and I'll get the job done."

"Don't you think that's a little simplistic in our modern age?"

"You think that's simple? Here's what I learned in the army: it really is do or die. You either achieve the objective or you don't. You win or you lose. There aren't any awards for trying real hard. Know why? Because usually those guys end up dead. If you're going to play the game, then you gotta win it. Simple as that."

"Simple as that," the host echoed. "Well. Nothing simple about being secretary of defense, and I know everyone on the Hill is pulling for you. Best of luck at the hearing."

My father nodded, acknowledging the compliment. "I'm just here to serve."

55

The next morning an email from Steven Edgars was waiting for me.

> Dear Ms. Porter,
>
> I'm happy to tell you everything I know about that fraud. Please advise on best way to contact you.
>
> Cheers,
> Steve

Through an exchange of emails we arranged to meet in Crystal City on Monday. He suggested lunch at a local burger joint. I demurred, afraid I might be recognized by one of my father's many friends who now populated the desks of the region's defense contractors or who had become some of DC's most powerful lobbyists. I suggested a hotel restaurant instead. Nobody ever ate at hotel restaurants. At least not for lunch. I was hoping he would be able to offer further insight into what had happened in Iraq.

I answered emails from colleagues at work for a while. Forwarded some files to people who would have to deal with them in my absence.

I glanced at my watch. Nine o'clock.

Time had gotten away from me. I borrowed June's car again; mine was still at the shop. I was due to pick up Alice from the vet's. When I got there, she seemed like her normal self.

As we wound through the parking lot on the way home, I could see the traffic light change to green at the far end. I sped up. When it turned to yellow I sped up even more. The light turned red as I passed the middle of the intersection.

At the edge of the parking lot, behind me, a gray car skidded to a halt.

Sam was in heaven when I got home. He'd been playing with Legos that Jim had found somewhere in the attic. I didn't think it had quite registered with him that all of his trains had burned up in the fire. He told me June had promised they could make cookies later.

"Cookies? But we just made Rice Krispies Treats yesterday. Did you already eat them?"

"No. It's just Miss June said she needed help."

"Why?" She'd seemed fine when I'd left. "Did something happen to her?"

"She just doesn't have a whole lot of kids to lick the scraper clean anymore. That's what she says. They've all grown up and moved away. And she says she's going to make me a cake on Monday while I'm at school! Any kind I want. And I sang her the concert song. She liked it!" The school's fall concert was on Wednesday night and his class had been practicing their song for weeks.

I expected him to be cranky after dinner when I asked him to put away the Legos, but he was so happy to have Alice back that he didn't protest. He got into his pajamas without any pushback and went straight to sleep.

Alice rolled from her side to her belly when I came back into the living room. Jim and June didn't have a fenced backyard, so I had to take her for a walk. It made me uneasy to be out in the dark. I tried to stay underneath the streetlights and I took my phone with me.

The neighborhood was respectable, friendly during the day. At night it was downright menacing with its looming trees and deserted streets.

My breath fanned in front of me as we started down the front walk.

Alice tugged on the leash and started off across the street toward the place where our house used to be. I yanked her back and stayed on Jim and June's side.

I walked her down to the end of the block. We'd just turned to start back when Chris found us.

"Georgie. Hi."

I kept walking, knowing every step took us closer to safety at Jim and June's. "Hey." It was too bad Alice knew him, otherwise she might have been a deterrent. I needed a strategy. And fast!

Moving away from the cars that were parked in front of the houses, I pulled Alice toward the middle of the street.

Chris kept pace with us. "I haven't really had the chance to catch up with you. Not since the fire."

"It's fine. We're fine." Just two more houses and I'd be safe.

"I've been worried about you."

Not as much, probably, as I had worried about him.

He put a hand on my arm.

I recoiled.

He put his hands up. "Sorry. I'm sorry."

I kept walking. "It's fine. I'm fine. Things are just a little tense right now."

"Sure. I understand."

I put a hand to Jim and June's gate, pressed down on the latch.

He caught me by the wrist.

I pulled it to my chest, but he didn't let go.

He stepped forward, toward me. "I just need to know, Georgie. Do you need help?" His eyes searched mine.

Help? Yes! I most certainly did.

The porch light turned on and Jim stuck his head out the door. "You all right out there?"

Chris let go of my wrist.

I slipped through the gate and latched it behind me. Held a hand up to Jim. "We're fine." I took a few steps up the walkway before I turned to answer Chris.

But he had already disappeared.

∞

Midmorning Sam and I were playing with Legos in the corner of the living room. It was Sunday—Samday.

There was a knock on the door. Jim answered.

I paused to listen.

It was a reporter wanting to know if he knew what had happened to JB Slater's daughter. She asked if Jim knew where she was staying or if he knew how to contact her.

Jim had fun playing Clueless Neighbor.

"Slater? There aren't any Slaters on this street. Did you try the next block over?"

"It would be Brennan. She married."

"Brennan. With a *B*?" He called out over his shoulder to June. "Honey? There's a reporter here asking about the house that burned down across the street. Were there any Brennans there?"

I glanced at Sam. He was intent on building a spaceship. I didn't think he'd heard anything.

June gave me a wink as she walked past us on her way to the front door. She joined Jim. "What's that?"

"Brennan. Were there ever any Brennans living across the street?"

"Wasn't that the previous family?"

The reporter cut in. "The house is listed in the property records as belonging to Sean and Georgia Brennan. Georgia is JB Slater's daughter. Do you know what happened to her? Or where she's staying? Her father's been nominated to be the next secretary of defense."

Jim nudged June with an elbow. "I was just telling this reporter that there have never been any Slaters there. At least not for the past thirty years."

June agreed with him. "I don't even know if I know any Slaters. Do you?"

Jim and June talked for a while about all the people they knew who *weren't* Slaters and the reporter finally gave up.

But word must have gotten out because they kept coming. June and I peeked out the window at one point in the afternoon and counted four different people canvassing the street, going from door to door. She sighed as she let the curtain fall back into place. "I don't think they're going to go away."

I agreed with her. "I might have to say something. Maybe if I give them what they're looking for, they'll leave."

We came up with a plan. She sent Jim out to gather them all up. That way, when I stepped out onto the front porch, they were all waiting on the walkway, cameras at the ready.

I explained who I was, confirmed that JB Slater was my father and that, yes, it had been my house that burned down.

A reporter tilted a microphone in my direction. "Do you know why?"

"You would have to ask the people who are doing the investigation."

"Are they treating it as an accident?"

"You'll have to ask them."

"Have you been in contact with your father?"

"My parents are aware of the situation."

"Is this connected in any way with his confirmation hearings?"

"I wouldn't think so. Generally, when senators have differences with nominees, they talk about them; they don't set out to destroy each other's homes. Sometimes a house fire is just a house fire. That's all I have right now. Thank you."

56

It felt oddly like a betrayal, the meeting I'd arranged with my father's enemy.

Steven Edgars looked just like the picture from his company's website. He had a square, ruddy face softened at the edges by a beard. His hair stood up at the top as if it hadn't quite realized it was no longer cut in a military high-and-tight.

"Mr. Edgars?" I held out a hand as he stood.

"Ms. Porter!" He gave me a searching look and took my hand in his. Giving it a couple of pumps, he squeezed it tightly. He gestured to a seat beside his. "Call me Steve."

I chose the seat across from him instead.

"Looking for new source materials, huh?"

A waiter brought us menus. We put the conversation on pause to inspect them and to order. Once the waiter had disappeared, I got down to business.

"I'd like to hear your version of what happened during Desert Sabre on the night of February 24th."

He scoffed. "My *version*? Listen, the truth doesn't come in co-ordinated colors. It either is or it isn't. Collecting 'versions' won't get you any closer to figuring it out; it'll just confuse you. So what I'm going to tell you is what actually happened. And it's the truth. You can have it, but you'll have to take it all. Understand?"

I nodded.

"Good." He leaned back into his chair with a scowl and fell silent as he crossed his arms over his chest.

"Can you start by telling me the rank you held at the time? What unit you were assigned to and what your duty was?"

"I was a brand-new captain, the company XO. That's executive officer."

"So with regard to General Slater—"

"Captain."

"Sorry?"

"He was a captain at the time."

"You were the same rank?"

"JB was my commanding officer, but yes, we were the same rank. I'd just become a captain and he was promoted early out of that war to major. But we were comrades in arms. Or so I thought at the time." He fell silent as the waiter returned with glasses of water.

I waited until he left before I spoke. "Can you take me back to that morning? Starting with when you got up?"

"When I got up?" He snorted. "I'd never gone to sleep. Have you ever been in the desert?"

"I've been to Palm Springs." My mother had held one of her fundraisers there for the survivors of military members who had been killed on duty. But I hadn't even finished speaking before he was dismissing my words with a derisive snort.

"A *real* desert. Where there's nothing but sand. Sand upon sand. Miles of sand. It's not like driving through Arizona or New Mexico, where there's sagebrush, cactus, and scrub brush to tie things down. That desert, the one over there, it's real. It's alive."

Okay then.

"It slowly eats away at you. Starts with sand across the road. Sand in the Hummers. In between the seats. In the engine. Sand in your pockets. In your boots. Inside your socks. Gets into your ears and your mouth."

I was getting the idea that he really did not like sand. At all.

"Annoying. But that's not all. Everything's different there. The sun. The night. Sounds. Stars. It's like you're trapped inside an hourglass, just waiting to be upended. You start wondering, just how far down does it go? I mean, how far down would you have to dig before you got to something else? Is that all there is? Just sand?" He paused. Stared, vacant-eyed, at something just beyond my shoulder.

Then he shifted, pinning me again with his ice-blue gaze. "So I was awake."

"Did you know where you were?"

"What do you mean? I was sitting there in the desert. Sure wasn't back home in Kansas."

"I mean where. *Where* were you? Exactly? Did you know?"

"We were where the division told us the satellites told them we were."

"Are you sure?"

"Well, yeah." His eyes tracked the hostess who was seating a couple at the other end of the room. Then he turned his attention back to me. "I mean, we all had compasses too, right? And the company had maps. But the real triumph of that war was that GPS worked. Granted, there weren't that many satellites back then, so it was limited, intermittent coverage, but still. Can't imagine a world without it anymore."

"So the war started. Did you know where the Iraqis were at that point?"

"Didn't matter. If we found them, we were supposed to neutralize them and move on. We weren't supposed to get bogged down or committed to any conflicts. The Iraqis we made contact with weren't the Republican Guard; those guys were the elite, the best of the best. Most of the guys we met that first day surrendered before we even fired a weapon. The real mission was supposed to happen the next day. We were supposed to make a breach through their lines so that everyone else could pass through it, *then* we were supposed to find and destroy the Republican Guard."

"So what happened?"

"What happened? What happened is we got so far out in front of our line that we actually made it through *their* line. By accident. How it works is, you start out in formation and then stuff happens. You're supposed to stay in communication with everyone so you know where the friendlies are."

"But?"

"But sand happened. And wind. And weather. It was a regular mess. Before you know it, we were out there in the middle of the desert. I'm looking around realizing we haven't seen anyone in a while. It's like we're on our own planet. Know what I'm saying? And it's not conducive to life."

"You were supposed to be scouting, weren't you? It wasn't unexpected that you'd be out in front of everyone."

"Sure, but problem is, we hadn't encountered anyone. Scouts go ahead of the main contingent until they encounter the enemy, and then they report back where he is. No enemy, no reporting back, no stopping. We could have gone completely through their lines into Kuwait and back into Iraq for all I knew. And then we start noticing the terrain looks a little sketchy. One of our trucks thinks they spot a mine. And that's when JB ordered us to stop."

"Do you know what the orders from headquarters were at that point?"

"No. But I heard later we were supposed to fall back. The general wanted to regroup and start up again with the sun."

"What happened next?"

"I'm wondering what's going on, so I go up to JB. He takes me aside. Turns out, he thinks we're smack in the middle of a minefield. But it's not on any map. JB orders everyone to stay put. We argued about whether to call in our position. JB, you can tell he's worried about how it's going to look. He has no idea where we are in relation to anyone else. Do we have support behind us or have we gone so far ahead of everyone into Iraq that we're on our own? But that's not the worst part. We're sitting out there in the desert just waiting to blow up, and all of a sudden, the guys with the infrared scopes start spotting people. Lots of them. All around."

"How many?"

"More than us."

"What did the captain do?"

"He leaves me in charge of the company and goes out there on his own to meet them."

"What about his RTO? Isn't he supposed to stick with the captain?"

He took a drink of water. "Supposed to. But JB ordered him to stay with me and the rest of the command group. If someone's going to shoot the captain, we needed to be able to tell headquarters about it. So JB's out there on his own."

"Does anyone else know about this?"

"Besides me, the RTO, and top? No. Thing about minefields is, you don't want anyone panicking. So JB goes out there, hands up. Talks to them. Then he turns around and tells us to put our rifles down. I'm thinking he's surrendered us, right? But then he goes out there again, talks to them some more. Brings one of them back with him. Guy opens a map, starts pointing to this and that. Turns out he shows JB a lane through that minefield, back to their position."

"Back to the *Iraqi* position? The Iraqis, who outnumbered you, led you back to their own position?"

"That's what it seemed like. JB takes the map and orders us to head out. So I argue with him. Why are we trusting the enemy? In the middle of the night? As we sit there in a minefield? Only due to the grace of God we hadn't blown ourselves up by that point."

"What did the captain say?"

"Said to trust him. Said it'd work out just fine."

"So you let the Iraqis lead you through it?"

"We did. JB said he'd convinced them the rest of the corps was right behind us and they might as well just cooperate."

"That's what he said? But it sounds like you didn't believe him."

"I did at first. The others thought JB had balls of steel, but I figured those Iraqis were like all the other units we'd come across. They couldn't surrender fast enough. They just wanted the war to be over. But then I get a look at them. They're weren't regular Iraqi army."

"How could you tell?"

"They cared too much. They had actual uniforms. Other thing? Their place wasn't bombed to crap. We'd been bombing the Iraqis every day since the middle of January, and that place hadn't been touched. Camouflaged pretty good. And it was state of the art."

"So you went there and did what?"

"Guy opens the gate and invites us in like it's some hotel or some-thing. Takes the captain on a tour."

"Did you go along?"

"No. But I saw enough to know their equipment, the weapons, they were top-of-the-line. Straight from Mother Russia. And recent."

"The Iraqis fought with Soviet weapons. That was widely known." At least that's what I'd gathered from my father over the years.

"Not those weapons. We fought all kinds of Iraqis for the next four days, and I never saw the kinds of things I saw there."

"Did the captain make any remarks about them?"

"Yep. He lined us all up and used them as target practice."

I felt my brows peak. "The Iraqis?" My father had ordered a slaughter?

"No. The installation. The weapons. Destroy everything. That was his order. We blew it all up."

"That was the overall mission, right? To destroy the Republican Guard."

"Right. That was the mission: to destroy them and their weap-ons so the pathway to Baghdad would be clear. JB kept us away from them, and could be everyone else thought they were Republican Guard, but I got close enough to hear some of them talking. They weren't speaking Arabic. They were speaking Russian."

57

I heard myself gasp.

Edgars sent me a wry smile. "He never talks about that when people ask him about the war, does he?"

Russians? Had my father made some sort of deal with the Russians? *That* might be a fact worth killing someone over. "The Russians were known to have sent military advisers to the Iraqis. They helped build up the army."

"Yes. But those people there that night weren't advisers. They were *soldiers*. A whole unit of them. They weren't there, out in the desert, to advise people. They were there to fight against us."

"Against us? On the Iraqi side? If that's true, then how come none of this ever came out?"

"Because our boys were focused on the firepower, not the personnel. And as we were blowing things up, those Russians disappeared."

"Where did they go?"

He shrugged. "Don't know. Poof! Vanished."

"Did you ask the captain about it?"

"He said to let it go. The next day we'd be heading out for the big battle and there was no time for prisoners."

"But you weren't satisfied with that explanation?"

"I saw what I saw. I heard what I heard."

"What do you think happened?"

He took another drink of water. "I think he made a deal. I think JB traded a lane through that minefield and their installation for the Russians' freedom. Think about it. It would be embarrassing, come dawn, if we'd been found miles in front of our line, in direct contradiction to the general's orders. And it would have created an international incident if those Russian soldiers had been discovered in that position. It would have given away their whole game and their lie about just trying to be honest brokers."

"Honest brokers of what?"

"You're probably too young to remember, but this was the Gorbachev era. It's still the USSR back then. They're warming to the West, right? But inside the Kremlin, there's people who liked things the way they were, and the way they were is that the Soviets were Iraq's allies. Big-time. They had a treaty with them. For a while there no one knew what the Soviets were going to do. *They* didn't know what they were going to do. What they *said* they were doing was trying to negotiate a peace treaty between Baghdad and the allies. But here's what I think. I think someone in the Kremlin wanted the good ol' days back. They liked it better when the Evil Empire was a force to be reckoned with. Someone wanted to fight. But the war accelerated too quickly. We got too far out in front. They weren't expecting it; we weren't expecting it. I think that's what happened." He sat back. "Hadn't heard that before, had you?"

"No."

"Didn't think so."

The waiter came with our food. We paused our conversation as he set the plates in front of us. There was something about Steven Edgars that I didn't like. I just wanted to get the interview over with and leave.

"Can anyone verify what you've told me?"

"JB could. But he won't. Never said anything about it in any of those TV interviews, did he? And now he's General Slater on the way to becoming the new secretary of defense. Think he'll tell anybody about it now?"

"There wasn't anyone else who figured it out the way you did?"

"Let me tell you what it's like out there in the middle of a war. You know there's only two outcomes: you survive or you don't. Any given moment, you're dead. So those times when you aren't dead, when you *don't* step on the mine, when the grenade *doesn't* explode, when you *aren't* hit by a bullet, you don't stop and think, *Why the heck haven't I died yet?* You tend to celebrate your incredible good fortune. Who was going to raise his hand that night and say, 'Pardon me, Captain, sir, but this doesn't make much sense. We were supposed to end up dead'?"

"So even if someone did put two and two together, the way you did, no one ever said anything."

"*I* said something. I took Slater aside and gave him a talking-to. Because what were we supposed to do after that? And how were we going to account for countermanding a direct order?"

"What did he say?"

"He said he'd take care of it. And he did. Once the commo got the communications going, JB had the RTO radio in that he'd made a breach. He had that map the Russians had given him; he gave it to the commo so he could tell headquarters right where we were. It identified the entire minefield. And there you go: he became one of the heroes of Desert Sabre."

"So to summarize, the truth is—"

"The truth is that Captain JB Slater illegally collaborated with the enemy. That's what happened. And you know what he always said in all those interviews he gave afterward? He said, and I quote, 'Truth is, I'd rather be lucky than good.'" Mr. Edgars snorted. "Rather be lucky than good. But here's the thing. He was unusually lucky during his career. There were those times in Bosnia and those others in Iraq—again—and then in Afghanistan. How many times did his units find the enemy where they weren't supposed to be? Or just narrowly miss being hit by air strikes? I'd say he had more luck than one guy deserved."

I tried to ignore the twist in my gut. Tried to view what he was saying about my father objectively. "Are you accusing him of something?" I wanted to be crystal clear about what he was saying.

"I'm saying that not only did he collaborate with the Russians that night in the desert, I think he also collaborated with them his entire career."

I tried not to show any outward emotion, but beneath the table, on my lap, my napkin was twisted into knots. "Do you have anything specific? Any proof?"

"Nothing but suspicions." He scowled.

"I would like to believe you, but I really need proof." He was talking about my father.

He blinked. "I just laid it all out for you, like I've been laying it out for everyone for years. And you know what I've gotten for my troubles? Nothing. Nothing but raised eyebrows and dismissals. JB Slater didn't get any smarter in the years after Desert Sabre. You'd think if you were going to cheat your way to four stars, at least you'd try to look competent about it. You know, when I first met him, I used to think that good-old-boy, country-hick talk of his was a prop. That he was using it to put people off guard. But the more I was around him, the more I discovered that he wasn't even smart enough to use it as a tool. It's the only thing he was ever truthful about as far as I know: he really was just a country boy from the backwoods of Arkansas who was lucky enough to marry Miss America."

"Miss Alabama."

"What's that?"

"His wife. She was Miss Alabama."

"You know what I did instead? What career path I took? I busted my butt for twenty years doing what they told me I should do."

At the beginning he'd come off as intelligent, though understandably bitter. At that point? Dangerously obsessed and slightly unhinged.

"Only 3 percent of second lieutenants are ever promoted to general. Did you know that? And do you know how many of those 231 generals have four stars? Seven. That is point-zero-zero-one percent of the active army. Know how many other soldiers deserved those stars JB Slater eventually got?"

I shook my head so I didn't have to say anything.

"All of them! *Every. Single. One.*" He picked up his knife and slashed into the steak he'd ordered. "Guess you can report to your father that I'm just a crazy relic from his past. No one will believe a word I say. Not enough proof to keep him from that fancy desk in the Pentagon."

"Sorry?"

"Your father. That's what you're here about, right? To do opposition research for his confirmation hearings?"

"I have no idea what you're—"

He leaned toward me over the table. "You can tell him there's no one who's listened to me for the past twenty-five years. Don't know why anyone would listen to me now."

I felt along the floor for my purse, grabbed the strap, and pushed to my feet. "I'm sorry, I—"

"Sad, what happened to your husband."

I shoved the chair toward the table and took a quick step back, in the direction of the lobby. "Thank you for your time."

"I feel sorry for your son. Sam, isn't it? You should probably tell Miss America to stop posting pictures on Facebook."

"I really don't—"

"At least you live in a nice part of Arlington. Good neighborhood. Nice homes. Good neighbors?"

I turned around and fled.

58

"Georgia. Georgia Brennan!"

Was he following me? Dodging the lunchtime crowds of government contractors and the al fresco diners eating at tables on the sidewalk, I took a quick look over my shoulder.

Yes, he was.

"Georgia Brennan. Wait!"

I plunged into a cluster of passersby, half stepping to match their pace and then sidestepping to move through them, away from the curb.

Then I heard a thud. The squeal of tires.

The diners on the sidewalk around me let out a collective gasp. They stood in unison as if they were controlled by a puppeteer. Steven Edgars lay sprawled on the street. As I watched, a gray car sped away toward the Washington Monument, which rose like a sentinel above Long Bridge Park. If he wasn't dead, he would be in the hospital for a very long time.

As several bystanders ventured out of the roped-off eating areas toward the street, I kept on going. Kept moving forward, kept putting distance between myself and Edgars. Because there had to have been someone watching us, someone who notified the people in the car that we had left the hotel. Someone who might still be out there, watching.

Edgars had told me my father collaborated with the Russians, but he'd offered no verifiable proof. If Edgars could no longer tell anyone what he'd heard—and since everyone at the Department of Defense had written him off as a bitter, angry person—I needed more than just his word.

But the things he'd said about my father had to be true. They made sense. And it was the only thing I'd heard that would make Sean worth killing. It would be devastating for the Pentagon if that information were revealed. They'd promoted a collaborator to their highest ranks. And on a personal level, if Edgars's information was revealed publicly, my father would be ruined. Past, present, and future.

What I still needed, however, was actual proof.

If I took Edgars at his word, maybe if I went forward through my father's career, dug into his follow-on assignments, I'd find some hard evidence that would link everything back to the Gulf War.

I'd almost made it to June's car when I keeled over, retching. A cold sweat had broken out on my forehead. I don't know how I even opened the door, but suddenly I was sitting in the driver's seat, hands clenched around the wheel. I closed my eyes.

In my mind I saw Steven Edgars lying in the street.

In my soul I remembered every time my father stood next to a flag talking about duty, honor, and country. Every time I ever heard him say, "God bless America." I thought of all the soldiers he had served with, all the people he had led into combat. And deep inside, I felt something shift.

I started the car. Left the garage.

I didn't have time for a breakdown. My father's confirmation hearing was in six days, and I was the only one who could stop it.

I went to the library, sat down at a public computer, then brought up the pages of Sean's notes on my phone. There was one name left from Desert Sabre that I wanted to find. Reginald Wallace. Top. He'd been mentioned in both interviews. I had to do some research to find his contact information, but I found an address in Maryland. The address led me to a phone number.

I stepped outside to call him.

Mr. Wallace answered. He wasn't available to speak just then, but he agreed to talk with me midmorning the following day, if I would drive out to see him. He didn't like telephones. Couldn't hear very well.

I chose a name from one of my father's other units. The one from Bosnia. But when I called and told him what I wanted to talk about, he hung up. The next name I chose from the unit did the same.

What had happened in Bosnia?

Though I only vaguely remembered the Gulf War, I remembered next to nothing about Bosnia. I typed *US Army* and *Bosnian War* into a search engine.

It came back with a lot of summary articles. Looked like the United States didn't really put boots on the ground in the region until the actual war was over.

I found another name identified with my father's unit, spent time on the internet, and came up with some contact information. I called the number I'd found and asked for Bobby Denunzio.

"Speaking."

I told him what I wanted to talk about.

"The Bosnian War?" His disgust was apparent, even over his New York City accent. "What a mess. Who ever heard of fighting a war with three sides?"

"*Three* sides?"

"Yeah. Give me a minute. Have to think about this." There was a long pause. I heard the sound of a TV in the background. "See, it used to be Yugoslavia, right? Remember that? Part of the Union of Soviet Socialist Republics. Well, those Soviets crammed lots of countries into one in order to make it. You had Bosnia and Herzegovina. That's actually one even though it sounds like two. You got Croatia. You got the two *M*s: Macedonia, Montenegro. You got Serbia and what's the other *S* one? Slovenia, right? Bunch of alphabet soup. So when the Soviet Union started busting up and everybody wanted out, well, those Serbs decided they wanted out too. But all on their own."

"This is before the war?"

"Right. So pretty soon it's a regular slugfest over there. Serbs on Croats on Bosnians. Only they used guns and bombs."

"And Major Slater was your commanding officer."

"Yeah. Now I told you there were three sides, right? So you got Serbs. And you got Croatians. Only—and this is the tricky part— you got your Croatian *Serbs* who, if Croatia decides they want their own Catholic country, well, those Serbs don't want to be a part of it. They want to be part of Serbia because Serbs are Orthodox. Now Bosnians are Muslim; they were the third side. Unless they were Bosnian *Serbs*, in which case they're Orthodox. So you got your Orthodox Serbs and Catholic Croats and Muslim Bosnians most of the time, but not always. And I don't mean to speak out of turn, but I'm a good Catholic boy and normally I'm on the side of the angels, you know? Except this time, the Orthodox Christians and even sometimes the Catholics, they were the bad guys. They were massacring the Muslims. So you got good guys who are bad guys and bad guys who are good guys. Couldn't keep 'em straight."

Maybe that's why I didn't really remember much about that war.

"And the politicians? They screwed it all up. At the end there, know what they did? The politicians went to the bad guys—those were the Serbian Serbs, the Orthodox types—and they basically said, 'Just tell us what you want. If we give it to you, will you just pack it up and go away?' That's basically how that war ended. Bad guys got everything they wanted and the good guys declared victory. Us grunts? We were going, *What was that all about?* All those cities destroyed? All those people killed? They were slaughtered. Serbs mowed 'em down and bulldozed them into mass graves. So if you were just going to give them what they wanted in the first place, then what was all of it for? Know what I'm saying?" He took a deep breath. "Sorry."

"So what were you doing there?"

"Me? I was finishing up my enlistment. We were fighting on the allies' side even though it seemed like we were helping the Serbs.

Stupid politicians. They were trying not to choose sides. But basically it was everyone against Serbia. Mostly."

"I was under the impression that there weren't any Americans on the ground until after the war ended. But you were there during the actual war?"

"Sure. Yeah. Serving under Major Slater."

"What did you do?"

"Mostly we were in Bosnia helping them communicate with the UN forces and the allies. We weren't supposed to be helping them *fight*, right? But we helped them out with comms. And we helped them spot military targets. When NATO dropped their bombs on the Serbs, it wasn't the U-S-of-A officially fighting. It was more like NATO just got lucky when they were dropping their bombs and magically hit important targets. That's what we did. We told 'em what to hit."

"Did you ever come into contact with any Russians?"

"Thing is, Russia said they were on our side, but you could tell their heart wasn't in it. 'Cause those Serbs, they were Orthodox. Russians were Orthodox. Know what I'm saying?"

"Did the major ever communicate with any Russians? Do you know?"

"You had to. You couldn't talk to a Serb unless it was the good kind of Serb. But Russians weren't Serbs even if they liked Serbs. So if you wanted to communicate with a Serb, you went through a Russian who knew how to get in touch with a Serb. That's the way it was. It was a crazy war."

"So the major had a Russian contact."

"Yeah."

"So this wasn't any secret."

"No."

Was this another dead end? If everybody knew, then my father had nothing to hide. Maybe Edgars had been wrong. "Were there ever any complications?"

"Well, it was like this. The Serbs were monsters. But we weren't necessarily there to fight them. We were there to support the Bosnians who were fighting them. For the Russians, it was kind of the same. So sometimes you had to do the dance."

"What dance?"

"You had to say, 'Hey, Ivan. We got to get from here to there. Do me a solid and don't let those Serbs drop a bomb on the road while I'm on it. That would be on such and such a date at such and such a time.' *That* dance."

"You coordinated movements."

"I wouldn't say coordinate. We *facilitated* things."

"And there were complications?"

"Well . . . I don't know." He paused. "I don't know."

"Can you tell me what happened?"

"I don't really know that anything did."

"What might have happened?"

"There was this, um, this group. This group of wounded. We were evacuating them. We assumed that it was all good. Turned out it wasn't. Serbs bombed the convoy. But see, that's the kind of thing that would have been coordinated. We would have told Ivan. He would have told the Serbs."

"How many people got bombed?"

"Lots. One of those Bosnians, one of the wounded, turned out he was one of their commanders. He bit it. And they got some of our guys as well. The good guys. The ones who were helping with the evacuation. It's not like that kind of thing didn't happen all the time. But usually it was just the Serbs bombing the other alphabet soup guys. That's what made that war so crappy. It happened *all the time*. Mostly all we were allowed to do was stand there and watch. But that time? That time it put a real dent in the Bosnian forces when their guy got killed and some of the good guys got killed too. Someone must have screwed up. I felt sorry for the major."

"Was that the only time it happened?"

"Happened a couple times."

"Were any other Bosnian commanders killed those other times?"

"Yeah. I mean, that was the tragedy, right? Not to mention allies. I mean, the Bosnians were fighting. You can kind of think, 'Well, that's the breaks.' But when the good guys got killed? It just wasn't right."

"Were you with the major's unit the whole time it was there?"

"No. When my enlistment was done, I got out. I didn't sign up to just sit around and watch people kill each other. That's not what I was in it for."

I thanked him for his time, and before he hung up, I told him to be careful.

"Careful? Me? Lady, I'm talking to you from Brooklyn. And not the good part. Born and bred. If anyone should be careful, it's the other guy."

I thanked him again and hung up.

I couldn't help wondering if maybe those bombings *hadn't* been a mistake. What if my father had passed information to the Russians? Not so they could keep the roads clear, but so the Serbs could bomb them and take the Bosnian commanders out?

59

My parents showed up just before dinner. They came bearing boxes.

"Just a few things," my mother said as she knelt on the floor and offered one to Sam.

It was almost bigger than he was, so I took it from her and set it beside him. She'd put all those years of charity work with disaster and military relief organizations to good use. It was filled with clothes. Shoes. A coat. A scarf and gloves. And down at the bottom were several smaller boxes.

Trains.

"Wow! Thanks!" Sam pulled them out and held them up toward Jim like prizes. "Want to play, Mr. Jim?"

"Sure thing, kiddo. But I want to show your granddad something first."

Sam didn't wait. While Jim walked down the hall toward his office, Sam dumped them out of their boxes. I knelt beside him, collecting the packaging.

Jim came back, a piece of paper in hand. "Just drafted up a little something." He tipped the sheet so my father could see it.

"Don't show the president!" My father flashed a grin.

"What is it?" My mother leaned over to have a look. "Well now."

I got to my feet and walked over so I could see too.

Slater for President.

Jim had drawn up a campaign logo for my father. Somehow he was able to hit all the right notes: patriotism, leadership, strength.

Horror swept over me. I hadn't realized until then just how lofty my father's ambition was. And just how close he was to achieving it. He had to be stopped.

My father extended his hand toward Jim.

Jim took it. Shook it. "Just a little nonsense." He winked. "I might be retired, but I can still have some fun."

My father chuckled. "Hey, mind if I keep it?"

"As long as you put it somewhere you can always see it." Jim tapped his forehead. "Keep it in mind."

"Sure, sure." My father clapped him on the back.

My mother put a hand on my arm. "There's a box for you too." She indicated one that my father had set near the front door. "I didn't know what you need, so I put in some toothbrushes, toothpaste. Some clothes."

What was she going to do when she found out about my father?

"There are a couple pairs of shoes. As well as a purse with some Visa gift cards to get you by for a bit." She gave me a look. "And some unmentionables. You know, we have a suite at the Hay-Adams. There's more than enough room for you and Sam."

"No."

"That way you wouldn't have to continue imposing on these kind people."

June must have heard our conversation. She walked over and put an arm around me. "It's no trouble at all."

∞

June invited them to stay for dinner. They left when I put Sam to bed. Just before I went to bed myself, I decided my best move was to call Sean. There was too much information to be conveyed in a text.

But the phone didn't go to voice mail. He picked up. In the moment before he spoke, I could hear talking. There was the sound of dishes, utensils. And beneath it all, there was music. "Yeah? Hey. I can't talk right now. Can't slip away. I'll get back to you." He hung up.

I stood there staring at my phone. We only had six days left to figure it all out and he didn't have time to talk? Couldn't slip away? I was trying to save his life and mine. And our son's! I wanted to throw my phone at the wall. But I didn't. Mostly because I was my mother's daughter; it wouldn't have been polite. So I powered it off and pulled my new pajamas from the box my mother had brought. Pondered my next move as I put them on.

But that music from the call refused to fade away.

That music.

I'd heard it before.

As I eased the blanket away from Sam and put a knee to the mattress to crawl into bed, I finally remembered where.

I put the blanket back, pulled my pajamas off, and put my clothes back on. I left my old phone on the dresser; Sam was safe with Jim and June, and there was no need to make it easy for anyone to track me through a known device. But I slipped my new phone into a pocket.

If Sean wasn't going to come to me, then maybe I could go to him. I glanced at my watch.

Ten o'clock.

Jim was still up, watching the news, when I tiptoed into the living room. He glanced up. "Sweetie? You okay?"

"I just need to go for a drive."

He searched my eyes before he answered. "Not a problem. Keys are on the table in the hall. We'll have some cocoa when you get back."

The restaurant I drove to was just one of dozens located in the shabby strip malls lining Columbia Pike. Redevelopment was relentlessly chewing up Latin American groceries and halal delis, and spitting out gleaming condos and sleek office buildings. But along that stretch of the Pike, restaurants were still numerous. On offer in that block were five continents' worth of food. Rai music competed with punchy mariachi. On summer evenings, when the doors to the restaurants were propped open, it was as good as going to the Smithsonian Folklife Festival down on the mall in DC.

When we first moved to the neighborhood, Sean and I must have passed the restaurant a thousand times before a taxi driver called it to our attention. *Best kebabs in town.* It soon became our go-to takeout, though I hadn't been since Sean had died.

My eyes swept the restaurant.

No Sean.

I was trying to be surreptitious, but the other three customers were looking quite pointedly at me.

I stepped up to the register and ordered what had, at one time, been my usual. After ordering, I took a seat in one of the darker corners, facing the kitchen. I listened, trying to imagine how the sounds would filter through a cell phone. The kitchen door opened and the strains of rai music drifted out into the dining room. It made me think of the desert. Of minarets and cool oases. The door swung shut, muffling the music.

He was there. He had to be.

I glanced at my watch. Ten thirty. I looked at the other two tables. Their occupants were eating with *plastic* utensils. From *paper* plates. My hopes spluttered and died. On the phone I'd heard the clatter of dishes. The slide of metal utensils against plates.

The music was right, but the setting was wrong.

60

I left the restaurant, clutching a bag of unwanted food, trying to push back my fears. I needed Sean's help to figure out what to do. After navigating the uneven sidewalk, I stepped over a broken curb and left the spotlight of the streetlights for the bleakness of the alley where I'd had to park.

The back door to the restaurant opened with a metallic scrape, flooding the alley with light. Music poured out of the door, along with the clatter of dishes. A man appeared, backlit on the doorstep, as a voice called to him in words that were indecipherable. He paused. Pivoted toward the interior as he answered. Then he bent, picked up a cardboard box, and carried it out to the dumpster. After balancing it for a moment on his thigh, he lifted the lid and hefted the box over the edge. As he turned, the streetlight drenched him in its glow.

"Sean." I whispered his name.

He was wearing a worn pair of jeans and a T-shirt. Fastened around his neck was a stain-blotched apron. With his bushy beard and longer-than-I-was-used-to-seeing hair, he fit right in with the restaurant.

He sent a sharp-eyed glance toward the edges of darkness and retreated to the building. As he took a pack of cigarettes and a lighter from his back pocket, I stood there fascinated. Sean didn't smoke.

Shaking a cigarette out, he put it to his mouth and cupped a hand around it while he lit it.

Had he smoked in his former life? Back when he'd been in the gang?

Holding the cigarette between two fingers, he raked his hair from his forehead. Massaging the back of his neck, he closed his eyes and leaned his head back against the wall.

I stepped forward from the shadows. "Smoking can kill you."

His mouth curled before he even opened his eyes. "I'm already dead." He tossed away his cigarette and came toward me. "They're closing in on me." Without breaking his stride, he took me by the arm, pulling me with him back into the shadows.

I'd come to talk to him, but right then I just wanted . . . him.

He glanced back over his shoulder. "You shouldn't be here. I think I'm being watched. That's why I can't meet you. It's too dangerous."

I put a hand on his arm and the other on his chest, reminding myself that he was real. This was what I was fighting for. I slid one hand to his shoulder. Used the other to tug at the too-long ends of his hair. "I know."

He closed his eyes. Bowed his head.

I moved my hand to his beard-covered jaw. This was where he was. This was what he was doing. I'd come to talk to him, but instead I stood on tiptoe and kissed him.

His lips were unyielding.

He smelled of cumin and grease and cigarettes. His beard was scratchy. My hands moved beyond the tangle to his temples, my thumbs splaying down toward his cheeks. Bringing his head toward mine, I kissed him again.

He exhaled, heavily. Then he removed my hands, pressed a fleeting kiss to my palms, and dropped them.

In the shadows, I couldn't read his eyes. I didn't want to let him go. I moved to embrace him.

He blocked me, slipping from my grasp. "I can't—" He stepped away, out of my reach. "I can't be here for you, Georgie. Not like this."

"I just— I need you." I approached slowly, took up his hand. Skimmed my other hand up his bare forearm.

His muscles tensed. "Don't."

"Sean." I kissed what I could reach. I kissed his shoulder, through the T-shirt. I stepped closer. Kissed his neck. Kissed just beneath his ear, a spot his beard hadn't reached. I kissed—

His hand fisted into my shirt, at my waist.

I put a hand up to his jaw. Encountered his beard where it used to be smooth. Pulling, just a tiny bit, I turned his head toward mine so I could press a kiss, just a single kiss, onto his lips.

His embrace came swift, fierce, so tight I couldn't breathe. He pulled me in to himself and then his mouth descended on mine. Hungry, desperate.

I wanted.

I wanted him. I wanted everything. Everything I didn't have. I wanted him turning to me in the night. I wanted him waking up next to me in the morning. I wanted him catching up our son and throwing him over a shoulder.

I wanted him.

I wanted us.

A shout came from the kitchen.

He raised his head. Answered in that unknown tongue. Then, breathing heavily, he let his forehead dip down to touch mine.

I kissed him again. Once. Twice. "What language?"

"Arabic." He kissed me back. Once. "I can't do this."

"Sean."

"I can't." Even if he hadn't been whispering, his words would have been hoarse. He gripped my forearms, tightening his hands when I tried to loosen their hold. Gently, he held me off. Held me apart. "I can't. Not again. Not until this is over."

"But—"

The man from inside the kitchen opened the door and called out. "I have to go."

I grabbed his head, pressed his forehead to mine. "My father met Russians out in the desert that first night. It wasn't the Republican Guard. It was a Russian outpost. Not advisers; soldiers. They were there to fight. They traded a way through the minefield and their position for their freedom. But there's no way to actually prove it unless my father admits it. In Bosnia, he met up with Russians again. He gave them information about the positions of Bosnian commanders to pass to the Serbs. The Serbs bombed them, along with some of the allies."

He stepped away from me, though he kept his gaze on mine. "That's what this is. That's who they are, who wants to keep this quiet. They're not FBI or DoD. They're Russians."

Once again, everything shifted. "I thought—I assumed—" I'd interpreted everything wrong. It wasn't the DoD trying to protect their own, hoping to cover for a mistake. It was the Russians. "My father is a traitor and a murderer." They were words I'd never imagined I would ever say.

"Yes."

"You were wrong, you know."

"About what?"

"About your parents. You said you couldn't save them. But you were young, Sean. You were just a child. It wasn't your job to save them."

He tried to move away, but I stopped him. "But Sam and me? This is going to work. It is. You're saving us. This is going to work and you're going to come back. You are not going to lose us."

He was watching me.

"Because I won't let you." I took a breath. Blinked back the tears that pressed against my eyes. "So tell me, what do I do? I need actual proof. How do I find it?"

"I don't even—" He broke off helplessly.

"I don't know how much longer I'll be able to talk to people. They keep getting—"

The man from the kitchen came out onto the stoop and yelled.

Sean yelled back. "I've got to go. This job is how I get the money to pay people off. I need to keep it. But we'll talk. Soon."

"But—"

He strode away toward the kitchen.

"—they keep getting killed." I said the words to no one at all.

61

June let me borrow her car again the next day; mine would be in the shop for the rest of the week. It turned out that Reginald Wallace lived about an hour and a half away, out past one of the small farming communities that populated Maryland between the border with Delaware and the eastern shore of the Chesapeake Bay. The land was cut by small streams and pocked by ponds. The trees were gilded, the grasses golden. It was one of those bright, burnished autumn days when the sun still gave off warmth.

But it was dry. The windshield soon collected a fine coating of dust. I pulled the lever for windshield washer fluid, turning the dust to mud. A few more pulls washed it all away.

As I followed my GPS through the twists and turns of the countryside, a gray car bobbed in and out of my rearview mirror.

There were a lot of gray cars on the road in the region, but there always seemed to be one in close proximity to me in particular. I was too paranoid to chalk up my suspicions to coincidence. If someone was following me, why oblige them by leading them straight to my contact? I approached the next T in the road without signaling and didn't slow down as I turned away from my intended destination.

The gray car turned the same direction I had.

I was starting to worry. It was one thing to be followed discreetly, another thing entirely to be followed brazenly. With one hand on the steering wheel, I widened the view on my GPS program to take a look at my options.

There were more streams in that part of Maryland than roads.

The longer I drove in the direction I was going, the closer I got to the Potomac River. The closer to the river, the fewer the roads. There looked to be only one possibility to escape being dead-ended.

I glanced into the rearview mirror.

The gray car was still there.

I looked back at the GPS. I was coming up on what had to be farm plots because they were bounded by roads that formed a grid of tight, even squares. I could turn down one and then, by making a series of turns in the same direction around the grid, I could resurface on the same road I was currently on. Then I could head back down it, in the right direction, toward Reginald Wallace's.

And if I took those turns fast enough, maybe I could lose the car behind me.

Of course, the driver of the gray car might intuit what I was doing, and if he was clever, he could use the same method. Only he could come at me from the opposite direction. And in that landscape of narrow roads and deep ditches, I didn't want to play chicken with anyone.

I gripped the steering wheel tighter. It was time to make a decision.

In three . . . two . . . one— I turned hard to the right. Glanced back to see the gray car do the same. I stepped on the gas and flew down the road, then gritted my teeth and got ready for my next turn. In three . . . two . . . one.

My back wheels fishtailed, fanning a cloud of dust.

No time to think. I just tried to counteract the fishtailing.

Was the gray car still there? I couldn't see for the dust. When it began to dissipate I saw that the answer was yes.

I'd broken out in a sweat. Making that first turn at the T had been a mistake. What I needed to do was get back to a main road. If anything happened to me, it was more likely to be noticed there. I was more likely to be found.

One more turn and then I could head back in the right direction. And once I hit that road, I was planning to hit my accelerator too.

Behind me, the gray car honked. Once. Twice.

What did he think I was going to do? Pull over?

I glanced back to see him turn off onto a rutted lane. Farther down a pickup truck waited. A man was standing in the bed. He straightened. Gave a wave to the driver of the gray car. Then he held up something dark. Something long and narrow.

Reflexively, I cringed.

It was something that looked . . . just like a fishing pole.

∞

It wasn't until I made that last turn that my heart started beating again.

Gradually, my fingers held steady. As I got back on the route to Reginald Wallace's, my muscles began to relax. As I turned off onto the narrow ribbon of a lane that led from the highway to his house, I was nearly run off the road by a car that shot past me in the opposite direction.

I hoped it wasn't Mr. Wallace; due to my detour, I was late. But after that, I crept around every bend of the road. I passed several other houses before I finally reached his.

The lane ended in a driveway that curved up to an old-fashioned white farmhouse and a tidy metal-roofed barn. I parked in front of the house, behind a sun-faded pickup. Then I walked up the front steps to the wide, covered front porch, rang the bell, and waited.

There was no answer. No sound of footsteps coming toward the door.

I rang again.

Nothing.

Stepping off the front porch, I walked over to the barn.

"Mr. Wallace?"

The sun filtered in through the open door, making the dust motes sparkle as they drifted through the air.

"Mr. Wallace?"

Over in the corner, a light shone from a workbench of sorts. Tools lined the walls.

He'd said he was hard of hearing, so I went in and walked toward the workbench, my feet scuffing against the concrete floor of the barn.

"Mr. Wallace?"

My view was blocked by a riding lawn mower. As I moved around it, I saw a body lying on the floor.

62

I froze. Then I dropped to the floor in a squat. Old men have heart attacks more frequently than they get murdered, but knowing what I did about my father and the Russians, I couldn't take any chances. What if he had been killed? And what if the killer was still there? I didn't want to be the next victim.

Keeping my profile low, I crept over to Mr. Wallace and shook his arm.

No response.

I stretched over him so I could see his face. Then I wished I hadn't.

Vacant eyes stared up at mine. A hole had been blown right through his forehead. I rocked back onto my heels and took a deep breath, forcing air into my nostrils and down into my lungs to try to keep from retching.

I had a sudden, nearly overwhelming urge to stand up right there and reveal myself. To shout, "I'm out. I'm done."

But the people who had killed Mr. Wallace wanted to kill Sean. And they wanted to kill me and Sam too. In fact, they almost had. So it wouldn't be over until we managed to get through.

I worked my way around to the entrance of the barn and then I stayed there, in a crouch, watching. Waiting. Listening for any sign that someone was still there.

How had the Russians known who I was going to talk to? They were there the day I'd talked to Steven Edgars. They were just ahead of me in coming to Mr. Wallace's. Actually, if I hadn't been late due to my detour, I might have walked right into them.

Somebody was watching me. And closely enough that they knew my habits. They knew when I went to work; they knew when I came home.

There *was* somebody. There had to be. They were watching me as closely as Jim kept watch on his neighbors. He knew everything that happened on our street. He was the first to notice visitors. The first to help me with the garbage cans or yard work. The first person I'd been turning to when I needed help.

No one knew more than Jim did.

And whose car was I borrowing? June's.

Which might make a person start to wonder.

Eventually I made my way back to the car.

There was nothing I could do for Mr. Wallace. And if I called for an ambulance or reported the killing to the police, then who would be their chief suspect?

Me.

As it was, I'd probably left far too many traces of myself in that barn.

I drove all the way up to Waldorf before I pulled off at a gas station and took my phone from my purse with shaking hands. I'd been making a tally. They'd killed Paul Conway. I assumed they killed Steve Edgars. They'd just killed Reginald Wallace. Who else was on their list? Who else had I talked to?

I called Mr. Ornofo.

It rolled to voice mail.

I hung up.

Just because he didn't answer didn't mean he was dead. But I wanted to be certain. I googled his name. It brought up the same pages on radiosport that I had accessed several days before.

I moved the cursor back to the search box. Typed in *Lee Ornofo death*. But I couldn't quite bring myself to tap the Search button.

It wasn't as if I would be summoning Death. Tapping Search had no bearing on whether he was alive. But still I felt like an executioner.

He was Schrödinger's cat. Both alive and dead as far as I knew. And I wouldn't know for sure until I could find more information.

I tapped Search, but it returned nothing new.

I deleted *death* and typed *killed*.

Nothing.

My hope renewed, I tried once more, searching *Lee Ornofo dead*.

It returned a link to an article published the day before in the Philadelphia *Inquirer*.

"Lee Ornofo, aged 65, found dead in his home."

Conway. Edgars. Wallace. Ornofo.

Four names. Four deaths.

I needed to find proof of my father's crimes and find it fast.

∞

As I drove, reason did battle with my paranoia. By the time I reached Arlington, I realized my watchers couldn't be Jim and June. They'd grown up in the area; they'd been living in their house for fifty years. And we'd moved in long before Sean started working on the Desert Sabre project.

Once I got back, I took out my old phone and pulled up my pictures of Sean's notes. I selected another name from my father's time in Bosnia. Perry Jenkins. On June's phone I searched for his name and his unit number. Got a hit on an oral history project that had been collected by Baylor University. Hoping they were focusing on veterans in their own state, I searched for all the Perry Jenkinses who lived in Texas. After calling several phone numbers, I found the right one.

I asked Mr. Jenkins for basic information, the same as I'd asked the others. Then I asked him what his particular job was.

"I kept the guns."

"What guns were those?"

"The ones the patrols would take. We were assigned with a unit of Russian paratroopers, patrolling along the zone of separation. That was the border between the Muslims and the Serbs. We were supposed to keep the Serbs on the Serb side and the Muslims from coming over."

"And how did the guns figure into it?"

"The Muslims would sneak over and, come to find out, they were hiding guns on the Serb side. They were stocking arsenals. Just 'cause we said the war was over didn't mean it was over for them."

"And what happened?"

"Depended on the night. Sometimes it was quiet. Sometimes they rushed the border. But once we figured out where an arsenal was, we'd raid it and take their weapons. My job was to keep track of the guns."

"The Muslim guns."

"Right."

"Was that difficult?"

"Shouldn't have been. There were a lot of guns, though. One night the patrol brought back about a thousand."

A *thousand*? "You said *shouldn't* have been difficult. Does that mean it was?"

"I don't know. Something funny was going on. We'd have *x* number of guns come in one night when the patrol came back, then a couple days later we'd only have *y* number of guns. Guns don't have legs, but there had to be some way they kept walking out."

"What did you do about it?"

"I told the major."

"Major Slater."

"That's right."

"What did you tell him?"

"I said those guns keep getting out. I think it's the Russians. I think they're passing them back to the Serbs."

"Why did you think that?"

"I had my suspicions. They were friendly with the Serbs. So that's what I thought and that's what I told the major."

"What did he say?"

"He said he'd take care of it."

"Did he?"

"I don't know. I got reassigned the next week."

"Considering what you told the major, didn't that strike you as odd? That you were reassigned?"

"Not really. I mean, the timing? Okay, maybe some people would say it seemed a little fishy. But the major told me he'd take care of it and he was always good for his word. He wasn't like some officers. And I'd just re-upped and requested assignment to a different post. Guess you could argue the point if you wanted to, but I didn't."

I called more names. Many of my calls went unanswered. And according to the search I did on my phone, several of the people on Sean's list had recently died. But those I got in touch with offered similar stories of my father's time in Qatar, Afghanistan, and through his rise at the Pentagon.

Putting the stories together filled out a pattern. If I'd harbored any hopes that he was just some pawn in a larger scheme, they'd been dashed. It was easy to see how his actions had been overlooked, though. His assignments had been discrete. Once they were over, he'd moved posts, changed positions, left behind the people he'd worked for and with. No one had been able to observe the pattern.

The impression he'd left over the course of his career? My father was a good officer who took care of his people. When circumstances seemed suspicious, every single person I interviewed gave him the benefit of the doubt.

But how much of a pass did one person deserve? And if he kept putting himself, and his men, in incriminating situations, at some point wouldn't any normal person start to wonder? If the pattern kept proving the pattern, then couldn't we just admit there was a pattern?

It almost made me feel for Steven Edgars.

The best defense for my father's actions appeared to be that he was a good guy and everyone knew it.

❦

My witnesses were dwindling; people on Sean's list were being poached. The Russians were trying to make sure the information about my father would not get out. But what could I do about it? The deaths were in different states, different localities, different jurisdictions. Nobody was going to be looking for a connection; I was the only one who knew there was one. And if I alerted someone to it? There were several problems with that.

Who would I tell? Sean and I were pretty sure the FBI wasn't after us, but until I could prove what was going on, we could take no risks.

But more importantly, how long would it take them to follow up?

And what would keep them from throwing *me* in jail? I'd spoken to Mr. Ornofo. I'd spoken to Mr. Abbott. And I'd been the one to find Mr. Wallace dead. That made me a prime suspect.

Should I warn the rest of the people on the list?

Morality warred with expediency. I only had five days left. Either I could spend my time building the case against my father, or I could spend it warning the people on the list that their lives were in danger.

How many people were left?

There had been almost two hundred men in his Desert Sabre company alone. And the further my father went in his career, the more people he had commanded. I could never hope to contact them all in less than a week. But I *could* hope to stop his confirmation hearing.

At least I knew the significance of what Sean had discovered and why people had been so interested in keeping it hidden. I had the truth. I might not exactly have proof, but maybe it would be enough to convince someone to start an official investigation. Even the *suspicion* of scandal had been enough, in years past, to roil Washington.

I borrowed June's computer again and put my notes together. Then I printed out a copy. There was one obvious way to set everything in motion, but it required that I swallow my pride. If it could bring Sean back from the dead and stop my father from being confirmed, it would be worth it. So I did it.

I called Jenn.

"Georgie?"

"I need to ask you for a favor."

She agreed to meet an hour later near the metro stop by the capitol.

∞

I stepped out of the metro train and onto a platform at the Capitol South station. Skirting tourists and government workers, I walked through the impersonal, brutalist concrete tunnel and took the escalator up to the street. As I emerged into the sunlight I squinted, turning as I ascended in order to get my bearings. A line of flat-roofed brick rowhouses stood behind me. The white stone Cannon House Office Building sat in front of me. Tourists milled around the entrance to the station, consulting their guidebooks and maps to no avail; there was no Capitol Building, Library of Congress, or Supreme Court in sight. Anyone who spent time in Washington soon came to realize, unless you knew exactly where you were going, it was almost impossible to get there.

Jenn was walking down the hill, toward me. She waved.

I waved back.

"So, favor?" Jenn asked as she approached.

I pulled my notes out of my coat's inside pocket and handed them to her. "Can you read this? Then pass it on to Senator Rydel?" He would be chairing my father's confirmation hearings and he considered himself the president's archenemy. If anyone could put to use what I'd found out about my father, it was him.

"Should I read it now?"

"No! No. Just read it later. Back in your office. Then pass it on.

It's about my father's confirmation hearing. I'm hoping the senator can do something with it."

"*Before* the hearing? The hearing's on Monday."

"I know. But it's important. Please."

63

Less than two hours later, she called me. We agreed to meet again that night at Northside Social.

Northside Social was as close to a subversive, college-style coffee shop as Arlington had. It wasn't the county's fault. People in Arlington didn't subvert. They did things the Arlington Way. They published letters to the editor. They set up working groups and advisory boards. And they generously funded things like veteran support services, affordable housing nonprofits, and free health clinics.

The coffee shop itself was perched on an odd, triangular-shaped lot that projected into a busy intersection. I bought my coffee and joined Jenn outside. The warmth of the day still lingered. She was sitting at one of the square black metal tables. It was located along the sidewalk, well away from the other customers.

I took a seat in the chair opposite her. "So did you talk to Rydel? What did he say?"

She leaned toward me. "First, let me ask you, how did you find out about all of this?"

"I have my sources."

"Are they DoD? FBI?"

"Does it matter?"

She looked at me for a long moment and then sighed. "Fair enough."

"You did show it to him, right?"

"I read it. And I did show it to him." She dug around in her tote, fished out my papers. "He read it. He agrees the information is explosive. Game-changing. But he can't do anything with it." She offered them back to me.

I took them, trying to make sense of her words. He wasn't going to do anything? "Why not? He's the chairman of the Armed Services Committee. He's the one who'll run the hearing."

"I know, but—"

"Is it because he doesn't believe in exposing espionage to the American people?"

"It's more complicated than that, Georgie." Her face registered frustration.

He wasn't going to do anything at all? "Know what? I'm tired of complications. What about integrity? What about justice?"

"I know you're upset about Sean, okay? What I did was wrong. But what can I say? I'm sorry. I really am. But you can't exact revenge by expecting Senator Rydel to hold up a hearing based on allegations that—"

"Who *are* you?"

"Excuse me?"

"*Who are you?* My friend, Jennifer Baxter, used to be interested in justice. She used to be a rebel. She used to talk about honor and integrity and working for the good of all Americans."

"That Jennifer grew up and went to Capitol Hill. You know what they say: You go to Washington to do good. You stay to do better."

"You're seriously going to sit there and tell me this isn't important."

She shifted. Glanced down at the papers in my hand. Rubbed her lips together. "I know it's important. I know what it says about your dad. But in context—"

"Context is just an excuse. You know it is. So tell me: What's going on?"

She said nothing.

"Jenn?"

She looked out into the intersection, then turned around and scanned the street behind us that served as a parking lot. Then she leaned forward. "There are things going on. Things you don't know about."

"Yes!" I hit the papers with the back of my hand. "Things like this!"

"No, I—" When she started speaking again, I could barely hear her. "You know how my dad is. Mr. Goody Two-Shoes."

I nodded.

"He made a mistake. It was after my mother died."

"What kind of mistake?"

"It involved what turned out to be a female Russian agent and a long weekend in the Hamptons."

My gut clenched. That would mean that this was about more than just my father. Bigger than just a secretary of defense nomination. "Jenn—"

She took my hand in hers. "And ever since, *ever since*, it's been okay. It really has. The Russians have *never* asked him to come down on a certain side of any case." Her gaze bored into mine. Searching. Begging. "It's not like that. It's just . . ."

"It's just that every now and then, he's asked to do someone a favor."

Her shoulders relaxed. "Exactly."

"Are you a part of it too?"

She stiffened. "I just need you to know, it wasn't me hitting on Sean that afternoon, Georgie. It wasn't my idea, okay? *I* never would have done that."

"But you did. You did do it." I pulled my hand away. "Just another one of those favors?"

"You have to believe me. It's never my idea."

"What else have they asked you to do?"

"It would have been really nice if you had taken me up on the offer to stay with me. After your house exploded."

"That wasn't— You weren't—" What was she saying? "The Russians wanted me with you? Why?"

She said nothing.

"Because if I was with you, then they could—" It felt like my brain had frozen. I was trying to work through the possibilities, but my mind wouldn't cooperate. "If we had stayed with you, then—" What was it the Russians were after? "Sean. We would have walked right into their arms and Sean wouldn't have had any choice then but to appear." And then the game would have been over. The Russians would have won. How close I'd come to taking Jenn up on her offer after I'd heard Sean in the crawl space!

She didn't seem surprised that I was talking about him as if he were alive.

"That's the reason you came on to Sean. Who else have you had to—"

"It's not like that." She sat back and her face warped into an ugly, unrecognizable mask. "If I didn't do what they asked, then my father would be in jeopardy. Can't you understand?"

I understood completely.

"And he's never hurt anyone. He's never done anything against the law. Not really."

"Who else?"

A tear slid down her cheek. She glanced away toward the street again and headlights glistened on her cheek. "It's never what I've wanted."

"Jenn. Listen to me. This is not okay. The Russians aren't Americans. This is standard high school government class stuff. They don't get a say in our government. They don't get to do things like this. You have to make a choice. Either you're for us—you're for liberty and justice and democracy—or you're not."

"It's not like that."

"Who? Who else?"

Her gaze drifted back to me. "They asked . . . They wanted . . . Senator Rydel."

The chairman of the Armed Services Committee who had presidential ambitions. The chief justice of the Supreme Court. The soon-to-be-appointed secretary of defense, who also hoped to be president one day. My breath caught. It was civics class all over again. What were the three branches of government? Executive, legislative, and judicial.

The chief justice had been the tie-breaking vote on cases of campaign finance and internet oversight. The senator, chairing one of the most powerful Senate committees, had made decisions on weapons systems, nuclear energy, and national security. And my father? He would have access to top secret government programs and intelligence. He would be charged with the readiness of the military, developing strategies and priorities, and prosecuting war. Or not.

My father and Senator Rydel were already being talked about as presidential contenders. One for the Democrats, the other for the Republicans. To the Russians it wouldn't matter who won. They had both been compromised.

It was a once-in-a-generation achievement. The three branches of government, which were supposed to function as a check and a balance to each other, rendered impotent because they were working together on behalf of our enemy.

She reached out and clutched my hand. "I didn't know about *your* father. I didn't know—"

"But think about what you did know. You knew they had your father and you knew they had your senator."

"I know. I know. What should we do?"

"Did Rydel read this?"

"Yes."

"So he knows about *my* father." My universe was rearranging itself; I was seeing things through new eyes, from a new perspective. There were different rules in operation now. If Rydel held my father's treason over him, then he could effectively make my father do whatever he wanted. And what the senator wanted was what Russia wanted. It was double jeopardy. The Russians could pressure my father from one side. The senator could blackmail him from the other. "Does the senator know about *your* father?"

"Yes." The answer came quickly.

"Your father knows about the senator."

"No. I would never tell my father that I had to—"

I held up a hand. Of course she wouldn't. That meant her father was in the same situation as mine; he could be pressured from two sides. But only the Russians knew about Rydel. "So the senator lets the president's nominee be confirmed as the new secretary of defense, and the Russians get access to the highest level of American military secrets."

"And my senator can't say anything about it"—she eyed my papers—"because he's in the same position."

Right. She'd drawn a very clear picture. "Then can you give this to someone else?"

"How would Rydel *not* know where the information came from? And how would my father not be exposed?"

"At this point, does it really matter?"

"I'm sorry." She swiped at a tear with the bottom of her sleeve. "For all of it. I'm so tired." She closed her eyes for a moment. When she opened them I read weariness in their depths. "I'm in this as much as you are. As much as your father and mine. If this blows up, then I'm in prison, federal prison, for life. If they don't execute me first. And . . . Preston?" She swallowed a sob. "I'd lose everything."

She was asking the wrong person for sympathy. "You've got to do something. You have to. Don't tell me you won't."

"But my father—"

"Your father is one person in a democracy of millions. Are you really telling me you're going to protect him at the expense of everyone else? That you're going to put one person above the principles we all say we subscribe to? How can you put his needs and his rights above all the rest of ours? That's not what we do here."

"But your father's in the same position. Don't you want to protect him?"

"This is what makes us different: I think the rules apply to everyone."

"But he didn't mean—"

"This is kindergarten stuff. It doesn't matter what he *meant*. What matters is what he *did*."

"I used to believe that too, then I got stuck trying to make him look like what he was supposed to be. I told myself it was okay because he's making a difference. He has real influence and—"

"He's been compromised by the Russian government!"

She shook her head. "There's no way for me to get out of this now." She grabbed my arm. "Give it to someone else. Do whatever you need to. Just please, do me a favor. Don't link it to Rydel. Or me."

I shoved the papers into my purse. Then I pushed my chair away from the table and stood to leave.

64

She stood too.

I was beyond caring what Jenn did, but as I rounded the table and started down the sidewalk, she followed me. A jogger was coming up behind us; I picked up my pace, heading for a wider spot in the walkway so I could let him go around.

Jenn called to me, "Just— Wait up!"

As I turned back, she paused and pulled out a chair from an empty table, indicating I should sit. "Please. Let's not leave it this way."

The man coming up behind us veered out toward the curb and began to jog around me.

I took a step toward Jenn to give him more space.

Instead of passing, he pivoted toward us, pushing me away from the table with one arm.

I stumbled and fell.

With his other hand he drew a gun from his hoodie pocket. It had a silencer attached and—

Jenn's eyes widened.

Out in the intersection, a car honked.

I was scrambling to my feet.

Jenn stretched her arm out toward the man. "Hey—" But her protest was stilled, her confusion calmed by a small, bright-red star that bloomed between her eyes.

My strength left my legs and they folded, leaving me stranded on the pavement.

As Jenn slumped forward, the man caught her by the arms and shifted her weight. He pushed her backward, propping her up in the chair.

My heart had stopped when I saw his gun, but it slammed back into motion. "What are— You can't just—"

A sweep of headlights illuminated the scene. It glinted off the star-shaped spot on Jenn's forehead and animated the reflective stripes on her running shoes.

He turned to me and for one long moment looked me straight in the eyes before slowly pulling his hood up over his head and jogging on.

Jenn just sat there, eyes wide open as a thin trail of blood snaked down her nose, onto her cheek.

The people sitting over by the front door kept talking. Cars passed. Out in the parking lot, a door slammed.

I pushed to my feet. My mouth kept opening and closing, but it couldn't seem to collect any air. Then my last ounce of breath came out in a keening cry and I doubled over as if I'd been hit in the gut.

Someone grabbed my arm. "You okay?"

Turning my head, I saw Chris standing there, hunched beside me. I didn't know how to answer.

He braced an arm around my back and pulled me straight.

I tried to recoil, but I couldn't.

"Walk!" The word was a command.

Cars passed, headlights sweeping through the asymmetrical intersection and glancing off the aluminum sides of the Silver Diner. Up ahead to the left O'Sullivan's, an Irish tavern, glowed in the night.

I shook my head. "I can't—I can't—"

Chris's arm came around my shoulder like a vise. He leaned down to talk in my ear. "Just walk!"

"I can't—I can't just leave her there."

Clamping me against his side, he lifted me and strode forward, past the coffee shop, toward the darkness of the parking lot where the glare of headlights didn't reach. The tips of my toes dragged along the ground. "You don't want to be there when they find her."

"They?" I wriggled out of his grasp. "What about *you*?" I beat at him with my fists.

He dodged my blows. "I didn't do anything."

Tears coursed down my face as I continued yelling. "You've been watching me for months now! You've been here the whole time! Why did you let them kill her?"

Catching my wrists, he spun, turning me toward him. Then held me to his side. "Hey! Calm down." He spoke the words into my ear.

I bucked, trying to break his hold. "You're the FBI. You're supposed to get the bad guys."

"I'm trying. That was my fault. I should have identified him as a threat."

I slumped to the ground.

He let me. Then, glancing down at me, he reached inside his coat and pulled out a gun.

I shut my eyes and curled up into a ball, bringing my knees up to my chest.

After a long moment, he hooked his hand around my elbow. "Get up. We're okay. It wasn't them. I think they're gone."

65

As he walked me to my car, he kept his hand hidden away inside his jacket. I panicked for a moment when I didn't see my car. Then I realized I'd driven June's to the coffee shop. Chris took the fob from my hand, beeped the car open, and shoved me in. Then he jogged around and got into the seat next to mine. "Talk."

I had to be very careful in choosing my words. "I found out my husband was one of your assets."

He said nothing.

What more could I say? I couldn't tell him that Sean hadn't died. He might suspect, but did he know for certain? And I couldn't let him know what I knew about my father. I had to tell *someone*, but I still wasn't sure if the FBI and the DoD were part of the problem. It hadn't been the Russians who'd taken Sean's files or gotten him reassigned. "He was killed in a hit-and-run accident."

"Yes?"

"It just seems suspicious."

"By which you mean a deep-state conspiracy?"

I shrugged.

"We're not—" He paused. Took a deep breath. "The FBI does not assassinate US citizens. We might jail them, but we don't murder them. Why on—" Another deep breath. "Let's live in reality for just a minute. I'd like to help you, Georgie. I think your life may be in danger." He gave me a long look. "But I need you to trust me."

"I can't."

"I'm being honest with you."

No, he wasn't. There was no Keith. I suspected there had never been a Kristy either. "It's difficult for me to trust people."

"I understand. But you seem to have the black widow's touch.

288

You talk to people; they die. What I need you to do is start asking yourself why. If it's not me—and believe me, it's not us—then *who is it*? Seems like you're the only one with answers right now." He got out of the car and left me to drive home alone.

∞

I had to pull over at the first intersection, so I could throw up.

And again at Glebe.

Jenn was dead. We'd been friends since high school. Granted, she hadn't turned out to be as good a friend as I had thought, but no one deserved to be murdered. And what about Preston? What was going to happen to her son?

What about my son? I tried not to let myself think about Sam. I was doing my best to keep him safe.

My eyes darted, scanning the street behind me, as I tried to determine if anyone was following me.

Should I return to Jim and June's? I didn't want to take danger back with me.

Should I try to hide? Try to lose them?

From Glebe, I turned onto Wilson Boulevard. As I approached the coffee shop again, ambulances were coming down the road in the opposite direction, lights flashing. Once they passed, I turned, repeating the loop.

By my next pass, police cars had joined the ambulances.

The Russians were after Sean. But they hadn't been the ones who cost him his job. Someone in the DoD had helped my father do that. With Sean's help, the FBI had been trying to identify him. Or her.

But what about Jenn? Who would kill her? The Russians? But why? Her death had to mean something. It had to fit with the other pieces of my puzzle.

Sean had wanted to investigate what he'd found out; Jenn had wanted to keep what she'd known silent. She'd been doing exactly what the Russians wanted. So why had she ended up dead?

Something else didn't fit: I'd seen the man who killed her. He knew I'd seen him. He *let* me see him and still, I was alive. Our house had blown up and still, I was alive. That was twice I should have died but didn't.

Why?

If the intruder in my house had been intent on killing Sam and me, he would have blown up the house when he was certain we were in it. But I'd been thinking about that. Alice had been at the vet's that afternoon and the car had been in the shop. Sam and I were in the basement. It probably seemed as if we weren't home.

The only logical conclusion was that they *hadn't* been trying to kill us.

Sean was right. They were trying to send him a message.

That made sense; that served a purpose.

But I kept circling back to Jenn. How would killing her serve a similar purpose?

If killing her was supposed to send a message to someone, who would it be?

I was missing a piece of the puzzle. Sean and Jenn had to fit, but they didn't.

It was like the gap between quantum physics and general relativity. The first described the smallest particles in the universe while the second explained its vastness. The problem was, neither could describe the other. When you tried to join them together, the theories fell apart. We all kept hoping that someone, somewhere could figure out a way to bridge the two and reconcile both branches of physics. There had to be a solution. We just didn't know yet what it was.

The Russians were after Sean; the Russians killed Jenn.

There had to be a connection. I just had to find it.

I texted Sean at the next red light.

Jenn killed

Have new info

Everything worse than thought

When I was sure no one was following me, I made my way back to Jim and June's.

∞

In the netherworld between wakefulness and sleep that night, I had a profoundly clarifying thought. I might not have understood the reason for Jenn's death, but one thing I did know. The gunman had let me see his face because, for some reason that was not yet clear to me, it didn't matter that I saw him.

Because I saw him, I could identify him.

I'd gotten what I'd been wanting. I had a face. I knew who to watch for. The contours of his features were seared into my memory. I could easily help a police artist draw a sketch that would help determine his identity.

If he could be caught and questioned, he could be the proof that the stories I'd collected about my father, the reports of his treachery, were true. In fact, that killer was the only real proof we had. And yet that hadn't mattered. For some reason they didn't think leaving me alive posed any risk. If I could figure out why, then I could make sense of Jenn's murder. Until then I had to do my best to keep Sam and me safe.

66

I drove Sam to school the next morning instead of walk-ing. Things were getting too dangerous. As I drove, I tried to prepare him for what he might hear at school.

"Preston might not be in class for a while. In fact, he may be switching schools." Jenn's ex lived in the north part of the county in a neighborhood with a different elementary school.

"Will he be at the concert tonight?"

"I don't think so."

"Why?"

"His . . . um . . . Miss Jenn died last night." I shot him a glance through the rearview mirror.

He was chewing on the string of his hoodie. "Like Daddy?"

"Right. Like Daddy."

"Did she get hit?"

"She did. Not by a car, though."

"By a ball?"

A ball? "No." Well, kind of. A small metal one.

"Because that's why we can't throw balls in PE. We might hit someone."

"She did get hit by something, sweetie." I realized my hands were gripping the steering wheel, my knuckles turning white. I flexed them, trying not to remember the way that bullet hole had bloomed on her forehead.

"Is she going into the hole?"

"She's going into the ground. She's going to be buried. And Preston is going to be really sad."

"Yeah." He went back to chewing on the string.

We pulled into the school parking lot and I drove all the way down to the end to find a spot.

I got out. Did a check of the area immediately around us. No one on the playground. No one suspicious in any of the vehicles immediately surrounding ours. The apartments that abutted the school property? It was hard to tell. There were too many windows. As I helped Sam out of the car, I shielded him with my body.

He grabbed my hand as we walked down the sidewalk. "Maybe Preston could borrow Alice for a while."

"Alice? Why?"

"She doesn't mind when you cry. And when you lie down next to her, she gives you a hug."

The last time I'd been in the classroom was for Bring a Parent to School Day. Back then the featured motifs had been apples and pencils and rulers. Now it was pumpkins and scarecrows and ghosts.

Bring a Parent to School Day!

I tugged Sam back as he went to put his things in his cubby. "Hey, do you remember Bring a Parent to School Day?"

"Yeah."

"Do you remember whose dad spoke after me? The one who brought you guys the comics and bookmarks?"

"Yeah."

"Whose dad was it?"

"Emma's dad."

"Is Emma here yet?"

He glanced around. "No. Yes!" He pointed to the door. "There she is."

There were several mothers walking into the classroom with their daughters at that point. I had Sam go over with me to make sure I talked to the right mother.

I introduced myself. "Are you coming to the concert tonight? I was wondering if I could meet up with your husband to discuss an article for his paper. I think I have a story he'd like."

We arranged to meet later that evening.

I kissed Sam on the cheek as I left. Told myself that he was probably safer inside the school than he was with me.

Sam whispered in my ear as I hugged him good-bye. "Grandpa and Grandma are coming!"

"Where? To what?"

"The concert."

"Tonight?"

He nodded.

"What?!" They couldn't come to the concert. Not when I was planning to pass information on my father to a journalist! "Why? How do they know about the concert?"

"I called them."

"How?"

"Grandma gave me their phone number. I know it by heart!" He proceeded to recite it.

"You called them? By yourself?"

He nodded. "Miss June helped me. They want to hear me sing."

I doubted it. No one in their right mind wanted to sit in a school gym for two hours and listen to a bunch of kids sing. "That's super nice of them."

On the way back up the hill, Sean texted me.

I'm thinking of getting back in touch with old friends

I took it to mean he wanted to go to the FBI. But I hadn't worked everything out yet. I texted back.

What if they aren't very friendly?
Not a good idea

I called my mother as soon as I got back to June and Jim's. "You guys don't have to come tonight. It was nice of you to offer, but—"

"We can't wait!"

"Really, Mom, that would definitely be above and beyond." And I didn't want my father anywhere near my son.

"Sam wants us to. I wouldn't dream of disappointing him."

"But what about the hearing? I'm sure Dad has a million things to—"

"You know your father. Everything that had to be done already is. So we'll be there tonight with bells on. We'll pick you up."

"How about we just meet you there?"

67

We ate dinner with June and Jim. After that, we met my parents at the school. We dropped Sam off with his teacher and then I led them to the gym where chairs had been set up in front of the stage. It smelled like fresh paint and basketballs. Footsteps squeaked as parents walked across the wood floors. Conversations echoed off the concrete walls and high ceilings.

I settled them in chairs as close to the front as I could find. Then I excused myself and went in search of Emma's mom. I found her sitting on one of the aisles toward the middle, holding a tablet up in the direction of the stage. She smiled as she saw me. Nodded at the tablet. "Just getting it ready to record."

The man I recognized as the journalist from Bring a Parent to School Day was sitting next to her, holding a bouquet of flowers.

She elbowed him. "This is Georgia. She's Sam's mom."

He extended a hand. "I remember. From career day." He had an open, genial face with intelligent eyes. "Hello, Sam's Mom."

I shook his hand. "Is there somewhere we can talk?"

He glanced at his watch. "If we make it fast. If I don't hear Emma sing, well, what's the point of going through the trouble of finding a parking spot?" We ducked out of the gym into the hallway. "My wife said you had a story for me?"

"I'm hoping I do." I pulled my notes from my purse. "If you wouldn't mind, can you read this? And then we can talk?"

He pulled a pair of reading glasses from the inside pocket of his coat. It didn't take him long. When he was finished, he refolded the papers and sent me a look over the top of his glasses. "If this is true . . ."

I let his question hang in the air for a moment before I answered.

296

"It is. All of it. And I would like to give it to you. I know there's no smoking gun or solid proof—"

"No, and—"

"—but I've lived in this town long enough to know that lots of people know things. And journalists hear things. Things like that"—I eyed the papers he was holding—"are never really secret. Someone knows. And sometimes all it requires to put a big story together is taking what you've heard and adding what someone like me knows and pretty soon, people are willing to talk and—"

He held up a hand. "Listen. I'm sure you're hoping for a big readership for this—before the hearing, right?"

I nodded.

"I have to tell you that's impossible. Not with the timeframe involved. The fact-checking alone could take—"

"But it's true. All of it is true."

"How do you know?"

"Because—" Because I'd lived it. And because my dead husband had told me so. And so had other people who had died because of it. "I checked as much of it as I could. And my father is General Slater."

"Your father!" He handed me back the papers as if he couldn't get rid of them fast enough. "I don't do family feuds. You might want to try one of the television newsmagazine formats instead. It would get great ratings."

"This isn't a feud. And I don't care about ratings. This is a matter of national security. It's a failure at multiple levels of the federal government. If this story doesn't get told, then—"

"Thing is, I can't just take your word for it. And your father is . . . Right now? After all the government, all the DoD scandals we've had? He's indestructible. And even if he wasn't, I get the sense that people have had enough. They're tired of watching a circus. They want someone to believe in. They've picked him. He's it."

"But—"

"And setting aside all of that, I would have to interview these people you've referenced. I would have to trace your story all the way back to the first Gulf War. Because with allegations like these, I'd be called up to the Hill. There would be congressional inquiries, and special committees would be formed. This would shake the administration. This one and the last four." He pointed to the papers in my hand. "That would be the next five years of my life. And if I don't do it right, then I put my paper, and myself, in legal jeopardy. So while I would love to take this story, and while I really hope you do find someone to publish it, I can't do it justice in time for the hearing. And my editor wouldn't let me."

"It's a story of national importance."

"It has Pulitzer all over it. If you'd given me a couple months' lead time?" He shrugged. "Stories of national importance are—" He broke off to bark a bitter laugh. "They're important enough that they have to be done the right way. I hope you understand."

68

My parents said they'd drive us home, but I wasn't about to let my father drive us anywhere. I begged off, telling them a walk would do us good. I figured there would be enough people walking back through the neighborhood that we would be safe.

My mother hugged me close before she let us go. My father bent down and gave Sam a high five. Sam asked for one "up high." He jumped several times to reach it, then kept on jumping even after he'd made it.

I let him keep at it so he could get out some of his pent-up energy.

My father leaned close to me. "Hey, I ordered a new train thing for Sam."

"Dad, you didn't—"

"For Halloween. Think you might have time to pick it up tomorrow at work?"

I hadn't told them I'd been fired, so I didn't have any excuse not to. "No problem." One thing he'd done right through the years: cultivate a relationship with his grandson. I wasn't looking forward to having to explain to Sam one day what his grandfather had done.

"Thanks, Peach."

Sam pestered me all the way home about when we could start trick-or-treating this weekend and what I would wear as a costume. He saved his biggest salvo for when we got back to Jim and June's.

"Mr. Jim! I was really good tonight. And Daddy said I can go to Gilman Street this year for trick-or-treating."

"Wow. Gilman Street! Put it here, kid." He held out his closed fist for Jim to bump. "If you get any Milk Duds, save them for me, huh?"

"Sure thing, Mr. Jim."

Gilman Street? Really? "I don't know, Sam. I think maybe—"

"That's what Dad said. I'm six."

"I know, but—"

"Dad said. He promised. He said when I was six."

"Hey. You know that church down the street? I think they're having a party that night. We could go there instead. I bet they'll have lots of candy."

Tears instantly welled up in his eyes. "But Daddy said—he *said*!"

We were coming perilously close to a mutiny. "I just don't know if it's safe." Strolling around outside in the dark? With Russians on the loose?

But then, I could make a reasonable argument that Halloween on Gilman Street might be safer than walking around outside any other night of the year. And what would be the alternative? Passing out treats with Jim and June? That raised all sorts of nightmares about costumed Bad Guys forcing their way into the house and doing terrible things to all of us.

"We come home when I say so, okay?"

He nodded.

"I mean it."

"I promise, Mommy."

"And you're holding my hand the entire time."

I texted Sean after Sam fell asleep.

> We need to talk
> See you soon?

He answered about half an hour later.

> I'll be on ice tomorrow
> Sounds like offense needs defense
> See you there

Offense. Defense.

It sounded like a sports reference. Thing is, I wasn't a sports fan. I'd always kept Sean company, though, on the couch at night when he'd watch his games. He only followed two sports: football and hockey. But hockey was his favorite. He used to take Sam to the rink sometimes when the Capitals, the town's NHL franchise, were practicing. They used one of the rinks at the Iceplex, where Sam skated.

Ice rink.

I'd figured it out.

I logged on to June's computer and googled the rink's website to access their events schedule. The Caps were practicing at the rink the next morning at ten thirty.

Bingo.

The next morning I went to the Iceplex, driving up seven stories to the roof of the parking garage. In a display of innovative community development of the kind prized by Arlington, it had been built right there on top. I walked in through the glass entrance, then slipped through the lobby and into the bleachers where I worked my way up and over a few rows. There were Caps fans and then there were *Caps fans.* Only the truly devoted would be at a rink midmorning on a Thursday to watch the team practice.

The players were doing some sort of shooting drill.

When they missed the net, pucks thwacked against the sideboards.

I flinched every time it happened.

Once, when one of the pucks hit the glass in front of the bleachers, I even threw up an arm. I couldn't help myself.

It was *cold.* As the players performed drills, I sat there on the metal bench watching. My feet went numb by degrees. So did my butt. I wished I'd brought a hat.

A man sat down next to me.

It wasn't Sean.

I slid down the bench a bit and watched for a while longer. When I started shivering, I decided to move inside to the heated mezzanine and watch from there. I took a seat on one of the benches that looked down on the rink.

One of the custodians was cleaning the windows. I moved my feet aside so he could pass. When he didn't I looked up, past the uniform, to see Sean.

"You have to stop showing up like this. It scares me."

"How else am I going to meet up with you?"

He had a point.

"No one ever looks at people who do the jobs they don't want to do. As long as I wear the right color, have the right props, I blend in and no one really sees me." He squirted some cleaner on the window and wiped it off with a cloth. "Tell me about Jenn."

"I was with her when she was killed."

He paused. Turned toward me. "What?"

"I'd put together my notes and given them to her so she could give them to Senator Rydel. I was hoping he could stop the confirmation hearing."

"And?"

"It's like I said. Worse than we realized." As he went back to work on the window, I told him what Jenn had told me, about both her father and her senator being compromised by the Russians.

"Then your father's part of a trifecta."

"But I don't think he knows about Jenn's father. Or her senator."

"This is big."

"We were leaving when they killed Jenn." I had to force myself to concentrate on the words I was saying. That way I couldn't dwell on the image in my mind. "She was shot."

"But they didn't get you."

"They didn't want to. They could have. The killer gave me a good, long look at his face. But then he left. They've been targeting those names on your list. They've been killing the people I talked to."

He sent me a glance beneath his brow and gave up on the window, setting the cleaner down on the ledge.

"They killed Paul Conway before I even had the chance to talk to him."

"They're trying to protect your father. And Jenn? That was a warning to me." He stuffed the cleaning cloth into his pocket. "I want you to take Sam and leave. Get out of town."

"I can't. We're so close. We've figured it out. It's just that I can't get anyone to take the story. If I could just find actual proof."

"The hearing is on Monday."

It's not as if I needed a reminder. "I know. If we just had proof, then I think it would be an easier sell. But I haven't found anyone who actually saw my father and a Russian together in an incriminating way. There was never anyone who caught them passing information or doing anything illegal. And yet people are getting killed to hide the connection. It's all there."

He was facing the window. Anyone watching us would have thought that his attention had been caught by the hockey practice. "Those Russians your father came across in Iraq couldn't have been the only ones. They had to have someone with the government in Baghdad, even if they weren't representing the official Russian position. They wouldn't have sent soldiers to fight without the Iraqis' knowledge. So maybe we need to come at it from a different angle, a different side. If we get proof that the Russians were there in the desert, then maybe someone rethinks what they thought they saw. Or maybe your father comes clean. Let me see what I can dig up."

"In three days?"

"It's not like the confirmation hearing is a firm deadline. Once the hearing's over, they'll still have to vote to confirm him. That won't be scheduled until afterward."

"Even then, it might not be long enough."

"It's all the time we have."

69

I drove down to the Crystal City Mall to pick up Sam's train after I left the rink.

We had to figure it out. If we didn't, the Russians would have the United States by the throat, and my husband would be one step closer to actual death.

While Sean dug through the past, I concentrated on the present.

My father still had to be communicating with the Russians. How could he not be in the run-up to the hearings? He was just days away from being installed at one of the highest ranks of federal government.

But how were they doing it?

The conversations of Russian nationals were routinely tapped. After the government controversies of previous years, everyone knew that. And we weren't in some cheesy spy movie where the characters wore black trench coats and talked over the phone in code.

They couldn't be using technology to pass information, could they? An anonymous Facebook account? Odd messages on Twitter? I thought about it as I waited at a light.

I had to assume they weren't. Russian digital movements could always be subject to hacking or tracking. But they still had to be coordinating. It couldn't be a face-to-face exchange. If anyone had any suspicions, they'd put a tail on a Russian, wouldn't they? And they'd notice whenever my father met with him. What they could use was a dead drop, leaving information for each other in a place to which both had access.

But then how would they signal each other to check it?

There had to be some bridge between my father and the Russians that I wasn't seeing.

I tried to flip the options, rotate the angles.

Something connected them to each other. Something had to connect them.

Something or some*one*.

My mother?

I discarded the thought as soon as it formed. My mother was too close to my father. Too obvious. If there was a person, it would have to be someone who knew them both. Someone who could receive a message and pass it on without suspicion.

One of my father's old aides-de-camp? One of his deputies?

No. They'd changed every couple of years and that would have been too risky. Each person drawn into the network would have meant more chances for the story to leak. For sure the FBI, the CIA, the DoD would have noticed if my father talked to a foreigner on a regular basis. And my father would have had to report that person on his security-clearance applications.

If it was a person, it had to be someone else. Someone different. Someone outside that world. Someone they could both contact, separately, without suspicion. It would have to be someone doing a job like Sean was doing. Someone unremarkable.

Dry cleaner. Plumber. Restaurant or hotel staff.

That seemed too cumbersome. And too geographically dependent.

I drove down the ramp into the parking garage, took a ticket, circled as I looked for a spot close to the elevator. Eventually I gave up and just pulled into a spot back where I'd first come down. As I sat there, thinking through the options, I raked back my hair, grabbing a fistful. Why couldn't I see it? The link had to exist. It had to.

Mr. Hoffman was busy with another customer, so I looked around while I waited. It was kind of funny that my dad had never pushed any army toys on Sam. He'd never bought him green men or guns of any kind. Which I appreciated. I had honestly never known how much my father loved trains. Not until Sam had come along. Maybe it was because I was a girl.

The customer left.

Mr. Hoffman greeted me. "You are here for the train. It's in the back. I'll get it."

I hadn't told him about the house. I didn't want him to worry more about us than he already did. I figured I had a few more weeks, until Thanksgiving, to figure out how to tell him.

He soon returned with it. "Your father has very good taste in trains." He put it into a bag for me to carry.

"I think Sam would agree. I'll let him know."

I'd meant to put the bag aside so that my father could give it to Sam, but I forgot.

Before I could stop him, Sam tore into it when he came home from school. It didn't take long before he was on his knees on the floor, fitting it into the track he'd built in the corner of Jim and June's living room.

I sat down beside him and asked him about his day. As he played, he told me about lunch and recess, which seemed to be his two favorite subjects. He was trying to put together a new crane, but he didn't seem very happy. He took one of the parts and hit the carpet with it once. Twice. Then he offered it to me.

"It's broken."

"What do you mean, it's broken?"

He shook it.

Something rattled.

"Grandpa always fixes them for me."

Always? "Do they usually break?" Those trains and playsets didn't come cheap. And European toys were supposed to be better made than most.

He'd set down the part and was absorbed in pushing a train around the track.

"Sam? Do they break a lot?"

"Yeah."

"Really?"

"What?"

Never mind. "Here." I held out my hand. "Let me see if I can find Mr. Jim's tools."

∞

Jim offered to do it for me, but they'd done so much for us. Too much for us. He finally showed me where his toolbox was and left me to it.

I shook the part. Whatever had come loose was inside. How to get to it was a bit of a mystery. It looked to be solid wood. I tapped at it with the handle of a screwdriver until I identified a hollow area. But it still took some looking to find a way to access it. There was an opening at the bottom about half an inch wide. It had been covered with a wooden plug. I pried it up with the screwdriver and then I tipped it upside down and shook it.

A thumb drive fell out into my palm.

70

Grandpa always fixes them for me. Sam's words echoed in my head.

Sam's toys were always "broken"; my father always "fixed" them.

That bridge between my father and the Russians?

Was it *me*?

The truth hit me with the force of a fist.

Was it—could it be—me?

I tried to view the problem analytically. Tried to insert myself—scientifically, objectively—into the equation. But even as I tried, I knew I couldn't really do it. It was a physics problem as much as it was a problem of perspective. The very act of measuring or even just observing something changed its very reality. Inserting myself into an equation would change it.

But what if I had always *been* a part of the equation?

I reined in my thoughts, stopping them from galloping away in panic and fury. I had already assumed the bridge between my father and his handler was a person. I had known the communication had to have been going on for years. One of them would have to contact someone, leave that person with some piece of information, and then that person—the intermediary—would pass it on to the other.

When had I started buying toys from Mr. Hoffman's? It was four years ago. Sam had been two. My father hadn't been around very often—he was working a job out of California—and Sean had been deployed with his reserve unit. I'd asked my father where he'd gotten the toys and he'd told me.

My father and Mr. Hoffman. That was the network.

I was the link to Mr. Hoffman. At least in one direction. I still didn't know how my father got information back to him. But that's why it hadn't mattered that I had seen Jenn's killer. I was one of them just as much as my father was. Just as much as the killer was.

The realization shattered my world—past, present, and future.

That bridge was me. More than me. It was my son too.

I put a hand to the floor and lowered myself to my knees.

Me.

I'd never known my father liked trains because the truth was, he didn't. Not especially. He'd just needed a way to get information from his contact. He'd used me, used his grandson too, as pawns in his scheme. What could be more innocent than buying a toy for a little boy? And those trains? They were perfect. The iterations of playset add-ons were infinite. And they were all made of solid wood that could easily be drilled to make a hiding place just the right size for a thumb drive.

My father and Mr. Hoffman.

And me.

There really were parallel universes. I'd been living in one. It was a place where enemies were friends and lies were the truth.

How many times had my father told me he'd ordered a new train set for Sam and wondered if I could pick it up for him so it would be there when he came to visit? I remembered all the times I'd brought thumb drives back to my house at his request.

My father had sucked me into his black hole right along with him.

No one really knows what happens inside a black hole. Its gravitational force pulls in everything without discrimination. Escape is impossible. Surrender is inexorable.

In that moment everything I was, everything I'd had, all of it disappeared into the vortex of my father's betrayal.

It had swallowed me whole.

On automatic pilot, I helped June with dinner. Like a robot, I moved through space and time, but I found myself curiously detached from reality.

My father was a traitor.

I was his accomplice.

That meant I was a traitor.

No wonder Jenn's assassin hadn't cared about me seeing him. He had nothing to fear from me. If I told anyone about him, tried to identify him, the trail of investigation would eventually lead to me. In the eyes of the law, I was just as guilty as he was.

It was a disorienting feeling, to know that you were absolutely Other. That you were completely different than you'd always thought you were. I felt like I was trapped in a body that was not my own.

After Sam was asleep I went for a drive. I ended up at Sean's restaurant. Once there, I parked, got out, and waited in the alley, hoping my husband would eventually appear.

Twenty, thirty, forty minutes later, once the cold had driven my hands deep into my pockets, he finally did.

The door scraped open. His form appeared on the stoop.

"Sean." I could hardly say his name without my voice breaking.

He squinted into the night. "Georgie?"

I moved into the light.

He nodded toward the shadows from which I'd emerged and I retreated back into the dark, where he joined me.

Looking down into my eyes, he put a hand to my cheek and smoothed back a lock of hair that had escaped my ponytail. "What happened?"

I reached out and grabbed hold of him, pulling him close, pressing my cheek to his jaw. "I need to know that you know me." I released him, raking my hands through his hair, and met his lips with mine.

He tried to step back. "Georgie, look, I don't think—"

But I didn't want to think anymore. I let my hands drop to his shoulders. From his shoulders, down his arms, to his belt loops.

His hands seized mine.

"Please." I turned my hands, meeting his palm to palm. I threaded my fingers through his. "Sean." I needed him to love me. No matter who I was, no matter what I'd done.

He took one last, long look at me and then gave in.

In a crush of lips and bodies, my arms around his neck, his weight pinning me to the wall, I found my redemption. But even as we rediscovered a long-dormant rhythm, as I arched against the wall, I wept. I wept without dignity, without restraint. And as we buried ourselves in each other, I let the old Georgie go. I would never be that person again.

71

The next morning I walked Sam to school. He wasn't in any mortal danger. And neither was I. He skipped along beside me in his Super Sam cape, oblivious to the world having turned inside out. He couldn't wait for his class Halloween party.

Chris was there with his Maltipoo just the same as always; he must have still been assigned to me. I hadn't told him I knew he didn't have a son.

But I'd been hoping to see him. I unfastened Alice's leash, took a deep breath, and then made my move. "I want to turn myself in."

He blinked. "What?" He took me by the elbow and moved us away from the other parents. "Turn yourself in for what?"

"Espionage."

He dropped my elbow. Stepped back, one hand up, fingers splayed. "I am not taking you in."

"I want to turn myself in for esp—"

"*Shut. Up.* As your friend, I'm telling you to shut up."

"But—"

"*Right now.*"

"But—"

"I'm going to pretend I didn't hear you, okay?"

"But I—"

"We haven't been watching you. I mean, we have, but not— You're not the one we're after. So just—" He put his hand up again. A warning. Then he glanced down the street, put his arm through mine, and dragged Alice and me off down the road. "Let's just turn this into a nice, normal walk, okay?"

"I am in this up to my ears. Over my ears." I tried to swallow the fear that had lodged itself in my throat. "Over my head. And I can prove it. I want to turn myself in so you can wire me."

∞

I spent the day in DC with Chris as I was questioned by the FBI. I gave them the thumb drive, then I sketched out the broad outline of my father's career and associations with the Russians. I explained Mr. Hoffman's role in it. I told of finding Sean's notes after he'd died and following up with the names he'd left.

I gave them the names of the men the Russians had killed.

I did *not* tell them I knew Sean wasn't dead. If things somehow went wrong for me, I wanted to keep him out there, free of surveillance, and able to care for Sam. I also didn't tell them about Jenn's dad or Senator Rydel. One thing at a time. The most immediate goal was stopping my father's confirmation hearing.

In exchange for cooperating with the FBI's investigation and providing names and details, they agreed to give me immunity from prosecution. That didn't mean, however, that I wouldn't have to testify about what I'd discovered. I agreed to it all. I agreed to everything.

I asked the agent who was questioning me, "Can you tell me— how long have you known about my father?"

"First learned of it from your husband. But the Department of Defense took it."

I wasn't supposed to know. "Then why haven't they stopped this before now?"

"It's complicated."

He didn't know the half of it.

"Your husband didn't trust them, so he came to us with the story."

"And you what? Sat on it?"

Chris was in the chair beside me. He put a hand on my arm. "We've been trying to corroborate it. You have to have grounds to arrest someone. You have to make sure a crime's actually been committed."

"Were you going to let my father be confirmed?"

He said nothing.

"You were?"

They said nothing.

"So why have you been watching *me*?"

They exchanged a glance. Chris answered me. "Because things weren't adding up." Which I interpreted to mean that, once again, Sean had been right. They suspected he wasn't really dead. "And we didn't have enough to put it together until now, okay? At this point all of this is still conjecture. But with you agreeing to be wired . . ." He left the possibilities open.

The other agent was sitting across from me. "You ready?"

I nodded.

"Here's the plan."

72

My parents came over that evening. Sam immediately took my father's hand and dragged him over toward the trains. My mother started talking about Halloween. "We just stopped by to confirm the plan for tomorrow night."

"Plan? For tomorrow?" What plan?

"Georgia Ann—it's Halloween! You can't tell me you've forgotten. So what time should we come over? For trick-or-treating?"

My father was surreptitiously picking up pieces of the new playset and shaking them.

"Georgia Ann?"

"Oh. Right! Um." I focused my attention back on her. "You guys don't need to come. We're not really going far."

"But I want to take pictures. And we thought we could take Sam to Fort Myer."

"Fort Myer?" I wasn't letting my father take Sam anywhere.

"Peach?" My father was trying to get my attention. He already had it. "Do you have the instructions that came with the set?"

I shook my head. "Sam tore into the box as soon as he found it. I threw it out. Sorry."

"I think there's a part missing."

My mother was still talking. "Military kids trick-or-treat too. Fort Myer can't be nearly as crowded. And your father has some friends on post there."

"Sounds like a great idea. Maybe we can do it next year."

My father stood up. "I'm going to take this set back to Hoffman's. There's something missing."

"But, Grandpa!"

He put his hand on Sam's head. "Don't worry, buddy. I'll bring it all back."

316

"Hey—Dad."

He turned.

"I wanted to talk to you about something." I was hoping to take him aside and confront him. They'd wired me. If I could get him to admit to what he'd been doing, then they'd have the proof we needed.

But he glanced at his watch. "Can it wait? We've got to get back downtown. We're meeting someone." He didn't wait for an answer. He handed my mother her purse and they left.

∞

Chris came by Jim and June's midmorning on Saturday. "You were right. We picked up Hoffman. He was in possession of classified information."

"Has he told you anything yet?"

"No."

"Did you get my father?"

He shook his head. "Have you heard from him?"

"Not today."

"We have agents waiting. They can take him in when he shows up."

"So what do I do?"

"You do what you planned. Wear the wire just in case. Go out trick-or-treating. I'll follow you and I'll get someone else assigned to you too."

"What if you lose me?"

"We won't lose you. Just take your phone with you. Keep it on. We'll track it."

"I don't know. Is this really a good idea?"

"There's no reason to skip going out. We have Hoffman. We'll bring in your father when he gets back to the hotel. And then it will all be over."

"But there's got to be more of them than just Hoffman. They knocked Sam down at the rink. They ransacked the house. And then they blew it up. Hoffman didn't do all of that. I don't think he did any of it." But the fact that he might have ordered it done? That chilled me. A man whom I'd considered a dear, sweet person—a friend even—had placed my family in danger.

"He's in custody now. We think we've identified the operatives. At this point they wouldn't dare do anything that might connect themselves to him."

∞

If I had thought it would help to tell Sam we were skipping Halloween, I would have, but what Chris said made sense. I chalked up my reluctance to residual uneasiness from being constantly on edge for the past few weeks. I tried to talk myself into being excited about Gilman. It was almost working until June dug up some costumes for Alice and me.

"We had these way back in the day." She beamed as she held them up.

Jim walked past.

She turned toward him. "Remember these?"

"Hey. Yeah. Sure! Underdog. Geez. How long ago was that on TV?"

"Wasn't *that* long ago. And look: Wonder Woman." She said it with a smile.

"Would you look at that! *That* one, I remember." He said it with a gleam in his eye.

Sam thought the costumes were terrific. He knelt and coaxed Alice into the red sweater with its blue cape.

"We used to have a Doberman." Jim winked in my direction as he helped Sam.

"So what do you think?" June asked the question with a raised brow as she held up the costume for me.

I was thinking that there was no way my wire wouldn't show

if I wore that costume. It was a Wonder Woman outfit from the Lynda Carter era. The blue hot pants had white stars on them. The top was a plastic breastplate piece that looked like it was molded to fit a Barbie doll. There were even gold-colored wristbands. "I don't think it will fit. But that's okay. I was just planning to go as I am."

June turned the costume around with a flourish. "It's adjustable. Look!" She pointed out the ties at the back of the breastplate.

"I have no idea what I'd wear underneath."

"But if you wear it you can do the pose!" She put her hands to her hips. "Remember?"

"I really don't think it will fit."

"But, Mo-om!" Sam wailed the word. "I'm Super Sam. You *have* to be Wonder Woman. You're my mom."

If he only knew how wonderful I'd turned out *not* to be. "I can't be Wonder Woman. I have to be Super Sam's Mom. I'll wear a sign that says SSM. You can help me make it." I held my breath, hoping that would sound like a good idea.

His face went stormy for a moment and then it cleared. "And you can walk Underdog just like you walk Alice!"

"Yes. Right!" Thank goodness he'd bought it.

73

It didn't take long that evening to visit our immediate neighbors. Sam, holding on to the plastic handle of the pumpkin June had bought for him, ran back and forth so that his Super Sam cape flew out behind him. I could tell he'd been practicing. A lot.

The blackened shell of our house was a blot on an otherwise picture-perfect block. The street past ours was mostly dark and the one after that too. I hurried us past them. It was only after we crossed the neighborhood's main artery that the party really started.

We heard a pulsing bass from three blocks away and could see flashes of light now and then above roofs as we walked. We hit the couple of houses that had lights on, then headed toward the end of the block where police had been posted. Joining the flow of people, we entered the throngs. I'd never been to Gilman Street on Halloween, but I'd heard about it.

Gilman Street was legendary.

If you lived there, you had to decorate. And not with cornstalks and harvest-colored ribbons. One of the houses turned its front lawn into a cemetery, complete with a vintage hearse and a skeleton on a motorcycle. Another house put up a false front shaped like the prow of a ship and outfitted it with pirate-themed decorations. The owners of a third house carved several dozen pumpkins and made a candle-lit, glowing arch out of them.

In a region populated by type A personalities, if you couldn't keep up with hearses and skeletons, then it was just better to buy somewhere else.

It was to Gilman that Sam insisted he wanted to go. Breathing a prayer that Chris was right, that we weren't in any danger, I grabbed hold of Sam's hand with my superglue grip.

At least I knew the FBI was following me. And my phone was stashed away at the bottom of Sam's pumpkin. If anything happened, it was more important that Sam stay safe than me.

As we joined the line of kids and parents moving at a snail's pace down the sidewalk, an unearthly shriek echoed through the night.

Sam's eyes widened. "Look!"

He was pointing to the roof of a house. A woman with long, stringy hair and a gown made of ghostly rags was wailing. Her eyes were ringed with dark circles. Her teeth had been blacked out.

"That's so cool." Sam breathed the words.

It was hideous.

"Do you think I can stand on the roof when I get big?"

"No."

Disappointment dimmed the glow in his eyes. "Why not?"

"There's a law."

He seemed satisfied with that answer. And as far as he knew, there were also laws about riding skateboards, staying up past nine p.m. on a school night, and stepping on worms that had stranded themselves on sidewalks.

Gilman Street probably was one of the safest places we could have been that night. We were surrounded by people. There were policemen posted at every block. And I'd brought Alice too. But still, anxious to return to Jim and June's, I tried to keep Sam moving down the sidewalk.

One of the houses on the block had set up a haunted house in their front yard.

"I want to do it!" Sam was hopping with excitement and there was a manic gleam in his eyes. I shouldn't have let him start sampling the treats he'd been collecting.

I tightened my grip on his hand. "No."

It seemed fairly innocuous. It had been set up in one of those long, narrow tents used at outdoor markets. There were multiple windows on both sides, which gave tantalizing glimpses of purple lights and bloody handprints. Eerie music wafted from the tent, and somewhere a fog machine was billowing vast amounts of creepiness.

"Can I go alone?"

"Absolutely not." I tried to keep walking.

He dug his heels into the sidewalk. "Please, Mom!"

"No." There was no way I was letting go of him.

"Everyone is going by themselves."

He had a point. But it was a flimsy one: nobody else had me as their mother.

"Please, Mom! I promise I won't be scared."

"I already said no."

We watched a pair of dinosaurs come out. Several Disney princesses. A pirate and a mummy ran past. A father in a Dracula cape strolled by.

Alice yanked on the leash.

I yanked right back.

A miniature Michelin Man, encased in rings of long white balloons, tottered along beside his mother.

Sam tugged on my hand. When I looked down at him, he was waving at someone.

I followed his gaze.

"Look, Mom! Granddad!"

74

What! Where?

Sam was jumping up and down, hand extended toward the Dracula that had passed us earlier.

He bent down toward Sam with a flourish of his cape and—

"No! Sam!" I tried to pull him away, tried to hide him behind me, but my father already had a grip on his other hand.

He looked at me over Sam's head. "You're hard to find, Peach." He wasn't smiling. Beneath his stage makeup taut lines stretched between his brow. His eyes swept the street ahead as he pulled us away toward a house on the other side of the street.

I tried to calm my fear. "We were just headed home. Do you want to come back with us? June said she'd have cupcakes waiting." Chris was out there somewhere. He said he would be following me. If we turned around, then it might bring us closer to him. Once he saw my father, he could arrest him and it would all be over.

He gestured with his chin toward the driveway. "How would you like to visit a secret hideout, Sam?"

He glanced up at me. "Can Mom and Alice come too?"

I gripped his hand even tighter. "You're not going anywhere without me, sweetie." Where was Chris? "But I really think we should go home, Dad. Sam's getting tired."

"No, I'm not!"

My father put his arm around my shoulders, enveloping me with his cape, as we skirted a candy line and blended with the shadows. He maneuvered us down the driveway and into the backyard. "There's a secret path to get there too. This way."

I didn't want to go anywhere with him. But the FBI was tracking my phone and they had me wired. Chris was on my tail. Only a minute more? Or maybe two?

At the oakleaf hydrangeas that seemed to delineate the property line, my father paused. "No need for a phone where we're going, Peach."

"I don't know what you're—"

"Give me your phone."

Considering the way he'd co-opted me into his spy network without asking, I decided not to press him. I dug it out from underneath Sam's candy and handed it to him.

He tossed it into one of the bushes.

We skulked across the next backyard, then down another driveway, leaving Halloween behind us.

The FBI had lost the ability to geo-track my phone, but I was still wired. "Where are you taking us?"

He shot a look at me over his shoulder and then reached back to grab me by the elbow. "Just keep up." Shedding the noise and the crowds, we stepped into relative peace. We were on one of the streets that didn't have sidewalks. It didn't even appear to have very many streetlights. It was narrower, less polished than the streets around it.

"Granddad?"

He grunted.

"I'm scared."

I squeezed Sam's hand. So was I.

My father led us to an old bungalow, built well back on the property. A dead willow oak leaned toward it, the moonlight filtering downward through its bare branches. The lawn was a battleground of insurgent kudzu and brambles; the shutters had tilted. At some point in the recent past, a hefty branch had splintered off from the tree and fallen through the top of a screened porch.

I pulled Alice with us down a front walkway made of paving stones that were sinking into the yard. We filed past parallel rows of boxwoods that had grown way beyond the bounds of clipped propriety.

In front of us, a storm door hung permanently open, providing easy access to the front door. My father put a hand to it. Pushed.

It swung halfway open and refused to budge any more.

He pushed Sam through and went in behind him.

As I began to slip through the door, Alice sat down on the top step, unwilling to go inside.

I tugged at her.

She wasn't having it.

I couldn't wait for her, so I dropped the leash and went inside. As I disappeared into the gloom, she must have thought better of staying out there alone. She scrambled in after me. The clicking of her toenails on the scarred hardwood floors echoed through the dark.

Where was Sam?

I'd entered a living room that had a gaping fireplace surrounded by built-in bookshelves. Walking farther into the house, I passed a pair of waist-high shelves marking off what must have once been a dining room.

"Mommy?"

Sam!

The dining room, in contrast to the living room, was bathed in pale, ethereal moonlight. It streamed in through a big bay window that took up the long side of the wall. And there, beneath it, sat Sam. I knelt beside my son, drawing him into my arms.

Alice padded over to lick his face.

"Are you okay?" Not waiting for him to answer, I held him away from me so I could see him. I positioned him in a splash of moonlight and smoothed an unruly lock of hair back across his forehead. "Are you all right?" I cupped his thin shoulders and drew him toward me in a hug. I wanted to fold him up and fit him back into my womb where nobody could ever harm him or steal him away again.

Ahead of us, somewhere, the floor creaked.

Alice barked, ears drawn back.

I straightened and placed myself in front of Sam.

My father emerged from a darkened doorway. He'd shed his cape.

I stood my ground. "Why are we here, in this falling-down house?" There weren't that many abandoned houses in the neighborhood. Hopefully that would give the FBI a clue.

My mother, dressed as Elvira, joined him. "We need Sean. We know he's alive. Where is he?"

We need? *We* know? Was my mother involved in all of this too?

"Grandma?" Sam grabbed my hand as his small, high voice pierced the gloom. "My daddy's dead." He stepped out from behind me. "He died. He's in the wormhole."

My mother's brow furrowed, marring her smooth, perfect complexion. "What?"

Sam eyed me. Glanced toward the ground. "He's in the wormhole."

I took over for him, bluffing for our lives. "I don't understand what you're asking. You think Sean is alive?"

They said nothing.

"Dad? You're the one who identified the body. You're the one who had him cremated. You both stood beside me at the funeral." If I could convince them that I thought Sean was dead, then maybe they would leave Sam and me alone.

How long had it been? Five minutes? Ten? Had Chris not seen us leave Gilman Street? I had to proceed as if he hadn't. As far as I knew, we were on our own.

Somewhere in the house, beneath us, something squeaked.

Beside me, Alice's ears lifted.

"Things weren't what they seemed. There was no body. Sean's alive. I know he is."

I said nothing.

"I need you to get him to come here. Tonight. Now."

"Sean's dead. He died in a car accident. I don't know what's going on, but I do know I can't speak to someone who's dead."

My mother and father exchanged a glance. I hoped that meant their certainty was wavering.

Alice got to her feet with a whine. Then she started digging at the floor.

I moved to grab her collar.

75

"Why is she doing that?" My father was not amused.

"I don't know." Not for certain. But the last time Alice did that, it turned out Sean had been in our crawl space.

"Get her to stop."

"Alice!"

Alice lifted her head, tail wagging, ears cocked.

I motioned for her to sit.

"Sean might be dead, but he left some notes behind, Dad. He wrote everything down. All of it." Rage—hot and violent—burned in my gut. "I know what happened in the desert." The FBI might not know where I was, but I was wired and they were still listening. They needed to hear my father admit to what he'd done.

His glance was colored by surprise. But he recovered. "What happened back then doesn't concern you."

"That's what they tried to tell Sean, isn't it? Why, Dad?"

"Everything I did, I did for the love of my country. Period. No matter what anyone told you, they'll never be able to say that I wasn't an honorable man."

"But, Dad, you—"

"Listen. Out there that night in the desert? I was just obeying orders. I was supposed to scout in front of the lines, report back any resistance, and keep going. We didn't encounter any resistance, so I kept going. Later that night, an order came to pause and regroup, but the message was garbled and it completely contradicted everything we'd been told at the start of the mission. So I can forgive myself for being suspicious."

"You disobeyed an order."

He licked his bottom lip. "There was a storm. We were in the desert. The comms weren't good, so I can cut myself some slack for that. My men were counting on me. Only I drove us straight into a minefield." He paused, eyes gazing out through the window. And then he refocused back on me. "When I saw those Russians surround us, I thought for sure we were done. I assumed they were Republican Guard. That's why I went out there by myself. Figured they might shoot me. But if they did, at least it would give the rest of the men some warning. Maybe some of them would be able to get away."

"Dad, why didn't you just—"

But he wasn't listening to me anymore. "Of course the Russian's offer was completely unexpected, and how could I not take it? It's not like people didn't know they armed the Iraqis. Not like we didn't know they advised them. Were they supposed to be actively fighting us? No. Would my battalion commander have liked to have known they were? Sure. It might have turned the whole thing into World War III. But that Russian swore up and down they were the only unit there. And he told me he'd show us their position so long as we destroyed it and they could get out without anyone knowing they'd been there. We were rolling over everybody; Iraq was collapsing. It was clear that we would win, so there was no point in fighting them. Why create an international incident for nothing?"

Beside me in the dark, Sam wrapped his arms around my leg.

"So think about it. In exchange for letting them go, I'd get safe passage through the minefield. I'd get the location of their position, and I'd be able to destroy it as well as get credit for creating that breach. And I knew that would make everyone forget that we hadn't fallen back like we were supposed to." He blinked. Looked at me. "You would have agreed to it too." He shrugged. "I figured it was pretty fair. They were on the losing side. He knew it, I knew it. Just a matter of time. He got the better end of the bargain. I thought so then, still think so now. And after Desert Sabre wrapped up, the war in Bosnia started. I think I was home for three months? Six? Something like that. Talked everything out with Mary Grace."

So my mother did know.

"She's the smart one. We figured I'd made the best of a bad situation. Then I ran into that Russian again in Bosnia. The Russians were all over the place. And they had all the intel. He shared some with me. I figured it was his way of paying me back for that favor I'd done him in the desert. He owed me one. Think he even said that. I said thanks, put it to work for me. But then I ran into him again."

I closed my eyes. I knew everything he was going to say.

"And he had some more information. And another favor to ask." He eyed my mother. "That's the one that made Mary Grace crazy. She swore up and down that I'd live to regret it. But by the time I talked to her, the deed was already done."

My mother's lips tightened.

He sighed. "That's the point when things started to change. Before that, the Russian gave me information like it was a gift. Know what I mean? After that, it was more transactional. And eventually, once I got to the Pentagon, the Russians assigned me to Hoffman. But it never involved life and death. It never involved the men."

My mother linked her arm through his.

"I promised your mother, swore to her, that I'd get out just as soon as I hit twenty years and retire. I would have, but they made me a general at year nineteen. So what could I do?" He looked straight at me. "I really need you to understand I'm not a traitor."

"But, Dad—"

"Sometimes the people at the Pentagon or the Kremlin just don't understand the way things look on the ground."

"But Bosnia, Dad. You gave the Russians details on convoy movements, didn't you?"

"We all did. So they could hand them off to the Serbs."

"You must have figured out that the Serbs were using them to target people and not to allow them safe passage."

"After the first few times that thought did cross my mind. But what could I do about it? I wasn't responsible for the Serbs' actions."

"But people died. Allies died."

"Sometimes in war, people get hurt."

"They didn't just get hurt. They got killed. And what about us? What about Sam and me? You almost got us killed. The Russians blew up our house."

"That wasn't me. That was Hoffman's doing. He arranged it. And it wasn't supposed to happen like that. It didn't seem like anyone was there. It was just that we wanted Sean to come out of hiding. He was the only one who knew about everything. Hoffman thought if he saw how serious we were, he'd contact us. It wasn't meant to hurt you." His gaze dropped toward the floor.

"All these years. How did you get away with it?"

"It was always a little tricky when I had to renew my security clearance. They ask a question about collusion, see my heart rate skyrocket. I explain about how many times I worked with Russians over the years. Just remind people of what they already know. I say, 'It just makes me nervous because someone looking at this could think I was a spy or something.' They laugh. I laugh." He stared out the window into the night. "In this business, you tell the truth as much as you can."

76

In the empty shell of that old, abandoned house, his words loomed large. But I couldn't let them stand unchallenged.

"You could have gotten out. You could have told them no."

"I did get out. But then defense companies put me on their boards of directors. And I started consulting. The companies kept my security clearance active. People wanted me to talk to them at their conferences and they wanted me to talk on their news shows, and all of a sudden I had this whole other career. But Hoffman was always there, asking for things." He glanced over at my mother.

"So when I found out that your Sean was uncovering my trail, who else could I talk to about it but Hoffman? I knew what kind of man Sean was. If the DoD hadn't given him a different job, he would have discovered everything. Then he would have told someone about it."

"So you're the one who got him transferred out?"

"That was me. Wasn't difficult to do. I still have some clout at the Pentagon." One side of his mouth lifted in a smile. "None of it's ever really been hard." He squared his shoulders, looked me straight in the eye. "Truth is, everyone wanted a hero, Peach." He shrugged. "I just gave them what they were looking for, that's all."

My mother stepped toward me, arm outstretched. "Your daddy never did any of it for the money."

They really didn't get it. Maybe it came from years of justifying their behavior. "Do you remember Sergeant Ornofo?"

"Ornofo?"

"Or Sergeant Abbott? Sergeant Wallace?"

"Yeah. Sure. E Company. They were with me in Desert Sabre."

"Now they're all dead."

"Oh. Well, I'm sorry to hear that."

"They're dead because they talked to me. About you. They were all murdered in the past two weeks."

"No." He shook his head. "No. I never—" He held up a hand. "I never—I never ordered anything like that. It wasn't me."

"You know what they said about you? They said you were good people. They said you knew how to take care of your troops."

"I didn't think . . . I mean . . . who would have known that . . ."

"Is that how you take care of your troops? You get them killed?"

My mother grabbed my arm. "Don't talk to your father that way!"

I pulled it from her. "Don't you get it? Let me explain it to you. Your husband betrayed our country. He raised me to tell the truth and be nice to people and keep my integrity, but you know what? He never did any of those things himself!"

My father began to bluster. "Now, that's not—"

My mother gasped. "Georgia Ann!" Her brows shot up.

"It's hard to do the right thing, you know? It takes sacrifice. And self-denial. And a whole lot of *not* having fun along with everyone else because you told me people expected more from us."

Mother's jaw dropped and then it snapped back. "Don't you sass me, young lady! It's not like—"

I held up a hand. "I believed everything he said. I believed it all. So guess what, Dad? I'm your worst nightmare. You'd better be careful when you start telling other people how to live. They just might take you seriously."

My mother's eyes were snapping. "Don't you even start, Georgia Ann. You are not the innocent in all of this. You are just as involved in this as we are."

"But *I didn't know*!" A sob burst out before I could stop it. I didn't know; I never knew.

My mother smiled her beauty-pageant smile, as if she were sharing an extraordinary talent. She gathered me into her arms as if I were a child. "Of course you didn't." Moonlight glinted off her teeth. "That was the genius of the thing." She pressed a kiss to my forehead and held me away. Her gaze had gone cold. "We're all in this together. So quit being so naïve. They already came for Hoffman. Your father got suspicious when he went to pick up some information this morning. Then Hoffman waved him off. So we don't have much time left."

My father offered me a hand. "We just need to fall in now and march along. Understand? We all live or die together."

My mother gestured toward the wall where two suitcases were waiting. "And don't worry. I've brought everything you need. So let's get moving!"

77

My father bent to pick up one of the suitcases. "We still need Sean, Peach."

"Don't call me that!"

He held up a hand as if to fend off my words. "I don't want him to get killed. I really don't. It's not worth it—not when we can all leave together. You must know where he is. Give him a call. Get him to come with us." He almost sounded like he cared.

Sam had hooked his fingers to one of my belt loops and was holding on tight.

"Sean's dead, Dad." I hadn't yet admitted to them that he was alive. And I wouldn't, as long as it kept giving them a question mark where they wanted a period. "So you're really doing this? You're running away from everything you've ever known? Why? You can't actually think the Russians are going to welcome you with open arms. You haven't succeeded. You were supposed to be the new secretary of defense. You've failed."

My mother took the suitcase from my father with her free hand, walked over, and pushed it into my arms. "We're going. Now."

My father put a hand to my mother's arm. "Mary Grace, maybe she's right. This is giving everything away. Everything we've worked for; everything we have. Maybe we should stay. Maybe we could—"

She shook his hand off and then her composure crumbled. Her eyes narrowed; her lips tightened. "Don't you even start! If you would have just listened to me in the first place! If you would have just listened to me, then we wouldn't be here now—"

I reached around and put a hand on Sam's back, pressing him to me. As unobtrusively as possible, I tried to back away from them. I needed to get us out of the moonlight.

We ran into Alice.

I stumbled.

They didn't even notice.

I took another step backward.

Alice retreated with us.

My father was trying again. "But I can get past this. We've done it before. We'll just frame it as international cooperation. Say the events have been misinterpreted. Pull out the battle-fog excuse. It'll work just like—"

"JB, you're *not listening*!"

I bent to the side, pulled Sam around, and quickly undid the strings of his cape. Then I spoke directly into his ear. "The bad guys are here. Understand?"

His eyes locked onto mine.

"You need to go hide."

Tying Sam's cape around Alice's neck, I positioned myself in front of Sam, praying they wouldn't notice him melting away into the shadows. And if they did look in our direction, maybe they'd mistake Alice for him.

My father kept talking. "I'll tell them. I'll just tell them everything. I'll explain. What I did, I did for the good of—"

"Save it." My mother turned to me.

I lifted my chin and squared my shoulders, trying to make myself as big as I possibly could. I didn't know what they'd do if they discovered Sam was gone.

"If you ever want to see Sean again, then he's going to have to come with us. And we're leaving. Now."

"He's dead. I'm his wife. Don't you think I'd know if he was alive?"

My father dismissed my words with a frown. "We just need you to do what we're asking, Peach. Your mother's right. We have to leave. We've got a car. And there's a boat waiting on the Eastern Shore. Once we make it to Cuba—"

The man speaking to me was not my father. The man in front of me was panicked, vacillating, and weak. Or maybe the man standing in front of me always had been my father. It's just that I had never truly seen him. I stood there looking at him through tear-glazed eyes. "Turn yourself in."

"What?" My parents spoke in unison.

"Turn yourself in. You said they already have Hoffman. If you turn yourself in, if you agree to testify against him, maybe they'll give you immunity."

"Do you really think . . . " My father looked at me as if he were hearing me for the first time. He walked toward me, in and out of the pools of moonlight.

My mother was already shaking her head. She grabbed my father with her free hand and spun him around. "No! Don't you even think of it."

"But—" My father stood there in the dark space between moonbeams, gaze fixed on her, eyes pleading. "But maybe it would work. Because it wasn't treason. It wasn't like that. Don't you remember, Mary Grace? That night I met that Russian in the desert, I was just doing him a favor. It didn't mean anything."

"Pardon me?"

"It was just—"

She stepped forward, reached into the shadow, and grabbed him by the collar. "What I need for you to do is keep the story straight." She dragged him into a pool of light.

"I didn't—I never— It's not like I ever gave them any information that was vital."

"JB."

My father tried to laugh. Moonlight reflected off his teeth. But the sound didn't make it out of his throat. "It's not like they ever asked me to kill the president or anything."

Their shadows, entwined and distorted, were projected onto the opposite wall.

"The story."

"It's not like—"

My mother put an arm around him. It looked like she was embracing him, but when she stepped back, I saw her pull a gun from his waistband. As my mother stepped back and raised her arm, a shadow sliced through the moonlight.

"—not like I was really a spy or—"

"Mom—" I lunged toward her.

She didn't even stop. She didn't flinch. I don't think she even blinked.

"—no!"

She pulled the trigger.

By the time I reached her it was too late.

Alice had sprung ahead of me, bolting from her haunches to her feet. She had planted herself between my father and my mother. I saw her barking, but I couldn't hear anything. The report of the gun had muted everything else.

He rocked back onto his heels as if someone had shoved him. Stood erect for a moment, straightening as if he were drawing himself up for a salute. Then his knees folded and he crumpled to the floor.

"Daddy!" I knelt by his side.

He sat there holding a hand to his chest. But he couldn't contain the blood that seeped out beneath it. He drew in great noisy gulps of air.

Beyond him, in the darkened doorway, I saw Sean emerge from the shadows. He stepped forward toward us.

I shook my head and inclined it toward the living room, where I suspected Sam must be hiding.

My mother stood over us, shaking her head. "He can't even die without making a mess of it."

He convulsed, folding into himself. Closed his eyes for a moment and then opened them. "Mary . . ." Blood burbled from his mouth.

"We're all in this together." My mother said the words to herself.

Then she turned her hollow-eyed gaze on me and swung the gun up in my direction. "We can't just leave you behind."

I raised my hands.

She shifted her gaze to my father.

"Grace . . ." His hand reached out toward her.

She frowned and focused her attention on me. "In a situation like this, you have to be able to keep the story straight." She dropped her arm, bringing the gun down to her side. "Now we don't have to worry about his side of it. So I just need *you* to focus on keeping the story straight, Georgia Ann. Get up." She brought her hand up and gestured toward the living room with the gun.

I stood and stepped away from my father.

She blinked.

My father moaned. "Help me . . ."

"I was not going to go back to Mobile and tell all those Sinclairs that they were right after all. That JB Slater would never amount to anything." Her gaze flicked to him. "All our lives, I've been trying to turn *you* into a hero. Well, that was my mistake. Now *I* can be the hero."

". . . you can't . . ."

"You're the one who can't." She raised the pistol and shot him again. In the head.

I closed my eyes. I never wanted to open them again.

But Alice whimpered, nudging my hip with her head.

My fingers closed around her collar. I didn't want her giving away Sam's absence or Sean's presence.

"Georgia Ann?" Her voice was testy.

I opened my eyes. Carefully, slowly, I put my other hand up.

"We need to go!"

"Yes. Okay. We need to go."

"So *move it*!"

I ordered Alice to sit. Then I extended my hand to my mother. "Better give me the gun."

"What?" She looked down at the gun in her hand. "Yes." Her gaze ricocheted over to me. "Yes. I suppose I should." But she made no effort to hand it to me. "We had it all planned. All we had to do was take care of Sean. In the beginning it was easy; no one listened to him anyway. Why should they? Then it turned out we didn't have to do anything at all. That car took care of everything. It was perfect until your father went to the morgue. No body? That was just too suspicious. Shame, though. It really would have been better if he'd died. He was the only one who knew."

"*I* knew."

She laughed. "Oh, sugar pie! We weren't worried about you." She reached out and patted my cheek.

I flinched.

"You've always done whatever we've told you to. That's what I told your father to tell Hoffman. And you and Sam had your own use. We figured Sean would come out of hiding if the two of you were in danger. And in the meantime, you gave us information. You led us to the people who could prove the story if they thought about it hard enough."

"How? How did you find all those people and kill them? You never had Sean's notes."

She shrugged. "You googled the names, though. Before you clipped the cable."

Realization hit me like a punch in the gut. I thought I'd been so careful.

She laughed. It was a laugh of surprised delight. A laugh that wouldn't have sounded out of place in a ballroom or at a charity fundraiser. "Hoffman took an impression of your house keys once when he visited. That's how they got inside that weekend we went to the beach. They wanted to add some audio and video feeds. That's what they were doing with the gas meter, but you didn't let them stay. The plan would have worked. I'm still not sure, though . . ."

Her gaze wandered over to my father. Then it swung back to me. "I don't know why it didn't."

"Mother?" I stretched out my hand. "The gun."

She straightened, pulling her shoulders back as she lifted her chin. "You and I did the right thing, Georgia Ann." She gestured toward him. "We discovered your father was a spy. Hoffman was the spymaster. Once we found out, there was nothing else we could do. We had to stop him, didn't we? That's the story. Don't forget it. What I need for you to do now is back me up on it. If we both say the same thing, then it's their fault, not ours. Do you understand me, Georgia Ann?"

I nodded.

She flashed her beauty-pageant smile again. "There's no reason for anyone to say anything now. It's finished; no harm done. We let it end with them. We'll just say that when confronted with espionage, we did the right thing." She handed the gun to me.

I took it. Cocked the hammer and pointed it at her. "One of us did, Mother. When confronted with treachery and treason, *I* did the right thing."

78

My parents were spies. Both of them.

And I was too.

It used to be, as I looked back on life with my parents, that I could explain them away with multiple excuses. My father was military. My mother was a Southern belle. I was an only child. They were helicopter parents. They hadn't been willing to let me go. I hadn't been willing to leave.

Used to be I could see every possibility but one.

But at that moment, I couldn't see anything else.

As a physicist, I'd always known that the answers to the big questions were staring at us. They were right in front of our eyes. We just couldn't see them because they'd camouflaged themselves in our reality. The key to unlocking the mysteries had to be things we'd seen a million times and always managed to overlook. They had to be assumptions we didn't realize we had made.

The assumption I'd taken for granted? The one I hadn't even known I was making?

It was me.

I was the assumption. I'd assumed that I was an interested but uninvolved bystander.

My mother smiled that beauty-pageant smile again. She reached out toward me with both hands. I didn't budge.

She held those hands up, palms out. "You don't want to do this, sugar pie. You know you don't."

"Sean?" I hoped he was still somewhere in the house. I needed him to call the police. My hand was starting to shake. I put my other hand up to reinforce it. I blinked. In that play of moonlight and shadow, my eyes had started playing tricks on me. I didn't know how long I could stand there like that, next to my father's body. It felt like I was just one "sugar pie" away from pulling the trigger.

But it was Chris who walked into the dining room at my call. "You're doing just fine, Georgie."

My mother's eyes widened when she saw him. "Thank goodness! I'm afraid my daughter's been under a lot of stress lately."

Chris positioned himself between me and my mother, but he was talking to me. "I have two other agents with me. You can put the gun down. They've got her covered."

I didn't move; they didn't know my mother like I did. They didn't know what she was capable of.

"I'm just going to take out a pair of handcuffs." He grabbed one of my mother's arms and cuffed it.

My mother was still talking. "I hope you're just doing this for my safety. The one you really should be worrying about is Georgia Ann."

Chris eyed me. "Just give me another couple of seconds and this will all be over. You okay?"

"I'm fine." I wasn't. I didn't know if I would ever be fine again.

My mother was full-on babbling by that point. "She's normally not like this. She wasn't raised like this. Not by me, anyway."

He turned my mother around, took her other arm, and cuffed it too. Another agent came forward and took my mother by the forearm.

Chris turned to face me. "Want to put that gun down now?"

My mother tried again. "If you're looking for the whole story, you'll want to hear it from me. It's best not to listen to anything *she* says." As she was led away, she sent a glance back in my direction. "I'm sorry, Georgia Ann, but this is *not* how I raised you!"

I followed her out to a waiting car.

Chris came along too.

I just wanted to make sure that she didn't smile her way out of anything.

As we stood there, Sean walked into the yard. He was carrying

Sam, cupping our son's head so he wouldn't see his grandmother's disgrace.

There was a bigger show unfolding in front of us than there had been over on Gilman. The county police had barricaded the street at both ends. EMTs, FBI, and DoD—anyone with a badge and anything to do with foreign intelligence, domestic crimes, or emergency medicine showed up, lights flashing, sirens shrieking.

The police took a statement from me. They took one from Chris too. He'd lost sight of me in the crowds. Once he realized we were gone, he tracked the phone. When he saw that I'd dumped it, he had to scramble. He'd arrived just after my mother killed my father.

When they were done with Chris, he joined me on the periphery as I stood there—shadows behind me, lights before me—waiting. We were there together when my father's body was carried out and my mother was taken away.

As the car drove off, Chris shifted and began to speak. "You know, you did the right thing."

"Sean did the right thing first. He tried to tell people what he found out. But no one wanted to hear it."

He glanced at me, blue and red lights reflecting off the planes of his face. "How about this time I make sure it gets heard. By the right people in the right places."

I nodded. "Turns out Sean isn't dead."

"Yeah. I saw him." He tugged at the leather brim of his baseball cap.

"And you aren't the father of a fifth grader."

"No." He slanted another glance at me. "I was always on your side, though, Georgie."

"How did you know? About Sean?"

"We didn't. We suspected. And it seemed like if he was alive, eventually he'd let you know."

"You made a good shadow. You were always there."

"In real life I'm just a normal guy who made a deal with his elderly neighbor. I take her dog for a walk every morning, and in exchange she lets me take out her trash every week and play handyman around her house once in a while."

I couldn't help smiling. "You're a nice man, Chris. If that's your real name."

"I can't really say."

∞

Finally, the police and ambulances had gone. All the other agencies had followed and even Chris had ambled away. At the end, there was just Sean and Sam.

And me.

Sean stooped to let Sam down. As his feet touched the ground, he slipped his hand into Sean's and stretched the other one out toward me. And suddenly Sam and I were both caught up in Sean's arms, locked together in his tight embrace. "It's going to be all right now. Everything's going to be all right."

I broke down, sobbing.

Sam put a gentle hand to my cheek and patted it. "It's okay, Mommy." He slipped an arm around my neck in a hug and then laid his head on my shoulder. "It's like I said the whole time. Daddy was just in the wormhole."

79

Sean's resurrection was a seven-day wonder. We decided to tell everyone that he'd been on a confidential mission and that I'd been given misinformation about his death; it was just a big interagency screwup. It was a testament to how many people in Washington had spent time either doing secret stuff or pulling their hair out communicating between agencies that people accepted it as true.

Jim couldn't seem to stop slapping Sean on the back. June couldn't bear to see him with an empty plate. We spent several nights, the three of us, sleeping in their guest room bed before moving into a furnished apartment. There, we waited for the insurance company to settle the claim on the house while we tried to get used to the new universe in which we were living.

As I was emptying the dishwasher one night, my phone rang. The old one.

I fished it out of my pocket. "Georgia Brennan speaking."

"Georgie? Hey. It's Ted."

"Ted." Ted? It took me a moment to place him. Ted. My boss. From work. "Hi."

"Hey. Yeah. Well, we've got it all figured out."

"All what figured out?"

"How to cover you. We straightened it out. We can put you on another contract for a while. Yeah. So I was hoping you could come back in next Monday. Start up again."

Come back? Start up again? "No."

"What?"

"No. I said no. I can't." In that former lifetime, when I used to work for Ted, I would have added, "Sorry." But I wasn't, so I didn't. I hung up instead.

I'd been putting out some feelers in the world of quantum science. It was a small community, so it didn't take long for word to get out that I was looking for a job. I wanted to work with people who were willing to look at things with clear eyes and challenge their assumptions. I needed to be with people who pursued truth with the same passion that Washington pursued power.

As the story hit the news, Russia insisted that Hoffman was a rogue operative and that he was not, and never had been at any time ever, acting as a government agent. To their credit, cable TV news analysts were nearly unanimous in decrying that statement as false.

Hoffman started to talk. He was a longtime Russian plant. They'd created an East German cover story for him, allowing him to "escape" through the Berlin Wall in order to set him up as a sleeper agent in the West. He'd run my father for years.

He revealed the locations of the dead drops my father used to pass information back to him and the part my mother had played in passing those messages. I had been the bridge between them, but she had provided the signal. Key words in her Instagram posts let Hoffman know when my father had a message for him. Key words in the comments Hoffman left, under a false name, on her blog let them know when he had information for them.

The gray cars I'd been noticing had been both FBI tails and objects of my paranoia. It turns out 20 percent of cars in the US are silver or gray. The fact that the car the Russians drove, the one that had killed Edgars, and the one I had seen on the way to Mr. Wallace's were also gray? Pure coincidence.

My mother's relations in Mobile quietly began to put it around that what my mother had done just proved her ancestry. Why else would she have killed her own husband? Everyone knew her branch of the family was slightly odd. It went back to the beginning, to the family's colonial roots. The French had been there way back when, so was it really any wonder? Everybody knew you could never trust the French.

She would have hated knowing they were saying that.

I had told the FBI to look into deaths associated with the veterans of my father's old units. Eventually the news got out that there had been a purge of personnel who had served under him, and a web-based conspiracy began to gather steam. The claim was that a third party had been bumping people off in order to smear my father's reputation. The false-flag theory became a rallying cry for crazies and crackpots across the nation that winter. They thought it incomprehensible that my father would have done all those things people were whispering about. And on top of that, it just didn't make any sense to them. He was General JB Slater, for goodness' sake!

In spite of everything, I wanted to feel bad for my mom and dad. I thought I *should* feel bad for them. They were my parents, after all. And the only grandparents Sam had ever known. But I was never really their daughter. I'd been a prop, a useful tool in their espionage toolkit. And they'd stood by while the Russians tried to kill my husband, hurt my son, and silence me.

I settled instead on pity. And disgust.

I rebuffed all requests for interviews. A few extra-zealous reporters tracked me down, but I stopped answering my cell phone and refused to open the door to anyone. And after a while, people went back to the familiar comfort of believing what they wanted and left me alone.

The army offered Sean his old job, but he declined. He'd decided to write a book on my parents instead. He wrangled with the government over his security clearance, but considering that he wasn't really dead and that his clearance hadn't yet expired, he was allowed to keep it. That meant he could include much of what we'd discovered, although the book would have to be vetted by the appropriate authorities. Though the finer details of my parents' actions hadn't yet been released, enough clickbait was circulating—"Beauty Queen Killer!" "Hometown Boy Gone Bad!"—that it was generating buzz. Though the book wouldn't be published until summer, it was already breaking records for advance sales.

At one point he asked me what I thought had happened. How a four-star general, the quintessential boy next door from Arkansas, could have become one of the worst spies our nation had ever known. I told him that my father had gotten lost one dark and stormy night in Iraq and he'd never managed to find his way home.

Chris must have been good for his word, because in January the Senate Intelligence Committee asked me to testify, offering immunity in return. Several lawyers with high-powered Washington reputations reached out to offer their services. I interviewed them all and chose the one who laughed when I made a joke about the theory of relativity.

As I got dressed the morning of the first day of the hearing, I chose my clothes with care. I needed to dress in order to elicit the response I hoped for. If I wanted to be taken seriously, I needed to look like I took myself seriously.

My mother had taught me that.

For all intents and purposes, I was the sole survivor of the JB Slater family. I was the one entrusted with my father's legacy. In some respects, he'd been a good father. In all respects, he'd been a bad patriot. He used to tell me that you only offer an excuse if you've failed at your duty. That's how I looked on his justifications for collaborating with Hoffman: they were all excuses.

∞

I'd only visited Jenn at work once or twice during all the years she'd spent on the Hill, so the maze of corridors in the Senate building was incomprehensible. As I walked deeper into the building, the bursts of camera flashes and the number of microphones shoved toward my face increased. My lawyer and her assistant played defense, clearing a path for me.

The hearing room was rife with cameras. As I sat behind a table at the front, most of them turned toward me. Though we'd asked for a closed hearing, the committee had denied the request.

Jenn's senator held a seat on the committee. His prematurely silver hair and those intensely blue eyes were instantly recognizable from the years he'd spent in government. As the chairwoman pulled the microphone toward her chest and began speaking, he looked at me.

I met Senator Rydel's eyes. Smiled.

A look of confusion marred his famously rugged features for a moment, as if he was wondering whether he knew me.

I was remembering the conversation I'd had with Jenn the night she was killed. After Rydel had read the information I'd provided, her father and mine had been in the same situation. The Russians had been able to blackmail them from one side and Jenn's senator from the other. But one thing had never been clear: Who was going to play that role, apply that pressure, to the senator? I hadn't yet mentioned his name to the FBI. With Jenn gone, he must have been thinking he was free and clear.

The chairwoman called the room to order and then introduced me to the committee.

As I scanned the senators sitting before me, incredibly, Jenn's senator winked at me.

"Ms. Brennan." The chairwoman smiled. "Don't worry. We don't plan to keep you long. Please rise and raise your right hand."

I stood.

"Do you affirm that the testimony you're about to give this committee is the truth, the whole truth, and nothing but the truth, so help you God?"

Did I ever.

AUTHOR NOTE

Several years ago I was listening to George Musser talk about his book *Spooky Action at a Distance: The Phenomenon That Reimagines Space and Time—and What It Means for Black Holes, the Big Bang, and Theories of Everything* on NPR. Something deep inside told me I *needed* to read this book. It's an instinct I've come to rely on. Long before I know what I'm going to write next, my subconscious is already at work on the story idea. So what else could I do but obey? Confession time: I am *not* a quantum physicist. I never even had the chance to take physics in high school. But I've never been able to choose my characters; they choose me. I did a lot of catch-up reading in order to weave physics into this book. It's no one's fault but my own if I didn't get it right.

Another subject that required research was the first Gulf War of the modern era. It took place from August 1990–February 1991. In response to Iraq's August 2 invasion of Kuwait, President George H. W. Bush authorized Operation Desert Shield on August 7. The United Nations Security Council gave Iraq's president a deadline of midnight on January 16, 1991, to withdraw from Kuwait. In the early hours of January 17, once the deadline lapsed, President Bush gave the order for the air offensive, Operation Desert Storm, to begin. Over 88,000 tons of bombs were dropped by coalition forces in over 100,000 sorties during a five-week period. The ground campaign, Desert Sabre (originally called Desert Sword), began on February 24. The ground war lasted only 100 hours before Iraqi resistance was destroyed and President Bush called for a cease-fire on February 28.

As mentioned in the story, General Franks, commander of the US Army's VII Corps, originally stressed that his troops should keep moving during the opening phase of the ground campaign and

351

should not become decisively engaged with the enemy. Everyone was supposed to keep to the plan. When the order went out that evening to pause, it was puzzling; pausing was the one thing no one was supposed to do. But Franks was worried about the possibility of friendly fire that night.

The Soviets were indeed present in Iraq, prior to and during the war, as long-time Iraqi allies. They had trained and equipped the Iraqi army. Under Soviet President Gorbachev's leadership, the Soviet military had been obliged to retreat from Eastern Europe, and the defense budget had declined. The prestige the military had maintained during the decades of Soviet power was gone. Is it any wonder that they attempted to carve out a place of power for themselves behind the scenes as they worked to broker a peace treaty? But were the Soviets actually present in the desert to fight alongside the Iraqis as I depicted? Not that I could find. And not that anyone ever reported. That was purely a product of my imagination.

The Gulf War left Soviet credibility badly damaged. The Soviet weapons Iraqis used were no match for the coalition's technologically advanced arsenals. The military training the Soviets provided the Iraqis had only led to their defeat. There was an attempted coup in the USSR on August 18, 1991, led by the KGB. It weakened President Gorbachev's hold on power. By December 8, the USSR was officially dismantled. On December 25, Gorbachev was "demoted," becoming only president of Russia.

As I was developing this story, I knew JB Slater's betrayal had to do with something that happened in the desert during the ground war. I didn't spend too much time early on trying to figure it out because unexpected things always happen during wars. I trusted that during my research I would come across something, some incident, I could work into my plot. Imagine my dismay toward the end of my first draft when I was reminded that the war was an undisputed triumph, meticulously planned and executed, using the most technologically-advanced weapons. And it lasted a mere 100 hours from start to finish. Yikes! I was ready to shred the whole manuscript.

All my fears were allayed, however, when I read about the poor weather conditions that first day of battle. I have never been more delighted to see the words, "It was a dark and stormy night."

The underlying theme of this story is, of course, the search for truth. I've spent a lot of time the past three years thinking about the topic. It's been alarming to watch as truth has lost ground to opinion. As a culture we have decided to base our beliefs not on the meticulously crafted scaffolding of verifiable fact, but on the flimsy foundation of things we wish were true. Worse, we've decided that everyone can have their own truth. But if your truth isn't true for someone else, then by definition, it's not actually true.

We are all more than entitled to our own experiences, which in turn can shape our world views, but truth is something that cannot be modified by any of us. Truth exists in the wild; no one owns it. It just *is*—whether we like it or not, whether we want it or not. And it doesn't depend on any of us for its survival.

As a person to whom words matter very much, the devaluation of truth scares me. It should scare you too. But I also believe that a longing for truth is embedded in the human heart. And if truth really does exist independent of you and me, I have faith that our search must eventually lead us toward each other.

ACKNOWLEDGMENTS

Writing a novel is a group project. I am incredibly thankful that when I proposed the idea of a contemporary suspense novel to my agent, Natasha Kern, she didn't even blink. She encouraged me. I am even more incredibly grateful that when I sent her my best first attempt at this novel, she didn't cry. Instead, she told me how to make it better and then referred me to Jennifer Fisher of JSF Editing. I will always be grateful that this story found its way into her capable hands.

Jocelyn Bailey deserves more praise than I can possibly give her. This story was above my abilities in many ways, and there were multiple points at which I could have fallen down during the editing process, but she kept believing I could pull it off. Jocelyn's enthusiasm and encouragement for the story made me do my best not to let her down. And then Erin Healy helped take everything to the next level and showed me how to be a stronger, cleaner writer. I am also thankful to Jodi Hughes who shepherded this book through the final stages of the publishing process.

And that's just the start.

Ryan Carpenter graciously talked to me about being a military historian and took me on a tour of the Pentagon. Mike Phillips shared with me his personal experience of coming across a land mine during Desert Sabre. Any discrepancies between my words and their reality are my fault, not theirs.

I could not have completed this book without the friends and neighbors who never failed to ask me how things were progressing and who were unfailingly patient in listening to me tell this story again. And again. Ginger Garrett, Maureen Lang, and Anne Mateer, author friends and fellow travelers on this writing journey—all cheered and commiserated as they reminded me that I was not alone. Or going crazy.

Crucial to this process were the readers who kept asking when my next book was coming out. And if I was ever planning to write more contemporaries. At long last, I can tell you that I am!

And finally, and forever, my family must be thanked. My husband, Tony, answered my questions about everything having to do with technology, computers, the federal budget, and government contracts. And my own sweet girl patiently put up with me during the weeks when I wasn't quite tuned in to all that was going on around me because I was listening to the voices in my head.

DISCUSSION QUESTIONS

1. What sound, scent, or image never fails to take you back in time to a memory of a particular person, place, or experience?

2. How have you lived your life: with curiosity, in hot pursuit of the truth? Ambivalent toward the truth? Afraid of what you might discover if you found out the truth?

3. You may have heard the saying "all truth is God's truth." Do you agree?

4. Is truth good or bad? Moral or immoral?

5. How far will you go to pursue truth? At what point does the pursuit become too costly?

6. In Chapter 52, Georgie is grappling with whether she can trust Sean. "Everyone trusted someone until they realized they couldn't. Everyone thought they knew what love was until they discovered they didn't. Everyone thought they knew the truth until they found out it was a lie. But how do you let go of one to take hold of the other?" Have you ever clung to a person who wasn't trustworthy, a love that wasn't true, or an idea that wasn't honest? Why? What role do the head and the heart play in those calculations?

7. Have you ever had an experience that led you to question everything? How did you distinguish the truth from the lies?

8. One of the most difficult challenges we can face is to change a long-held belief to fit a newly acquired set of facts. It's less difficult to alter that new set of facts to fit the long-held belief. In other words, it's much easier to lie to ourselves than admit that we were wrong about something. Why do you think that is? Can you think of a time when this tension played out in your life? Which choice did you make?

9. How do you define the word *heroic*?

ABOUT THE AUTHOR

Siri Mitchell is the author of fourteen novels. She has also written two novels under the pseudonym of Iris Anthony. She graduated from the University of Washington with a business degree and has worked in various levels of government. As a military spouse, she lived all over the world, including Paris and Tokyo. Siri is a big fan of the semicolon but thinks the Oxford comma is irritatingly redundant.

SiriMitchell.com
Facebook: SiriMitchell
Twitter: @SiriMitchell

FINDING
OUR WAY

Edited by Rueben P. Job and Neil M. Alexander

FINDING
OUR WAY

--- ✦ ---

Love and Law in
The United Methodist Church

Abingdon Press

Nashville

FINDING OUR WAY:
LOVE AND LAW IN THE UNITED METHODIST CHURCH
Copyright © 2014 by Abingdon Press

Library of Congress Cataloging-in-Publication Data has been requested.

ISBN 978-1-63088-169-6

14 15 16 17 18 19 20 21 22 23—10 9 8 7 6 5 4 3 2 1

MANUFACTURED IN THE UNITED STATES OF AMERICA

CONTENTS

CONTRIBUTORS

Frame: An introduction about the guiding vision and theological framework as we seek together to be faithful to God and to our covenants. By Rueben P. Job, retired, from the Iowa Area, and by Neil M. Alexander, who is publisher for The United Methodist Church.

PART ONE: OPTIONS

Enforce (our *Book of Discipline*): The *Discipline* interprets scripture and contains the rule of law for UM congregations and elders. When sacred promises are violated, leaders must uphold the spirit and letter of the law and follow the process defined by the *Discipline*. By Gregory V. Palmer, who serves the Ohio West Area.

Emend (our lives and our *Book of Discipline*): The General Conference legislative process must be engaged to emend the *Book of Discipline*—or not. This is the responsible and thoroughly United Methodist way of moving through disputes and reaching consensus. By Hope Morgan Ward, who serves the Raleigh Area.

Disobey (our *Book of Discipline* but obey the Bible): Scripture and the sanctity of love are a higher authority than the *Book of Discipline*. Therefore, the current impasse must be broken by loving acts of conscientious fidelity to higher principles. By Melvin G. Talbert, retired, from the San Francisco Area.

Disarm (the incoherent conflict between personal and social holiness): In many kinds of conflicts, in marriage and in war, the conflicted parties drop their weapons or grievances, agree to a cease fire, and search for a peaceful way to resolve their disagreement. By Kenneth H. Carter Jr., who serves the Florida Area.

PART TWO: RESPONSES

Order (our teaching and actions): Our sacred trust depends on keeping our promises. By J. Michael Lowry, who serves the Fort Worth Area.

Unity (to transform the world): When two elephants fight, the grass suffers. By John K. Yambasu, who serves the Sierra Leone Area.

Diversity (to embrace our differences): By Rosemarie Wenner, who serves the Germany Area and is current president of the Council of Bishops.

PART THREE: STEPS

Trust God (to discern a way forward): Immerse ourselves in an intense process of prayerful discernment. This approach pleads for the guidance of the Holy Spirit and asks all to open themselves without condition or pre-judgment to the insight and inspiration that comes through deep prayer and listening. By Rueben P. Job, retired, from the Iowa Area.

FRAME

Rueben P. Job and Neil M. Alexander

We have choices to make. We make important choices in how we honor God, follow Jesus, live together, work for justice, love mercy, and treat each other. We make choices when we search for, live out, and bear witness to the truth.

Of late we see an increasing preference for polarizing declarations about what is and is not consistent with Christian teaching. We hear competing appeals to strictly follow or completely abandon some dictates of the United Methodist *Book of Discipline*. In these and other ways people are drawing lines in the sand and demanding that folks choose a side on which they will stand.

For more than forty years, deep conflict and struggle have marked our dialogue and governance about the church's teaching on same-gender relationships and the celebration of marriage. And now some say the time for holy conversation is over and it is time to rally around various viewpoints and stand their ground.

Where might this intensifying battle of words and wills lead us? We see the raw emotions, angry characterizations, polarizing rhetoric, the fracturing of relationships, and a growing sense of alienation from God and each other born by decades of debate. Do we expect that choosing to do more of the same or increasing the level of confrontation will lead to a result that is better than our current turmoil? Will exacerbating the current melee move us much closer to God's kingdom that beckons? Some say yes.

As a retired bishop (Rueben) and The United Methodist Church's publisher (Neil), we observe the denomination we love grappling with issues of importance that not only confound but also threaten to divide us. We hunger for our church to wrestle with hard questions and decisions in a spirit of humble commitment to passionately follow Jesus, as we engage each other with generosity, gracefulness, and mutual respect.

Perhaps the result of the current turbulence will be schism. If so, this would not be the first or last case in which a parting of the ways is the upshot of church struggles over belief and practice. Perhaps the result will be no change or partial change in the current language in the *Book of Discipline*. Perhaps the outcome will be something none of us yet imagine. We hope, pray, and work toward a respectful, rigorous, genuine, and prayerful dialogue that could lead in time to a consensus that is Christ affirming, life giving, and makes plain to all the abundance of God's extravagant love.

We offer these "letters" to the church from some of the bishops who have been set apart for a ministry of servant leadership, which includes "an enquiring mind and a commitment to the teaching office" as well as leading "the whole Church in claiming its mission of making disciples of Jesus Christ for the transformation of the world" (2012 *Book of Discipline*, ¶¶403.1.b and 403.1.c). We respectfully acknowledge that persons we love take issue with the propriety of bishops weighing in on such matters by offering contrary perspectives, saying that in fostering this dialogue we emphasize the wrong disciplinary assignments or draw mistaken conclusions about the proper role of bishops. Such is the state of our human condition, that almost every idea, plan, and action is subject to multiple interpretations and disputed claims of relevance or accuracy.

We submit that the thoughtful, honest, and respectful airing of views and claims about authority are in the very best tradition of the Methodist and the Evangelical United Brethren founders whose heirs have come together to form the people called United Methodist.

Engaging the "other" to discover and occupy common ground is part of the DNA of United Methodism. We look first to Philip William Otterbein, who in the second half of the eighteenth century was a part of the lively ferment of religious life in North America. He was an emphatic, theologically precise, and most particular preacher who led churches at a time when spirited debates over doctrine and ecclesiology flourished.

At a gathering around 1767, Church of the Brethren, Mennonite, and other preachers were vying for the attention of those in attendance. Preachers sharing the same farm setting offered competing sermons simultaneously to as large a crowd as each could attract and to whom their unamplified voice would carry. "Otterbein listened intently to [Mennonite] Martin Boehm's preaching . . . [and] was greatly moved. At the end of Boehm's sermon, Otterbein went forward, embraced Boehm and exclaimed, 'Wir sind Brüder!' ('We are Brethren!')" (J. Bruce Behney and Paul H. Eller, *The History of the Evangelical United Brethren Church*). Therein a bridge was established that spanned the doctrinal and ecclesiological boundaries of the day and led to the formation of the United Brethren Church.

We see a similar reach across the chasms that divide us in John Wesley's "The Marks of a Methodist":

> By these marks, by these fruits of a living faith, do we labour to distinguish ourselves from the unbelieving world, from all those whose minds or lives are not according to the Gospel of Christ. But from real Christians, of whatsoever denomination they be, we earnestly desire not to be distinguished at all, not from any who sincerely follow after what they know they have not yet attained. No: "Whosoever doeth the will of my Father which is in heaven, the same is my brother, and sister, and mother." And I beseech you, brethren, by the mercies of God, that we be in no wise divided among ourselves. Is thy heart right, as my heart is with thine? I ask no farther question. If it be, give me thy hand. For opinions, or terms, let us not destroy the work of

3

God. Dost thou love and serve God? It is enough. I give thee the right hand of fellowship (cited by Thomas Langford in *Wesleyan Theology*).

We do not present the essays in this volume as if they are either the beginning or end of what has and will be an ongoing and spirited struggle for clarity about beliefs, teachings, practices, warmed and cold hearts, faithful obedience, and accountability. This collection is one contribution in the midst of a continuing search for clear vision and faithful living.

A number of bishops from regions across the worldwide United Methodist connection were invited to contribute. Our timing and other priorities made it difficult for some to participate. For that reason, and because we are fully committed to the value of continuing this holy conversation, a website will welcome and post additional input and responses by more bishops (www.ministrymatters.com /FindingOurWay).

Providing a setting for ongoing participation is important. Disparate contexts in various regions of Africa, Europe, the Philippines, and the United States require and deserve attention that one volume cannot accomplish. In the preamble of the Social Principles we read, "We affirm our unity in Jesus Christ while acknowledging differences in applying our faith in different cultural contexts as we live out the gospel" (*Book of Discipline*, preamble to the Social Principles, p. 104). Unity is not a static state but the ever renewing, dynamic quintessence of varied expressions as in joyful obedience we offer our lives to God. We need more light and clarity about the challenges and choices facing our diverse denomination as together we strive to find our way forward.

The bishops in this conversation draw from deep wells of insight, experience, conviction, and the gift of helping us read our landscape. They draw wisdom from scripture, reason, tradition, and experience. The generous response of those taking part plus others who provided expert counsel is greatly appreciated. All involved have enthusiastically agreed that any royalties that accrue will be donated to the Imagine No Malaria fund.

As they worked, we encouraged the writers to stay intently focused on their assigned theme and avoid blurring the lines between their content and that of the other contributors. Our aim is to present a thoughtful and distinct perspective in each chapter for study and reflection. We asked each writer to articulate the best case for a particular perspective on finding our way, while not softening the edges of differing points of view. Their contributions make apparent the core values and essential choices that alternate paths represent.

Yet we encourage readers to discover points of intersection among the contributions and to entertain ways to mix and blend perspectives. It is likely readers will see merit and insight in several or even all of the ways forward discussed in these pages. Indeed, we expect the conversation may uncover more ways to frame these matters and prescriptions for how United Methodists might respond.

We see this discussion as a part of a process, not as the summation or conclusion of a debate. We don't intend to advance one view over another. We seek together to remember who we are, to renew our solemn promises, and to fully claim our identity as followers of Jesus Christ.

By reflecting on the ties that connect as well as on the issues and words that divide us, we find hope in our common baptism as the central covenant that ultimately defines and binds us. Through baptism "we are initiated into Christ's holy church. We are incorporated into God's mighty acts of salvation and given new birth through water and the Spirit. All this is God's gift, offered to us without price" (*The United Methodist Hymnal*, p. 33).

In the Baptismal Covenant "we renew the covenant declared at our baptism, acknowledge what God is doing for us, and affirm our commitment to Christ's holy church."

We have choices to make. The word *choice* is a pivotal term in the controversy over homosexual practices and same-gender marriage for both the individuals involved and the church that seeks to love and serve them. We know that love without law can cultivate relativism and a lack of accountability, while an emphasis on the law without love can descend into arrogant judgmentalism. What some view as choice others view as a given fact of nature. Where some offer encouragement, others withhold affirmation. We may choose to celebrate or abhor a holy union; to enforce a prohibition or choose to rely on what we view as the spirit of the gospel. The word *choice* helps to make apparent the profound tension between freedom and obligation.

There may always be contrary interpretations of the meaning of sacred texts, varied conclusions about the appropriate lessons to be drawn from life experience, and conflicting assessments about how best to advance the teachings of the church and the ordering of its ministries. The resulting discord will challenge us and might prove to be both agitating and a gift. In whatever ways we engage and respond, we are called to choose at all times to walk humbly, embrace faithful love, and do justice along the way.

Seemingly incompatible views about church law concerning same-gender relationships and what it means to love God and neighbor are tearing at the fabric of our United Methodist connection. We implore you to invest all of your heart, mind, and being in a rigorous and fulsome exploration of differing perspectives about how to move forward. We pray in that journey together we will make room for hearing the thin, quiet voice of God as we rely on experience, reason, and tradition, all understood in the light of scripture. And we pray that our response to each other will be loving, thoughtful, respectful, and honest as "we affirm our unity in Jesus Christ while acknowledging differences in applying our faith . . . as we live out the gospel" (*Book of Discipline*, preamble to the Social Principles, p. 104).

PART ONE

OPTIONS

ENFORCE

Gregory V. Palmer

We would rather not need yet another book about why some followers of Jesus Christ have reached an intractable impasse over this or that controversy. But unpleasant controversy is part of being both human and Christian, so this is not a new place for Christian thought or practice.

The current impasse for United Methodists Christians is human sexual practice and homosexual practice in particular. For more than four decades our psychic, emotional, spiritual, and political energy have been focused in one way or another on this conversation. To say it more accurately, this is a conversation where people don't actually talk to each other. We really are not in dialogue. We are and have been talking past each other for a long time.

Like every reader of this volume, I am weary. But I could not say no when given the chance to participate in a real conversation. I nearly said no when asked to reflect on the point of view in this chapter, to enforce the *Book of Discipline*, wishing I could be assigned one of the other points of view. But I am convinced that no matter what one's personal yearnings and convictions, a real conversation does not occur until each and every point of view can be taken up

9

thoughtfully. So I choose to participate in spite of any derision and scar tissue that may come my way. More importantly, I believe in the church that is built upon the life, death, and resurrection of Jesus Christ our Lord. I believe in The United Methodist Church, while not blind to its failings. It is the church in which I have a heritage and a hope.

I struggle with the word *enforce* more than a little. It is a harsh word because it underscores juristic practices. The word gives too much attention to the reality that our entire process for accountability—to live within the covenant that binds us together and frames our life—seems as if it is imported from Western civil law. I am more drawn to the term *uphold*. The two words may convey the same range of meaning for many, but the term *uphold* is a term that we United Methodists prefer in our liturgical life together. In our liturgies, many solemn promises are made and many aspirations are expressed. We are called to uphold (support) the church and each other, even as we "exercise" the discipline of the church.

Portions of our *Book of Discipline* may be a bit too dependent on language, processes, and rubrics from civil litigation, and when that is the case, we sacrifice the sensibilities that define a church. *Enforce* presses down upon a people. *Uphold* is about lifting and paying attention to important choices. *Uphold* is about implementing. It changes the tone. Given that we are stuck, we must make every possible effort to change the tone of our conversation and our practice. Even small and insignificant tones can make a difference. As one who is called to interpret the *Book of Discipline* and to see that it is meaningfully implemented, tone is critical. The choice is between using our book about church covenant as a club, a bat, or about opening it and inviting people to gather around it for conversation about mission and mutual accountability.

ORDER

United Methodists choose to order their common life in a particular way. Every church does this. The ordering is established for the sake of the mission. A pattern is set so that the church knows where it is going and how it is going to get there. The template provides a means to address as many contexts and situations as can be anticipated, whether they are missional opportunities or occasions when congregations or individuals choose to operate outside of the agreed upon pattern for our common life. A book of polity exists to state history, doctrine, mission, and processes to sustain its ongoing life in witness to the world. One of the characteristics of order or orderliness is that we have applicable rules and regulations that can and should be applied fairly and without distinction for the sake of the mission.

> The *Book of Discipline* and the General Rules convey the expectation of discipline within the experience of individuals and the life of the Church. Such discipline assumes accountability to the community of faith by those who claim that community's support.
> Support without accountability promotes moral weakness; accountability without support is a form of cruelty (*Book of Discipline*, ¶102).

Every four years the General Conference of The United Methodist Church convenes to open the *Discipline* once more. Nearly one thousand delegates, half lay and half clergy, deal with a truckload of petitions, each addressing a specific paragraph in the *Discipline*. The delegates review the template, the pattern for our common life and witness, and render a judgment that this is who we are and what we should do in witness, mission, and ministry going forward for four more years. To be sure, it is a legislative experience accompanied by all of the bane and blessing of such a representative and democratic process.

It is by no means a perfect process. Any observer or participant of a United Methodist General Conference may wonder if it is a desirable process. But it is the process for setting the pattern or template that we agree to support. A less than perfect process is not likely to yield a perfect product. Even the *Discipline* assumes some imperfection. The Episcopal Greetings in the *Discipline* offers the following reflective and humble statement: "Each General Conference amends, perfects, clarifies, and adds its own contribution to the *Discipline*. We do not see the *Discipline* as sacrosanct or infallible, but we do consider it a document suitable to our heritage. It is the most current statement of how United Methodists agree to live their lives together" (p. v). This basic language and sentiment has been a part of the Episcopal Greetings of the *Discipline* for a number of successive quadrennia. We know that we are still on our way to perfection. This is as it should be. Acknowledging imperfection is not an exercise in self coddling or making excuses for ourselves. It is rather a humble acknowledgment of reality and a prayerful yearning for the help of the risen Christ in the power of the Holy Spirit to help us become what we cannot and will not become without divine aid or assistance.

As a constitutional requirement, every four years we tend to "amending, perfecting, and clarifying" how we want to live our common life going forward. As new knowledge and fresh consensus emerge, the General Conference has not only the right but also the responsibility to respond on behalf of the whole United Methodist Church by affirming what is in the *Discipline* or by stating anew and afresh how we will live and organize our common life and implement the mission in every expression of the church. And if, for example, we want to reopen the *Discipline* more frequently, the means is already present through a constitutional amendment. Within our order and polity the means and processes already exist to make changes, even dramatic changes.

Our capacity to move together and speak with a clear voice on anything is threatened by an unwillingness to live with and within the order or pattern that we have set for ourselves on any particular issue. Of course, dissent from particular positions that the church holds is not news, and it is not especially unwelcome news. Diversity of opinion is expected and welcome because it may point the way to a conversation that the church needs to have. Even with dissent, where the church stands on any matter is yet another occasion for the position of the church to be restated, reexamined, and even reformed.

More importantly, a failure or unwillingness to live within our agreed covenant potentially undermines all the work of the General Conference. It seeks to substitute my wisdom or that of my tribe for the work and wisdom of a larger, deliberative body. It makes me and my viewpoints the center of the church's wisdom.

THE COMPLAINT PROCESS

The church in its wisdom through the General Conference has a prescribed process to deal with breaches and violations of our covenant life. It is referred to as the complaint process. The procedures for the process are outlined in ¶363 in the *Book of Discipline*. While this section of the *Discipline* focuses on clergy, note that complaints can be filed against laypersons, too. In this process we assume that our life together in the church and through the responsibilities entrusted to us are a *"sacred trust."* When it is alleged that a clergyperson has "violated this trust," and a person or persons write and sign a statement to this affect, it sets in motion a review of the ministry of the clergyperson:

> This review shall have as its primary purpose a just resolution of any violations of this sacred trust, in hope that God's work of justice, reconciliation and healing may be realized in the body of Christ.
> A just resolution is one that focuses on repairing any harm to people and communities, achieving real accountability by making things right in so far as possible and bringing healing to all the parties (¶363).

This background and aspiration for trust is important.

I believe the complaint process is an invitation to a conversation—though that conversation may not be welcome by all parties involved. The conversation and the review is an opportunity to seek clarity. Such clarity might indicate that a complaint is misplaced. There may be misunderstanding and misinterpretation of words and actions. With such clarity the parties involved can seek ways to move forward and heal the wound that opened between them. Not every disagreement meets the test of a chargeable offense. But the complaint process can create space to air and redeem a real relational disruption in the church.

In other cases, the review precipitated by a formal complaint does indicate that a chargeable offense is a real problem for the church and the parties involved. When a chargeable offense is alleged, allowing the complaint process to work, actually engaging it in pursuit of *just resolution* creates healthy boundaries for complainants, for respondents, and for the church, especially the local church(es) involved. There are ground rules for the process and framing for the congregation. A path is laid out, and none of the parties involved, especially those charged with implementing the process, should be left to their own devices in making up the rules as they proceed. Defined roles and time lines are to be observed. At every juncture of the process, all that are party to a complaint are enjoined to give themselves over to that which will make for a just resolution. So I say enforce, uphold, implement, and use the process that we have available for the good of the whole body.

Formal complaints and the attendant process are not the only means at the disposal of the church to address the challenges of disorder, dissent, and disagreement. But not allowing this process to work in the healthiest of ways when appropriate or demanded by complainants is short sighted at best. Thus the punditry that urges no more complaints or no more trials is mistaken about the discipline and governance of a complex religious body. Here is why.

In the first place, the frustration with complaints and trials in the present day is only focused on one issue, the focus of this book. To cast aside the process available to us for but one chargeable offense is to elevate this conversation above other violations and offenses in terms of moral importance. It suggests that complaints and trials are okay in the case of other chargeable offenses, but not if the complaint is based on one of the chargeable offenses related to human sexuality. The plea to stop the trials would have a more melodious ring if we as a church would call into question the entire judicial process, no matter what the breach in behavior, and ask ourselves: Does the church have a more excellent way of addressing matters of accountability? Have we imported something from another realm of conflict resolution, much like David trying to wear Saul's armor, which does not fit who we are and who we are called to be? Perhaps the next General Conference could spend time conceiving a new way forward in accountability processes for lay and clergy alike, rather than tweaking an already broken system that is often poorly administered—all good intention notwithstanding.

Secondly, it is simply untrue and inaccurate to convey that the process we have, however imperfect, for adjudicating complaints inevitably leads to trials. Any portrayal of the process as a type of inquisition or hunt for heresy is a form of pandering or fear mongering, whether intended or inadvertent. Furthermore, the *Book of Discipline* in "Division Four—the Judiciary," Article IV, ¶58 states: "The General Conference shall establish for the Church a judicial system that shall guarantee to our clergy a right to trial by a committee and an appeal, and to our members a right to trial before the Church, or by a committee, and an appeal." Therefore, while trials are not inevitable and certainly not desirable, to decree and declare that trials simply will not occur is a denial of rights to clergy who are at times falsely accused. Can we deny this right to some in the service of protecting or preserving the rights and guarantees of others? The right to trial is primarily intended to allow persons against whom there are chargeable offenses every opportunity to plead their case and establish their innocence. And, let's face it, there are church leaders who want trials for themselves or others as a platform or stage from which they can declare how they see the issues.

Whether as an outcome of the supervisory process or a trial, the worst of our fears need not be confirmed before the process is allowed to work.

A church which rushes to punishment is not open to God's mercy, but a church lacking the courage to act decisively on personal and social issues loses its claim to moral authority. The church exercises its discipline as a community through which God continues to "reconcile the world to himself" (*Book of Discipline*, ¶102).

Given the current process, could we enlarge the vision of the good that might come from the complaint process? Could it move beyond being a mere tool that creates boundaries and guarantees rights? Might we see the process, appropriate to the nature of the complaint, of course, as a means of having a larger conversation? This process is not the only means to have the important conversations that ought to command our attention. But might they be a means that transcends a pro forma process to get at crucial things? To rule out use of the complaint process is to shut down conversation rather than invite it. To dismiss the process may be a refusal to engage. For example, many times when I receive a complaint from a parishioner about their pastor, about the work of ministry, I always ask the complainant and the respondent if they are willing to meet with the other to have a facilitated conversation to see if they can resolve their differences. Of course, I wonder and I sometimes know why such conversations have not taken place already or have not been fruitful to date. But I have the opportunity to keep making every effort to encourage others to make a good faith effort to engage and keep conversation open. If I too easily treat every complaint as unworthy of such effort or deem it unimportant, I have become complicit in not playing a part in God's intention to redeem and reconcile all human relationships.

Some elders, local pastors, and deacons have had complaints filed against them for presiding at services that celebrate or bless same-gender unions. To ignore or short-circuit the complaint process that could lead to trial is to participate in shutting down a conversation that the church needs to have in a variety of venues, formal and informal. It is to assert that I am wiser than the church.

Feeble and fragile though it is, the *Discipline* should be observed because we are a community that makes solemn promises. We are born of and sustained by the promises of God, who has been made known in Israel and in the life, death, and resurrection of Jesus Christ. We affirm promises in our covenants because God continues to keep the promises that God made. In baptism, confirmation, and church membership we make promises to God as households and as individuals. The church makes promises to God and to households and to individuals. In the ongoing life of the church we make promises to each other especially as we are called and privileged to take on certain roles in ordered ministry.

Of course, one of our ongoing challenges individually and collectively is to struggle with integrity to discern in any given situation or context the most faithful response when some of our many promises seem to clash with other promises we have made. Not keeping our promises willfully or inadvertently undermines both the community and the mission. Even when we feel that the way in which we have approached particular matters of faith and practice is in need of a fresh look and a new approach and articulation, we have promised to go about the change in a particular way. In refusing to uphold our promises, we make a mockery of the process and the promise. We could well be unreliable partners for future covenant-making and promise-keeping. We depend on each other to have a truly hopeful future.

EMEND

Hope Morgan Ward

The North Carolina Annual Conference began a Unity Dialogue in 1998. For over fifteen years, the Dialogue has continued. Faithful leaders stay at the table, engaging in conversation across differences.

In fifteen years, there is no memory of people changing their minds. There is better and richer fruit: The rancor of earlier times in conference plenaries subsides, deep friendships continue across divisions of view and opinion, and the ability to engage difficult conversations is strengthened.

The North Carolina Conference *emended* our life together through this process. We modified it through God's grace that flows when we convene and engage. The term *emend,* used in the parlance of editing and publishing, helps us reflect upon what happens in our life together. We revised our life from within. We persevered in the United Methodist family to make it better, more whole, more life-giving.

The more familiar term *amend* describes the process of adding something to our life that was not previously present. In this way, that which is amended becomes better, stronger, wiser. *Emendment* captures our journey more accurately. From within, there arises a greater capacity to live well with differences.

A JOURNEY OF EMENDING

In his first quadrennium in North Carolina, Bishop Marion Edwards engaged leaders in response to increasing combativeness in regard to the issue of homosexuality. It was his great hope to help us live in healthy and life-giving ways with divergent opinion and conviction. He shared his vision during the 1998 annual conference session. Before leaving the site of the annual conference session, he worked with leaders to nominate people across the spectrum of Christian views on homosexuality. We identified twenty-five leaders, diverse in view on this issue and representative of the age, gender, ethnic, and geographical diversities of the episcopal area. We identified an excellent facilitator and gathered for the first Unity Dialogue in August 1998.

The meetings were difficult. The first task of the group was the creation of a covenant for gatherings and conversations. There were divergent views on the purpose of the dialogue, spoken and unspoken. Upon reflection, we all would confess to carrying secret hope that we would convert others not of our view to change sides in the push and pull. Working toward good group process, inclusion of all voices, and articulation of outcomes was demanding. Some leaders resigned early on, seeing little fruit and little need for dialogue. As director of connectional ministries and the staff person relating to this effort, I approached every gathering with anxiety. In my spirit were ebbs and flows of hope and dread. My experience was shared by every person committed to the process and engaged in it.

A quarterly meeting pattern was set for the Unity Dialogue. Across the years, we gathered regularly for Bible study, reading and reflection, witness and conversation. Communion at the Lord's Table was—and continues to be—the center of every Unity Dialogue.

Together we spoke of the strong cultural milieu beyond the church, the historical stream of Christian teaching on this matter, the impact of this subject within our ecumenical and interfaith relationships. We examined over and over the seven biblical texts that deal directly with homosexual acts. We acknowledged the violent victimization described in some of these texts. We noticed the centrality of the call to loving relationship and the absence of comment on homosexual acts in the Gospels and in the words of Jesus. We considered the reality that loving, committed, covenant relationships between persons who were homosexual were unacknowledged in ancient times. We studied the creation stories, asking: Do these creation accounts describe the desire of God for mutuality among humans or the delineation of heterosexuality as normative for all? We acknowledged that nowhere is there direct biblical affirmation of homosexuality. In all these conversations, there was strong push and pull as we spoke from entrenched positions.

Unity Dialogue participants all testify to having at times the sinking feeling that we were going nowhere, accomplishing little. Participants, however, had a common sense that this was important work, witness, and engagement. We discussed a number of times the question: Is it time to quit? Each time, the decision was made to keep on gathering, talking, and praying together.

Early in the Unity Dialogue process, open gatherings were held in regions of the conference to include more persons in the experience of dialogue and to engender unity across our differences. Bishop Edwards spoke at each gathering, sharing his heart, expressing his sense that the wording of the *Book of Discipline* was biblically faithful, yet clearly acknowledging that he was called as episcopal leader to seek the unity of the church through listening and engaging with all people. A panel of diverse witnesses shared in each gathering. Each panel included the witness of homosexual persons, family members of homosexual persons, and persons articulating with deep conviction the varying views about biblical obedience in this area of our life together.

The panel discussion was followed by break-out groups, led

by trained facilitators. In facilitating one such group, I remember vividly a father and mother who came from beyond the bounds of our annual conference, having heard of the opportunity to dialogue about homosexuality. Their daughter had, the week previous, told them of her homosexual orientation. They were lost with no place to go, nowhere to turn. They came with hope to speak of this very real and pressing life experience in a place that would be safe. In the group we held this story with reverence and surrounded this family with prayer.

The regional gatherings ended at the Lord's Table, with a clergy member invited from the region to preach. Many years later, I remember and give thanks for the leadership of a bishop who owned his perspective while opening his life's energies to convene, listen, and bless.

In July of 2012, I was assigned as bishop to the Raleigh area after serving two quadrennia in the Mississippi area. The North Carolina Annual Conference is my home, and I have the unique experience of being sent "forward" to a place I have known and loved—and from which I had been absent for eight years. At the 2013 annual conference session, the North Carolina Annual Conference approved a resolution, imploring "the General Conference to change the language used in the Social Principles, and to affirm the place of LGBT (Lesbian, Gay, Bisexual, and Transgender) members within the church, lest they risk losing not only those members but any and all members with family or friends who are LGBT."

The resolution noted as one stream of rationale the statement of the sixty-first annual conference session of United Methodist Youth, acknowledging "that the church is divided on the issue, but feel that such language is harmful not only to the groups that it attacks but to the future of the church, as such language is alienating to both present and future members."

The debate on this resolution took place with comments affirming and comments resisting. The tone, however, was remarkably changed from our memories of rancorous debate. After the annual conference session, as bishop I received very little pushback, only a few letters of objection. This movement toward gentling the culture and conversation of our church has deep roots in a long and sustained process of engagement.

The North Carolina Annual Conference is not of one mind on the issue of homosexuality. Laity and clergy, and the communities in which our churches bear witness, have strong views. I do give witness, however, to a change of tone within our United Methodist family. I believe it is a gift of God that has come to us through grace and a process of disciplined convening and conversation.

In the debate on the resolution to *emend* the language of the Social Principles, a clergy member rose to ask the question, "Is it too early in the quadrennium to petition the General Conference?" I ruled that it was not. However, the question is instructive.

The conversations that we need to convene, the dialogues in which we need to engage, take time and demand perseverance and patience. It is essential that we name the ongoing work of dialogue as we move from the rhythm of the quadrennial cycle. We engage with passion and energy in the months prior to General Conference, we fall exhausted into the months following General Conference, and we then cycle back toward the next opportunity to engage. This is unhealthy and unproductive.

It is time to *emend* our life together.

GENERAL CONFERENCE AS THE STEWARD OF WORDS

The stewardship of language is an essential ministry of the church, enriching the quality of our life in mission. In London, on the altar of St. Brides Church—the Printer's Church—are carved the words, "The Word Became Flesh." Words and faith are inextricably bound in our faith that proclaims Jesus Christ as God's Living Word.

Words are a gift. Used well, words bless us and help us grow. The

Bible abounds in exhortations to speak slowly and thoughtfully and lovingly.

New words capture our imagination and expand our thinking. Learning and the use of words are inseparable. Therefore, John Wesley observed with hyperbole that it is impossible to grow in faith without reading. We are born in an instant, he further observed, but we grow by slow degrees. Words form faith, and faith is expressed in words.

We find security in words. I learned this lesson dramatically as a listener designated in our conference to observe the process toward the publication of *The United Methodist Hymnal.* As I studied the history of hymns, I learned that John and Charles Wesley engaged in heated debate over hymn texts. Will it be "O God, our help . . ." or "Our God, our help . . ."? Hymn texts have been altered through the years. However, the suggestion that texts be altered now, that hymns be omitted, that hymns be added, elicit amazing resistance and anger. As a young pastor engaged in this listening process, I heard overattachment, felt heated anger, and witnessed obsessive clinging to words. More recently, I have pondered the *emendment* of the original Swedish text of "How Great Thou Art." The words we sing, "When Christ shall come, with shout of acclamation and take me home, what joy shall fill my heart," were originally, "When Christ shall come, with shout of acclamation and heal this world, what joy shall fill my heart." *Emending* is both a promising and a dangerous opportunity.

We feel at home hearing some words. We feel exiled in hearing other words. These reactions are evidence of our humanness. Our whole beings are beautifully formed by God the Creator when well-chosen lovely words flow over us. Our whole beings are bruised and bent when poorly-chosen hurtful words flow over us. It is a high calling to use the best language to express our partnership in Christ's mission.

It is essential that we engage in good dialogue about our language. It is important that we ask right questions about our language: Do the words constrict and constrain? How are the words heard in the whole community, by individuals within the community, by people beyond the community? Do the words move us into fruitful ministry in the world? Do the words propel us up and out? Do the words hold us back and keep us down? Are the words used consistently or exclusively? Are the words scriptural? Are the words just? Are the words accurate? Are the words good? Are the words life-giving?

The General Conference is entrusted with the stewardship of words, the phrasing of the *Book of Discipline.* With this trust comes the task of continually *emending* our life together.

It is imperative that the General Conference engage this responsibility with faithful courage. The times in which we live call for leaders who have capacity to articulate for this current age the path forward. Life in Christ is dynamic. The constancy of Christ—yesterday, today, and forever—continues in the rhythms of our life together, as we rise and subside, expand and contract, articulate and *emend.*

In John's Gospel, Jesus describes himself as the door, or the gate (John 10:9). Those who enter by that gate will come and go and find pasture. The image of a door or gate infers a fence or enclosure. In the network of fencing, there is a path for coming in and going out. The psalmist blesses this movement, singing the promise of God's presence gracing us by day and by night, keeping us from harm, watching over our lives as we come and go now and forever from now (Ps 121).

These images of movement are graceful and inviting. They draw us into all our comings and goings with God who is our guide. They remind us that our life together is not static, that new words emerge, that even word meaning changes over time. Our calling is to be attune to the divine rhythms of day and night, resting and rising, coming and going.

As we acknowledge these divine rhythms, we find renewed courage. We are able to recognize our attachment to words and places and times. We are able to name the constraint of our humanness as we are overattached. We find that we are clinging to words and phrases as if they contain eternal truth.

Biblical images cannot be grasped in the way that words or phrases can be held, tight-fisted. As we embrace the rich biblical image of coming and going, we resist the temptation to adhere rigidly to formulaic language. Our grip loosens, and we pray and think more deeply. Sequences of words, easily retrieved, widely known, may be of diminishing value in this present time. As we relax our hand and wait with open palms, God gives what is needed for this moment.

Words and phrases are channels of eternal truth. They are tools to express what we see, hear, and comprehend now. Indeed, we "see through a glass, darkly" (KJV) or we see a partial "reflection in a mirror" (1 Cor 13:12). As we recognize our humanness, we acknowledge that all our words are subject to review, to affirmation, or to *emendment*.

EMENDING IN OUR LIFE TOGETHER

Many years ago, a wiser and more seasoned leader in our annual conference gave good advice. I commented with dread about some aspect of the *Book of Discipline* (being little acquainted it with it in practice). He said, "Oh, no! Think of it this way: The *Discipline* is your friend."

His wisdom helped me to befriend the *Book of Discipline* and to allow the *Discipline* to befriend me. I am helped by the guidance of the *Book of Discipline*, rooted deeply in our heritage, *emended* and *amended* through the quadrennial process of the General Conference. I am connected in mission and in ministry through Disciplinary words, concepts, and ideas. I link and lead with authority beyond myself as I seek to be faithful to our Wesleyan life together as expressed in the *Book of Discipline*.

At the same time, the *Book of Discipline* frustrates. A compendium edited by a committee of 996 persons cannot avoid frustrating those who seek to be guided by it. Inconsistencies and tensions, processes needing perfection, and language yet imperfect vex and exasperate.

We do keep trying. Which says it best: Disability leave? Incapacity leave? Medical leave? The changes in language reflect our good effort to honor the personhood of all as we name what needs to be named, to say what needs to be said.

As Wesleyans, we most helpfully understand discipline as a graceful reality in our lives and ministry. The means of grace embraced as scriptural by Wesleyans are living interactions: baptism, the Lord's Supper, worship, prayer, Bible study, engagement with the poor. In the same way, discipline is most faithfully understood and engaged as cooperation with grace.

Language powerfully forms our life together. Words have power to restrict our imagination or to expand it, to liberate our whole beings or to hold our selves captive, to hurt others or to bring healing. In common parlance, discipline connotes constraint. In Wesleyan parlance, discipline is the pathway to expansive spirituality, liberation, and healing.

Grace and discipline are two lively and profound words that arise from our heritage while grounding our community and empowering our partnership in Christ's ministry into the world. Our life together as United Methodist people bears always the streams of grace and discipline. Might the *Book of Discipline* become a greater means of grace in our lives as we partner in Christ's ministry?

Might we approach the next General Conference with clear-eyed awareness that the language we now have is not working well for us? We are a divided church in need of healing to give the radiant witness of unity observed by those outside the early church: "See how the Christians love each other." In loving each other, there is faithfulness to Jesus's prayer that we may be one so that the whole world will believe.

The *Book of Discipline* is a guide and a tool. The purpose of the *Book of Discipline* is to create structure, culture, and guidance for the life together of United Methodist people.

We have wrongly framed the issue: Improving and modifying the current wording of the *Discipline* need not create winners and losers. None of us need hold with a death grip current wording on this or on other issues. We continue to seek the light. *Emending* the *Discipline* is opportunity for all to grow in faithfulness, to acknowledge that God has something better for us than we have dreamed or imagined. To hold any particular wording in the *Discipline* as good and final for all time is the antithesis to the spirit of the journey toward Christian perfection that Wesleyans so wonderfully articulate, embrace, and embody.

A Path toward Emending

The Connectional Table shifted the agenda of the fall meeting in 2013 in response to a disruption staged by Love Prevails, an advocacy group for full inclusion of LGBT persons in the life and ministry of The United Methodist Church. Following the meeting, Love Prevails proposed four concrete actions.

In response, a task force was created by the Connectional Table to consider a path forward, partnership possibilities, and clear communication. The task force met and created a path forward. The path includes an invitation to theologians from the United States and the central conferences to engage the Connectional Table in critical theological reflection on human sexuality and the mission of the church. These presentations and discussions will be live-streamed and archived, embodying transparency while providing an educational resource for the church. Partners were identified for this path forward, including the Council of Bishops Task Force on Sexuality-Gender-Race, the Council of Bishops Committee on Faith and Order, United Methodist Communications, the Commission on General Conference, JustPeace, and ecumenical partners who have gone through similar conversations.

The Connectional Table task force is clear that a process, a path, a journey will be essential. Christian unity amid diversity is the challenge of every generation. It is clearly before us at this time in the history of our church.

The path forward continues to focus on the sections on "human sexuality" and "equal rights regardless of sexual orientation" in the *Book of Discipline*. Commitment will be sustained to provide content that offers differing interpretations and opinions in regard to biblical teaching on human sexuality. Resources will be sought and developed for sustained conversations convened throughout the connection.

The path forward embraced by the Connectional Table embodies an attempt to engage in dialogue, to resist silence and entrenchment, and to move forward together in the unity that is not uniformity. The higher unity sought is the unity the Holy Spirit gives, always a gift to be received and embraced.

I share this effort in the hope of encouraging other paths to be created in every arena of our shared United Methodist life and witness. Let us not be afraid of convening and conversing. Conferencing is our deeply rooted United Methodist way of moving through disagreements and disputes. As we review our history, we rejoice and we change our hearts and lives, seeing instances of faithful and fruitful engagement as well as instances of avoidance, evasion, and injustice.

The psalmist sings of God redeeming and gathering all from the east and the west and the north and the south. While our whole beings wander, hungry and thirsty, God hears our desperate cries and leads us to a spacious place (Ps 107). This spacious place is the place we seek, and God still desires to lead us there. The beautiful psalm begins in thanksgiving to God for faithful love that endures forever. We are called to believe where we cannot see, to stretch toward more than we might dream or imagine.

In biblical criticism, *emend* is used to describe the process of making textual changes to create an alternate reading that makes more sense in the context of the passage. Our calling in this time is to work together with perseverance and patience, to lead the church without fear, to hold the vision of the spacious place that is prepared for us.

Emending of My Life
in the Midst of Our Life Together

At the 2009 session of the Mississippi Annual Conference, a worship team planned an evening worship service to embody our theme: "Arise, Shine: Open Your Doors!" We invited churches and ministries to bring a door to the annual conference session. The response was glorious, and a team of carpenters created stands for 250 doors—front doors, antique doors, modern doors, screen doors, back doors, narrow doors, wide doors, Dutch doors—decorated to embody the missions and local churches across our annual conference. One church simply took the hinges off the youth room door with mission photos collaged across its surface. They brought it for the display of doors that encircled the convention center.

The planning team invited three teams of witnesses, each embodying persons who have a hard time finding welcome in United Methodist churches. The first two witnesses were young people. The second two witnesses were married, an interracial couple. The third two witnesses were lesbians in a committed relationship.

The third witnesses evoked great anxiety, anger, and fear. The local newspaper was pleased to have a cover story as well as a follow-up story, demonstrating unprecedented interest in United Methodist ministry. I held listening sessions across the annual conference to receive the response of many clergy and laity and to respond to the reality as I experienced it. In the witness of Connie and Renee, listeners attached very different meaning to what they heard: Some heard defiance of scripture and church law. Some heard personal courage and deep love of the church. Some heard derailing of the work of the church. Some heard focus on the work of the church. Some heard a call to arms. Some heard a call to peace. Some were angry and hostile. Some were supportive and joyful.

Advocacy groups within the church took note of the witness, using it for their purposes in varied and interesting ways. In the midst of this troubled time, I called the witnesses at their home to offer them pastoral encouragement. As the conversation concluded, Renee recited Ephesians 3:20, which says: "Glory to God, who is able to do far beyond all that we could ask or imagine by his power at work within us; glory to him in the church and in Christ Jesus for all generations, forever and always. Amen."

In the amazing and brave witness of these daughters of the living God, I continue to find inspiration and courage. The current language of the *Book of Discipline* is inadequate, formulaic, and harmful to persons and to our life together as United Methodist people. It impedes our witness. It runs counter to the resonant Wesleyan "all"—the favorite word of Charles Wesley—describing the expanse of God's embrace.

There are a myriad of diversities in our lives and in our witness. All have fallen short of God's glory, and God loved the world so much that Jesus Christ was sent to live and die for us that all might be gathered back to God. It is time to humbly acknowledge the Lordship of Christ over us all, to live well with each other, and to leave judgment to God. It is time to embrace a new way of being a global church, with greater flexibility for regions of the world to create faithful Wesleyan ways forward. Our lives individually are too short and our life in community is too important to compromise either with less than complete obedience to God who created us all, loves us all, and redeems us all.

THE CHALLENGE OF EMENDING OUR LIFE TOGETHER

They say it cannot be done, that the breaches are too deep, the sides too entrenched.

I offer as counter the response of Mary to the angel Gabriel, "Nothing is impossible for God" (Luke 1:37). This good world God creates is full of people God graces with courage, integrity, humility, and wisdom. And many of these good people are United Methodist.

Let us rise up and be the people God creates us to be.

Let us remember key biblical texts of the Wesleyan movement, including the Sermon on the Mount, particularly the Beatitudes, and the texts that direct us to orient ourselves to mission with the poor.

Let us be courageous in convening dialogue that will challenge and confound even as it leads over time to rich blessing.

Let us take the time to create a way forward in our communities, our conferences, our church, and our world.

Let us look to our ecumenical partners and learn from their experiences.

Let us tell the truth—that faithful Christians disagree on these matters—remembering that truth-telling is one practice of thriving communities (Christine Pohl, *Living Into Community: Cultivating Practices That Sustain Us*).

Let us be realistic and give up the false hope of uniformity of opinion. We seek a higher, a better unity. This unity is God's gift, given through the Holy Spirit.

Let us engage hard questions and decisions in a spirit of generosity, gracefulness, and mutual respect.

DISOBEY
(BIBLICAL OBEDIENCE)

Melvin G. Talbert

MY JOURNEY

I come from a humble beginning. My parents were sharecroppers. My father could neither read nor write; he never completed the first grade. Yet he was a wise man. My mother completed elementary school through the seventh grade. She was the prayer warrior in our home, always reminding us to pray before going to bed each night and giving a prayer of blessing before each meal. Every Sunday morning she would like an alarm clock kneel by her bedside and begin praying aloud. The praying would continue until each of us had prayed. My parents were devout Methodists in our small rural church. Dad's favorite expression was, "Your word is your bond." My early life was influenced and shaped by my parents and by the people and leaders in my church, the public schools, and the larger community.

As I matured in age, I saw the wisdom of my dad's expression. For me it translated into a favorite principle that guided me throughout my life and ministry—"Do the right thing." I have not always succeeded, and I am not perfect. I have made mistakes, bad decisions, bad choices, and bad judgments with people in many situations. However, the people in my relationships, especially in my church, never gave up on me. They nurtured me in the Christian faith; inspired, encouraged, and challenged me to do good for myself and for others. I love my church. It has provided for me a biblical and spiritual foundation for living faithfully into my favorite guiding principle during challenging times and situations.

In my early faith development I was practical and simple. My theological concepts of God and Jesus Christ were nurtured not by the preaching of our pastors but by the theologically informed writings in the curriculum resources used in our Sunday school. Those practical materials in the middle of the twentieth century did not introduce me to homosexuality as an issue. It was not on my radar screen. Race was the big issue. So all I heard about homosexuality in the church and in the community was negative and very judgmental. No one in my community of friends and associates was identified as homosexual. But in retrospect, there were single individuals, well-respected professionals and religious leaders, who might have been gay or lesbian. Of course, the culture was such that if one had been identified as homosexual, that would have meant professional, economic, political, and social suicide for that person. To survive, homosexuals were forced to live in secrecy.

At the age of twelve I had my first encounter with the effects of racism. My dad drove up to a filling station (which is what a gas station was called then) and asked the white twelve-year-old boy to fill our gas tank, saying, "Boss, will you fill up my gas tank?" My blood began to boil. As soon as my dad drove away from the filling station, I snapped at him, saying, "Daddy, why did you call him boss?" For several miles, there was silence. When I glanced over to see the face of my dad, tears were streaming down his cheeks. He quietly said to me, "Son, one day you will understand." We never spoke of that event again. But many times I have thought about it. Sometimes I imagine saying to him, "Yes Dad, I do understand that you had to accommodate yourself to the role of second-class citizen to put food on our table. And because you did, I love you dearly. Your love for us was your priority. You wanted us to have all that we needed. Thank you for putting us before yourself." That experience taught me to have empathy and patience, while at the same time I resolved to do the right thing.

I got a chance to make a difference and do the right thing when elected as a delegate to General Conference in 1968. It was an historic conference because it approved the merger between The Evangelical United Brethren Church and The Methodist Church. It abolished the racially segregated Central Jurisdiction that was created in 1939, and it created the General Commission on Religion and Race to advocate for and monitor the process of moving toward a more racially inclusive church. This new entity, The United Methodist Church, made significant strides toward becoming a fully inclusive community for all persons at every level of its ministries without regard to race, gender, class, age, or status. Specifically, that merger removed all laws and structures that discriminated against or marginalized women or African Americans. However, removing restrictive laws and structures does not necessarily ensure full inclusion. Racism and sexism are still alive and well in our church and society. As a faith community we are not perfect. But we are by God's grace in the process of becoming perfect. The long and hard road toward full inclusion continues.

The 1968 General Conference also created a special Commission on the Social Principles. Its task was to examine the existing Social Principles from the merged churches and develop a new set of Social Principles for The United Methodist Church. It was a privilege to serve as a member of that special commission. Our first challenge was to understand the historic context for the Social Principles of those former churches and to access their significance for those churches and the social context of society at that time. We were amazed to discover the credibility of those statements for the churches over several decades. For example, we learned many believe that the 1908 Social Principles of The Methodist Episcopal Church influenced more social legislation in the United States Congress (House and Senate) than any other single document over five decades. When The Methodist Episcopal Church spoke, people listened.

THE ISSUE

In the course of drafting the new Social Principles, the issue of homosexuality was a hot topic. After considerable thought, study, and reflection, we came to the conclusion that "mother dominance" was the primary cause for homosexuality. So we drafted a statement to account for that theory. Fortunately for us, during the same time we were preparing our draft of the new Social Principles for presentation to the 1972 General Conference, *The New England Journal of Medicine* released its findings on the causes for homosexuality. That medical report shot holes in our report and destroyed with scientific evidence a theory of "mother dominance" as the cause of homosexual identity. This evidence brought us back to ground zero. We realized that we were not prepared to issue a definitive statement on homosexuality. So we chose to prepare a general statement similar to the statement in the 2012 *Book of Discipline*, ¶161F, which reads, "We affirm that all persons are individuals of sacred worth, created in the image of God."

When we presented a new statement of Social Principles to the 1972 General Conference, a motion was made from the floor and adopted, which amended the report. This action added a new barrier of exclusion. We intervened in 1968 to correct an action taken in 1939 which segregated Black people into a separate jurisdiction (the Central Jurisdiction). And in 1972 we created a General Commission on the Status and Role of Women to advocate for and monitor the process of full inclusion of women in our church.

But in 1972 we acted to construct another wall. We voted to identify homosexual practice as "incompatible with Christian teachings." This derogatory language is directed toward our sisters and brothers who are lesbian, gay, bisexual, or transgendered (LGBT).

In ten subsequent General Conferences, efforts were made to remove the offensive language regarding homosexual persons from the *Book of Discipline*. During these years, rather than remove the disparaging language, the General Conference chose to harden its position by overreaching into the historic authority of ordained elders in performing their pastoral duties (see *Book of Discipline*, ¶¶340.2.a(3) and 341.6). When a bishop ordains an elder and orally instructs that person to "take authority" (*The United Methodist Book of Worship*, p. 678), that means ordained elders have the right, privilege, and freedom to exercise judgment or discretion in performing daily pastoral duties and discharging pastoral responsibilities, which includes marriages. The *Discipline* delegates the accountability of ordained elders to the clergy session of the annual conference, the covenant group which grants the elder permission to serve. But in the case of ¶341.6, the General Conference voted to usurp the historic authority of the annual conference by directing the elder to discriminate against same-gender couples when exercising day-to-day pastoral duties. Likewise, congregations are directed to discriminate against same-gender couples by denying them the use of church facilities for hosting same-gender ceremonies, even though the same-gender couples and homosexual persons of sacred worth are not (legally) denied by the *Discipline* their membership and many leadership roles in United Methodist congregations.

Currently, our General Board of Discipleship provides liturgical resources for pastors who may choose to use the facilities of congregations to bless animals, fowls, inanimate objects, and more. Are not our LGBT sisters and brothers of sacred worth like all God's creatures?

We tend to identify homosexuality as the issue we have been struggling with for more than forty years. But on closer examination, the issue for United Methodists is probably not homosexual identity but rather same-gender marriage, where an identity is put into practice. Let's take a closer look at language and laws in the *Book of Discipline*. The derogatory language in ¶161F reads in part, "The United Methodist Church does not condone the *practice* of homosexuality and considers this *practice* incompatible with Christian teaching" (emphasis added). The legal consequence of this principle is found in ¶304.3: "Therefore self-avowed *practicing* homosexuals are not to be certified as candidates, ordained as ministers, or appointed to serve in The United Methodist Church" (emphasis added). In ¶341.6 the *Discipline* reads, "Ceremonies that celebrate homosexual unions shall not be conducted by our ministers and shall not be conducted in our churches." The legal language, however, in ¶613.19 is contradictory. It states that church funds cannot be used for teaching about homosexuality because The UMC intends "not to reject or condemn lesbian and gay members and friends."

The disciplinary language regarding chargeable offenses for elders in ¶2702.1(b) reads, "*practices* declared by The United Methodist Church to be incompatible with Christian teachings, including but not limited to: being a self-avowed *practicing* homosexual; or conducting ceremonies which celebrate homosexual unions; or performing same-sex wedding ceremonies" (emphasis added). With the exception of ¶613.19, all the above-mentioned paragraphs refer to the *practice* of homosexuality. It appears that the issue is not homosexuality. Rather, the real issue pertains to intimate sexual relations between persons of the same gender who are consenting adults and who seek human wholeness and fulfillment as human beings created in God's image. What exactly is it about *practicing* homosexuals that makes them unfit as candidates for ordination or being appointed to churches or ministries in our church? What is it that makes it necessary to prevent clergy from celebrating holy unions or performing same-gender marriages in our churches? It appears to me that the dispute is about intimate sexual relations between persons of the same gender. This dispute does not make sense to me. The *Disci-*

pline's ¶161F in part reads, "We affirm that sexuality is God's good gift to all persons. We call everyone to responsible stewardship of this sacred gift." Homosexuals are persons. They desire and deserve intimate sexual relations as "God's good gift to all persons." And when same-gender couples choose to marry, they are choosing to exhibit "responsible stewardship of this sacred gift." It is just and the right thing to do for a church to bless the decision of same-gender couples who love each other and choose to live in a monogamous relationship for the remainder of their lives. Homosexuals desire the same sense of sexual fulfillment and worth as do heterosexuals. This is something our church should celebrate.

TO DO THE RIGHT THING

While witnessing this continuing struggle for more than forty years, and while remaining open to the inspiration and guidance of the Holy Spirit, I felt called to offer another way of following Jesus Christ faithfully. I did this because our General Conference remains embroiled in a political impasse where opposing sides refuse to compromise.

I became quite weary a few months prior to the 2012 General Conference. I gave serious thought to simply moving from the scene to enjoy retirement and my grandchildren. I began making excuses such as, "I'm too old, and I'm facing some difficult health challenges. Maybe I should just hang it up and let others provide the necessary leadership." In the midst of that personal struggle, the Spirit spoke to me in a clear voice, saying, "Have you ever heard of Moses? You know that he was 80 years old when I sent him to Egypt. Mel Talbert, get off your —— and do the right thing." With renewed vigor and hope, I embraced the challenge of going to the 2012 General Conference. I was ready to do what I felt God's Spirit calling me to do. Early in the General Conference, I was hopeful that we might get the derogatory language and the restrictive laws removed from our *Book of Discipline.* But as time passed, while consulting with various individuals and groups, it became clear that we would not be successful in accomplishing this mission.

The defining moment occurred for me when a motion by Adam Hamilton and Mike Slaughter failed at the 2012 General Conference to simply "agree to disagree" on the issues of homosexuality. After much prayer, discernment, reflection, and consultation with colleagues, friends, and associates, I knew the time had come for me to use my influence as a bishop of the church. I must speak a word of hope and challenge to my LGBT sisters and brothers, who have been dehumanized and marginalized too long, and to my church, which continues to do harm to LGBT sisters and brothers by retaining the derogatory language and by enforcing laws that are wrong, evil, immoral, and unjust.

All along, I had been prepared to speak, whether we were successful or not in accomplishing our mission. So at noon on May 4, 2012, at the site of the General Conference, I released a statement, an excerpt of which follows:

> As I stand before you today, I declare that God has already settled this matter. All human beings are created in the image of God. There are no exceptions. We belong to the family of God. . . . At the same time, I declare to you that the derogatory language and the restrictive laws in our *Book of Discipline* are immoral and unjust and no longer deserve our loyalty and obedience. . . . So, in the light of actions taken at this General Conference, I believe the time has come to call for and invite others to join in what I am calling "An Act of Biblical Obedience" based on the twofold commandment of Jesus (Mark 12:28-31).

I concluded my statement with these words: "And if the opportunity presents itself, I will perform a same-gender wedding."

WHY BIBLICAL OBEDIENCE?

Why did I call for biblical obedience? I have three simple reasons: First, I affirm the actions and decisions of more than 1,100 clergy across the connection, who had signed the statement "Altar for All," declaring publicly their intention to perform holy unions or same-gender marriages, even if the church's restrictive laws were not changed. They deserved to know that at least one bishop was willing to stand in solidarity with them. They needed to have a public statement of affirmation from at least one bishop who felt their cause was right and just. Some leaders would consider this ecclesial disobedience. But I prefer to call it "biblical obedience," because thousands of church leaders know that we are obeying the teachings of the Bible when we affirm same-gender couples.

Second, my concern is to address the erroneous assertion that progressive theologians and religious scholars and church leaders are not biblical. I am open-minded, progressive, and biblical. I am Wesleyan to the core. My theology is grounded in scripture, tradition, experience, and reason, which is how John Wesley practiced his reading of the Bible. Progressives refuse to surrender the Bible to the religious people who are afraid of persons whom God made and who are different from us. For centuries the Bible has been used to justify slavery, to justify the inequality of women in society and in the church, and to support laws that discriminate against people of color or who immigrate to our communities from other lands and places. Our Protestant and Wesleyan theology is grounded in the prophetic tradition of the Old Testament, and in the life, teachings, and ministry of Jesus, who confronted the empires in the New Testament. We believe in God as revealed in the Old and New Testaments. We believe Jesus Christ is God's Son who came and lived among us full of grace and truth. We believe in salvation. We believe Jesus died for our sins. We believe in the resurrection. We believe Jesus Christ is savior and Lord. The Bible is our book, too. Through the Bible we experience the liberating and redeeming love and grace of God, which embraces all humanity and creation—excluding none from the distribution of God's grace. The Bible teaches and the Spirit reveals to us that all God created is good. We reject using the Bible to dehumanize or demonize anyone.

41

Third, through biblical obedience I stand with LGBT people in our church to join in a peaceful and loving struggle to defy the official stance and laws of our church. I called on sisters and brothers, laity and clergy, to join in an act of "biblical obedience." Even while many in our church are evangelists who use the Bible to exclude seekers who are different than them, we believe that including same-gender married couples and single persons with a homosexual identity will renew and revitalize churches for faith, witness, and service.

WHAT IS BIBLICAL OBEDIENCE?

Church law in the *Book of Discipline* is in tension with God's love and grace.

First, simply stated, biblical obedience is responding to the witness of the prophets in the Old Testament. Consider this passage from Micah 6:6-8:

> With what should I approach the LORD
>   and bow down before God on high?
> Should I come before him with entirely burned offerings,
>   with year-old calves?
> Will the Lord be pleased with thousands of rams,
>   with many torrents of oil?
> Should I give my oldest child for my crime;
>   the fruit of my body for the sin of my spirit?
> He has told you, human one, what is good and
>   what the LORD requires from you:
>   to do justice, embrace faithful love,
>   and walk humbly with your God.

Through the prophetic witnesses in the Old Testament, we obey God's requirements for loyal love as we do the right thing. Of course, this simple biblical imperative is extremely demanding and challenging.

Second, biblical obedience embraces the heart of Jesus's teaching ministry. Mark's Gospel says it well:

One of the legal experts heard their dispute and saw how well Jesus answered them. He came over and asked him, "Which commandment is the most important of all?"

Jesus replied, "The most important one is *Israel, listen! Our God is the one Lord, and you must love the Lord your God with all your heart, with all your being, with all your mind, and with all your strength.* The second is this, *You will love your neighbor as yourself.* No other commandment is greater than these"(Mark 12:28-31).

Jesus echoed the message of the prophets when he responded to the legal expert. Jesus remained a devout Jew. His life, teachings, and ministry embraced the prophetic tradition and witness of the Old Testament. Jesus spent his whole life breaking barriers, crossing boundaries, loving and welcoming the outsider, and extending love and grace to everyone he met.

Biblical obedience requires and inspires members of the faith community to search their hearts to determine if they are ready to put their lives on the line for a just cause. Are we followers of Jesus— or not? For me this kind of justice is personal. When I sat and would not move from lunch counters in the 1960s in defiance of Jim Crow laws that legalized discrimination against African Americans, banning them from using public accommodations designated for whites only, I was ready to die for the cause of civil rights—for future generations. When I spoke to the crowd at noon on May 4, 2012, in the Tabernacle during General Conference, I chose to put my reputation and my whole life and ministry on the line in solidarity with LGBT sisters and brothers and with straight allies, clergy and laity, who believe that full inclusion of LGBT sisters and brothers in all the ministries of our church is a cause that is just and right.

Across the connection, many leaders insist that church laws must be upheld, especially by bishops. I agree with this claim as a general principle. I spent all my life supporting and defending the actions and decisions of our General Conference. I love my church. I will always be grateful for the many opportunities and privileges my church granted me to witness and serve in places throughout the connection and around the world. Through National and World Councils of Churches, I have represented my church in ecumenical delegations to heads of state and churches in more than twenty countries, including places such as Cuba, South Africa, North Korea, and Iraq. I have led and been involved in religious pilgrimages to visit the Pope, the Russian Orthodox Church in Moscow, and churches in other places. In all these situations and occasions, I was proud to represent and defend my church and to proclaim the stand and position of our church regarding democracy, freedom, and justice. The United Methodist Church has done and continues to do great things around the world.

Yet there comes a time when the justice we proclaim beyond our church to the world must be made manifest in our relationships with each other. While I believe in the democratic principle of majority rule, the Bible also says "Don't take sides with important people to do wrong" (Exod 23:2) or to put it another way, "You shall not follow a majority in wrongdoing" (NRSV).

It is time for people of faith in our church to remember their baptismal vows. One of the baptismal vows reads as follows: "Do you accept the freedom and power God gives you to resist evil, injustice, and oppression in whatever forms they present themselves?" You or someone on your behalf answered, "I do" (*The United Methodist Hymnal*, p. 34). Even as an infant, when our parents or sponsors responded for us, that does not let us out of this solemn promise. Each time the "Reaffirmation of the Baptismal Covenant" is celebrated in our congregation, the elder at the appropriate point calls on the congregation to "remember your baptism and be thankful" (*United Methodist Hymnal*, p. 52). It is time for members of the faithful in our church to remember their baptism and do what is right, even if that means rejecting and defying the unjust laws of our church.

The derogatory language and the discriminatory laws against LGBT sisters and brothers in our church are wrong and should no longer deserve our loyalty and support. We are called to act and live as though they do not exist.

THE IMPLICATIONS OF EMBRACING BIBLICAL OBEDIENCE

What are the implications of embracing biblical obedience? First, obeying scripture means that loyalty to God is a higher priority than loyalty to our church's laws. To be clear, the language regarding marriage (¶161B) and regarding homosexuality (¶161F) is not found in scripture and does not account for the contemporary understanding of who LGBT people understand themselves to be. And the discriminatory laws prohibiting clergy and congregations from being in full and inclusive ministry to and with LGBT people (¶341.6) are oppressive and conflict with other sections of the *Book of Discipline*, which urge congregations to be in full ministry to all persons and urge parents not to condemn or abandon their children who are gay or lesbian.

While serving in Nashville as general secretary of the General Board of Discipleship in the mid-1970s, I was invited by a board member to participate in a special weekend experience in Boston. The event began Friday evening with dinner and ended by noon on Sunday. Participants were told in advance that the event would include a mixture of gay and straight people. We agreed in the introductory session we would reveal only two things about ourselves: our name and the city where we lived. I was homophobic at that time. I carried with me into that event the biases, prejudices, and misconceptions regarding gays and lesbians I had been taught by my church and my culture. So while I kept the nondisclosure, I formed opinions about who I thought was gay or lesbian or straight in the group. Then I waited for my biases and prejudices to be confirmed on Sunday morning when we revealed our vocations and sexual identities. I experienced a personal moment of transformation. My biases, prejudices, and stereotypes were exposed. I began seeing and accepting gays and lesbians as they really are—persons of sacred worth created in the image of God. In that moment, I promised God and myself that I would never again judge gays and lesbians based on false biases, prejudices, and stereotypes. That weekend set me on a path toward transformation. I know now that gay, lesbian, bisexual, and transgendered persons are among the most loving, caring, and gifted persons I have ever known. They are persons who love and serve God and neighbor just as much as you and me.

When I was elected bishop in 1980, I promised those who elected me that I would be a bishop for all the people for whom I would have episcopal oversight. Of course, I did not always know precisely what that meant in every given situation. I had to live into that reality. As a bishop, I was intentional in seeking conversations and relationships with LGBT church members. We developed a trust relationship. They became some of my strongest advocates. On one occasion when we were discussing the reality of life for LGBT people in church and in society, I responded to the discussion by saying, "I hear you and I understand what you are saying, but why do you have to talk about it?" One of the participants responded to my question with another question, saying, "Bishop, have you ever heard of Black Power?" I raised my hand with a clinched fist, saying, "Oh yes!" To which the participant said, "Then why do you have to talk about it?" I went away from that experience saying to myself in the words that one of my grandsons would often say, "I got it!" If LGBT persons, according to church law, cannot speak openly for and about themselves, who will speak for them?

When my church continues to sanction derogatory language regarding human beings and directs its pastors and congregations to discriminate against same-gender couples who choose to marry, it is time to speak a prophetic word of challenge to my church. It is time to use "the freedom and power God gives [me] to resist evil, injustice, and oppression" wherever they exist. In this instance, it is in my own church, which I dearly love. Out of a spirit of love and loyalty I implore my church to do the right thing.

It was my privilege to serve as the bishop for an annual conference where the laity elected a self-avowed practicing lesbian as lay leader. She was an outstanding professional person in her church and in the community. She and her partner invited my wife and me to dinner in their home. We broke bread together. Knowing that we loved sports, they occasionally invited us to join them for dinner prior to going to a Sacramento Kings basketball game. Getting to know this couple was one of the most pleasant and joyous experiences of my life. It was no surprise to me when their pastor came to me and said he had decided to perform a holy union celebration for this same-gender couple who were members of his congregation.

Of course, I reminded him of the laws of our church regarding this matter. Yet I told him that if I were in his shoes, I would probably do the same thing. I took a public stand declaring to our congregations that the position of our church was wrong. (The decision to perform the same-gender holy union resulted in more than sixty-seven elders and pastors from that conference and from across the connection to join the pastor in celebrating the same-gender holy union in the Sacramento Convention Center in 1999.) The Committee on Investigation refused to turn the complaints against these clergy into chargeable offenses. According to church law at that time, this meant the matter was settled.

Second, embracing biblical obedience means a willingness to accept the consequences of choosing to obey God when church laws conflict with God's commandments about love, grace, and justice for all. When Jesus healed the blind man in John 9:1-41, the man was lifted up as an example of why "faithfulness to the grace and truth available in Jesus, not faithfulness to the law, is the decisive mark of true discipleship" (comment on John 9:28-29, Gail R. O'Day, *New Interpreter's Bible*, vol. 9, p. 659). As another example, while disobeying Jim Crow laws, along with hundreds of others, including the late Rev. Dr. Martin Luther King Jr., I was arrested and jailed for attempting to eat a meal in a public restaurant designated for whites only. I had made the commitment to nonviolence, which meant I was willing to die for that cause. Being in the same jail cell with Dr. King for three days and nights changed my life forever. My radical and hate-filled ideas regarding all white people were replaced with the transforming concept of love, which requires loving your enemy and doing good to those who would hurt you or who would do evil things to oppress you. To paraphrase Martin Luther King Jr. from his Christmas sermon in 1957: You can bomb our homes and threaten our children and hurt us, but we will wear you down by our capacity to suffer. And we will love you. We will love you until that day comes when finally we win you over. When we do, we'll have a double victory, for you will be changed and our world will be changed.

Biblical obedience means doing the right thing, no matter what. It means laying your life on the line, giving priority to God's call and the teachings of Jesus. It means loving those with opposing views while constantly doing the right thing.

THE WAY FORWARD

In the spirit of love that comes from suffering, the way forward is to participate in grassroots, emerging biblical obedience movements that will challenge our church and its leaders at every level to do the right thing. Across our connection, especially in the United States of America, holy unions and same-gender weddings are performed by leaders at all levels of our church. Most rites are done privately or secretly. In many situations, bishops and other judicatory leaders choose not to take notice of what is going on. Yet for those who choose to do the right thing by performing such ceremonies in public, some are treated as criminals, with complaints filed against them, and for others trials have been held or are pending. And for many others, they are simply ignored or shunned.

Sisters and brothers at every level of leadership in our church live in partnered relationships and provide extraordinary leadership and service in a variety of settings. Yet they are forced to live in silence. Each day they live in fear that their cover will be blown, and they and their partners will face the wrath of hate, discrimination, rejection, humiliation, suffering, and pain. Something is wrong with this picture.

Our situation would be much different if we lived into and practiced our lofty motto: "open hearts; open minds; open doors." The integrity of our church is at stake. Our constituents, especially our young people, are demoralized by our hypocrisy. They expect us to be authentic in what we believe and teach. In conference settings across the connection, elders preside at the Lord's Table. We announce that all persons are welcome. We do not really mean that everyone is welcome at the table when we exclude those who are bold enough to identify who they are, while we welcome those who choose to hide their true identity in order to serve others and do what God has called them to do. We must stop it!

All over our dearly loved church we encounter a cloud of suspicion and fear. Some of our brightest and best clergy leaders find themselves trapped, and they choose not to risk speaking truth to their people because they fear the wrath of their people, their bishop, and their district superintendent. The younger generations among our constituents are simply biding their time. They will stay in love with God and wait for their opportunity to change the church laws, or they will disengage from our congregations and find their religious aspirations fulfilled elsewhere.

As straight allies and LGBT sisters and brothers we will continue living, loving, and suffering until we are all changed. Rather than focusing solely on removing the derogatory language and unjust laws from our *Book of Discipline* through the actions and decisions of General Conference, we will continue focusing on congregations and other groups at the grassroots level who are choosing to do the right thing. As descendants of those who founded this church, we are not leaving. This is our church. We believe God is calling and challenging us to do the right thing in local settings where people are open and excited about doing what is right and just for all. In these congregations, and in our communities, there is joy, excitement, enthusiasm, and waves of young families who are alive, vital, and growing in faith and love.

In recent years I have heard and received many stories of United Methodist constituents who are baffled at why our church is so unwilling to acknowledge its oppression and discrimination against a marginalized people in our churches, among our families, and in our homes. They are our mothers and fathers, our aunts and uncles, our sisters and brothers, our daughters and sons, our nieces and nephews, our beautiful grandchildren—all created in God's image.

After presiding at the wedding for Joe Openshaw and Bobby Prince in Center Point, Alabama, on October 26, 2013, my photo performing the wedding appeared on the front page of *The Tennessean* newspaper along with an article containing several comments by me. Approximately two weeks later, I received an inspiring e-mail:

Dear Bishop Talbert, Thank you for your love and understanding of God's children. My (young) son told us he was gay this year. I was worried about the high incidence of suicide, depression, and drug use often associated with gay youth. I've come to understand that much of that is caused by society's telling them that they are wrong, that God made them wrong. I do not and never believed in a God who hates someone just because they are who He made them. It makes me sad to think what God must think of the way people have twisted His message of love and acceptance.

Because of people like you, my son came out at a really good time. The discussion and acceptance of gay marriage has meant so much to our family. Even in rural ——, where we live, my son has been loved and accepted by his friends and family, facing no discrimination or unkindness, only love and support. He has more friends than he has ever had before, as he is finally comfortable and genuine with those he loves, and who love him. I am fully aware and grateful of the fact that brave individuals like you have made this possible. You stood up, and so many have been able to stand, as well. God bless you!

I responded to the e-mail, in part saying,

Dear ——. It's stories like your story that bring joy to my life. I rejoice in hearing that my witness helped your son realize that God loves him the way he is. But most of all, he now knows that you love him just as God created him.

I received similar stories of affirmation and support from across the connection. We are in the business of saving lives, one person at a time.

Why must human institutions, including the church, have some class or group of people as enemies to demonize? We are much more productive as a church and as congregations when we practice what we preach regarding our open table and open hearts. As participants and servers we are not called in scripture to judge each person who breaks bread with us at the Lord's Table. We are called to share with everyone the abundance of God's love and unmerited grace. We each come to the table, heterosexual or LGBT, as sinners seeking transformation. Sharing God's grace with every human being is the responsible pursuit of biblical obedience. Wherever injustice and oppression appear, we solemnly promise to disobey unjust church laws because we give priority to Jesus's commandment to love each other as much as we love ourselves.

DISARM

Kenneth H. Carter Jr.

THE UNITY, MISSION, AND INTEGRITY OF THE CHURCH

One facet of our present condition as The United Methodist Church is that we likely do not agree about the issue most in need of definition. For some it would be scriptural fidelity; for others, inclusiveness; and for yet others, the renewal of the local church. Since there are passionate advocates in each of these tribes, I suggest there is an issue foundational to each of these concerns: the unity, mission, and integrity of the church. The scriptures are interpreted, faithfully, within the church. For inclusiveness to have practical meaning, there must be an actual community with the capacity to receive new persons. And if there is to be a future with hope, we cannot simply maintain the status quo.

At present we lack a desire for unity, an intentionality for mission, and a commitment to integrity. First, the symptoms of our current reality can be found in the harm persons are doing to each other (in print, social media, ecclesial gatherings, the larger culture). Second, we see the symptoms in the regionalism of the church, wherein smaller and more progressive jurisdictions are overrepresented in leadership on boards and agencies, while larger and more moderate jurisdictions in the United States fund this work, to a great extent, and include congregations that are increasingly disenchanted. At the same time, more conservative jurisdictions outside the United States are increasingly the shapers of denominational polity.

In this emerging context, which is increasingly fragile, there is a deep sense of mistrust. And so when a bishop from one jurisdiction acts in a different regional jurisdiction in violation of the *Book of Discipline* and in defiance of the request of that bishop, the distrust and division become more sharply pronounced. That this bishop who violates the *Discipline* is then only accountable within his own jurisdiction, without any real dialogue with or accountability to the context where the action occurred is yet another symptom of a broader problem.

The symptoms of our lack of unity and integrity as a denomination are the result of a deeper condition: our theological incoherence. One side of the issue has a theology of prevenient grace and social holiness; another has a theology of justifying grace and personal holiness. Our resulting communication does not move us more deeply toward any kind of solution to the present impasse. We are actually talking past each other.

United Methodists are blessed with a rich and deep theological tradition. We believe that every person is created in God's image. We acknowledge that human sin disfigures this divine image. The result is alienation, confusion, and estrangement. We confess our need to change our hearts and lives, to turn toward God. In the language of the parable, to change our hearts and lives is to come home to the father's house (Luke 15). That turning, an act of faith and itself one dimension of the work of God's grace, is met with an unconditional love, the saving (justifying) grace of God. We are saved by grace and not by something we did to make us proud (Eph 2:8-9). We respond to this gift of saving grace by continuing on the journey toward becoming more like Christ. In this process, God's image is restored in us. God is love, and we respond by loving God and loving our neighbor. Our response, again empowered by God's grace, is sanctification. This is the call to holiness, which is both personal and social in its expression.

This rich and deep theological tradition is profoundly biblical and finds expression for us in the writings of John and Charles Wesley and their descendants. In the truest and highest sense it could be described, to borrow a phrase of the Yale theologian Hans Frei, as a "generous orthodoxy."

Our present denominational crisis is rooted in the reality that our theology (what we teach, what we preach, what we believe) is often neither generous nor orthodox. Our current incoherent social teaching is the result of the present theological chaos. We are polarized, and here we mirror the culture, as Methodists so often do, and the result is a division into two theological camps.

One camp has a theology of prevenient grace and social holiness. Everyone has dignity, although here there are unconscious limitations, and we are called to change the world. In its extreme form this can be an ideology totally void of boundaries, and it leads to what Dietrich Bonhoeffer called "cheap grace," and what H. Richard Niebuhr defined as "Christ without a cross." In its practical expression, the outcome is a kind of works-righteousness. This works-righteousness is a difficult path, because the world resists all of our efforts to bring about change, and a malaise or depression ensues. This depression, in the words of a wise church consultant, is killing the mainline church in the United States. In our common life, this malaise manifests itself inwardly in experiences of discouragement and self-loathing and outwardly through expressions of displaced anger, blaming, and shaming.

Another camp has a theology of repentance, justifying grace, and personal holiness. If every person simply said and meant the words of the sinner's prayer, all would be well with our souls. This orientation takes one aspect of the evangelical movement and separates it from the necessary social and contextual realities that shape us and call for our engagement, a calling that runs like a thread from the eighth-century prophets to Jesus's sermon on the mountain to the letter of James to the journals of John Wesley. This collective voice within our denomination can sound exclusionary and judgmental, and the result is a sharp definition of who is included and who is not.

These theological camps align comfortably (and conveniently) with two dominant political movements, which find institutional expression in the political parties of the United States. The political parties, in turn, find their ecclesiastical counterparts in the respective caucus groups within our denomination, which are religious subsets of them. But neither captures the fullness of our rich and robust theological tradition as Wesleyans, which includes a grace that is more pervasive than we can imagine, in space and time, and a holiness that is more comprehensive than we are inclined to grasp.

The recovery of a coherent theology of grace and holiness and a rejection of the partisan political captivity of the church could lead us to a coherent social teaching. Coherence means that we have clarity and intelligibility and the quality of holding together. We have a clear and generous orthodox theological tradition as United Methodists, but we have lost our way. We are in desperate need of a coherent social teaching.

ALIGNMENT AROUND CORE VALUES

How do we find our way? We might begin with definition of our core values as denominational leaders. These are unity, integrity, and covenant. The unity of the church, for which Jesus prays in John 17, is rooted in the gift of the one God; the integrity of the church is grounded in the congruence of who we are and how we behave; and the covenant identity of the church is shaped by all that God has done for us in Christ and all we pledge to do in response for the world.

Our confusion around unity, integrity, and covenant is often a function of our inability to articulate God's call in our lives (individually and collectively). In his classic, *The Purpose of the Church and Its Ministry*, H. Richard Niebuhr describes four dimensions of God's call: the call to be a Christian, the secret call, the providential call, and the ecclesiastical call.

The *call to be a Christian* is related to our baptisms and is the experience of everyone who hears and acts on Jesus's words, "follow me" (Mark 1:16-20). This call is also expressed in discovering and sharing our spiritual gifts and through participation in the body of Christ.

In the *secret call*, we hear God speaking to us and leading us. There is a sense of guidance and direction. Sometimes we fight the call, and yet in time we may surrender or yield to the call. It is important for those in active ministry to return again and again to the call experience (Gal 1:12).

The *providential call* is related to the discernment of our gifts and God's grace. Here our varied callings in life may come into conflict: our responsibilities as parents or adult children, our need to be located in a geographical area, the sense of timing and sequence. In the providence of God a door may open or close.

The *ecclesiastical call* is the journey taken by persons who embrace a set-apart ministry. In The United Methodist Church, the ecclesiastical call happens in staff/pastor-parish relations committees and charge conferences, where the laity are present and help us to hear God's call. Later this call is tested in district committees and conference boards of ordained ministries, where the clergy are more present in the evaluation of call. Finally, a clergy session affirms the ecclesiastical call, and a bishop ordains to deacon or elder or licenses to local pastor.

The fullness of a calling combines each of these dimensions. In a culture of individualism, it is common to claim that the "secret call" is preeminent and not to be questioned, but in fact this is an impoverished definition of call. God's call is both internal and external; it

57

finds voice in the human heart and the confirmation of the church, where it is "acknowledged and authenticated" (*Book of Discipline*, ¶304.1). As a movement of the Holy Spirit, the call is both inner witness and external validation. An individual is convicted, and a community receives a pentecostal outpouring: Both are expressions of the Holy Spirit. The fullness of God's call is the resonance of the inner and outer witness.

In my role as a bishop, the church asks me to "guard the faith, seek the unity, and exercise the discipline of the whole Church" (*The United Methodist Book of Worship*, p. 703). I find that this ministry is often about reflecting on experiences of call: how a clergyperson feels led to remain in a congregation or itinerate; how another clergyperson wishes to express sacramental ministry; how an elder may have gifts for ministries of superintendency; how leaders (clergy and laity) are gifted to be in mission in ways that strengthen the annual conference; how a bishop deliberately violates church law. In my own discernment, I find myself again and again returning to Niebuhr's four dimensions of call: The call to be a Christian is foundational, but it is too important to be assumed. The secret call motivates and inspires but is not sufficient in and of itself. The providential call acknowledges human factors and the contingencies of life. And the ecclesiastical call takes seriously the resources of scripture and tradition and our covenant with each other.

Some Christian traditions give much greater prominence to the secret call: The Quakers would be an example. Some Christian traditions place the ecclesiastical call in a congregational context: The Baptist and United Churches of Christ would be examples. United Methodists differ from these traditions in that we are connectional and episcopal. The experience of call is always lived in tension with the needs of a sending church and a polity that ensures pastoral leadership for every congregation and continued appointment of all elders. Clergy are related to each other in the orders of deacon and elder, and local pastors in a fellowship. Churches are connected to each other in annual conferences. Clergy and churches are placed in relationship to each other through appointive processes that are consultative. The ecclesiastical call always moves us more deeply into relationship with each other, and this is a sign of maturity, a means to our unity.

E. Stanley Jones, in *The Christ of the American Road*, describes three stages of the church: *dependence, independence*, and *interdependence*. As a bishop, I am in conversation at times with clergy and churches who wish to be independent—they deny the reality of the ecclesiastical call. I remind myself and sometimes I remind a brother or sister that we have made promises to God and to each other. This is the discipline of our shared life, and having chosen to be United Methodists, we believe that this is the way that leads to life. The path to maturity and holiness is one of interdependence, not independence. When clergy (including bishops) violate the discipline of our shared life, or privilege other calls above the ecclesiastical call, relationships are fractured, and indeed the result can be schism. As Bruce Marshall of Southern Methodist University has noted, "There is a faithful dissent that genuinely builds up the church, but also a false dissent that harms the church."

The discernment of this distinction lies in how we hold together doctrine and discipline, remembering that "our theological task is both individual and communal" (*Book of Discipline*, ¶105). This theological task finally incorporates matters of unity, integrity, and covenant. As a church we are always "on the way," and thus the body of Christ is broken. As disciples, we are moving "toward perfection." We have not achieved it. As individuals who live in community and churches who live in connection, we make promises to each other, and by God's grace we keep them.

PRACTICES THAT SUSTAIN OR STRENGTHEN CORE VALUES

As a pastor I would occasionally notice the absence of a formerly active parishioner, and a thought would cross my mind: *I wonder*

59

where that family has been lately? I would then encounter her at the athletic field, or him in a grocery store, and an inevitably awkward conversation would ensue. The reasons for leaving would unfold: a contentious relationship, an unpopular social position, an unmet expectation in worship, a judgment—harsh or restrained—about someone's morality.

In a culture that teaches us to self-identify according to preferences real or perceived, I understood. And yet, as a pastor, I always hoped for something more. As a bishop, this drama is repeated on a larger stage. The situation involves the expectations of clergy and laity, movements and obstacles related to justice, the desire to be unshackled from institutions, even as those same institutions supply the resources that are wanted and even needed. I've read the literature on our need for community and the powerful forces that undermine it. I have experienced the joy of unity and the beauty of diversity. And I have known their painful absence.

So what motivates us to live in community? And whatever might inspire us to stay in community, or remain as one denomination, with those who hold starkly different positions than us on matters of great importance?

In the Gospels this reality is narrated in Jesus's parable of the wheat and the weeds (Matt 13:24-30). We sometimes yearn for a vineyard that would be more holy, just, or pure if those with whom we have conflict are no longer present. There was evidently a temptation in the early church among the Zealots or the Pharisees or in the Qumran community to define communal discipline by weeding out "followers of the evil one." In Jesus's teaching, we are urged not to undertake any kind of weeding out or uprooting. This is finally and in time the work of God. In the vivid image of Jesus's parable, we grow together, wheat and weeds, in the church. This is a calling to live together, patiently aware of our own imperfections and those of others. At times we live together in the midst of an experience that is moderately discomforting; at other times, our relationships are strained by matters at the core of who we are and aspire to be.

In our denomination, the most divisive matter is the LGBT question, which is at times framed as an issue and more often lived in family and parish relationships. I should insist here that the straight person is not interpreted as the wheat and the gay and lesbian person as the weed. To say that the wheat and the weeds grow within each of us is to acknowledge our acceptance of grace and our need for confession. The warning about removing the weeds from the wheat is not to condone passivity or complacency. Rather, in removing the weeds, one will also uproot the wheat. How does one speak out of conviction about one dimension of a person's life, without doing harm to him or her or a family? At our best we struggle with our finitude and with the possibility of God's grace!

To add complexity, the seed (God's word) speaks differently to each of us, and the shallowness of a local church's soil can be a function of the desire to be relevant or the steady stream of messages that distort the thin, quiet voice. Most pastors and judicatory leaders would agree that we are not in a place that positions us for the substantive conversation that is so often needed. Contributing factors to this environmental condition are the lack of catechesis in many congregations, inadequate theological formation of youth and their parents, weakening denominational infrastructures (support for camps, campus ministries, church-related colleges, and theological schools), a market economy whose mobility diminishes relationships, and a surrounding culture that is increasingly secular, materialistic, and individualistic. The difficulty in having a mature conversation around issues of human sexuality (or racial profiling and "stand your ground" laws—I live and serve in Florida) is shaped in part by the shallowness of our spirituality, the fragmentation of our community, and the weakness of our congregational life.

We are tempted to flee from those who challenge us. The "homogeneous unit principle," which came in for ridicule outside the church-growth movement, turns out to define us when we simply want to hang out with people who think, vote, pray, and behave like us. This may not be a conscious decision. It simply requires less energy.

And yet, perhaps we hope for something more. And yes, perhaps the Gospels call us toward the creation of something better. So we live together, wheat and weeds. At its best, the church is a kind of "greenhouse" where we are planted, cultivated, pruned, and thus transformed. To live together is a gift of grace, to remain in a real church, in some local context, is to participate in the means of grace. This is an essential activity in our maturing as disciples until the harvest where God is both a gracious and just redeemer. So we discern, judge, and evaluate. As Reinhold Niebuhr noted in *Justice and Mercy* (p. 56), "while we have to judge, there is a judgment beyond our judgment, and there are fulfillments beyond our fulfillments."

The practices of humility and patience, from a human point of view, can seem somewhat passive and even indifferent, particularly when the energies that flow toward opposing convictions threaten to fracture the community. And yet, we trust in the slow and steady shaping of providence; we hope for what we do not see; and we "grow side by side until the harvest" (Matt 13:30).

I would encourage Christians who cannot accept gays and lesbians, in orientation or in practice, to place the judgment of them (and all of us) in God's hands. As the Apostle Paul asks in Romans 8:34, "Who is going to convict them?" And I would encourage gays and lesbians to be patient with their brothers and sisters in the church who have not walked their journey. This is not a justification for continued injustice. And yet it is also true that sexuality itself is a mysterious, complicated, and emotionally charged subject. Rational conversation and dialogue will emerge only if those who disagree come to the table hearing the admonition of James: "Be quick to listen, slow to speak, and slow to grow angry" (Jas 1:19).

Patience is here understood not as a false tolerance of difference. I am speaking of the patience of God toward us and the calling we have, as disciples of Jesus Christ, to more fully reveal God's image to each other. Such patience is the fruit of the Spirit (Gal 5) in families and in congregations across our denomination. This patience is an essential mark of our mission with gays and lesbians, which itself is grounded in generous orthodoxy. Patience resides in our participation in the lifelong experience of grace, which is the power of God to transform us.

In "The Character of a Methodist," John Wesley commented that "as to all opinions that do not strike at the root of Christianity, we 'think and let think.'" And in "A Plain Account of the People Called Methodists," he insists that "*orthodoxy*, or *right opinions*, is at best a slender *part* of religion, if it can be allowed to be any part of it at all." His sermon on the "Catholic Spirit" is focused around a question and an answer taken from 2 Kings 10:15 (KJV): "Is thine heart right, as my heart is with thy heart? . . . If it be, give me thine hand." Wesley's interpretation of this verse of scripture is worthy of our reflection:

> "If it be, give me thine hand." I do not mean, "Be of my opinion." You need not. I do not expect nor desire it. Neither do I mean, "I will be of your opinion." I cannot. It does not depend on my choice. I can no more think than I can see or hear as I will. Keep you your opinion, I mine; and that as steadily as ever. You need not even endeavour to come over to me, or bring me over to you. I do not desire you to dispute those points, or to hear or speak one word concerning them. Let all opinions alone on one side and the other. Only, "give me thine hand."

He compares the catholic spirit to the universal spirit or universal love and concludes:

> Lastly, love me not in word only, but in deed and in truth. So far as in conscience thou canst (retaining still thy own opinions and thy own manner of worshipping God), join with me in the work of God, and let us go on hand in hand.

In the language of the Wesleyan tradition, a generous orthodoxy toward God is expressed through a catholic spirit toward each other, for the sake of our common mission in the world.

RHETORICAL CLARITY (AND CHARITY!)

The letter of James includes a significant passage about the nature of our speech and its effect upon others (Jas 3:5-12). When we are speaking to each other, or characterizing each other, particularly around matters related to human sexuality, we fulfill the spirit of the first General Rule to do no harm by paying close attention to our words and their impact.

So how might we engage each other with rhetorical clarity and charity? We begin with an intention of seeing the best in each other. Those on the political right might view those with whom they disagree as being motivated by Christian convictions of justice and compassion. Those on the political left might in turn view those with whom they disagree as being grounded in a traditional and ecumenical interpretation of scripture.

The more clearly we can frame our perspective in the resources with which we share in common—scripture and tradition—the more constructive will be our debate.

In addition, we will benefit from a rhetorical charity. This guides us to debate and discuss our passionate convictions about human sexuality with civility and to treat each other with dignity, which excludes blaming, shaming, and bullying. This is not to suppress speech—it is simply to seek a higher way of being in conversation with each other.

PEACEMAKING AND RECONCILIATION

As followers of Jesus in the United Methodist tradition, we profess our faith and we come into membership in the body of Christ. Across many years of leading confirmation classes in local churches, I would remind the students (and congregations) that these two realities—a personal relationship of faith and trust and a corporate commitment to each other—are inseparable. Therefore, what if the fullness of the gospel is confessing *and* reconciling? What if the fullness of the gospel is my own personal experience of a grace that saves me and takes me from the old life to the new life (Eph 2:8) <u>and</u> my inescapable participation (Eph 2:14) in the breaking down of the dividing wall of hospitality that separates me from my brother and my sister?

This is more than "Let's just get along." It is more than tolerance; it is even more than inclusivity. It is the fullness of the gospel; it is the fullness of grace. And in the call of the church, to serve as a bishop, I was asked to work on this unfinished business. I know this, because it happened less than two years ago. I remember saying the words in public. This work continues now in a residential area (Florida) that possesses an almost dizzying diversity: Anglo and Cuban and Haitian, native African Americans and transplanted African Americans, very large churches and very small churches, and some of the most liberal and conservative, connectional and congregational people I have ever met in my life. And they are all United Methodists!

Many of them are saying, in their own way, "Breaking up is hard to do, but it is the right thing for The United Methodist Church. Don't you think that is where we are headed, bishop?"

Sometimes I wonder. And then I remember the words I often find myself saying each morning, words found in the *Book of Common Prayer*:

Lord Jesus Christ,
    you stretched out your arms of love on the hard wood of the cross
    that everyone might come within the reach
        of your saving embrace:
So clothe us in your Spirit
    that we, reaching forth our hands in love,
    may bring those who do not know you
        to the knowledge and love of you;
    for the honor of your Name.

So are we going to guard the faith and seek the unity of the church? Yes, of course, because we have made that promise, and we have integrity. Because of who we are and what the church has asked us to do, there are days we find ourselves stretching out our arms of love on the hard wood of some cross, leadership taking the shape of a cruciform life, in the words of the theologian Robert Cushman.

But it surely goes deeper than what we have promised to do in the current cultural climate. It surely goes deeper than a decision that flows out of an electing body or ordaining board of a conference. Our expectations are grounded in the nature of God who is one, as represented in the prayer of Jesus for his disciples in John 17. It is the plea we make each time we say the epiclesis: "Make us one with Christ, one with each other, and one in ministry to all the world" (*The United Methodist Hymnal*, p. 10).

Is there a future with hope? In ourselves? Maybe not. In our issue-silos? Surely not.

Consequences of Status Quo or Schism

Responsible leaders who care about their institutions must give some attention to scenario planning. What are the possibilities and consequences of remaining in the status quo or moving toward division and schism? There is a growing energy in the polarities at the edges of our denomination, in gathering, in fundraising, and in outreach toward what was once a middle ground. There is a weakening of the impulse toward unity, and this is reflected in the Council of Bishops.

The path toward division is one that our sister churches in the American mainstream have already traveled. Each has experienced dramatic membership loss as a result. I am aware that The United Methodist Church includes annual conferences in Africa, the Philippines, and Europe, and yet the conversation is relevant because the US churches support the global infrastructure. The implications of division would be significant for initiatives across the global church, and this has also been the experience of other mainline churches in the United States that have divided.

So how did we arrive at this precipice, and what is happening? It helps me to ask a more relevant theological question: How could a denomination die to self?

We have been, for a generation, an institution in decline. It may be that we have been in a season of purgation; perhaps God is pruning us (John 15). We often use the rhetoric of inclusivity, and yet we are prone to stay in our preference groups, with people who live in our regions, who support the causes we champion, who think theologically the way we do, gathering in increasingly smaller numbers.

Clearly, our denomination has been on a path of slow death for a generation. The last General Conference, along with the responses of the Judicial Council, was an exercise in resistance to change. Our resistance to change included an unwillingness to acknowledge our present realities: We have a massive infrastructure that marginalizes the local church, a complex polity around human sexuality that does not take into account the experiences of many of our gay and lesbian members, and a lack of accountability among the bishops who have failed to unify the church.

Is the path to slow death inevitable? The alternative is deep change. The deep change will begin as we cease demonizing those who disagree with us. There is diversity within the body of Christ. The deep change will occur as we privilege the mission (purpose) over our preferences. The deep change will include the acknowledgment that we do not have unity in the church; we have an unstable coexistence, a kind of secular tolerance of each other.

Where will a slow death take us? It may guide us to loosen our polity, allowing for geographical and ideological variation among annual conferences, particularly around who may be ordained and married and accounting for civil laws when these are relevant. It may allow us to flatten our denominational structures. This movement was the will of the body at the 2012 General Conference, even as facets of it were overruled judicially. Slow death might lead us to a common cause between those on the left, who want more local autonomy, for social reasons, and those on the right, who want more autonomy for evangelical reasons. The loosening of polity, around human sexuality and participation in apportionments, would be a sign of deep change, and yet we are presently experiencing what Robert E. Quinn describes as a "slow death" (*Deep Change: Discovering the Leader Within*): We are losing gay and lesbian members shaped as disciples in our congregations, and we are not able to do critical mission at the local level because of a support of structures at the denominational level.

If we are unable to do the work of peacemaking and reconciliation, and if the energy (and resources) continue to flow to the polarities of our denomination, and if our regional differences continue to become more pronounced, we may indeed be headed for a division or schism. I reflect on this possibility not as a suggested way forward but as a reckoning of the painful cost of our fracturing, a cost that we do not always adequately consider. The result might be the creation of two or three institutional expressions of what is now The United Methodist Church: progressive (Reconciling, MFSA), evangelical (no denominational label, Willow Creek association, larger churches, Good News), and mainstream (most connectional and aligned with our present structure). Some of our present institutional framework (the publishing house, the Board of Pensions and Health Benefits) would then serve two or three clients, rather than one. And as David Watson of United Theological Seminary has noted, we might allow for mutual recognition of orders across these traditions within a more loosely organized Wesleyan family, just as we do now with the Lutherans and Episcopalians.

I write specifically about what a new relationship might look like because I think it is beneficial for leaders in The United Methodist Church to contemplate. We reflect more on the church we idealize (one that fits our theological and political convictions) than on what a different church might look like. There is much to be lost in a new scheme. As imperfect as our polity is, we have accomplished significant mission together. At the top of my list would be Africa University, the United Methodist Committee on Relief, and our support of theological education. The dismantling of our connection would involve casualties and would in all likelihood, if previous General Conferences are a witness, be a violent process. None of this would glorify God or advance our stated mission: to make disciples of Jesus Christ for the transformation of the world.

One part of finding our way may be the creation of structures for the possibility that there may be, in time, a reunion of those who separate in the shorter term. This has happened before and might well again, in the mystery and providence of God. Church history is a stream that moves in measurements of decades and centuries, not news cycles.

Finally, leaders must do the work of Jesus in the way of Jesus. The end—whether that is doctrinal purity or being on the right side of history—does not justify the means we take to arrive at our preferred destination. As we read in 1 John, we cannot say that we love God, whom we have never seen, if we do not love our neighbor, whom we have seen. The calling to live in peace with God and with each other is a challenge to the people called Methodists; and yet we have the promise:

> Because of our God's deep compassion,
> the dawn from heaven will break upon us,
> to give light to those who are sitting in darkness
> and in the shadow of death,
> to guide us on the path of peace (Luke 1:78-79).

PART TWO

RESPONSES

ORDER

J. Michael Lowry

These words are spoken in examination of every woman or man who steps to the altar to be ordained an elder in The United Methodist Church: "In covenant with other elders, will you be loyal to The United Methodist Church, accepting its order, liturgy, doctrine, and discipline, defending it against all doctrines contrary to God's Holy Word, and accepting the authority of those who are appointed to supervise your ministry?" *(Book of Worship*, p. 676). In the lexicon of our life together as a church we have long understood that an elder is ordained for "word, sacrament, and order." Indeed, the word *ordination* comes from the Latin word *ordinare*. It means to "put in order." Seeking to find our way forward in the current crisis engulfing Untied Methodism (as well as most other Christian denominations in the United States), any of the options suggested virtually beg for a deeper consideration of the meaning and importance of order in the life of faith and the life of the church.

THE IMPORTANCE OF ORDER

The United Methodist understanding of being ordained to "order" has never been taken to imply that proper advocacy of change in church life and rule is to be muzzled. Nor have we countenanced a rigid adherence that stifles appropriate dissent. Rather, by order we mean a sense of unity built on the common coherence of doctrine, mission, and discipline. Indeed the word *discipline*, from which we get the title of our church law book, is often used as a synonym for order.

The concept of church order and discipline comes from a firm biblical foundation. In the Pastoral Letters (1 and 2 Timothy, Titus), Timothy is instructed to protect what he has been given in trust (1 Tim 6:20). In 2 Corinthians the apostle Paul urges the church to "put things in order" (2 Cor 13:11). Paul admonishes the Thessalonians, "So then, brothers and sisters, stand firm and hold on to the traditions we taught you, whether we taught you in person or through our letter" (2 Thess 2:15). The famous debate at the Jerusalem Council in Acts 15 is a debate over order, the doctrinal discipline of the church. These brief scriptural references merely hint at the depth of biblical conviction that order is a central concept to the life of the church.

Order contains within its essence a doctrinal character (what we teach) and a disciplinary character (how we shall act together). It is not to be regarded lightly or set aside casually. In the life of any organization, or, more accurately, any living organism such as the church, the boundaries must be permeable enough to breathe and simultaneously firm enough to contain the essence. Order helps accomplish this crucial function. Justo Gonzales perceptively reached for this essential balance when he used the image of foul lines on a baseball diamond (in a DISCIPLE BIBLE study video) to denote what is in the faith (in some sense orthodox) and what is outside the faith (in some sense heretical). In baseball there is a great deal of room within the foul lines. We may argue at length and with passion about the meaning of the Trinity. But should we reject the concept of the

Trinity as a central teaching of the Christian faith, we have stepped outside the foul lines.

Our current rage against order and struggle about order is by image a contentious argument about the foul lines and indeed about the very nature of whether foul lines properly exist. Our debate in the United States is acerbated by the rampant individualism of our culture. Such individualism has infected our very understanding of what it means to be a covenantal community.

THE COST OF DIS-ORDER

Passionate advocates for change to the United Methodist prohibition against same-gender marriages (*Book of Discipline*, ¶2702.1.b), who act out a conviction of biblical obedience, have chosen to stand trial and risk losing their status as an ordained clergyperson in The United Methodist Church.

Actions of courageous and prophetic civil disobedience are a part of our deepest faith convictions. We affirm that biblical obedience is a calling over and above civil and church laws. Yet standing courageously on the ground of biblical obedience does not settle the issue. First of all, there is sharp and deep disagreement in the life of the church as to whether or not violation of the church's prohibition on same-gender marriages is actually based on a biblical faith. In facing the issue of same-gender marriage, we experience deep division over what it means to be biblically obedient. It is not obvious to a simple majority of the church (as demonstrated in repeated General Conference votes) that refusing to obey church law is being biblically obedient.

Secondly, it should be carefully noted that when civil disobedience is invoked, Christians have been willing to bear the penalty for such disobedience. This has long been a principle of civil disobedience. The need for order is not ignored but rather embraced on a higher level through the witness of being willing to face the penalty incurred. Presently, the position of biblical obedience, which evokes actions by some of civil disobedience against church law, is corrupted by the lack of meaningful penalties applied to those engaging in disobeying church law. It is now acceptable for some advocates, some church juries, and some bishops to settle for a twenty-four-hour suspension of the guilty clergyperson. Such a meaningless level of accountability has the effect of giving a person an extra day off for violating church law established by General Conference. Such actions offend the very integrity of the advocated biblical obedience.

Thirdly, the cost of dis-order in the life of the church is heightened in multiple ways. As indicated in the prior paragraph, the integrity of the witness against what is perceived to be biblically unfaithful is itself cheapened. More significantly, the church's discipline is itself under attack. The concept of covenant is degraded. Put bluntly, people (clergy, laity, and churches) that refuse to pay sections of their apportionment are often directly challenged for a failure to abide by our disciplinary covenant (church law), while many who break covenant and discipline in defense of their position (a minority position in the life of the church) on same-gender marriage are given what amounts to a free pass. It appears that our disciplinary covenant is applied to some but not others. Some people make statements such as, "if the *Discipline* doesn't apply to them, why should I have to follow it?"

Apportionments should not become a weapon, because it is wrong to use this issue to harm ministry to persons in need. Failure to realize the connection is naive at best and casually reckless at worst.

There is a high price tag to dis-order in the church. Covenant promises are compromised. Injustice becomes the charge by multiple parties, which leads to a culture of victimization. Missional resources are diverted or depleted. The ultimate cost of dis-order may be The United Methodist Church itself. The high cost of dis-order challenges us to find a different way.

76

UNINTENDED PROGRESSIVE COLONIALISM

Colonialism is defined in a dictionary as "the control of one country over another area and its people" and as "control by one power over a dependent area and its people" (Merriam-Webster). We face a situation in the governing arm of our church where many, quite possibly a majority in the United States, conscientiously object to church discipline as enacted at General Conference. However much I might admire a refusal to follow church law in this matter, I sense a deep disrespect for what a church democracy has adopted. A potential majority of the church in the United States is telling a clear majority of representatives outside the United States that their votes do not really count or matter on same-gender issues. The refusal to abide by a majority vote is a form of unintended progressive colonialism.

I believe neither that colonialism is intended nor that there is any intent to nullify the votes of those living outside the United States. However, current actions to ignore, dismiss, or marginalize (by lack of meaningful discipline) church doctrine has the effect of saying that the majority outside the United States don't really count as much as those from the United States. Living in a democracy at times means abiding by a law we disagree with. For example, I strongly disagree with the current position of US law with regard to immigration. Many activists who want to change the law are engaged in civil disobedience. They are arrested and charged. Nevertheless, votes in Congress (and those who elect members of Congress) are not ignored or negated through a disagreement with our laws. The deep progressive argument in the United States for change on same-gender marriage in The United Methodist Church appears to be an attempt at negation.

Attempts to disobey church law are a form of unintended colonialism because the actions of a more prosperous and powerful part of the church would dictate policy and order to overrule representative convictions throughout most of the central conferences.

CAN THE CENTER HOLD?

I respect and find myself swayed by leaders in our church, and my colleagues in this book, who take various positions while also eloquently calling for an end to the conflict. I am deeply attracted to the proposal offered at the end of this book by Rueben Job to "trust God" through a process of discernment. And yet as compelling and indifferent as this vision appears, in subtle ways it contains the seed of antinomianism. An antinomian position "holds that under the gospel dispensation of grace the moral law is of no use or obligation because faith alone is necessary to salvation" (Merriam-Webster). The steps call for a cessation of church trials and celebrations of same-gender marriages but without an affirmation of church law and doctrine. Even with gentle, loving discernment language, the assertions to "trust God" appear weighted and biased toward an eventual change of church law and doctrine. Change in favor of an endorsement of same-gender marriage and ordination appears to be the hidden assumption of this proposal. The conflict will not end if those who support the current position in the *Discipline* simply need time and prayer to come to the truth.

Take the argument a step further. Imagine after a period of prayerful discernment the church perceives that God is calling us to hold to the current position as the discipline most truly loving and faithful to the gospel. Does anyone seriously think that all (or even most) who currently disagree with the current position would return to a stance embracing graceful inclusion without access to marriage and ordination?

And yet, given the deep rift and despite my doubts about our willingness to engage in fully discerning prayer, trusting God may truly be the stance we can take. Radical discerning prayer is threatening to all of us because it opens us to the possibility that we might be wrong or that God is calling us to a different path. This challenge to deep prayerful discernment delivers us back to horns of the dilemma: (A) Many find our current doctrinal stance immoral and intolerable. (B) Many believe the current doctrinal stance to be biblically faithful. A simple majority (B) embrace a conviction "that all persons are individuals of sacred worth" and "that God's grace is available to all" and insist that "we commit ourselves to be in ministry for and with all persons" (*Book of Discipline*, ¶161F). The majority (B), however, reject endorsement of same-gender marriage and "the practice of homosexuality."

We face the reality of deeply divergent understandings of biblical faithfulness. The two basic spectrums of conviction are incompatible. The pain and passion are strong and raw all across the spectrum, from the far right to the far left. Our penchant for "holy conversation" can further disguise an attempt to convince those who disagree with us of how right and righteous we are (and how right and righteous our position is). We do well to remember, from the experience of coming to faith in Christ, that changing a core foundational mind-set is rarely a matter of winning an argument. So each of us need a little (no, a lot!) less certainty and a little (no, a lot!) more humility in our judgments.

William Butler Yeats in 1919 published a poem, "Second Coming," following the first World War. The poem contains an image that we often use to understand global dis-order: "Things fall apart; the centre cannot hold."

Can the center hold for our disciplined United Methodist order? Not without a re-ordering of our life together.

A CALL TO RE-ORDER OUR LIFE TOGETHER

Scott Jones, bishop for the Kansas area, observes, "unity rests in coherence of doctrine, mission, and discipline." The painful reality is that we lack coherence in doctrine. We don't have deep clarity on mission. (We agree to "make disciples," but we don't agree on what it means to "make a disciple.") And we are locked in a struggle over discipline. We do not have unity.

This pessimistic assessment of global unity is distant from how ordinary Christian lives are actually lived on the ground in congregations and communities, which means our lack of coherence should not deter us. We have been here before. We are a people of the resurrection. As we look to a future with hope (Jer 29:11), what form will this new future take? In wrestling with the form of the future, we must not casually think schism is a good thing. Our history from the Civil War should teach us that separation is rarely amicable. The factious litigation in other Protestant denominations should serve as a warning to us. The option of simply trying to muddle through with dis-order has a price far too high.

It is time to re-order our life together. Perhaps the form will be more of a confederation than a connection. Perhaps our order admits and permits regional differences in doctrine. Perhaps we have no option other than to "trust God" even as we struggle.

Can the center hold? I do not think so in our current configuration. Rather I think there is a marvelous second coming over the horizon of our passionate convictions and misplaced aspirations. "Surely some revelation is at hand" (Yeats). There is a new order waiting to be born, and we who struggle so much with dis-order must open ourselves humbly and faithfully to God's new order.

UNITY

John K. Yambasu

In 2014, I received a letter from the Council of Bishops asking me to join a group of colleagues "to lead honest and respectful conversations regarding human sexuality . . . to clear theological understanding of the mission and polity of The United Methodist Church." After thoughtful and prayerful discernment, I accepted that invitation and later the invitation to contribute to this volume because I have hope that God will usher in an era of healing, restoration, and unity for our nearly broken relationships among the people called United Methodist.

At the same time, I admit that writing from an African perspective on such a sensitive topic can be an overwhelming challenge. Rather than adopt a judgmental attitude, I attempt to address the issue from the perspective of a God who is the owner of his church, a God who knows and feels our pain, and a God who is at work in the world to raise us up again and lead us in new directions when we come to the crossroads or when we stumble and fall.

The issue of homosexuality dominates almost every major conversation in the church across the connection, especially in North

America, to the extent that it has become a major tool in the hands of the devil to distract the whole church from the main purpose of our existence. Our purpose is clearly articulated in the denomination's four areas of focus:

• Developing principled Christian leaders for the church and the world

• Creating new places for new people and revitalizing existing congregations

• Engaging in ministry with the poor

• Combating the diseases of poverty by improving health globally

At the 2012 General Conference, the entire conference was halted for nearly three hours as supporters of LGBT brothers and sisters seized the floor of conference to signal that they ought to be heard. As I looked at the faces of many delegates on that conference floor, I saw a hue of mixed feelings: sympathy, desperation, anger, frustration, disappointment, fear, and tears. For hours, the conference proceedings were hijacked. For hours, we could not focus on addressing the issues for which we gathered. In the end, neither our LGBT brothers and sisters nor our heterosexual brothers and sisters won the fight. All of us lost. To me it was a shame. It was a heavy blow to a church that prides itself on being a "united" and "global church" with over twelve million members around the world.

I returned home from that conference with mixed feelings. The question, "Where is our church heading?" frequently took control of me, and I am still struggling with that question. It appears that we have lost our true sense of identity. We stand as a denomination at the crossroads. We stand as a denomination ripped apart by sexual orientation: United Methodists fighting United Methodists. As we say in Africa, "When two elephants fight, the grass suffers." The United Methodist Church is a house fighting against itself, and scripture tells us that such a house cannot stand (Luke 11:17). With disagreement about homosexuality, we now live in a broken and hurting church.

RACE

Before and after the civil rights movement, race issues dominated the social, economic, and political landscape in the United States. The whole world witnessed and still experiences its devastating effects in almost every aspect of life. It caused deep divisions and intense pain and anguish. It disrupted the economy of the nation. As a result of the nationwide violence and social instability that ensued, both victim and perpetrators attempted to justify the reason for their actions. The whole nation was ripped apart by two colors: black and white. This division continues to be a reality. We continue to experience the ugliness and unacceptability of racism in the huge numbers of black men and women that populate the prison halls in the United States. We continue to bemoan institutional racism in the still countless numbers of homeless African Americans on the streets of the United States. We continue to live with and accept as "normal" the massive inequalities among white persons and black persons in institutions of higher learning and in the employment market. We continue to witness the indiscriminate extra-judicial killings of people of color, most of whom do not receive the appropriate constitutional justice they deserve. In short, racism is still rife in the United States, and in other parts of the world, and its consequences are enormous. We have compelling reasons why the church must rise up once again and muster the spiritual and political strength to eliminate this menace in all its shapes and forms. The struggle to end racism and bring about healing and wholeness is a fight that the global church cannot afford to lose. It is costly, but the church must remain relentless in this struggle and defeat this evil no matter the cost. To reengage in this struggle is certainly not merely an option but a compelling mandate from a God of love who is eager to see justice flowing "down like waters, and righteousness like an ever-flowing stream" (Amos 5:24). Our world again needs a Rosa Parks or a Martin Luther King Jr. to appeal to the moral and spiritual conscience of the world and declare that racism is evil.

HOMOSEXUALITY

Much like racism, homosexual identity and practice is a single issue that generates excessive animosity in the church. Never in our history have we had such widespread disagreement over the issue. Never in our history have we experienced this level of civil disobedience to our *Book of Discipline.* Though they promised during ordination and consecration to uphold the *Book of Discipline,* on the grounds of "moral conscience" and with the language of "sexual orientation," some clergy and bishops, with support from some laity, have resorted to civil disobedience by either engaging or participating in ceremonies to bless same-gender marriages. Never in our history have we experienced so many judicial actions against our own brothers and sisters for participating in practices that are "inconsistent with Christian teaching" from the scripture. Never in our history as a church have we experienced such disunity, pain, and hurt over our practices and teachings.

As I take a personal look at our church, I sometimes wonder about God's presence in the midst of this disagreement. Is our church becoming Ezekiel's "dry bones" in the valley, dry bones in search of prophets and prophetesses, lay or clergy or bishop, to rise up and speak resurrection hope into our lives? Is there any hope of the church ever reviving from this state of disunity and pain? Could this not be the time, perhaps more than any time in our life, when every United Methodist needs to go down on his or her knees to ask for God's divine intervention to save the unity of our church?

Our denomination seems gripped by a deep and unfathomable fear of disintegration. From many concerned members of the church, I am asked whether there is any hope for our church coming together again.

HOPE

My answer is yes.

The Bible tells us that God is able to do far more and immeasurably greater things than we can ever ask or imagine (Eph 3:20). And I know that God has a plan for the people (Jer 29:11), against which the forces of hell on earth can never prevail (Matt 16:18).

From church history we recall that homosexual practices are not the only issue over which the church has experienced division. The early church became divided over the issues of circumcision, racism (Jew and Gentile), and spiritual matters (speaking in tongues and prophecy). Paul and Barnabas had sharp disagreement over Silas and Mark (Acts 15:36-40). In our recent history, the church became divided over the issue of slavery. But the good news is that through all these times and seasons, God carved out a plan and purpose for his church—and here we are still alive to see each other's faces.

God knows exactly what he is doing in and for his church. God alone knows where he is leading his church, and any attempt by any individual or group of people to thwart God's plan will be fruitless. God is still at work in the church, carving out a future we may not know. I believe that The United Methodist Church has a hope for a better future, far better than we now think or imagine. Scripture abounds in introducing a God of hope to the world. God can and will surely save our denomination from doom. If the denomination could come together and join others in the fight against racism and thereby usher in "peace and good will" to all Americans and if in these very times, in spite of our differences, the whole denomination can come together and agree to raise $75 million to fight malaria in Africa (thereby saving millions of lives of children through the Imagine No Malaria campaign), I believe God's spirit is going to lead us into a new era of evangelical and pentecostal spirit, to the point where we forget about who we are fighting for and focus on who we belong to as a people with "one faith, one hope, and one baptism"—called by God to bring about a living hope in our world.

The Bible tells us that weeping may stay all night, but in the morning comes rejoicing (Ps 30:5). We may be in a state of fear and anxiety, we may be going through a momentary time of tears and uncertainty about what is happening to our church, and indeed we may be sailing on stormy seas gripped by the fear that our boat will sink. But in the midst of all these storms, I can hear Jesus say, "Don't be afraid. Be strong and courageous because I am with you."

By faith, I can see from afar that soon the storm will subside, and we will begin to sail on calm waters. We will speak in new tongues—tongues of hope, tongues of joy, tongues of spiritual holiness, tongues of great and powerful revivals with biblical truth—to the point where God will move us beyond our present into a future with hope. I believe that what is ahead of us is more important and more glorious than what we are now experiencing. As United Methodists, we still have "a story to tell to the nation." We still have "souls to rescue and souls to save." I believe that in the midst of our fear, brokenness, and hopelessness, God will breathe his breath upon the church and usher in a new vibrancy across the globe. Yes, I do so believe.

CHANGE THE WORLD

While some of us in Africa may say that homosexual identity or practice is not an issue for the church, it affects places in our African societies. For example, as a result of widespread poverty, some young boys and girls are "initiated" as sex workers into homosexual practices as a means of survival. To be sure, sexual slavery of any kind is abhorrent to all of us, no matter where we live in the world.

As with any culture or country in the world, it is apparent that ordinary citizens, business investors, and senior politicians are practicing homosexuals but are afraid to identify in this way for fear of reprisals. Whether we like it or not, we may one day learn that we have a homosexual son, daughter, or spouse in our family. It is a fact, like it or not, that homosexual practices are a part of every culture throughout the world.

Here is my position on this matter. I believe that the Bible is the infallible word of God. The Bible provides direction for all those who proclaim Christ as their Lord and Savior. I believe, therefore, that sexual promiscuity, homosexuality, and adultery are inconsistent with the teachings of scripture. I think this is the prevailing view in our denomination. This is what missionaries from the United States and England taught us when they took Christianity to Africa. They built churches, schools, and colleges, and we learned what the Bible teaches. We believed and internalized it. It became part of our social and spiritual makeup. Just as God instructed the Israelites to pass on the Ten Commandments from one generation to another, so the church in Africa has passed on this teaching from generation to generation. For us to now be told by the church in the United States that what we were taught in the Bible is not true could be traumatizing for the African Christian.

Nevertheless, we cannot afford to "excommunicate" or resort to any form of discrimination against those of our brothers and sisters with whom we disagree on this matter. I personally denounce any attempt by the church or by individuals to perpetrate any form of discrimination or hate against homosexual or heterosexual brothers and sisters. Rather, we must take it as our responsibility to engage each other through frank, open, and loving dialogue—with the hope of ushering in a spirit of Christian reconciliation in the church.

We need to stop this fight. As finite beings, we are certainly too frail to fight for God. Furthermore, God is so big, so almighty, that God need not fight for himself. We must remember that we are not weapons for a fight but living tools in God's hands to bring about transformation in the world. We are Christ's body called to live out our faith in a world where there is so much hurt and suffering. There are more important issues that must concern us. There are lives to rescue, hungry people to feed, sick people to heal, and a world to bring to Christ. In the midst of our diversity, we can still imagine God's divine power working to breathe life and hope in our situation.

We can trust that God is able to take us over this deep cliff of uncertainty to a future filled with hope.

My grandmother told me a traditional story that I have since read on the Internet. I was a twelve-year-old boy growing up in a polygamous family of seven siblings who were born to different mothers. With barely enough to share, we often quarreled and sometimes fought each other for the limited food and other resources available in the home. The quest for survival reached the point when hate began to gradually creep into the family, not only among us siblings but among our mothers who did everything possible to ensure that their child received the best out of the situation.

> *It was the coldest winter ever. The porcupines decided to group together to keep warm. This way they covered and protected themselves; but the quills of each one wounded their closest companions.*
>
> *After a while, they decided to distance themselves one from the other, but because of the cold they began to die, alone and frozen. They had to make a choice; either accept the quills of their companions or disappear from the earth. Wisely, they decided to bear the pain and go back to being together. They learned to live with the little wounds caused by the close relationship with their companions in order to receive the heat that came from the others. This way they were able to survive.*

The story of the porcupine is a lesson that the church needs to learn. Homosexuals and heterosexuals, gay and straight, need to accept the imperfections of each other and come together in prayer. God, through his divine grace, will lead us into the place where we will all sit in the same pews and with one voice shout, "In Christ there is no east or west, no north or south."

DIVERSITY

Rosemarie Wenner

By virtue of their election and consecration, bishops are members of the Council of Bishops and are bound in special covenant with all other bishops. In keeping with this covenant, bishops fulfill their servant leadership and express their mutual accountability. . . . The Council of Bishops is thus the collegial expression of episcopal leadership in the Church and through the Church into the world.

—2012 Book of Discipline, ¶¶422.1–2

This is who we are as the Council of Bishops of The United Methodist Church. We are a council composed of nearly 160 individual bishops; 66 of us lead an episcopal area; the others are retired but work in many assignments within the council and the church. The council is a diverse group of bishops living and working on four continents—men and women of different races and diverse theological positions. In our diversity we represent the church. And as a diverse group of people, we must find a way to offer collegial and collaborative leadership to The United Methodist Church, which defines itself as part of the church universal.

How do we lead, recognizing the fact that both United Methodist clergy and laity represent the church at General Conference, and the bishops who comprise the Council of Bishops have diverse and even contradictory opinions on questions related to human sexuality, as well as on many other conflicting issues? As an officer of the Council of Bishops, here is my answer, and here is what I have experienced as a member of the council.

KEEP THE MAIN THING THE MAIN THING

"God's grace is available to all!" This is the crucial phrase in the paragraph on human sexuality in the Social Principles of The United Methodist Church (2012 *Book of Discipline*, ¶161F). In Council of Bishops meetings, I hear this sentence quoted over and over again when we discuss conflictive issues. Methodists emphasize grace. We strongly believe that we are saved by grace and that we are shaped and transformed by grace, day by day, so that we live into a fuller understanding of the gospel and share God's redeeming and renewing grace with all of God's people. Because of our emphasis on grace, we are people on the way, journeying toward perfection. And we are a mission movement, living the call of "making disciples for Jesus Christ for the transformation of the world" in and through vital congregations. As a strong expression of our conviction that God's grace is for all, we see ourselves invited through Christ to the Communion table, and we invite *all* to the table.

As bishops of the church, we remind ourselves and the people in our congregations of the impact of what we are saying and doing by emphasizing grace. We often say: "God's grace is available to all," and we then act as if "all" means "all who are like us." Or: "all who at least seek to become like us!" All means *all*! By following Christ, we are sent to people who are strangers to us. We must find a common language to engage each other. If not, we will not be able to tear down the walls that divide us. We will live with misunderstanding and disagreement. And yet we do believe that God is already there;

God's grace is at work in people who are strangers to us just as it is working in us. By following Jesus, we will be led to live and act in a grace-filled way. This is neither easy nor comfortable. All the biblical descriptions of discipleship teach us that following Jesus means to leave our comfort zones by overcoming barriers, risking to give away what we want to save, and finding life through death. We lead the people to become disciples and to make disciples of Jesus Christ. This purpose is the main thing! And we serve the church with a humility that is worthy of Christ's example.

LEARN TO EMBRACE DIVERSITY

Living with diversity and with conflicting opinions is challenging and sometimes painful. It is hard to accept that we are not of one mind in our biblical interpretation about the practice of homosexuality. By majority vote in the recent General Conferences, we have said in the Social Principles: "The United Methodist Church does not condone the practice of homosexuality and considers its practice incompatible with Christian teaching" (*Book of Discipline*, ¶161F). Many United Methodists, however, have a different perception, and they also support their interpretation with biblical references. I continue to invite all parties to respect each other as fellow Christians; to engage each other in prayer, biblical study, and theological reflection; and to work for a more appropriate expression of what we can say together. This is a long and difficult journey, given the fact that we are a church that serves in many different contexts on four continents.

As church leaders it is crucial that we model how to live with diverse opinions and how to strive for more clarity in a respectful way. We must admit to each other that many United Methodists, including some bishops, interpret the Bible in such a way that supports the use of God's good gift of sexuality only according to God's will if practiced in a faithful and loving relationship between a man and a woman. They seek to love and respect people of other sexual orientations, they welcome everybody into the church because the church is a community of sinners that need forgiveness, but they cannot accept the practiced sexuality of people in the LGBT community.

Other United Methodists, including some bishops, interpret the Bible in a different way. They see the biblical references to homosexuality as expressions of a different cultural and historical background. For them, people of all sexual orientations are created in God's image, and for them everyone is invited to live out the good gift of sexuality in loving, caring, and trustful relationships.

In Germany I know faithful United Methodists from each side of this spectrum. I invite all of them to engage with each other in prayerful Bible study and respectful dialogue. People all over the world and from all sides of this issue experience frustration and pain, because we have talked for years and yet we continue to struggle. Most of all, those who are lesbian, gay, bisexual, or transgendered are hurt because they see themselves excluded based on decisions at General Conference. As leaders we recognize their pain, and we encourage all to continue the journey and to embrace the diversity of viewpoints. It is painful to disagree, but at the same time a lively church stays connected because all of us believe that God's grace is available to all.

BROADEN THE PERSPECTIVES

In its meeting in November 2013, the Council of Bishops recommended "that the Executive Committee initiate a task force to lead honest and respectful conversations regarding human sexuality, race and gender in a world-wide perspective in our shared commitment to clear theological understanding of the mission and polity of the United Methodist Church." One might ask why there are several topics named and not just the questions on human sexuality. I am grateful that the council broadened the perspective: We are not only struggling with the fact that we have different opinions on human sexuality. Our progress in overcoming racism and sexism is too slow, as well. And there is not a single cultural and theological approach to all of these topics. People in various parts of the world bring their history, their traditions, and their contexts to the table. In Germany, where I live, the state law still makes a distinction between the marriage of a man and a woman and the "officiated legal partnership" for gay or lesbian couples. We have lively debates as well as legal disputes about whether this is appropriate or not. In other countries it is still taboo to talk about sexual practices at all.

Every time when we meet at General Conference we come together as people with a broad spectrum of theological opinions and contexts. This global mix of cultures and norms must intensify our awareness of how different we are from each other as we talk about these divisive questions. I encourage us to use our direct contacts that have been established through partner conferences, mutual visits, and global migration in order to learn more from each other. And we can intentionally make use of new means of communication. The aim is to listen, learn, and understand and not merely try to convince each other that one's own position is right.

In some ecumenical dialogues the partners practice a model that might be helpful for us as well: The representatives of one denomination explain how they understand the other denomination. This approach takes into account that all are one in Christ, although there are different and even conflicting views on essential questions. This is a core Christian belief: We are not called to become the same, one like the other. We are called to be one in reconciled diversity.

Look again at the topics that the task force of the Council of Bishops prefers to consider. We will not become one race. And there is for sure no reason to support a hierarchy of races or to establish walls or even fight against other human beings because they belong to a different ethnic group. There is more than one gender as well. There are biblical references that would support a gender hierarchy, and we still continue to engage in a Christian dialogue about how men and women are equally created in God's image.

Yes, there are many nations on earth, thousands of language groups, all of them creating unique cultures. People who are shaped by the Western culture tend to see their culture as the dominant one. It is very hard for me as a German to overcome biases and generalizations toward people from other countries and cultures. But this is a Christian call. The New Testament describes the Christian community as a community of equals with regard to the value of all the factors that divide people: gender, race, nations, social status, and yes, sexual orientation.

There is no reason to give one human the right to see himself or herself as dominant over other humans. All of us are gifted, and all of us need redemption. We must learn to respect each other and to help each other grow in our discipleship. Christian unity is not a status where finally all are the same. Jesus teaches us that unity is a way of following Christ's example and learning from him how to love the other just as he or she is.

I am afraid that because of our long history of conflicts related to human sexuality we very often narrow our perspectives. Many key leaders seem to lose energy and are too tired to invest time in new dialogues with even more diverse people. The approach chosen by the Council of Bishops will probably take a very long time. I am convinced, however, that our focus on the core of what Christian unity means will teach us how to live in diversity, seeing Christ's face in the other and from there engaging in a robust search for how to interpret the Bible in a way that leads us toward love, justice, and reconciliation.

PRAY AND WORK FOR HEALING, RECONCILIATION, AND A LESS PAINFUL WAY FORWARD

Bishops are called to serve as shepherds of the whole flock. We seek to minister to all the people in our various areas, no matter who they are or what their opinions on divisive questions may be. And the Council of Bishops as a collegial body serves the entire United Methodist Church. This is one of the reasons why individual bishops, as well as the Council of Bishops, have been hesitant to debate in public the issues that have the potential to divide us. Many of us see ourselves called to proclaim what we agree upon rather than our disagreements. We are currently asking ourselves whether we serve the church well by being silent on divisive questions. Perhaps we could model a constructive and respectful way of debating pressing questions?

Although many conferences throughout the denomination report good examples of how to engage with each other in meaningful dialogue, there is a lack of helpful experiences on a global level. In fact, until recently, General Conference was the only place where United Methodists from all over the globe discussed questions of human sexuality with each other. Many groups, including the Council of Bishops, offer leadership to shape General Conference so that we may manage to navigate through rough waters. At General Conference we worship and pray together, we celebrate our worldwide connection, we speak of Holy Conferencing or Christian Conferencing and—despite our desire to do no harm but to do good—we undergo a difficult and sometimes hurtful process of decision-making according to rules that create winners and losers.

The Constitution of The United Methodist Church says clearly that the General Conference is the only body to define the discipline of our church. Bishops as well as all ordained clergy are supposed to uphold the *Book of Discipline*. The Council of Bishops over and over again has said that we accept that role. In addition, we are called to offer pastoral care for those who are hurt by the process because they see themselves misinterpreted or excluded by our current church law. In all of our actions, as bishops we seek to work toward healing and reconciliation in order to overcome the brokenness of our church.

This is true even in situations where individual bishops do not uphold the *Discipline*. In the fall of 2013, the Council of Bishops recommended following the processes outlined in the *Book of Discipline* for rebuilding sacred trust if pastors or bishops fail to uphold the *Discipline*. The procedures outlined in the *Book of Discipline* in dealing with a complaint are aimed at "a just resolution of any violations of this sacred trust, in the hope that God's work of justice, reconciliation and healing may be realized in the body of Christ" (¶363.1). Even if such a just resolution cannot be achieved in the supervisory response process and judicial proceedings are undertaken, it is again the same aim: "The judicial process shall have as its purpose just resolution of judicial complaints, in the hope that God's work of justice, reconciliation and healing may be realized in the body of Jesus Christ" (¶2701).

This procedure is difficult to explain, however. Many church members fear or hope that disciplinary processes aim to punish or even to exclude or condemn those who are under complaint instead of intensively seeking common ground in order to continue the Christian journey together. The low trust level in our connection makes it difficult to gain acceptance for a supervisory response process that take place in a safe space where complainants and respondents as well as those in charge of leading the process engage in listening, praying, and seeking solutions.

It saddens me that the path the church has agreed upon as a way toward reconciliation is not well known and sometimes even is not respected as a way to resolve conflicts. We might need to find alternative ways to resolve the conflicts that arise because of our different opinions. Before and beyond all our efforts to work for healing, I encourage our entire denomination to use every means of grace: prayer, bible study—alone and with others—worship, Holy Communion, fasting, and sharing love with friends, strangers, and yes, even enemies. It certainly shapes us when we pray together, read and reflect on the Bible, gather together at the Communion table, and share God's love with people at the margins.

AGAIN: KEEP THE MAIN THING THE MAIN THING

I am convinced that we need to learn to live with our diversity related to human sexuality. No matter what decisions are made at the next General Conference, we will continue to live as a denomination where people have different opinions on this issue and on many other difficult questions. The Council of Bishops offers its leadership for a church that sees diversity as God's gift. It is also challenged to value diversity as a blessing and to work to understand each other. As a worldwide body, we seek to raise awareness among ourselves and in the conferences throughout the connection concerning the cultural and theological diversity represented among United Methodists who live in places as different as Kinshasa, Manila, Moscow, and Los Angeles. And neither in Kinshasa nor in Los Angeles are the people called United Methodists of the same opinion on divisive questions. We will have to discuss whether we see the practice of homosexuality as a core question that has to be answered in a unified way. If we could find the freedom to live with different answers, we could surely learn to live together in a less hurtful and harmful way. This agreement would require bold steps from all the various groups that have organized themselves in order to move the church forward. There are bishops who seek to reach out to those various groups. They talk with people from all sides and seek to invite all United Methodists of good will to engage in direct talks rather than addressing each other through the media.

I remind my colleagues not to forget those United Methodists who live on other continents beyond North America. They may well be the ones who could help us to build the needed bridges. To learn how to talk with each other in a Christian way, I encourage us to reread John Wesley's sermon on the catholic spirit and his *Letter to a Roman Catholic* as a model of how to we could move forward. John Wesley did not agree with parts of the Roman Catholic doctrine. He saw the need for further theological diversity. Nevertheless, Wesley wrote:

97

But if God still loveth us, we ought also to love one another. We ought, without this endless jangling about opinions, to provoke one another to love and to good works. Let the points wherein we differ stand aside: here are enough wherein we agree, enough to be the ground of every Christian temper, and of every Christian action.

And in his sermon, "Catholic Spirit," he encouraged his listeners:

Though we can't think alike, may we not love alike? May we not be of one heart, though we are not of one opinion? Without all doubt we may. Herein all the children of God may unite, notwithstanding these smaller differences. These remaining as they are, they may forward one another in love and in good works.

This is the main thing for us as United Methodists: We help each other to grow in love and in good works, so that we focus on our purpose to "make disciples for Jesus Christ for the transformation of the world." I pray and work for a future where we will find ways to embrace our diversity on many issues, including human sexuality, allowing us to think differently. Perhaps we may even be able to live with different answers concerning clergy who live in faithful and loving homosexual partnerships and those who choose to conduct same-gender marriages. We seek to find such ways so that our faith, love, and hope will be fully engaged in being a mission movement that transforms the world.

PART THREE

STEPS

TRUST GOD

Rueben P. Job

O n Baptism of the Lord Sunday where our family worships, the congregation observed the day as we gathered for the early morning Communion service. After the beautiful music, the scripture reading, and a moving sermon titled *Remember*, an open invitation was given for all to come to the altar to receive Communion and have the sign of the cross made on our hands as we remembered our baptism.

I was baptized as an infant in a township schoolhouse where an itinerant preacher came to conduct worship services. Twenty years later I took the vows of membership in a congregation of the Evangelical Church thirteen dirt-road miles from our family farm. I do remember this solemn promise, how important it was to me, and how the transformation that began on the snow-covered prairies of North Dakota continues today.

While kneeling at the altar rail with others, I opened my eighty-six-year-old hands and received Christ's body given for me and Christ's life poured out for me. The sign of the cross was made on my hands, and I returned to the pew where I was surrounded by family and friends.

Then I watched as about a hundred persons of every age, every economic and social class, every hue of skin color, those needing assistance to walk, and those bound to wheelchairs made their way to the altar and received Christ's body and life and the sign of the cross with water.

After eighty-six years, while watching the constant stream of souls moving to the altar, it is natural to think about what it will be like as we transition from this life with God to the life with God to come. In this momentary vision I could see multitudes moving toward the promise of eternal life with God. They came from every country, every culture, every political persuasion, every gender, and every economic and social class, and they knew they were all God's dearly loved children redeemed by their faithful savior. They sang as they walked in unity and harmony and made their way to the welcome-home feast that awaits us all. And of course as this vivid scene faded from my awareness, I wondered, *What am I doing now to be at home in that happy crowd, moving toward the greatest celebration any child of God can ever experience?*

Then I thought of the congregation where we worship. I became aware of the faithful efforts on the part of many who seek to prepare us for that joyful journey with the multitudes who are moving toward home and the completed kingdom of God in the life to come.

This congregation is in many ways like others in the denomination we love and serve. There are similar tensions and questions, but in most cases there is always an honest, robust, gentle, and protracted time of prayer, study, and reflection before any issue is considered ready for decision. Our congregation is extreme in its diversity and equally extreme in its love and welcome for all who gather for worship, study, prayer, reflection, food, and community and then are sent out into the world to give themselves for others.

Together we yearn for a faithful church where our deep commitment to God in Christ results in a love for God and neighbor that is unconditional in every way.

Together we yearn for the peace and joy that transforms our lives and results in a calm, confident embrace of every issue in good times and hard times.

Together we yearn for a relationship with God in Christ that is so intimate and powerful that we will be able to live in constant awareness of God's presence, guidance, companionship, and comfort.

Together we yearn for a congregation and a denomination where love for God and neighbor is so real, vibrant, and active that any and every issue can be faced so openly, prayerfully, honestly, and respectfully that it will lead to the unity and faithfulness that is worthy of the name of the One we claim to follow.

DISCERNMENT

I confess dismay when I observe the denomination we love gripped at all levels by the issue of same-gender relationships.

Often the tone and content of the arguments that are made on all sides of the issue of same-gender relationships are far from being compatible with Christian teaching. For over forty years we have observed and often participated in this strident approach to finding a fair, just, civil, loving, honest, and effective way of dealing with different sexual orientation and same-gender relationships.

The arguments for censure, threats of division, and immediate punishment reflect a commitment to law over grace or truth over love, which is contrary to what Jesus taught and lived. When Jesus healed the blind man in John 9:1-41, he was lifted up as an example of why "faithfulness to the grace and truth available in Jesus, not faithfulness to the law, is the decisive mark of true discipleship" (see p. 47).

Why do we find it so difficult to follow Jesus, who emptied himself to be faithful? Why have we chosen to reject the way of our redeemer, our teacher and leader? Why do we turn away from the call of the One who died for our salvation?

If we are not willing to find a faithful way forward, which way shall we go? In our thoughtful moments we know that the path we are on will not bring us closer to God in Christ, does not reflect God's kingdom, for which we pray, and is really unworthy of us who want to be followers of Jesus. Among many others, I believe there is a better way that is faithful to our tradition and faithful to all who are concerned about this issue that has so long divided us.

In *A Guide to Spiritual Discernment*, I observed, "The church is not perfect. Sometimes we wish it were. Sometimes we even think it is. There are those moments of Christ in action through the church that move us to joyous thanksgiving. There are also the moments that painfully remind us that the church is made up of persons like ourselves. We are the body of Christ, the church. And we are a mixture of motives, hopes, faith, fears, anxiety, and who have been shaped by family, culture, education and the church itself. And we carry all of who we are into the church. So it is not surprising to us that the body of Christ is broken and fractured. The conflicts, halting discipleship, fragile faith, timid witness, and qualified commitment are a natural outgrowth of who we are as individual Christians.

"While we may look at the church in its various expressions with joy at times and dismay at others, we must remember that new life is possible. Transformation can begin today. Resurrection power is available to us and can be invested in the church this very moment. With God's help we can initiate change this very day!

"This is true because the first line of defense against further brokenness is within each of us. My efforts to stop the brokenness and take the first steps to reform and transform the church must begin with me. My prayer for a holy church marked by righteousness and love can be answered only as I yield my life to the way of Jesus Christ and the power of the Holy Spirit. The transformation begins with me. What a liberating thought! I am not powerless and without options. With God's help I can surrender my life to the transforming, life-giving power of the Holy Spirit and in that very moment begin the journey toward the wholeness and faithfulness I want to see in the church."

At the next General Conference, all decisions of polity, rules, language, and budget will be discussed, presented, and decided. Our *Book of Discipline* is more than eight hundred pages long and covers our origins, history, constitution, theology, rights, and responsibilities. It is our principal guide on who we are and how we live together as a denomination. It is a complex document created over a long period of time and subject to revision every four years.

As one would expect over this long period and in a document of over eight hundred pages, some paragraphs and rules seem to be in conflict. One of those areas of conflict seems to be between our Constitution and some of the language about gender issues involved in our current discussions.

Our Constitution begins with this affirmation in the preamble:

> The prayers and intentions of The United Methodist Church and its predecessors, The Methodist Church and The Evangelical United Brethren Church, have been and are for obedience to the will of our Lord that his people be one, in humility for the present brokenness of the Church and in gratitude that opportunities for reunion have been given.
>
> Therefore, The United Methodist Church has adopted and amended the following Constitution (2012 *Discipline*, p. 23).

Then Article IV of our Constitution declares that the church is inclusive, which appears to be in conflict with much of our debate about gender issues. It reads as follows:

> *Article IV. Inclusiveness of the Church*—The United Methodist Church is a part of the church universal, which is one Body in Christ. The United Methodist Church acknowledges that all persons are of sacred worth. All persons without regard to race, color, national origin, status, or economic condition, shall be eligible to attend its worship services, participate in its programs, receive the sacraments, upon baptism be admitted as baptized members, and upon taking vows declaring the Christian faith, become professing members in any local church in the connection. In the United Methodist Church no conference or other organizational unit of the Church shall be structured so as to exclude any member or constituent body of the Church because of race, color, national origin, status or economic condition (*Discipline*, ¶4).

Between General Conference sessions bishops have the responsibility to rule on any issues of law that may arise. These decisions are all subject to review and approval or rejection by the Judicial Council.

This is no ordinary time in the life of our church, and this is no ordinary conflict. Therefore we cannot seek a remedy in the ordinary way that has led to generations of deepening division and distrust. This is not a time to wait and see what happens. It is a time for a radically new approach. That approach is to place our trust in God and seek God's direction until together we discern a way forward. Discernment is not a call to "just pray about it." Rather it is a call to radical, risky, and complete trust in God rather than trust in our own ingenuity or rhetoric. The way of discernment will not be easy to accomplish, although it will be easy to dismiss.

My plea is that we will take the risk at every level of the church and help each other to seek and trust God's wisdom rather than our own. I believe there are simple steps we can take now to prepare us to receive God's guidance to a faithful, fair, just, and loving solution to our division over issues of sexual orientation and same-gender relationships.

To take these simple steps will take an enormous amount of humility and trust in God's sovereignty. We will need to become vulnerable enough to claim our own fallibility and sinfulness and confess we are not in a position to declare any person by any name other than God's dearly loved child, which is how we identify ourselves.

This humility must be coupled with a radical faith and trust in the immanence, power, providence, good will, and love of God.

Can we do this? Of course we can. But only with God's help! After the baptism of Jesus, he was

> led by the Spirit into the wilderness. There he was tempted for forty days by the devil. . . . Next the devil led him to a high place and showed him in a single instant all the kingdoms of the world. The devil said, "I will give you this whole domain and the glory of all these kingdoms. It's been entrusted to me and I can give it to anyone I want. Therefore, if you will worship me, it will all be yours." Jesus answered, "It's written, *You will worship the Lord your God and serve him only*" (Luke 4:1-8).

Unfortunately, we did not practice the faithfulness of Jesus, and we fell for the outstanding offer of evil, and we really believed we could have it all. We were sure that with our cleverness and skill and the wisdom of the world we would solve every problem because we could win any struggle and have it our way. But we miscalculated our weakness and the impossibility of the offer being true and therefore achievable.

We forgot that even after forty days in the wilderness, hungry and weary, Jesus never fell for the devil's promise. His relationship with his dearly loved Abba was so strong, sure, intimate, and trusting that he never flinched in the days of his temptation, even though he knew where his relationship with his dearly loved Abba would take him.

He clearly did not want to face the humility, shame, and agony of the cross. But his trust in the God he knew as loving Father was so great that he never once turned away from his call and mission as he set his face to Jerusalem to begin the final days of his mission. Is it possible for us to have a trust and confidence like that? Perhaps not exactly like that, but it is possible for us to have trust and confidence that mirrors the trust and confidence of Jesus. We can be faithful to our call as Jesus was to his.

However, somewhere along the way, we seem to have stopped really listening to the radical call and promise of Jesus. Did it happen so slowly that we did not know that we were being taken in by the empty promise that we could have it all? Did we really believe we were intelligent enough and had the ability to solve any problem or reconcile any conflict on our own?

Or did we become so entangled with our busy lives and our busy churches that we just slowly drifted out to sea and did not even notice that we had left the land of promise where with God all things are possible?

Or after forty-two years of trying to find our way on our own, does it really matter how we got where we are? Because we all know we are at an unhealthy place and a place we do not want to be.

Today we are deeply pained to find ourselves in a church we dearly love that is severely wounded, divided, politicized, and draining energy and resources in our struggle over same-gender relationships to the neglect of our witness for Jesus Christ.

Can we find a way forward that leads us closer to God's kingdom for which we pray? A way forward that mirrors the life of Jesus? A way that binds us ever closer to God in Christ? A way that is closer to rather than farther away from the way of Jesus? Is there such a way forward? Jesus says there is, but we cannot do it on our own. We cannot buy our way there with the wealth of our affluence, and we cannot find our way there with the wealth of our intelligence, our propaganda, or our masterful communication skills.

Though we are stunned by inability to save ourselves, the Gospels tell us the first disciples were just as stunned about who can be saved when Jesus reminded them that *"What is impossible for humans is possible for God"* (Luke 18:26-27).

The faithful church we yearn for is possible, even in this divided and politicized world. The peace, unity, and harmony that we yearn for is possible. The calm confidence to face any issue in good times and hard times is possible.

But these results will not come from the path we are on. Today we taste the bitter fruit of forty-two years of trying the same way to resolve these difficult issues. We can be sure the results will not change as long as we continue using the same methodology. The results will change only when we are ready to give up the lesser gods of our own making and promise once again to follow the one true God we have come to know and love through the birth, life, ministry, death, and resurrection of Jesus Christ.

THREE BASIC STEPS

To give up the gods we have made will require deep humility, an incredible trust in God, and the courage to lose everything and die to everything else for what is the primary call of our lives.

This proposal is worked out in three basic steps:

The first step: Immediately stop the propaganda.
The second step: Declare a moratorium on celebrations and trials regarding same-gender unions.

The third step: Begin a practice of prayer and discernment that leaves our preferences outside as we enter this extended period of seeking only God's direction.

Are we strong enough to seek this way forward? Or are we too much in the grasp of the lesser gods of this world to follow the God who is loving creator, faithful redeemer, and reliable sustainer of all that there is? Only you and I can decide. And the good news is that we do not do this alone. The One who we have promised to follow has promised us, "The Companion, the Holy Spirit, whom the Father will send in my name, will teach you everything and will remind you of everything I told you" (John 14:26).

The first step is immediately stopping the propaganda war and recognizing every person as a dearly loved child of God who is therefore included and welcomed as equal at every level of the life of the denomination. This will mean an end to hurtful words and messages we use about each other. When we place another person in our judgment cage, they can never escape unless we open the cage. And not only does such a judgment cage keep them in the prison of our opinion, we blind our eyes so we can never see the real person. We see only our warped opinion of who this child of God really is.

To do this we will need to step back from spouting words and laws as if we speak for Moses, and turn to the words, call, and demands of Jesus who we seek to follow. We will remember that the person whose opinion is different than mine is one of God's dearly loved children, and to demean that person with hateful words and actions signals a deep fracturing of God's family and a great divorce from the way of Jesus.

The second step is to declare a moratorium on all celebrations and trials regarding same-gender unions. We are in a period of great turmoil and peril and relentlessly moving toward unsustainable confrontations and polarization. As much as we yearn for resolutions to these matters, surely we *can trust God and invest* the time required to find a faithful way forward together. We do this as Jesus's dearly loved community, pleading with all to suspend the fighting and seek higher ground. And we can do this without jeopardizing our *Book of Discipline* or the covenants we have made with each other. This pause will give us time to reflect on where we are going in this conflict but most importantly time to listen quietly and peacefully to the voice of God who calls and speaks to us. But it requires humility with the will to listen and the faith to believe that God has a word for us that leads us to the promised land.

These first two steps will release an enormous amount of energy, creativity, and money to invest in the crying needs of the hungry, thirsty, sick, stranger, and prisoner that Jesus told us to care for if we wish to inherit the God's kingdom and even experience it here and now (Matt 25:31-46).

These first two steps are necessary if we are to stop destroying each other and the church we love. The priority is the pearl of great price that, if practiced, will transform our relationship with God and therefore lead to the transformation of our lives, our congregations, our denomination, our witness to the world, and our faithfulness as disciples of Jesus Christ.

And that priority is prayer. If prayer is to become that priority in our lives, we must be willing to give up the deceptive idea that we are strong enough and wise enough to control our lives without divine intervention. This will also mean giving up the limitations we place upon God's interest in or power to bring about change, new life, resurrection, or any marvelous gift that may be beyond our ability to conceive, create, or accomplish.

If we can accept prayer as our priority, then we will have the courage to set aside two years prior to General Conference as a period of concentrated prayer and discernment by every individual, every congregation, and every institution of our denomination. This is no small endeavor, and it will require a radical shift in our practice of prayer. Prayer will not be seen as an additive to life but as a way of living every day in companionship with the One who made us, wooed us until we were aware and heard the call to salvation and discipleship. We will remember that God first loved us and invited us into the relationship of prayer.

At their request Jesus taught the disciples how to pray and how to live a life of prayer. He walked in constant companionship with his dearly loved Abba and taught the disciples the essential elements of that relationship. Through the power and presence of the Holy Spirit, we can become those who live a life of prayer, and our congregations can become a house of prayer (Matt 21:13).

INDIFFERENCE

If we are serious about this period of prayer as a time of seeking a new way forward, then we must remember to practice rigorous *indifference.*

Indifference means we must empty ourselves of our own preferences, as hard as that will be. Do we really want to know God's will more than anything else? An affirmative answer can only come from those who love God so deeply and have learned to trust God so completely that they know this is the only real remedy for our confusion and conflict.

Some may argue that we cannot arrive at a decision if we set aside our preferences. However, centuries of using this practice have proven that setting aside our preferences does enhance our capacity to hear God's preference. Of course this means no one "side" will win because everyone will win. Isn't that the desirable outcome we seek?

It also means we are likely to discover a way forward that we have never thought of and certainly never thought possible to find. Our limited vision and hardened position make it nearly impossible to think outside the boxes we have created.

And this is where our utter humility and unwavering trust must be called upon as we are asking God to guide us to a place where we can all find a way forward and not just a way to confirm our position. If I do not trust God, I will trust my own voice and my own ideology that tells me I already know the right way forward. And we know where that attitude has led us.

But if we have really been indifferent to our own preference and have committed ourselves to what we believe is the call and claim of God in Christ on our lives, we will still proceed with a great deal of humility. Our witness will be clear, honest, gentle, and faithful to Christ.

Our witness will be what we have heard in our period of discernment, but we will never say to each other, "This is the right way for you, and you must follow it too." Of course, we will invite everyone to consider what we have heard and the path we have decided to follow. But it would be sheer arrogance on our part to tell others that it is the only way to fulfill their call. Ultimately that decision is always between God and the individual. Together we will listen, share insights, and discover a way forward that is fair, equitable, just, and faithful to Jesus Christ and can be adopted by all of us.

But this can *only* happen if we are each willing to trust God in Christ to the extent that we believe God can bring us to that remedy and provide the power and presence of the Holy Spirit to guide us as we find our way into God's promised kingdom.

What I am proposing is a radical departure from our efforts of the past four decades, and I consider it to be an urgent call to a new level of faithfulness on the part of bishops, superintendents, individuals, congregations, lay and clergy leaders, institutions, and annual conferences. This will strengthen rather than weaken our covenants with each other. These covenants began with our baptism and guide us today. It will give us a unified opportunity to renew our solemn pledges and practice our solemn promises as together we seek God's guidance for a faithful way forward.

Some will say, "It will never work."

Jesus said, "Ask and you will receive."

God's presence and power are as available to the contemporary church as they have ever been. It is up to us to claim that power and presence as we seek healing for our deep and infectious wounds.

Of course God in Christ wants to hear our requests for all things, but when the request is for God's guidance, direction, and help in finding that way, *we do not first tell God what that way is*. Rather, as together we seek God's way, we ask for the Holy Spirit's promised presence to teach us everything we need to know and then trust God to keep that promise. So all of us change our practice of judging each other or trying to find another argument to win a debate, and we concentrate on listening for and obeying God's direction.

What will happen when we adopt this way of earnest and humble listening to the only One who can help us? The major transformation will be in our relationship to God in Christ. The transforming and intimate communion with God will be restored and renewed. We will once again realize we are walking in God's holy presence every moment of every day, and prayer without ceasing will become a reality instead of a desire. We will each be reminded that we have a responsibility to permit that holy presence to guide and sustain us. We will seek to position our lives in such a way that we will be aware of that holy presence and allow that presence to shape every part of our lives and all of our relationships.

The more we sense that holy presence, the more we will become like that holy presence. The more we become like that holy presence, the more we will find ourselves fulfilling the request of Jesus to love God with our whole being and to love our neighbors as we love ourselves. The transformation in our lives moves to the transformation of all of our relationships, and we begin to see clearly that everyone is God's dearly loved child just as I am God's dearly loved child. Then what seemed like an impossible concept becomes available and achievable. Indeed, all things are possible with God.

If conferences use these years prior to General Conference for deep and discerning prayer, they will be guided to choose delegates that are committed to end forever the discord that today deeply wounds and divides our denomination at every level.

If congregations also use these years for deep and discerning prayer, they will be led to ending discord at every level of their life together, and they will become a magnet that draws young and old to the inviting and life-giving reality of unconditional love.

If individuals will also use this time for deep and discerning prayer, they too will be brought to a place of full acceptance of themselves as children of God. They will have eyes to see each other as God's children—nothing more and nothing less.

Then for the first time in four decades we can experience release from this crippling discord that has robbed us of the gift of community and unity of purpose and witness. Our life together will then be so attractive that multitudes will be drawn to us and want to join us because they see what they themselves want to experience.

Our resources will then be focused on those whom Jesus identified as our mission, and the poor will be accepted, loved, and cared for; the prisoner will be visited; the sick will be healed; and diseases like malaria and HIV/AIDS will be overcome. Each of more than forty-two thousand congregations on four continents will become a source of light, life, and hope in their community, and the world around them will be changed.

The early church reported incredible events as signs and wonders (Acts 4:32-37; 5:16). The formation and transformation taking place in these communities was remarkable and gave clear witness to God's active presence through the power of the Holy Spirit in their midst. The Holy Spirit not only blew away the barriers that separated and the sin that enslaved but filled this new community with compassion that led to an unprecedented witness to the world.

This same transformation can happen to us as we yield our way to God's way and begin in earnest living a life of prayer and discernment. We too can permit the Holy Spirit to blow away the sin that blinds us and the barriers that separate us and then become available to accept the grace of forgiveness for the sin, the breaking down of barriers, and the healing of our wounds. Grace Adolphsen Brame says, "Most of us pray that God will do something to us or for us, but God wants to do something in us and through us" (*Receptive Prayer*, p. 9). Are we ready for that radical transformation?

> O begin! Fix some part of every day for private exercises. You may acquire the taste for which you have not. What is tedious at first will afterwards be pleasant. Whether you like it or no, read and pray daily. It is for your life: there is no other way . . . Do justice to your own soul: give it time and means to grow. Do not starve yourself any longer. Take up your cross and be a Christian altogether. Then the children of God rejoice (from a letter to John Tembrath as quoted in *A Wesleyan Spiritual Reader*, p. 13).

To build and expand on this period of prayer, we will look to the next General Conference not as a battleground but as a setting to acknowledge and extend efforts to help the church engage in study and prayer. Our goal together could be to ensure that we provide study, prayer, and reflection resources to be used by every individual, congregation, and institution of the denomination in preparation for the 2020 General Conference.

When these prayer practices are followed we can expect annual conferences to elect delegates that have practiced three years of faithful prayer and discernment. And we can expect those delegates to be open to the Spirit's guidance and together be brought to a loving, just, and faithful way forward on these issues and so many more. We really can have a loving, unified, mission-focused, joyful, and Jesus Christ-focused denomination. God is ready for this transformation. It's up to us to be open to God's intervention in our individual lives and in our life together.

If we as United Methodists are to become a praying people, we will need a pattern of prayer to guide us and keep us faithful to this essential part of our life together. Our *United Methodist Hymnal* provides beautiful orders for daily prayer and praise, found on pages 876–79. These prayer options are not offered as a rule that must be followed but rather as an invitation to give faithful attention to developing and continuing a vital and intimate relationship with Jesus Christ, a relationship that will sustain us in every experience of life and make it possible to trust God completely as we learn to be at home with God in Christ wherever we are and in whatever circumstance we find ourselves.

You may already have such a pattern of prayer that serves you well, and you may wish to continue that practice. However, if you do not have such a way of prayer or you are seeking a better way to remain faithful to your life of prayer, you will find that our hymnal offers rich and rewarding resources for all who seek to live a prayerful life.

Trust God.